D0057902

UNCORRECTED PROOF—NOT FOR SALE

Title: TRUE HOLLYWOOD LIES
Author: JOSIE BROWN
Classification: TRADE PAPERBACK FICTION
Publication Month: OCTOBER 2005
Price: $12.95 U.S./$16.95 Canada
Index: No
Illustrations: No
Page Count: 336 pages
Trim: 5-5/16 x 8
ISBN: 0-06-081587-6
ISBN 13: 978-0-06-081587-5

AVON
TRADE

An Imprint of HarperCollins*Publishers*

Josie Brown

TRUE
HOLLYWOOD LIES

AVON
TRADE

An Imprint of HarperCollins*Publishers*

TRUE HOLLYWOOD LIES. Copyright © 2005 by Josie Brown. All rights reserved. Printed in the United States of America. No part of this book may be used or reproduced in any manner whatsoever without written permission except in the case of brief quotations embodied in critical articles and reviews. For information address HarperCollins Publishers Inc., 10 East 53rd Street, New York, NY 10022.

HarperCollins books may be purchased for educational, business, or sales promotional use. For information please write: Special Markets Department, HarperCollins Publishers Inc., 10 East 53rd Street, New York, NY 10022.

FIRST EDITION

Interior text designed by Diahann Sturge

Library of Congress Cataloging-in-Publication Data

Brown, Josie.
    True Hollywood lies / by Josie Brown.—1st ed.
        p. cm.
    ISBN 0-06-081587-6 (alk. paper)
    1. Triangles (Interpersonal relations)—Fiction.   2. Hollywood (Los Angeles, Calif.)—Fiction.   3. Children of celebrities—Fiction.   4. Motion picture industry—Fiction.   5. Fathers—Death—Fiction.   I. Title.

    PS3602.R715T78   2005
    813'.6—dc22

                                                                2005002554

05   06   07   08   09   JTC/RRD   10   9   8   7   6   5   4   3   2   1

To Martin,
the source of all my inspiration and passion.

Acknowledgments

As a first-time novelist, I thank my lucky stars that I have Al Zuckerman as my agent, and that I am smart enough to realize that he is so much more than that to me: He is also my guru and my valued friend.

I am blessed to be working with Lucia Macro, my editor at HarperCollins. Her humor, honestly, and inspiring words are the reasons why she is one of the most beloved editors in publishing.

Others at HarperCollins have been an enthusiastic cheering squad. Their belief in this book is why it was such a joy to write. Much thanks to Carrie Feron, for her warmth, courtesy, and vision; to Kelly Harms, who was the first to fall in love with Hannah—although I suspect she was somewhat smitten with Louis as well, for all the wrong reasons; and to Pamela Spengler-Jaffee, who sings its praises to all the right people.

Helen Drake was *True Hollywood Lies'* first reader and ardent enthusiast. Emily Kischell's insights gave Hannah her poignancy. Bonnie and John Gray, Allyson Rusu, and Angela and Tom Johnson have been this book's unwavering champions since they first heard about it. I thank you all for being my dear friends.

Sharon Rusu and Guy Goodwin-Gill, my soul mates from across the pond, graciously took time out from their very busy schedules to vet my British slang. For this I owe them a really great bottle of Sonoma cabernet sauvignon. Must be hand-delivered, of course. Let's meet in Ferney-Voltaire, shall we?

And to my children, Austin and Anna, for their constant love and faithful support.

Orbit: *The path of one body around another due to the influence of gravity.*

Part One

Luminosity

Absolute brightness.
The total energy radiated into space,
per second, by a celestial object such as a star.

1

Black Hole

*When a star appreciably larger than the Sun
has exhausted all of its nuclear fuel,
it will collapse to form a black hole—
"black" because no light escapes its intense gravity.*

In the Hollywood you know, here's how the world ends:

The ice caps melt.

A meteor hits the earth.

Aliens invade.

In the Hollywood I know, here's how my world ended:

I buried the only man I ever loved: my father.

I discovered that my boyfriend of the past two years was a lying, cheating louse.

And the money that had allowed me to pursue my one and only passion—astronomy—vaporized into thin air.

And it all happened in less than 72 hours.

I guess I should start at the beginning. And since this story takes place in the land of fairy tales, I'll give you the fairy-tale version first, courtesy of Hollywood's official newspaper, *Daily Variety:*

THE KING IS DEAD

Leo Fairchild, the most charismatic film actor of the latter part of the 20th century, has died. By most accounts, he was sixty-eight.

Fairchild succumbed to a heart attack late Thursday night at his palatial Bel Air estate, Lion's Den. His fourth wife, former actress Sybilla Lawson, and his daughter, Hannah, were at his side. He was pronounced dead at 1:50 A.M. at Cedars Sinai Medical Center, said his attorney, Jasper Carlton. A private memorial is planned for today.

"Leo Fairchild was a true original," said a bereaved Jack Nicholson, a contemporary with whom Fairchild shared adjourning courtside seats at Los Angeles Lakers basketball games. "He had that special magic, that elusive alchemy that convinced audiences he was their hero, their best buddy, that noble guy we all wished we could be . . ."

Leo X. Fairchild started out as a child actor in the 1940s, working with such esteemed directors as William Wyler, John Huston, Joseph L. Mankiewicz, and Billy Wilder. While the adoring spotlight fades on most child actors by the time they enter their teen years, Fairchild—tall, fair, and possessing a square-jawed handsomeness—matured seamlessly into a boyish teen heartthrob, then took on roles that seemed to mirror his personal escapades as a playboy raconteur, for which he won three Golden Globe Awards and two Academy Awards.

> Fairchild's celebrity continued to burn brightly
> through the 1960s cinematic auteur era—he was a
> favored leading man for such directors as François
> Truffaut, Bernardo Bertolucci, Francis Ford Coppola
> and Martin Scorsese—and into the twenty-first cen-
> tury, as he played muse to such pop-culture-infused
> art house giants as Quentin Tarantino, Spike Lee,
> John Woo, and M. Night Shyamalan.
>
> Fairchild leaves prolific credits, some of cinema's
> most memorable moments, and—if the tabloids are
> to be believed—a string of broken hearts . . .

Truly touching.

However, not exactly accurate—at least, not the part of how Leo died. I'd like to set the record straight, here and now:

First of all, my dad, Leo Fairchild, was called to meet his Maker while he was screwing the latest love of his life—a 19-year-old starlet currently playing the eldest, ditziest daughter in a Disney Family Network sitcom—at that legendary celebrity hangout, the Chateau Marmont.

The staff there was able to convince the other hotel guests that the hysterical, high-pitched shrieks emanating from his playmate were in fact the whimpers of Sharon Osbourne's pooch Minnie, which, they insisted, was in a nearby suite, being supervised by Hollywood's most renowned canine midwife while giving natural birth.

Then, as a pacifier, they offered the human whiners a suite upgrade or a complimentary massage, whichever they preferred.

By doing so, Marmont staffers were guaranteed that the inquisitive guests were preoccupied while the starlet—her screeches stifled amid stiff gulps of an expertly mixed French 75—was whisked out of Leo's suite, down the back stairwell, and into a waiting Humvee limousine. At the same time, Leo was being bagged and tagged by discreet personnel of the renowned Hollywood Forever Cemetery before taking *his* last ride in a limo. (You've got to hand it to the hotel's staff: no one handles a celebrity death like those folks. Just another example of how practice makes perfect.)

Second, it *is* true that his current wife, Sybilla Lawson—a former beauty queen who considered herself an actress because of one walk-on she had in a '90s made-for-TV movie—was at Lion's Den, Leo's obscenely humongous Roman-Greco palace in Bel Air, which she insisted he build for them. Considering her usual martini-induced state of unconsciousness, however, if Leo had indeed died there, it might have been another 16 hours or so until she'd discovered him—and that is a really big maybe, given her propensity to stay in her bedroom for days on end and her assumption that any other prostrate bodies lying around were also suffering the slings and arrows of an outrageous hangover.

And, to my regret, I wasn't at Leo's side either. Quite frankly, he had been dodging me for the past month, PDAing lame excuses for ducking out of our weekly Thursday-night dinner dates at the Sunset Lounge. And thanks to his cell's caller ID, he could easily ignore my many concerned voice messages. I couldn't figure out why, although I had some inkling: He didn't know how to tell me that he'd decided to pass on the project pitched to him by my current boyfriend, Jean-Claude, a fledgling (albeit fully financed) independent producer of French-German-Swiss-Hungarian extraction.

Leo was wary of any man-boy I brought home. This made sense when I first started dating. After all, like most daughters, for the most part I chose guys who were anti-Leos. Having moved through my fair share of slackers, nerds, and pseudo-intellectuals—none of whom earned more than a derisive sigh from Leo—I took it up a notch and began dating third-rate actors: all sincere dudes and hard workers to the one, but they were still guys who were never destined to score beyond the second male lead in a made-for-TV movie, or be the nameless "Man in Video Store" or "UPS Man" in blockbuster films employing casts of thousands.

"Hannah, my darling," Leo would sigh. "If you're going to date someone in The industry, at least find someone who'll earn the right to share our legacy."

Translation: find a guy whom Leo would be proud to call his son-in-law.

I thought that was what I was doing when I started dating Jean-Claude: handsome, wealthy, European, and itching to get involved in producing small films with meaningful messages. However, Leo thought (although he didn't say it in so many words) that Jean-Claude was just another Eurotrash hanger-on looking for a free ride; that I was playing Lisa Marie to Jean-Claude's Nick Cage—which, once again, made Leo the King in that scenario.

Still, I denied this vehemently and clung to Jean-Claude, knowing we would someday prove Leo wrong.

Ironically, the night Leo died, it was Jean-Claude who gave me the news.

"Where are you, Hannah?" he asked tersely.

I was annoyed because he should have known the answer to that: not three hours earlier, bored listening to him and his ex-pat buddies with obscure royal titles and dwindling bank accounts commiserate under a murky L.A. sky about the stuck-up L.A. women promenading poolside at Skybar (specifically, the ladies ignoring their well-worn pickup lines), I quite distinctly remember telling him that I was going to head over to the Griffith Observatory with my telescope. Whenever I could get away (which, considering Jean-Claude's predilection for barhopping, translated into every night of the week) I went planet hunting—that is, seeking out undiscovered planets circling suns in other galaxies.

My current target was the red dwarf star known as AU Microscopium—or "Mic," as we called it—which was moving in tandem through the galaxy with its sister star, beta-Pictoris, through the constellation Saturn. For nearly a year, I had spent every spare evening glued to the eyepiece of my telescope, watching that particular patch of ebony sky and carefully measuring every wiggle or flicker emanating from Mic for proof that some yet unnamed celestial body—a new planet—was in fact shadowing it.

This "silly little hobby" (Jean-Claude's declaration, not mine) was something he indulged me in—particularly if there was enough eye candy to distract him from my absence.

His frantic call put an end to all that.

"It's Leo," Jean-Claude said, in a dire tone. "I think you'd better get over here as fast as possible."

"Where? Skybar?" I was confused. It was a wannabe's hangout, not one of the usual watering holes that established players like Leo often frequented.

"No—uh, Lion's Den," he murmured distractedly. "Look, I don't have time to explain. Please," he choked, "just get here!" He then heaved a soft sigh into the phone and hung up.

That was how I came to realize that my father had finally left me for good.

I didn't jump into my car immediately but instead kept my eye on Mic. It seemed to quiver ever so slightly. At least, I thought so. Then again, through all my tears, it was hard to tell.

Leo's memorial service was held at dusk in the Beverly Hills Hotel's Crystal Garden. The setting sun's soft rays, bouncing off the hotel's pale pink stucco walls, provided a healthy glow to the complexions of the many stars in attendance.

No doubt that was greatly appreciated.

True to the claims that Leo had been "a thespian bridge between Hollywood's Silver Screen era and that of a newer, rawer epoch in filmmaking" (not my proclamation, but that of *Premiere*), the turnout was a Hollywood *Who's Who:* Barbra was there (in classic black Karan, of course), as were Nicole, Renée and Charlize (in funeral frocks provided by Prada, Lacroix, and Marc Jacobs, respectively); the two Toms (Hanks and Cruise); Nicholson, Pacino, De Niro, Scorsese, as well as the two Stevens (Spielberg and Soderbergh), and both the Coen *and* the Farrelly brothers. Also milling about was every up-and-coming actor, mobster, gangsta/rap singer-cum-actor, Playboy bunny, limo driver, bartender and waiter who had ever crossed Leo's path.

The eulogies were touching and numerous. Everyone had a "Leo" story. Both Toms waxed poetically about being "discovered" by Leo, and how his mentorship had changed their lives, while Madonna sobbed, albeit dry-eyed, "He was like a father to me." (Of course, this immediately gave credence to the old rumor that the two had been more than "just friends" in her romantic hiatus between Sean and Warren in the summer of '89.) Everyone's head nodded in unison, leaving one with the impression that the "grand-père of cinema" *(Newsweek)* had mentored, bullied or screwed his way into the heart of anyone who had ever stepped foot on a studio lot.

Having relieved the semi-comatose Sybilla from the process of planning and coordinating Leo's funeral, I had not yet allowed myself the opportunity to acknowledge my own grief. By the time Warren and Gene began rhapsodizing on and on about some ill-fated bad boy shenanigan that the three of them had attempted during some on-location shoot in which Leo was once again the cockeyed hero, I couldn't contain myself anymore; I let my tears fall freely along with everyone else's.

(Well, admittedly, most of the puffy eyes in the crowd were from the many eyelifts that had been performed that week. Still, it's the *thought* that counts.)

Long after the final guests had successfully maneuvered the paparazzi gauntlet and been whisked away via remotely-summoned limos, and after said paparazzi had finally snapped their final photos (including some of the catfight between Sybilla and the Disney Channel junior diva, which Jean-Claude was kind enough to break up), and after the waterworks display put on by Wife #3, a former soap opera diva, had finally trickled out (ironically, just seconds after the CNN cameraman had packed up his gear), I finally had the chance to collapse in anguish.

I stumbled into the private hospitality cottage that had been rented in tandem with the Crystal Garden for use by the bereaved. At first it appeared that the small but elegant space was totally empty. As it turns out, it wasn't. Sybilla had also decided to take her consolation there. I knew this because I could hear her wailing in the cottage's bedroom.

I sighed. In truth, I didn't like the woman. While wooing Leo, she had been sickeningly sweet to me, hoping to inspire me to be her ally in that cause. I hadn't obliged. I'd had my reservations about her, but I'd never shared them with Leo because he was a big boy and could make up his own mind in that matter, with or without my blessing.

To my chagrin, once they married, she did her best to keep the two of us from seeing each other, or else she readily excused herself from our get-togethers. So as not to feel like a third wheel, Jean-Claude made it a point to bow out as well, which is probably why our Thursday-night dinners were so comfortable—that is, until Jean-Claude made it his life mission to produce Leo's next movie, which is why Leo made it his goal to avoid Jean-Claude's entreaties in every possible way.

Speaking of Jean-Claude, where was he? I wondered. Sybilla's wailing was excruciating. Since the moment she had heard of Leo's death, Jean-Claude had taken it upon himself to give her a shoulder to cry on, so I couldn't really blame him for finally ducking out.

I tapped gingerly on the bedroom door. No answer. I tried again, a little bolder this time. Her convulsions only grew louder.

Wow, I thought. I guess she really *did* love Leo!

That was where I was wrong. Peeking through the bedroom door, I was able to confirm that, yes, Sybilla *was* hysterical with emotion—however, it was the ecstatic kind that only happens when you're enjoying illicit wild monkey sex with someone who makes it his business to play women as if they were Stradivarius violins.

That virtuoso was none other than Jean-Claude.

Both of them looked up at the same time. It was as if the three of us were suspended in a time warp. Then, in slow motion, the desire in their faces melted into guilt. Still, it was no match for my own look of horror, I'm sure.

I ran out the front door, ignoring Jean-Claude's pleas as he grappled with the pants tangled at his feet. He caught up with me as I was unlocking my car door. "Hannah, please—" he stuttered. "It's not at all what you think!"

"What, are you crazy?" I screamed. "I know *exactly* what was happening in there."

"I was just—consoling her! It meant nothing, I swear!"

"It may have meant nothing to *you*, but *she* was sure enjoying herself! Believe me, Jean-Claude, that was no performance. Sybilla isn't that good of an actress."

He nodded resignedly. "All right, Hannah, you want the truth, you'll have it: Sybilla and I—we love each other."

"You—you what? Since when?"

The thought suddenly struck me: *Had Leo known about it?*

"I won't lie to you. We've been in love for quite some time. We were just waiting—well, for the right time to tell you."

"And Leo, too?" I spat out the words.

He frowned. "Yes, we were going to tell the both of you."

I couldn't speak. It was as if someone had knocked the air out of me. Finally I murmured, "When would that have been? After he completed your film?"

Jean-Claude didn't answer.

"Well, then maybe he was right not to want to do it."

"Don't be so sure he wouldn't have. Sybilla would have talked him into it."

I winced at the inference: that *she* could have made Leo do something that I could not.

"In fact, we were planning it as a comeback vehicle for her, too."

"For *Sybilla?*" The thought was so ludicrous that I laughed in spite of my anger. "Why, she couldn't act her way into an infomercial! Marriage to Leo saved her from having to be turned down for—for a position as a QVC hostess!"

"You're cruel, Hannah." With that, he turned and walked back toward the cottage. I wanted to call out—I don't know, I guess I wanted to curse him, curse them both . . . or, maybe, ask him what I had done wrong to deserve *this*.

Instead I got into my car and fumbled to put the key in the lock. I couldn't quite keep my hand from shaking in order to achieve that goal, so instead I sat silently, watching the fronds on the stately palm trees scattered throughout the hotel's lawn rustle to and fro from the gentle breeze blowing in from the ocean.

My cell phone beeped. The caller ID showed that it was Jean-Claude calling. A shiver of hope ran through me: *Maybe it was all just a big mistake, a bad, stupid dream! Maybe he realized how much he'd hurt me, how much I really meant to him. Maybe—*

I clicked it open.

"Hannah, my sweet—" Sybilla.

I almost dropped the phone. "What do you want, you conniving bitch?"

"Just to warn you," she cooed. "The will is being read tomorrow, and if I were you, I wouldn't make any trouble."

"Don't threaten me, you two-timing stepmother-fucking whore."

"Ouch. That hurt—*you*, dearest, and tomorrow you'll find out *exactly what I mean.*"

The line went dead.

It was my turn to wail, which I did: loudly, angrily, and only because I knew that the chorus of sprinklers humming up and down the hotel's emerald lawn was drowning out my sobs.

The bereavement calls came in all night. No matter who it was from—one of my dad's many friends, acquaintances, enemies, ex-wives, former girlfriends, new girlfriends, etcetera, etcetera—it started out the same way: asking me if there was anything, *anything at all* that they could do *for me* . . .

Very, very kind.

Within a sentence or two, however, they'd choke up as they reminisced about the first time they ever met Leo. Then the sniffling began, at which point the tables were turned, and I was now consoling the caller: "That's okay, Matt—" (or Brad, or Tobey, or Meryl, or Sharon or whomever). "Oh, I know, I know. He *was* the greatest. He always loved you, too. Yes, *really!* He mentioned you all the time . . . Yes, I know, he was like a father to you, too. I guess we can console ourselves that, Leo being Leo, is charming the pants off a different crowd now . . ." Or something to that effect.

Sometime between the second and the seventh call, I got smart and decanted a bottle of Château Lynch-Bages 2000 Pauillac (Leo's cardinal rule: a good hostess stocks her bar with at least one one-hundred-dollar bottle of wine), and I allowed myself to take a sip before picking up the phone each time.

The final call came about ten o'clock at night. By then the bottle was long gone, and I no longer felt the obligation to man the Mother Teresa hotline, so I let it ring. But whoever was calling wouldn't give it a break. I finally resigned myself to that fact and picked up the phone.

"Hannah, I'm glad you're home. It's Jasper." Jasper Carlton is—was—Leo's attorney. He is also the third and only Carlton of the venerable old Beverly Hills law firm of Franklin, Carlton, Gregory, Churchill, Carlton and Carlton who is still living and breathing. As such, in Hollywood his representation is like a rare stock, or akin to buying a thousand shares of Microsoft in '82; in other words, golden.

I felt an immense flood of relief. I didn't know what Sybilla had up her sleeve, but whatever it was, if there was someone who could launch a successful counterattack, it was certainly Jasper.

There was another reason I was glad to hear his voice on the other end of the phone: I hadn't yet taken the opportunity to thank Jasper for his unwavering loyalty to Leo all these many years, despite my father's errant behavior, including the now legendary tiffs with studio heads, the public bickering and estate plundering by Leo's four wives, and his innumerable affairs, including the one that had led to the birth of Leo's "one and only love child" (my most unfortunate nickname, courtesy of *Star* magazine) with the one woman whom he *hadn't* married: my mother, Journey Sterling.

In many ways, Jasper is not your typical Beverly Hills lawyer, although that isn't evident by his trendy attire. His suits may be Brioni (his one concession to a client base that considered itself cutting edge), but his heart is very much classic Brooks Brothers, and it showed in the formality and honesty with which he treated his clients.

"Jasper, I'm glad you called," I whispered, my voice breaking. "More than anyone, you were always there for Leo, and I thank you for that."

Obviously touched by my kind words, Jasper sighed. "Don't be so quick to thank me, kiddo."

"What do you mean?"

"About eighteen months ago, when you first started dating that French fellow—"

"Jean-Claude?"

"Yes, that guy. I saw him at the funeral today."

I laughed harshly. "Well, you don't have to worry about him any more, Jasper."

"I know," he answered, pointedly.

I blushed hotly, glad that Jasper couldn't see me through the phone. "How?"

"I'll get to that. As I started to say, about eighteen months ago, Leo came in to see me. To change his will."

"I don't get it."

"Apparently he was upset, thought this lad was trying to take advantage of you. He felt that, in order to protect you, he should make some changes to your trust fund."

"What—what kind of changes?" Suddenly I felt cold. I sat

down, hard. Thank goodness there was actually a chair behind me.

"Your trust was to continue *only* until his death." Jasper let this sink in.

I didn't know what to say. I hadn't known that Leo had felt so strongly about Jean-Claude. In fact, I had assumed we had cleared whatever hurdles had stood between the two men in my life. Obviously I had been wrong.

And once again, Leo had read the situation right.

Jasper continued. "Well, last week he came into my office again, requesting that I draw up another new will. In it, you were to be included again. Sybilla was going to be cut out."

"I think I know why," I muttered.

"Yes, I can imagine. Neither Sybilla nor Jean-Claude seems to have a discreet bone in their bodies."

So, Leo *had* known after all! I dropped my head, ashamed at my own naivete.

"However, Hannah, he never got around to signing it."

"What? What does that mean?"

"For right now, it means that the current Mrs. Leo Fairchild will inherit his full estate. However, you would have every right to contest that will."

"I can't even think about that now, Jasper. It's—it's just too soon."

"I know, kiddo. I just wanted you to be aware of the true situation before the will is read tomorrow."

"So that's what she meant."

"Who?"

"Sybilla. I—I just found out about them today, I mean her and Jean-Claude. She told me not to 'make waves,' or else I'd regret it."

"Sounds like she knows she'll have to accept a settlement of some sort," he answered thoughtfully. "Still, I think that under the circumstances, we're going to have to move fast. I'll ask the court to freeze whatever assets there are. But the way your stepmother is already spending it, there may not be much left when all is said and done. Which brings us to a very important question: how are you fixed for money?"

I grimaced. "My rent is paid up for the month, but it's slim pickings after that."

I didn't mention that I'd recently splurged on my new convertible Beetle with all the bells and whistles, along with a summer wardrobe from Fred Segal's to go with it; or that I was still paying off the $4,000 I'd borrowed for my telescope, lenses, mount and other stargazing paraphernalia. "I haven't exactly been very frugal, I guess. And you know I don't have a job. I've been concentrating on my planet hunting."

Jasper cleared his throat, which I interpreted to mean that he viewed my astronomy project as just another harebrained example of TFB (trust fund baby) busywork.

"Can you type?"

"Sure, slowly, with my index fingers."

His silence spoke volumes.

"I see myself more as a people person," I backpedaled brightly. "You know, hostess with the mostess. And I'm *great* with details."

"I know. You came through like a champ in planning Leo's funeral. I can't even imagine how things would have gone off if that addle-brained stepmother of yours had taken the reins. You know, Hannah, I always felt you were the one thing in Leo's life that made him proud. You were his anchor, whether he was willing to admit it to himself or not."

A knot formed in my throat. Jasper's kind words made me both happy and sad at the thought of Leo. "So, what do you have in mind, Jasper?"

"I've got a new client who needs some help. Don't worry, it's not a lot of office work. His manager can make arrangements to handle that kind of stuff."

I silently waited for the punch line.

"What he needs is a gopher—you know, someone who can run errands for him, help him run lines, be on the set with him to make sure he's got everything he needs—"

"You want me to babysit an *actor?*"

"Well, yes, in a way. You'd be his personal assistant."

I couldn't help but laugh. "Are you serious?"

"Frankly, yes I am. It's Louis Trollope. You know, the one they call the new British heartthrob. He's a young Hugh Grant, but with a Colin Farrell edge."

"Colin is Irish."

"That's beside the point, my dear. The point I'm trying to make is that Louis is hot *right now;* the wet dream of the month. And because of who *you* are, you'd be perfect for the position: you won't be star-struck, you understand the importance of discretion, you can't be intimated—"

"You can say that again." My mind flashed on all the screaming matches I'd had with Leo. In most cases I had stood firm, to his chagrin. Of course, those times had usually ended with me hiding in a bathroom, upchucking my pent-up inclinations to run, hide, and cry myself to sleep over our colliding obstinacy.

"And," Jasper continued, "you're already familiar with actors and their—well, let's just call it their 'idiosyncrasies.' "

"I don't know if that's a compliment or a slap in the face."

"It's neither. It's just a fact of your life. So, why not capitalize on it?"

I saw his point, but I didn't exactly like it.

Sure, I could handle whatever some up-and-coming actor could throw at me; if Leo had given me nothing else, he had given me a ringside seat on high-profile notoriety. But *that* had been a living hell. Now that I was free of it, why would I want to relive history with a cardboard copy of Leo?

I wasn't *that* desperate. At least, I hoped I wasn't.

I let loose a loud sigh. It had been an exhausting week, and I was ready for it to be over. "I don't know, Jasper. I really don't think I'm cut out for it. But thanks for thinking about me." My lack of sincerity was palpable, I'm sure.

"I understand, sweetie, believe me I do. But the money is decent—six thousand a month—and it won't be forever, just however long it takes for Leo's estate to be straightened out. If anything, the hubbub around this kid might help you keep your mind off of it. And he's not a bad sort—at least, not yet, anyway. You might actually enjoy yourself." He paused. "Take a day or two to think about it. If you change your mind, call Svetlana in my office, and she'll email over exactly what you need to know about the job. In the meantime, I'll do my best to keep Leo's widow at bay."

"You're very sweet to be concerned about me, Jasper. But don't hold your breath." With that, I said good-bye.

And pulled the phone out of the wall in silent protest.

Then I walked over to my telescope. Peering through the lens, I suddenly realized that I was too dizzy to be standing up, so I stumbled off to bed.

The good news: If I was going to get wasted, at least it was happening on a $100 bottle of red.

The bad news: It was probably the last expensive bottle of wine I'd ever drink.

Here's the part where you get my backstory:

Let me start off by saying that it's not easy being a trust fund baby. First of all, everyone naturally assumes you're lazy because you don't have to work in order to make your rent money.

In most cases, that is *so* wrong. Of course, many of us work! It's just that we are usually working at something that doesn't come with a salary attached. I mean, many TFBs are struggling actors, artists or musicians.

And a lot of us do charity stuff (in other words, those who can't, volunteer). We TFBs put the "junior" in Junior League, regardless of our age.

My own form of hereditary atonement is astronomy research for UCLA: I do mapping of late-type stars that are found at the center of the galaxy. And because I'm a volunteer, it's initially assumed I'm a saint—that is, until people find out that I'm the daughter of Leo Fairchild, and then they change their minds based on a new assumption: that I'm too stupid to use my family's connections or trade on my illustrious name to get a *real* job.

Well, they're wrong. I'm not too stupid. I'm just too *stubborn*.

Maybe that's because I've always felt that my birth was in fact an accident, the result of too much hashish and a defective condom shared between a man old enough to know better (Leo was forty-two at the time) and a girl young enough to be his daughter—Journey, my mother, who was all of nineteen.

I must admit, when he heard he was going to be a proud papa, he did try to do right by us. At the time, he was between wives (numbers One and Two), so why not?

But hey, it was the late '70s, and a chant murmured in a Mount Tam redwood grove at sunrise in front of a bunch of stoned acolytes does not a union make—at least, that was the conclusion Leo reached just prior to my first birthday. So he offered Journey her freedom ("It wasn't our karma, sweetheart"), along with generous child support for me.

He deduced, quite rightly, that my mother was not the kind to make palimony waves. She left Los Angeles for Northern California without a backward glance. In truth, she couldn't stomach the town anyway: her love beads and New Age values were out of place with the true Hollywood: lies, doublespeak and business-as-usual backstabbing.

Besides, Leo's wandering eye hurt even more than his callous dismissal of their union.

For the first sixteen years of my life, I lived with Journey on a tiny houseboat docked along the Sausalito waterfront, a pseudo-bohemian enclave that welcomed free spirits with open arms. For a little kid, it was a virtual play land: our homes—made out of anything that could float, from tugboats to abandoned barges to hobbled-together skiffs—were anchored so closely together that we could play tag by hopping from one gangplank to another.

We appreciated that our parents were, for the most part, big kids, too: artists, musicians, writers, poets and activists who were not tied to work schedules or deadlines, laughed at conformity, and deviated from mainstream answers in favor of any and all alternatives.

There was a caveat, however: while encouraging our own sense of freedom, adventure and experimentation, they expected us to accept it wholeheartedly from them as well.

By the time I became a teenager, I was finding this harder and harder to do. To Journey, I wasn't merely her child, but also her soul mate, pal and confidante. I was always expected to be there: panhandling alongside her at the ferry terminal as the nine-to-five commuters were on their way to work in San Francisco's financial district, or hawking Journey's handicrafts—poorly made candles, painted rocks, and recycled denim made into tiny purses—at the dusty Marin City

Flea Market, whenever Leo's monthly stipend ran out, which it did all too often, particularly after one of Journey's infamous monthly houseboat parties, where the thick pot haze did little to obscure the pairing-off of errant spouses or significant others.

When I turned thirteen and asked Journey if I could join her in a toke, she made a big deal out of my request, insisting that we throw a "joint mitzvah" to celebrate the occasion. All I remember about it was how ill I was afterward—and how Journey was too stoned to wake up and comfort me.

By my fifteenth birthday, I'd had enough of Journey's way of life. I now had a thirst to know more about how others lived—specifically, my father, beyond what I had gleaned from his old movies, tabloid clippings and our too few daddy-daughter phone conversations and my occasional visit to his many homes in the Southland.

All my life I had been taking care of Journey. Now I wanted someone to take care of *me*.

She was not all that open to my suggestion that I live with Leo until I turned eighteen. "Despite being a total shit head, he *is* your legacy. But still—"

"I know all that. But he's also half of who *I* am. Shouldn't I give him a chance to be something different, at least to *me*?"

Neither of us thought that there was a snowball's chance in hell he'd agree to my scheme. I mean, who would want a goonishly tall, gawky, pimply, flat-chested Jane Austen–enthralled teenage girl with crooked teeth and terrierlike hair hanging around the house? Particularly when the average age of his current flock of busty, burnished and blond girlfriends was twenty-three: for sure legal, but still young enough to trade clothes, CDs, and secrets with his daughter.

You could have knocked both Journey and me over with a feather when, through his assistant, Tammy, I got the word to

"Come on down to L.A." Journey bought my ticket on Southwest the very next day.

The morning I flew out of San Francisco was cold and foggy. An hour later I departed the plane into brilliant sunshine, my eyes blinking to adjust as I hopped into the waiting limo Leo had sent to pick me up. I felt like a butterfly emerging from its chrysalis.

That adjustment took three years, and Leo made it a truly eye-opening experience: Not only was I versed on how to choose fine wines, tie a tuxedo bow tie, and tell a great script from a real stinker but I also learned how to lie with a straight face—to his agent, his latest director, the press, studio heads and, most importantly, to Leo's various and sundry girlfriends.

Leo marveled, "Honey, you're a chip off the old block. A natural-born liar!"

Although on the surface his compliments seemed more heartfelt than backhanded, *they really weren't.*

I also learned that I, too, was not immune to Leo's duplicity, which usually occurred when I needed him most. My 104-degree fever and strep throat couldn't keep him from a Lakers game, although he claimed he had to "stay late on the set" and sent Tammy in his place to take me to the hospital. (There I was in my hospital bed, flipping channels with my remote, when I came upon Channel 9 as its camera panned the Lakers' court. And there Leo was, in his floor seat, right next to Jack.) And on my seventeenth birthday, he missed my party because he was "on location"—in Palm Springs, I later learned, with the woman who would soon be his third wife, the soap star.

Then there was the time he showed up for my apartment-warming party immediately after my graduation from high school but disappeared an hour into it, claiming he had to meet his agent and a producer on the Fox lot. A couple of hours later, changing out of my bathing suit in the pool's clubhouse,

I overheard two of my so-called girlfriends comparing notes on his sexual prowess in the apartment complex's hot tub.

After that I skeptically parsed everything he said to me. Doing so wasn't easy on either of us: Leo wasn't used to others so obviously calling his bluff, and I was too hurt to realize that my pointed inquisitions were only exacerbating the problem between us.

To some extent, moving out of his house helped our relationship. He was much easier to love from afar—and far more tolerable when we did get together.

I also found another way to drown my sorrows: while I might not have been able to trust another woman to like me for myself as opposed to my proximity to Leo, I could always count on the fawning attentions of every sales clerk between Rodeo Drive and Melrose Avenue. Love me, love my credit card—which Leo paid in full—was my motto. We both accepted this as his grudging penance for absentee parenting.

My saving grace: astronomy, which I discovered through a UCLA extension class. Looking up into a cobalt sky at millions of tiny white dots, and grasping hold of the concept that these other worlds were millions of light-years away and far beyond our reach, put the frailty of our humanity—even Leo's—back into perspective for me. It's why I spend hours hunkered over a telescope in the hope of discovering something so spectacular.

Even Leo got it. Once he surprised me, tracking me down at one of the viewing platforms outside the observatory. I was so engrossed in a star shower that I hadn't hear him come up behind me. He just stood there, silently watching me until I looked up.

It would be an understatement to say that my father had a way with words. Coming out of his mouth, the phrase *Pass the salt*, was not a simple request but a truly moving experience of passion, verve, and elocution—which was why most of the world's renowned film directors had salivated at the chance to pay him millions of dollars to hear him say "Pass the salt," or other phrases just as mundane.

To me, he simply said, " 'You teach your daughters the diameters of the planets and wonder when you are done that they do not delight in your company.' "

"That's beautiful," I stuttered, still surprised to see him.

"Samuel Johnson said it." He gave me a kiss on the cheek and took a turn at the telescope.

It was the only time in my life that I felt my father totally and completely understood me.

And then he was gone, as unreachable to me as any supernova moving through the cosmos.

And there I was, alone on planet Earth, with overdue rent, a car payment to make, foreclosure eminent on my telescope, and a very big Fred Segal's bill landing in my mailbox any day now.

Not to mention a lawsuit in the making.

I'd weathered Leo and survived. How bad could life be looking after Louis Trollope?

2

Supernova

*A rare celestial phenomenon, involving the explosion
of most of the material in a star,
resulting in an extremely bright, short-lived object
that emits vast amounts of energy.*

It took the court exactly two weeks to freeze Leo's assets so
that the disputed will could be reviewed some time within the
next six months (God willing).

However, it took less than 24 hours for Sybilla to shuffle
about a fifth of the estate—Leo's cash stash, family jewelry
and heirlooms, and various safety-deposited trinkets—into her
own private Neverland, never to resurface again.

On the seventh day, I rose, came to my senses, and took
Jasper up on his suggestion.

Oh well, better late than never.

At my behest, Jasper's Svetlana set up my interview with
Louis Trollope that afternoon at four-thirty sharp, then couri-
ered over the formal job description for the personal assistant

position. Enclosed with it were a trove of articles that were anything and everything ever written on Louis, as well as a little note from Jasper containing a quote that he obviously thought would help me put my situation into perspective:

> If you run into a wall, don't turn around and give up. Figure out how to climb it, go through it, or work around it.
>
> Michael Jordan

The first thing that popped into my mind was the question of whether Michael Jordan was a client of Jasper's firm, but I immediately put that thought to rest: it wasn't Jasper's style to cheerlead a client's branded words of inspiration.

However, had the note come from Leo's agent instead, Randy Zimmerman, of ICA—International Creative Agency—I would have had no doubt that this was in fact the case. A complimentary pair of Nike sneakers in my correct size would have also accompanied it, along with a lascivious request to watch me try them on, sans any other attire.

That was because Randy was the ultimate swine.

On the many occasions in which I'd pointed this out to Leo, he'd responded by paraphrasing his favorite president, Franklin Delano Roosevelt (and, needless to say, with a spot on accent): "He may be a pig, but he's *my* pig."

Any way you shake it, in Hollywood, your ability to negotiate several $20 million deals earns you that kind of loyalty.

A placement firm that specialized in such positions had obviously written the job description that was also enclosed. Its criteria were daunting enough to intimidate the unqualified but sufficiently covert to entice a real bootlicking go-getter. In part, it read:

PERSONAL ASSISTANT: *Seeking an exceptional candidate who can enhance our client's lifestyle and creative objectives. Must be responsible, flexible, an excellent problem solver, have a strong work ethic, and be the model of honesty and integrity. The ability to maintain the highest level of security and confidentiality at all times is essential. You will be on call 24 hours per day, 7 days per week. Responsibilities will cover a wide range of duties, as you will be overseeing our client's complex lifestyle issues. Thus, you must have the ability to multitask while still remaining organized and focused on the tasks at hand. If you are an excellent planner with strong problem-solving skills, and thrive in a fast-paced environment, then you may be a great asset for this creative artist. However, you must be prepared to face adversity.*

What does this mean? Should I have trained with Special Ops?

You must also be fluent in etiquette and proper protocol when dealing with business and personal associates of our client. Exposure to European graces is a plus! You will be responsible for all details that allow your employer to stay focused, on time and on track by ensuring that creative and personal needs are met. Must feel comfortable working out of home in an exclusive area of Hollywood. Duties include phones, some Internet, travel arrangements, and general organizing. Must have reliable transportation and valid driver's license. Some travel, light cooking, and running errands. Experience in personal training and interior design would be beneficial . . .

There was more, running almost as long as the U.S. tax code, but I won't bore you with the rest. Suffice it to say that a combination of Mother Teresa, Miss Manners and Mary Poppins would be a perfect candidate—*maybe*.

Who was this guy, anyway? The pope?

And Jasper thought this gig was up my alley? It was worth it to interview, just to prove him wrong.

My appointment with Louis Trollope took place at his house, which sat high in the Hollywood Hills. It was a typical actor's bachelor pad, which is to say it was a ramshackle stucco cottage with a Spanish tile roof, hidden deep inside a grove of madrone trees and overrun with bougainvillea. And, while it was merely adequate in the area of creature comforts, it received exceptionally high points for its breathtaking views of the city and the ocean beyond.

I had zigzagged my way up Mulholland Drive, then turned back north onto Laurel Canyon Boulevard. I was going faster than I should have, but only because his house was almost as far as Fryman Place and my Beetle was running on fumes. Already the winter sun was setting, and I wanted to get there and back as fast as possible, reasoning that it would be better to coast downhill on empty in twilight than after dark.

Svetlana's directions ended at a nondescript driveway on a tiny dead-end lane off LCB. A tall wooden gate blocked the driveway. I pressed the security phone's intercom button three times before getting a response: something garbled came out, but it ended with "—love."

"I beg your pardon?" The last thing I was expecting was a term of endearment. I prayed he could hear me better than I had heard him.

"Shit!" came his response. At first, I didn't know what to

think. Had my question offended him in some way? Or did he have Tourette's syndrome? Or was this just a sneak preview of his usual demeanor?

"Sorry, love, that wasn't meant for you. Somehow I—I disconnected my cell phone by mistake. Bloody piece of crap! Please, come on up the drive. Park anywhere."

"No problem. I'll be right up." The Beetle had been idling in neutral, which was supposed to conserve its last pitiful vapors of gas. I waited until the gate swung open far enough for the Beetle to squeak by and crawl toward the house.

In the driveway were a Humvee, a Prius, a deep red Ferrari F430, and a Harley Davidson custom VRSCSE Screamin' Eagle V-Rod: the right accessories to suit any mood or event. These were the prerequisite toys of the male *célébrité dans la mode*, evidence that Louis Trollope had arrived, at least by Hollywood standards.

The front door was wide open.

"Hello?" I called from the foyer.

At first I didn't see him. Walking boldly through the entryway and into the living room beyond, I barely missed stumbling over a khaki camel-hair ottoman. Coming in from the outside, it took a while for my eyes to adjust in the cool semidarkness of the room. With its rough-hewn beamed ceiling, dark stained batten-and-board walls, large suede chairs and several oversized leather settees clustered around a carved antler coffee table piled high with movie scripts, Louis's cottage was so obviously Beverly Hills designer Dodd Mitchell's take on a gentleman's hunting lodge.

Finally I made out his silhouette. And although Louis hadn't said a word, I just knew he had been watching me from the moment I had entered, clearly relishing the opportunity to observe without being observed himself—a rarity for him, I'm sure.

Now that I was standing there in front of him, he gave me his complete and utter attention: the equivalent of 1,000 watts of unadulterated star power.

"Hello to you, too. I'm quite charmed to make your acquaintance," he said, offering his hand to me.

I had to admit, the celebrity magazines have Louis Trollope pegged right: "For being a guy's guy, it's easy to see why he's such a chick magnet . . ." *(GQ)*, what with his being "ruggedly handsome and roguishly charming . . ." *(Ladies' Home Journal)* and possessing "startling azure eyes that, when focused on you, make you feel that you are the only person in the room—not to mention cheekbones to lust for . . ." *(Redbook)* as well as ". . . the cutest bum on either side of the pond" *(British Vogue)*. Over all, he's "just a wicked wet dream!" *(Cosmopolitan)*.

And there I was, bathed in the spotlight of his smile.

It would have been easy to bask in its warmth, but my intuition warned me not to get too used to it, or I might get burned.

I shook his hand, and I swear, when I touched him, a current ran through me like a bolt of lightning. It was all I could do not to melt into a ball of jelly at his feet.

If Louis felt it too, he didn't show it. I was surprised just how much that disappointed me.

The soft, insistent moan of his cell phone broke the spell.

"Damn! It never stops!" he muttered again. "Why doesn't the world just leave me alone?"

He looked as if he wanted to throw the phone through the plate-glass window and into the pool that lay just outside. Then he thought better of it. Instead he sighed and tossed the phone into the piles of pillows nestled on one of the humongous leather couches, where the buzzing was immediately muffled in buckskin-encased goose down.

I couldn't help feeling a bit sorry for him, knowing as I did that, should his wish ever be granted, he would rue the day.

"Jasper claims that you're the answer to my prayers." His voice was warm, the words silken.

I blushed, not knowing how to answer him. "I'm sure it was said simply out of kindness," I murmured modestly.

"God, I hope not! I'm in a jam. Tell me you're my angel of mercy. *Please.*"

His eyes locked onto mine again with what he intended to be a soul-searing gaze.

"Well . . . well, I—I don't know if I can live up to all of your expectations. That was quite a daunting job description."

"It's rubbish. It was dreamed up by one of those agencies that finds zookeepers for spoiled, pampered Hollywood brats." He raised one eyebrow skyward and leaned back suggestively. "Our relationship would be a bit more low-key, casual. You'll come to know me intimately—of course, I don't mean that in an incestuous way. More like a doting sis, mind you."

(My god! He's flirting with me!)

Noting that his charm had brought about the desired result, Louis chuckled conspiratorially, then eased me onto the settee alongside him. I fell between the cushions—thankfully not onto the cell phone, which had finally stopped growling.

"Things are going crazy around here. I'm finishing up a film right now, and I've been offered three more movies, all wanting to go into production immediately. And, just my luck, they're all great roles, but different, you know? That's why you are so important to me."

You had me at "Hello to you, too" . . .

Stop it! Been there, done that!

To break his spell over me, I nodded my head, as if to indicate that, if it mattered to him, then it mattered to me, too—which he already took for granted.

"One is the lead in the *Lords* prequel: instant box office, of course, before the first frame is even in the can. But I'm dying to work with Brownstein, you know, that kid who ran away with all the offers at Sundance this year? He and I are talking about something small, edgy...smarter than the usual garbage thrown out by the studios." His face took on a faraway look. Then a self-satisfied smile appeared. "And, I'm sure you've heard the rumors that I'm considering the lead in the remake of the *Mad Max* series."

I nodded again, enthusiastically, although, in truth, I hadn't heard.

"They were such classics! It was such a breakthrough role for Mel Gibson," I said encouragingly. "I'd imagine it would be that for you, too."

"What do you mean, 'breakthrough role'? I've *already* broken through." The smile faded. His eyes went dark with wariness. Flippantly he added, "You know, Mel wanted *me* for the lead in *The Passion*"

"Oh, *really?*" I feigned belief, but lacking the performance skills of even a reality TV show contestant, I don't think I fooled him. He really couldn't blame me for doubting the claim. I mean, come on already: he was too buff and too blond for Jesus—even a digitalized Hollywood version.

"I'm for real, I swear! But his sodding agent talked him out of it. Said I was too young for the role. That guy had it in for me because I fired him the year before! Too bad Mel hadn't done the same." He ran his fingers through his golden tendrils, spiked with just enough hair goo to flop forward on cue.

Frankly, I had a sneaking suspicion that, even when the movie was being made, Louis already had a few years on The Second Coming. However, diplomacy (and credit card angst) gave me reasons to keep my mouth shut while Louis rationalized that bit of fate.

"That's okay. It wouldn't have worked anyway. Me as Jesus! What a hoot! I would have had to play it totally Method any-

way, and that would have been hell, what with the whole
Christ story being such a *downer* . . . you know, that whole cru-
cifixion thing."

He paused for emphasis. "Besides, the character has no sequel potential, right? I mean, where do you go from there, *The
Resurrection?* I guess it just wasn't my karma to get the role."

It was a line taken straight out of the Leo handbook. Ah,
how some things never change!

"Besides, I usually play winners, you know? That's how directors see me—at least, that's what they say in *Hollywood Reporter.*"

To prove my empathy, I tossed off this lame consolation:
"Oh, well, as they say, 'Don't go believing your own press clippings.' "

"Why? What have you read? What have you heard?" Louis
turned deadly serious.

"Oh—uh, nothing. Nothing! Really."

"You can tell me. Believe me, you won't hurt my feelings."
He purred the words, but that famous smile had frosted over. I
shivered unconsciously.

"Nothing, I swear! I never even look at the tabloids. Or the
trades, for that matter." Oh well, no more fun and games, I
thought.

My chagrin must have been obvious to Louis, because suddenly he was the Sun God again, all warmth and smiles. "That
will change quickly enough when you work for me."

Didn't I know it! One of my first memories of Tammy,
Leo's assistant, was of her hands, ink-stained from having
scrutinized tall stacks of tabloids for articles about Leo, which
she would then cut out and paste into a scrapbook. "For posterity, babe," Leo would murmur to me, winking coyly. Then,
as an excuse for this egocentric ritual, he added this cautionary
note: "My legacy is yours too, you know."

Yeah, right, sure.

Even if I hadn't believed him, Sybilla must have, because the only things she had released to me thus far had been Leo's twenty-four scrapbooks, a half-century of Tammy's handiwork. Sybilla's limo driver had unceremoniously dumped them on the front porch of my Venice Canal cottage on an unseasonably scorching hot morning. I had been at UCLA, so by the time I'd gotten home that night, rivulets of Elmer's glue had already cascaded down the steps into small gooey puddles strong enough to pull my left sandal off my foot as I'd stumbled over Leo's legacy in the dark. The clippings, yellowed and brittle, had either stuck together like Siamese twins or dissolved into shreds of confetti. It had been another week before the porch had finally lost its eau-de-Montessori-preschool fragrance.

When you work for me, Louis had said.

Suddenly I bolted upright at the implication. "I beg your pardon?" I murmured politely.

He took my stupor for the usual shock and awe he invariably elicited from the masses, all in a day's work.

"I have a gut feeling about you. I think you'll work out. It's a go, then? You won't break my heart, I hope?"

Break *his* heart? If he kept up this level of charm, he'd be calling an ambulance for *me*.

Don't be a fool. It's Leo all over again.

So here he was, practically begging me to take the job. Yet, as flattering as that was, I knew deep down inside that Louis would have made the same offer to anyone short of a two-headed circus freak who had walked through his front door by now.

At the same time, he *had* called me his angel of mercy.

Besides, Beetle and Fred Segal bills wait for no woman. And the legal fees for fighting Sybilla's raid wouldn't be cheap, either.

Reluctantly, I nodded my consent.

"Fabulous, love! Just fabulous!" He practically glowed with appreciation. "By the way, I'll need you to start as soon as possible."

"Okay, sure. What time will you want me here tomorrow?"

"No, I mean like *now*. My dirty laundry is in the bedroom. Scoop it up like the good girl you are, and take it down to the dry cleaner's. Put it under your name, of course. I'd hate to see my tighty-whities on eBay. That happened to Clooney, had you heard? Then go down to the BH Ralph's and pick up some food. I'm having a little get-together for that closed-circuit fight. Just four or five mates, nothing too big. I'm Zone, so keep that in mind with what you pick out. Get some deli, too, and some beer."

He was no longer the attentive wooer. With that dismissal, the moratorium on his cell phone ended. It was recovered from its cushioned nesting place, already flipped open, and autodial as he headed off in the direction of the pool. His pantherlike restlessness virtually shouted, *I've got things to do, places to go, people to see, so get lost.*

"Which way to the bedroom?" I called out archly, hoping that my tone conveyed the message *I may be at your beck and call, but I'm certainly not your slavey!*

No response. I couldn't tell if that was the result of his not hearing me, or the fact that he was ignoring me outright. Naively, I chose to believe the former.

"And, um, before I leave, shouldn't we discuss the terms of my employ—"

Placing one hand over the mouthpiece of his cell phone, he turned back around. On his face was a look of mild exasperation intended to make me feel guilty for asking.

"Call my manager, Genevieve. She takes care of those kinds of details. Jasper's person will have her number."

He had spoken.

And now I was *his* "person."

I nodded resignedly, a gesture as empty as an air kiss, since he was already psychically light-years away from me.

I'd officially been pulled into his orbit. And yes, I know a black hole when I see one . . .

I was off and running. In less than three hours, I had to accomplish the following:

a) Have Louis's laundry at the dry cleaner's down on Ventura before they closed;

b) Make it over to Sunset Boulevard, to Louis's manager's office, to pick up a care package (Louis's phrase, not mine) containing everything I ever needed to know about managing Louis's life; and

c) Stop off at the Beverly Hills Ralph's for the appropriate snacks for Louis's closed-circuit TV boxing event gathering with his posse (again, his term). In doing so, I must consider the following: Zone (Louis), legitimate vegan (for another guest), and gourmet carnivore (for the two or three other guys). By that description, I assumed Louis meant that anything that ever suckled a mother or flown the coop—be it a cow, buffalo, deer, open range chicken, duck, or ostrich—was fine to bring home, as long as it had been fully prepared by either a name chef or a trendy deli, as opposed to Mickey D's or the Colonel.

Once Louis's little shindig was underway, I planned on perusing his care-and-feeding package so that I would know exactly what I should be doing over the next two weeks. This was, of course, based on the assumption that the Supreme Being would answer my fervid prayers so that it would be necessary for me to know Louis's agenda only that far in advance.

As I hightailed it down Laurel Canyon Boulevard, I autodialed Svetlana for Genevieve's telephone number—something Louis did not know by heart, as he only autodialed it from his cell. Being the doll that she is, Svetlana forwarded the call directly to Genevieve's office so that I would not have to program it in as I maneuvered the twists and turns of the road. After playing Twenty Questions with Genevieve's assistant and holding for what seemed like ten minutes, I was finally deemed worthy enough to be put through to her.

"Thank God you've finally called!" Genevieve fairly barked by way of a salutation.

"I'm sorry. I just left Louis now. It's the first opportunity I've had—"

"Yeah, okay, whatever. Look, just get over here pronto. I've got to pull out by six. I'm attending a benefit with Liza at eight—"

"Minnelli?" I asked more out of politeness than interest.

"No, Doolittle," she answered haughtily. "Of course, Minnelli! Is there any other?"

Her snobbery brought out my own. "Oh well then, tell Liza that Hannah says hi. We met at my dad's house, when they were filming *Overture* together."

Silence. I assumed she was putting two and two together. When she made the connection, she replied with an icy sweetness, "Why, of course! *Leo's* little girl. Jasper said something about your possibly needing this job. So sorry about your loss. But hey, don't worry: that's one card you can play for a while . . . well, at least for another year or two. Make it here before six, okay?"

Once again the line went silent. This time it was from her having already rung off.

Fuming, I revved the Beetle's engine as it rounded another curb. So, I was "Leo's little girl," with no identity of my own? That bitch! *Needing* this job, eh? Ha! They needed me more than I needed *them.*

And as for my playing the fame-by-association "card"—

Well, damn it, admittedly she was right. I had tried to pull the oldest Hollywood shuffle: name-dropping as one-upmanship.

Tears welled up in my eyes. What was wrong with me? Was I suddenly so scared about my future that I needed to cling desperately to Leo's past?

Unable to see the road in front of me, I pulled over to the curb and turned off the engine. Across the street the hillside dropped off completely, allowing for a spectacular view of the whole L.A. basin. Despite being enveloped in a thick, gauzy haze of smog, the city lights twinkled—albeit up to a point, where they broke off abruptly, indicating where the Pacific shoreline began and civilization as we like to imagine it left off.

I could just walk away, I reasoned, and begin fresh some-where else, where no one knews me—

—but that would mean leaving behind all the things that were important to me: my little cottage on the Venice Canal that I now called home; my star project; the one or two friends I had who loved me for myself, as opposed to my pedigree . . .

And my past.

Because in truth, I could never walk away from my history with my father.

Then again, why would I want to? Just because some Holly-wood handler had hurt my feelings?

The *hell* with *that!*

I was through with hiding—from myself, from what I was, from what I had the potential to be. It was time to use my connections, to allow every ace I'd been dealt to be played.

And hell yeah, I *would* play the Leo card! The fact that it trumped all others at this point in my life meant that, from now on, it should only be turned over on an as-needed basis—and certainly *not* to impress industry bottom feeders, like Genevieve What's-Her-Name, Manager to the Stars.

Decisively, I put my hand back on the car key and turned the starter. The engine groaned for a minute, then puttered to a halt. I looked at all the digital readouts on the dashboard until I found the problem:

No gas.

Great, I thought. Now I have to walk all the way down Laurel Canyon Boulevard and over to Hollywood Boulevard for a gas station, then walk back up with a gas can.

Groaning, I laid my head down on the steering wheel, which tooted loudly from the weight of it. The sound, jolting me upright, echoed through the canyon. It was a not-so-subtle reminder that my future actions would have as many consequences as my inability to act had had in the past.

It was going to be a long night.

3

Open Cluster

A group of young stars that were formed together;
possibly bound together by gravity.

Grudgingly I grabbed my pocketbook, got out of the car and locked it behind me. For the interview I had dressed in a short black skirt and matching top, with some low-heeled sling-backs; not exactly hiking attire. Feeling it would be easier to walk barefoot than in my tight little shoes, I quickly took them off. Barefooted, I started gingerly across the street, figuring it would be safer to walk against the traffic. That way, if I were to get hit, at least I'd see the person who did it.

It didn't take long for someone to try. Just then a motorcycle crested the hill. I froze, not sure whether I should keep moving forward or turn back toward the car. Before I could make up my mind, the motorcycle swerved and fell over, skittering to a halt a mere six inches from me. Its rider, still holding onto the bike, had been dragged sideways along the blacktop.

"Omigod!" I screamed. I hadn't meant to kill anyone. I'd only meant to save my favorite pair of Jimmy Choos.

I kneeled over the crumbled form, a man in jeans and a

leather jacket. Scared, I fumbled to release his motorcycle helmet. He slapped my hand away, then took it off himself.

"Forget it! Forget—what the hell were you doing out in the middle of the road, in the dark, anyway?" he roared angrily.

Despite the scowl, the two-day growth of stubble and a bad case of helmet head, he was certainly decent-looking: mid-thirties in age, dark, curly hair, a lanky frame and deep-set brown eyes.

To put it mildly, I wouldn't have thrown him out of bed.

Motorcycle Guy turned his head slowly from side to side, as if making sure his neck wasn't broken. As he rose off the pavement, he brushed the dust off his jeans. There was a big rip at the knee, where blood was trickling through.

He may have been mean, but at least he was alive. A sense of relief washed over me, followed by a mild rinse of indignation.

"Well, quite frankly, I was trying to get to the other side. Hey, listen, it wasn't my fault entirely. You must have been doing at least sixty! Besides, pedestrians are supposed to have the right of way."

"Pedestrians aren't usually strolling down LCB," he said caustically as he heaved the bike back up on its wheels.

"They are if they've run out of gas." I closed my eyes, let out an involuntary sigh, and hobbled back across the street. Now that I knew the guy was still breathing, I could quit playing angel of mercy and begin the trek down the hill.

"That Beetle there?"

"Yeah, that's mine."

"Oh." Motorcycle Guy scrutinized me for a moment, as if weighing whether or not I was worth the hassle of helping, considering his luck with me thus far. Being no fool, I wanted to swing the vote in my favor.

"Look, I'm—I'm truly, *truly* sorry about getting in your way."

"Thanks." Then silence.

Great, I thought. So, you want me to grovel, huh? Sure, okay, I can grovel, if it means not walking four miles down a hill and back up before my night has even started.

"I don't imagine—I mean, would it be too much if—"

"If what?" He cocked his head to one side, then stared down at his watch. "Damn! My watch stopped."

"Oh! I'm sorry. Look, I . . . I guess I owe you a watch, huh?"

"Nah. Forget about it. Some dude on the street sold it to me."

"Oh. Well, uh, the offer stands if you change your mind. Say—"

He threw the leg with the bloody knee over the seat of the bike, then turned the ignition, revving the engine a few times to make sure it caught.

"Say!" I yelled over the bike's growl. "Um, would it be too much—"

"What?" he yelled back, with a sly smile. "Can't hear you!"

"I said, would it be too much to ask for a ride down the hill! You know, to get some gas."

"Humph!" He stopped for a moment and glanced skyward, as if seeking his answer somewhere on the tail of the Big Dipper.

"Look, I know you were headed in the opposite direction, but still . . . pretty please?"

" 'Pretty please.' " He looked back at me. "Does that often work for you?"

What a *punk!* What a sonofabitch jerk! That was it for me. Angrily, I shrugged him off and headed back down the hill. I could feel him staring at me, but I wasn't going to give him the satisfaction of looking his way ever again.

I heard his bike roar up the hill.

As the sound of his bike echoed through the canyon, I stopped for a moment, totally defeated. Damn! What else could go wrong tonight?

I had made it about a mile down the road when I once again

heard the low rumble of a motorcycle. It was pitch dark now. Still, I could make out the headlight on the bike, crawling toward me up the hill. As it came directly upon me, I saw that it was Motorcycle Guy once again. Apparently he'd turned around somewhere further up on LCB and cut over to Hollywood Boulevard on one of the side streets that bobbed and weaved down the hill. A two-gallon gasoline canister was tied to the back of his bike.

He paused as he came alongside me. "Jump on," he said gruffly. Still, he was smiling.

Happy and relieved, I nodded silently, and as ladylike as I could in my very short skirt, I climbed on his motorcycle. Hesitantly, I put my arms around his waist. A minute later we were at my car. I popped the tank lock, and he angled the canister hose so that it drained directly into the tank.

I reached into my purse and pulled out a ten-dollar bill. "Please, take this. It's—it's the least I could do, for all your trouble."

"Nah, I wouldn't feel good about it. Besides, I hadn't done my Good Samaritan move of the week yet, so you lucked out."

"You can say that again. This is the only break I've had all week."

"That bad, huh?"

"Yeah. My father just died, my stepmother is raping the estate, and I've just started a new job—oh jeez! I've got to get going!"

"Oh." He actually seemed disappointed. "You have to go to work? Right now?"

"Yep. My boss is a real slave driver. Hey, but who knows? Maybe he'll fire me for being late my first night on the job." I laughed, then extended my hand in thanks. "Seriously, I mean it. I don't know how to thank you."

He took my hand in his. A sizzling current ran up my arm, and my heart started palpitating wildly.

Twice in one day! How could that happen?

I let go, embarrassed, and jumped into the Beetle. It started up with a cough but pulled away from the curb with ease. Motorcycle Guy just stood there, watching me drive off. Not anxious to break the connection, I waved into the rearview mirror. Then, glancing at the car's clock, I noted that it was already a quarter after six!

Damn! I sped down the hill.

It wasn't until I hit Sunset that I realized I hadn't asked him his name.

I got to Genevieve's office too late for a face-to-face encounter, which was fine by me. Her assistant, who was just as anxious as her boss to get on with her own evening agenda, was tall, too tan for March, and wearing too-tight Sevens with belly-baring bandeau top. She handed me an overflowing paper bag and shooed me back out onto the street.

"Everything you need to know is in there," she murmured breathlessly, locking the heavy carved double doors behind us. Without a backward glance, she then drove off down the block, most likely to meet her friends at a "be seen" bar on the Strip—perhaps Ashton's place, Dolce, or maybe the Concorde.

Lucky, lucky girl.

Although I still had the Ralph's run to make, I took a quick peek inside my goody bag and found the following:

- My salary was to be $4,166.67 per month, or $50,000 per year (if I lasted that long), paid to me by Genevieve's management company. On the ninetieth day of my employment, I was to be assessed for a raise that might take me to $72,000, depending on Louis's recommendation. That was a bit disappointing, considering Jasper had sold me on this gig based on the fact that I'd be making six thousand a month. Well, beggars can't be choosers, I reasoned. Hopefully before then Jasper would straighten out the estate mess, and Louis's opinion of me wouldn't matter . . . unless I wanted it to.

- A Blackberry, to keep a digital accounting of Louis's calendar, along with a printout of his itinerary thus far for the next 12 months. I'd have the grand chore of inputting all of this into it. Having never used one, I figured it would take me a year just to figure out how to do so.

- A list of the foods on his Zone diet, thank God— although possibly, due to all the Zone worshipers within proximity, the BH Ralph's probably kept a list of foods and recipes on file.

- Two cell phones—one gray, one red—taken out in my name, although it would be used expressly for calls for and from Louis. The gray cell was for his business calls, while the red cell's number was given out to the privileged few who were accepted into the most private part of his universe. I was also instructed to program Louis's cell with both my home phone number and the red phone's telephone number, in order for him to be able to reach me at all times.

- A typed directory of all the important people in Louis's life. Should anyone on this stellar list call Louis, I was to put them through to him immediately. They included:

- Jasper;
- The odious agent Randy Zimmerman (yes, Louis shared both Leo's lawyer *and* his agent. Talk about déjà vu!);
- Genevieve;
- His acting coach, the renowned Candida Sage;
- His publicist, Monique Radcliffe;
- His nutritionist;
- "Dr. Manny" (Manolo) Lipschitz, celebrity therapist to the stars:
- His physical trainer;
- His chiropractor;
- Mickey Fairstein, realtor to the stars;
- His life coach, Eduardo Larken;
- The various members of his posse;
- And, of course, his current girlfriend, Tatiana Mandeville, the Russian-French Übermodel who had graced the cover of last year's *Sports Illustrated* swimsuit edition, and whose universally renowned pout was adjacent to Louis's own beneficent smile in practically every magazine article I'd already perused while delving into Trollope-iana.

- A list of people who, upon calling, should be told that he was "out of range," but that he would return the call as soon as possible; I was then to ask him if he wanted to return the call and when, and follow his directive. These included certain directors, producers, A-list actors, sundry celebrities of all walks of life and claims to fame, as well as some A-list journalists and talk show hosts, including Oprah, Diane, Katie, Jane, and Barbara.

- A list of people who would never ever get a call-back, come hell or high water. Of course, they were never to know this. On that list were *The National Enquirer, The Globe, The Star*, the entire producing and reporting staffs of *Entertainment Tonight, Extra, Inside Edition*; Joan and Melissa Rivers; most definitely the *Weekly World News*, and a motley crew of over-aggressive fans and stalkers. Someone named "Sam" (no last name given) was also included (previous posse member? stalker extraordinaire? long-lost brother?), as well as the fourteen girlfriends he'd dated prior to Tatiana. (Obviously, good-byes were something Louis took seriously.)

I had my work cut out for me.

The Ralph's run netted six bags of groceries for a whopping $485.23—a bit pricier than the usual fare for a guy's night out, I was guessing.

Unless it was being delivered by a couple of third-rate hookers.

I couldn't pull into Louis's driveway because he never answered the intercom when I rang up, so I parked out on the street. Grabbing two of the bags, I began the trek back to the house.

As it turned out, there was no room to park in the driveway anyway, what with all the boy toys parked willy-nilly behind Louis's own collection of hot wheels. There was a black Lamborghini Murciélago, a bright yellow Lotus Esprit, and I recognized the red Hummer—a twin of the one Louis owned—belonging to Randy Zimmerman. Up until last year, Randy had owned an Aston Martin Vanquish, same as Leo. The trade-in was a sure sign that the auto Randy drove in any given year mirrored his idolatry of his client *du jour*.

The front door was opened a crack. Still, I knocked before entering. No one answered, but I could hear the fight announcer's voice and raucous men's laughter wafting out from the living room.

I found my way to the kitchen and dropped the bags on the counter. I considered whether or not to make another run out to the car but thought it best to make my presence known first. I headed out to party central.

The lineup in Louis's living room looked like a lad mag dream cover shot, something along the lines of "Hollywood's Young Turks at Play." Sprawled comfortably among the leather and suede sofa groupings with Louis were Ethan Blount, an indie director who had recently gone mainstream in a big way, having had the foresight to secure the film rights of a popular cult trilogy belonging to a well-known Japanese sci-fi/fantasy author; T.H.E. Mann, the gansta-hip hop artist known for his chart-busting X-rated rap lyrics and his trend-setting line of men's clothing, who had successfully transitioned into movies as the lead of a new "urbanized" James Bond series ("Jamez Bondd"); Bennett Fielding, a hot young TV sitcom actor whose very first movie role had been the comic relief in Louis's last film; the ever-leering Randy Zimmerman.

and Motorcycle Guy.

Motorcycle Guy? Here?

He did a double take too, then let loose with an ear-to-ear grin.

Very nice!

I glanced away, but I couldn't help but smile, too.

"Ah, and finally, here is the most important lady in my life," Louis declared with a flourish. He didn't bother to get up, though. He just tapped the picture-in-picture feature on his remote control so that a *Man Show* wet T-shirt contest could be viewed at the same time as the boxing match.

"For the next forty-eight hours, anyway," Randy sneered.

"Or until Tatiana hears you've said so," Bennett chimed in then guffawed, as if he'd been auditioning for the role of class clown.

"Don't mind them, dearest. They're just jealous because you're not only capable but beautiful as well—whereas Ethan's assistant is some techno-nerd like himself, T's assistant is his very pregnant wife's ever-watchful brother, Bennett's girlfriend won't let him have one of his own, Randy's assistants are usually out the door in a minute and a half, or end up in the psych ward because he's so abusive, and Mick doesn't have the cash flow *or* the stature to rate his own Hannah. Well, that's just too bad, eh? They'll just have to admire you from afar."

From the looks on their faces, he'd gotten across his underlying message: *Lay off; she's all mine.*

"Besides," Louis concluded, "*someone* has to take care of my dirty laundry. Believe me, it's not something Tatiana aspires to."

It was on the tip of my tongue to say, *Guess what? It's not what I aspire too, either!* Instead I smiled benignly—and groaned inwardly. In my haste to make it to Genevieve's before six, I had forgotten to drop his laundry at the dry cleaner's. I made a mental note to myself to do so first thing in the morning, and to beg the clerk to have it back the same day. Of course, I would make up the difference and take the loss.

This job was already costing me money!

"Hannah, meet my guys: Bennett Fielding, Ethan Blount, T.H.E. Mann, Randy Zimmerman, and Mick Bradshaw."

I shivered at the sound of Motorcycle Guy's real name. It was almost as if that charge I'd felt when he shook my hand on Laurel Canyon Boulevard had been reignited at the center of my spine, and, in a flash, had worked its way back up and somehow wound its way back into my heart.

(*Stop it, Hannah! He's in Louis' orbit, which means he's out of your range*).

It took a moment, but I came to my senses and murmured a bright, "Nice to meet you all." Before I could turn to leave, though, Randy drawled out, "Oh, *I* know Hannah. We're old friends, ain't we, sweet thang?"

His suggestive tone raised the hairs on the back of my neck. Randy expected one of two reactions: for me to slink off because I was too embarrassed to answer him, or for me to be flattered that he wanted to hang out with his wang out.

What, was he *kidding?* All his arrogance earned him from me was a look that should have turned him into a SnoCone.

"Dude, that ain't *no* way to treat a lady." T.H.E. got up and proffered his hand. "These boys have the manners of a pack of hyenas. Don't be giving 'em no mind, sweetie. And you can call me T, if I can call you Hannah."

"Thanks. Please do, and I'd be honored to do the same." I smiled up at him, willing to forgive and forget all those nasty rumors about his having pistol-whipped the head of his music label as his way of expressing his "disappointment" over the lack of promotion for his latest CD, or that, just a nanosecond before I'd entered the room, he had commented on how he'd like to "twang the G-string" belonging to the third contestant from the left.

"You'll have to excuse me. I've got to bring in the rest of the groceries."

"Need any help?" Mick had asked nonchalantly enough, but he still had that shit-eating grin on his face, which made it all the more difficult for me to keep a silly smile off mine.

"There are only four more bags," I said hesitantly. "It's nothing, really—"

"I don't mind. I need to stretch my legs, anyway."

"Sure, okay. Thanks." I was glad to see that the others were preoccupied with the pre-fight commentary as Mick followed me out the front door.

"I can't believe you were on your way *here*."

"Yeah? Well, I can't believe that *you're* Louis's new assistant."

Simultaneously we both said, "You should have seen the look on your face—" and burst out laughing at the serendipity of it all.

It was too dark outside to see much, and it seemed totally natural when Mick grabbed my hand and steered me up the driveway toward the gate. Halfway there, he bumped into Randy's Humvee and yelped: he had hit the knee with the open wound from the motorcycle fall.

"Gee, I—I can't apologize enough for that."

"Hey, it's just a scratch, really. Besides, if I hadn't fallen, we would have met under totally different circumstances. That might have changed everything. Fate, you know?"

I didn't know what he meant by that, but I liked the way it sounded. "I guess you're right," I answered cautiously. I was glad that it was dark and he couldn't see how happy hearing that made me, because I wasn't yet ready for him to read me so openly.

Besides, there was still the issue of my working for Louis.

"So, how long have you known Louis?" I asked as casually as possible. I opened my car door, then grabbed two sacks of groceries and handed them to him. I picked up the last two bags and locked the car door.

"For a couple of years. I was the script doctor on *Fast Eddie*, his first American film."

"Oh, yeah? I remember that one."

"Yeah, well, he had the role pegged. You know, 'fast-talking bloke taking L.A. by storm.'"

"Sounds like total typecasting."

"Seems to have turned out that way. Anyway, that's when we started hanging out together. I also wrote *Dead End*, which he starred in."

"I know. It just came out, right? That's the one that may get him an Oscar nod. Wow, you two have a great relationship: artist and muse."

"Not really."

"You're *not* great friends?"

"No. I mean, yes, we *are* close buds, but he's not my 'muse.' I wrote it several years ago, before I'd even met him. In fact, it was my first script, and I had another actor in mind for the lead. That guy turned me down, though, and it sat in a drawer for years. Louis read it and pushed the studio to get it made. I owe him a lot for that."

We'd walked into the kitchen undetected. The boxing match had just started, and curses, whoops and whistles were flying out from the living room. I opened a few cabinets until I found ones containing the plates and trays I needed, then began unwrapping the prepared dishes. Mick seemed in no rush to get back to the guys, which was fine with me.

"Of course, being the grateful friend that I am, I guess I'll have to tell Louis what you really think of him."

Was it that obvious? I turned around, startled. "How do you know what I think?"

"You told me, remember? At the scene of the accident. You called him a 'slave driver.'" He let loose with another teasing grin.

I laughed. "Who do you think he'll believe, you or me?" I blinked my lashes in mock innocence.

"That's a good question," said Louis.

Neither Mick nor I had heard him enter. We both stared at him, like two guilty children caught playing doctor or something. He looked from one of us to the other, not sure what to make of our little game.

"I didn't know you two knew each other. Gee, Hannah, you seem to be *very* popular."

"We just met tonight," I explained. "Unfortunately, on my way down the hill, I ran out of gas, and Mick stopped to help."

"Oh." Louis turned back to Mick, bemused. "So *Hannah* is the girl you almost ran over. *Interesting.*"

"Yep, she's the one." It was Mick's turn to be embarrassed.

"Why? What did you say?" I asked Mick, confused.

"He said, 'I almost ran over the best piece of ass I've seen in a long time.' Of course, had I known he was talking about *you*, Hannah, I would have said, 'Too bad, because you can't have her, she's mine.'" He laughed. "By that, I mean only during your waking hours. The last thing I am is a slave driver, right?"

I knew better than to answer honestly. With calm precision, I picked up the loaded tray and carried it into the living room.

I did my best to stay out of the living room for the rest of the evening. Even when I was called to bring in more poi blinis with smoked salmon (care of Wolfgang Puck takeout), wheat-free tofu-topped pizza (ala Cheebo) or British Columbia salmon (Zone) with a pitcher of Goji Himalayan Juice or Lagunitas Draft Micro-Brew to go with it, I ignored Randy's jibes, Louis's sudden attentiveness, and most certainly Mick's apologetic glances.

To keep myself busy, I went over Louis's itinerary for the next day with a fine-tooth comb, making notations as needed:

5:00 A.M.: Wake-up call

6:00 A.M.: Limo to Columbia Pictures

6:30–7:00 A.M.: Makeup, Bldg K

7:00 A.M.–6 P.M.: On Set *(Breakneck)*, Studio 1002

12:30 P.M.: Lunch in Dressing Room (Zone!) and *Entertainment Tonight* interview with Mary Hart

8 P.M.: Premiere of Ethan Blount's latest film, *Tales of the Crystal Universe*, at the Arclight on Sunset

10:30 P.M.: After-party for *Crystal Universe* at the Viper Room

Does the guy ever sleep? I wondered. Apparently he did not, which meant that I wouldn't be getting much shuteye either for the next couple of months. Or time with my telescope, which was an even bigger crime in my book.

Sighing, I then put my mind to perusing Louis's itinerary for the rest of the week. Based on that, I would have to coordinate the following:

- Leave Sunday for New York, via the studio's private jet, to promote *Dead End.*

- Monday: In the early afternoon, Louis would be photographed by Annie Leibovitz for a *Vanity Fair* cover; in the early evening he would join James Lipton for an "Inside the Actor's Studio" interview, which was to be taped in front of an audience filled with film students and cinephiles. *(So that Louis could prepare a full arsenal of appropriate responses and interview postures—unabashed modesty, unwavering intensity, wise cynicism, perhaps a faraway glance that bespoke a bittersweet longing—Monique, Louis's publicist, had included several DVDs of previous "Actor's Studio" interviewees for him to study. This stash included interviews of the two Toms, Harrison, Johnny, Sir Ian, Benecio, Sir Anthony, Paul, Colin, and the pinnacle of all Lipton interviews, as determined by the "LGF", a.k.a. the Lipton gush factor: the Barbra interview. It would be my job to study the tapes beforehand and make notations that might be of interest to Louis.)*

• Book him into the Ritz Carlton, and accept *only* the Ritz Carlton Suite. *(Oh, just great. And what if the Ritz Carlton Suite was already booked? Would Louis stand in the lobby and pout until it was made available? Or, as his "person," would I be made to stand there and pout in his place?)*

• Book Prudence K. for an in-room massage. Ask for "Barry" at the concierge desk; he will know how to find her. DO NOT ASK VIA SWITCH-BOARD!!! *(Hmmmm. . . .)*

• Have four dozen yellow tulips sent to Tatiana, via her modeling agency.

• Have a late, albeit romantic, supper brought up to the suite—Zone, of course. *(Can Zone meals be romantic? If not, should I switch menu to South Beach? I mean, South Beach is more romantic sound-*

*ing than Zone, so would it not follow that it would
taste more sensual, too? Hard to say.)*

- Next day: fly Virgin Air, upper class, to
Heathrow, where Louis would complete voice-
over production on his last British film, a dark
take on Daphne du Maurier's *Rebecca*, starring
Louis in the Olivier/Maxim de Winter role. It's
considered edgy because it ends with Louis's
character actually being tried and hanged for
killing his first wife. (This was Louis's idea: "Up-
dates the plot somewhat, don't you think? Besides, it makes the role Oscar-worthy . . . well, it's
at least a shoo-in for an Olivier, right?") *(Would he
want me in London with him? At least my passport is
current, thanks to Jean-Claude's insistence that, as a
girlfriend of a jet-setter, I should always be at the
ready for a transcontinental jaunt on any given whim.
That was another way in which our relationship did
not live up to his promises: the furthest I ever got with
him was Cabo San Lucas—and on my dime, surprise,
surprise . . .)*

- Book Louis into the Portobello. Accept *only* the
Round Room! *(Ah, the hotel of rock stars and
fashionistas—which meant I'd have yet another chance
to play "My celebrity is more important than your
celebrity!" Would Louis's name pull rank? And what
would be my punishment if it did not?)*

- Limo Service: Regency Limo, ask for Alfonse.
Accept none other!

- Ask Alfonse to arrange for in-room massage from
Ernestine J. *(Considering Louis's after-flight mas-*

*sage rituals, it shouldn't be a big deal to get the names
and telephone numbers of his favorite masseuses from
Barry and Alfonse for the PDA. Make mental note to
do so . . .)*

- Next day limo service to Notting Hill Sound Studios.

- Zone luncheon.

- Break for British *Cosmo* profile interview: "A Man for All Pleasings . . ." to take place with a photo shoot by Mert & Marcus, at a King's Cross Studio.

- Back in recording studio, until 6 P.M.

- Heathrow to LAX via Virgin.

- Limo home.

I could already see that working with Louis was going to put a major crimp in my star search. Oh well, maybe I'd have the energy to sneak out tonight, after the party, I thought.

But first things first. I called the limo service that Genevieve's directions stated was Louis's preference, and requested his favorite driver, Malcolm.

"I'm sorry, miss, but Malcolm is already booked for tomorrow morning. However, he will be available later that evening to take Mr. Trollope to the premiere and the after-party."

"Oh." I was in a quandary. Was Louis the type to throw a tantrum at things like that? I guess I'd find out the hard way, tomorrow. "Please send the next-best substitute, then . . . someone-um-unobtrusive."

Yeah, right, *that* was sure to appease Louis!

Despite the fact that everyone except Randy claimed early studio calls, Louis's shindig didn't break up until two in the morning. Mick stuck his head in to say good-bye and (I'm guessing) to apologize, but I would have none of it: I feigned being tied up on a phone call to London ("Yes, yes, Mr. Trollope will of course require the Round Room, on the twenty-eighth. Please put the room under his usual pseudonym, E.A. Presley") and dismissed him with an impatient wave.

My message was crystal clear: The game was over. We had both lost.

Louis came in to say goodnight as I was washing the last of the plates and silver. "So, what time will you need me tomorrow?" I asked brightly.

He laughed, as if the question had been a joke. "You'll meet me here and ride in with me to the studio, of course. My assistant is *always* written into my movie contracts."

"Sure, of course." It was a cool trick: My presence on the set ensured that my salary was to be covered by the producers during the weeks of the shoot schedule—a savings to Louis's bottom line.

Which meant that I, too, would need an early wake-up call—that is, if I went to sleep at all. Six o'clock was only three hours away. If I ran every light between here and Venice, that would still take me, minimally, forty minutes, and forty minutes back. . . .

That was *ridiculous!*

As if reading my mind, Louis offered, "Of course, you *could* sleep here—"

(Oh, I get it. And, no!)

"Uh, look, Louis, if this is going to work, then I think we should get something straight right up front—"

"Hannah, it's *okay.*" One eyebrow arched upward, contradicting his angelic countenance. "I thoroughly apologize for that ungentlemanly behavior earlier this evening, at your expense. It was *very, very* cruel of my friends, and of course, of me. You don't yet know my sense of humor, which, I'm sure, made it even more unseemly." He paused and ran a hand through his professionally tousled hair. "Look, I'm being honest: I, too, want our relationship to stay strictly professional. I've—well, I've seen it otherwise, and I know it never works out. *Never.*"

His emphasis was comforting—and, I had to admit, disappointing at the same time.

"I know I can be a bit demanding. And with all you've been through this week, I'm sure that the last thing you need is some whiney bloke sending you up and down this bloody hillside on a whim."

I couldn't help but laugh out loud. He joined me, and for once I felt thoroughly at ease with him.

"Okay, look, we've got to be up in less than three hours. Go ahead and catch a nap in the cabana. It's got everything you'll need. G'night, sis."

With that he leaned over, gave me a very chaste kiss on the forehead, and headed off toward his own room.

He didn't need to wait for my answer. He already knew it.

Despite the sumptuous amenities in the cabana (feather mattress, down pillows and comforter, and 700-thread-count Egyptian cotton sheets on a Dux 7007), I tossed and turned all night, running over my mixed feelings about both Louis and Mick.

Here was my conclusion:

First of all, I could not deny that I was attracted to Louis. And, unless I was totally delusional, he was also showing signs of attraction—which scared me, because, in my book, he already had three strikes against him: in the past five years he had been involved with what averaged a different woman every three months; the fact that he was currently dating the number-one swimsuit model in the world, which should have made me come to my senses quickly; *and* then there was the "actor" factor.

Bottom line: Take the paycheck but pass on any inevitable heartbreak.

Next on the agenda was the issue of Mick: Louis's best friend was making no bones that he saw something in me.

Did I mind? Heck, no!

Did Louis mind? Heck, yeah—and he wasn't afraid to mark his territory.

Should what he want really matter to me? No, not really . . . except that, for some odd reason, I *did* care. It was as if, knowing that Louis just might . . . just *might* . . . I dunno, maybe, like, really like me . . .

(I can't deny the fact that you like me! You really, really like me.)

. . . as opposed to Mick, who might actually . . . fall in *love* with me.

And with that thought, I dozed off with dreams of men on motorcycles revving wildly in my head.

4

Welcome to the Galaxy!

Galaxy: *Vast star systems containing thousands*
of billions of stars, dust and gas, held together by gravity.
Galaxies are the basic building blocks of the universe.
Globular Cluster: *A spherical cluster of older stars,*
often found in galaxies.
Dwarf Star: *A star having relatively low mass,*
small size, and average or below-average luminosity.

The limo was late.

Of course, Louis was pissed. This, despite my letting him sleep in an extra quarter hour. ("Whah . . . wake-up time already? Love, you're yanking my wanker, right? Be a doll . . . another fifteen, eh?")

And despite refusing the breakfast I made him—Zone, of course. ("Sorry, love, I'm not a morning man . . . no pun intended, so don't take that in the wrong way, right, my darling? How about something simpler, say, a nice cuppa Jamaican Blue Mountain? What, none in the house? Perhaps you can go down the hill and see if Ürth or the Bean or *something* is open at this ungodly hour . . .")

And despite my warning that Malcolm would *not* be his driver. ("What do you take me for, love, some kind of Hollywood prima donna pouf? Ballocks, worst-case scenario, you'll drive me down in the Ferrari. . . . What do you mean, you can't drive a stick shift? Wasn't that in your job description? . . . Oh, it *wasn't?* Not that it would have made a difference, love, because you *know* I can't live without you . . .")

By the time the driver arrived—he claimed to have gotten lost finding the house—Louis was sullen. He did not say one word during the whole ride to the studio. When we finally got there, he jumped out before the driver even had a chance to pull over in front of his dressing room. Stymied, I jumped out too. Before the door slammed shut, I was able to follow him in.

He was already undressing. Having taken off his leather jacket and T-shirt, he turned toward me, his rippling biceps, expansive chest and washboard abs bare except for a burnished tan, courtesy of his daily poolside vigils. On Louis, these perfect features weren't just a cliché but primo romance novel cover art in the flesh.

I stood there, speechless and embarrassed at my intrusion on his privacy, and perhaps for my own modesty and in light of none coming from him.

Grinning wickedly, he taunted, "So, you like beefcake for breakfast, do you, love?"

"I'm—I'm sorry. I just thought—well, I thought that perhaps we should talk about what got you so upset." I blushed and turned to leave. "But I know you have to get ready for your first scene. I'll—I'll wait outside."

"No, I'd prefer you'd stay." I could hear him unzipping his jeans in preparation of putting on a less movie-star-like/more cop-like pair of pants he was to wear on the set. "Help me run some lines, okay? Say, could you hand me that?"

"What?" I cautioned a peek. He was wrapping himself in a robe, and he grinned devilishly when he saw the relief in my face.

"That script. There."

I lunged to where he pointed—a bookcase beside the couch. "What page?"

"It's marked. Here—"

With catlike grace, he walked over to me and stood so close that our faces were almost touching. He ran his hand over mine *(could he feel it shaking?)*, moving it toward the earmarked page I had missed. His robe fell open slightly—enough that I couldn't help but notice the not-so-slight bulge in his dark gray RIPS boxer briefs. Fumbling with the script, I dropped it on the floor. As I started to pick it up, his arm snaked around my waist. I stopped cold.

"Why are you so nervous? I'm not going to fire you."

"It's not that," I mumbled. "I'm just . . . I'm just—"

"You're afraid I'm going to make love to you, aren't you?" he murmured teasingly.

"No! Not at all." *Yes, that's exactly it.*

"If we did make love, here and now"—he paused, as if finding that thought tantalizing—"I *would* have to fire you. We both said that, right? And we meant it, didn't we?"

"Of course. I know that," I stuttered, confused. "Uh, Louis, look, I had no right to just walk in here like this. It's just that I could tell you were mad, and I know it was because of the early wake-up, the breakfast, the limo—"

"Don't you feel I have the right to blame you for all of that?"

"Well, yes . . . I mean, no. I mean, well, how was I supposed to know that you're grumpy when you don't get enough sleep, or that you don't eat breakfast in the morning, or that you only drink Blue Mountain, or that Malcolm was already booked?"

"Stop me if I'm wrong, Hannah, but isn't that your job?"

"Yes, it is—but *only* as of fourteen hours ago. So perhaps you could cut me some slack!"

We were eye to eye again. I saw a million expressions cross his face. He settled on stoic indignation—an Oscar-worthy choice, I might add.

"Fair enough," he retorted. "But grant me the same courtesy."

"What do you mean by that?"

"I mean that, yes, I understand that I can be a bit testy, particularly when it's this god-awful time in the morning. And, yes, I didn't warn you that I don't eat food before noon, or that my beverage of choice wasn't in the house. And I'm not pissed at losing my driver this morning—well, maybe I am a *bit* miffed that I lost him to some junior executive on his way to LAX, or whatever." He stopped to catch a breath. "Still, has it crossed your mind even once that maybe—just *maybe*—it's not *any* of those things that have me pissed? That maybe it's just the natural anxiety I'm feeling for having to carry this lousy movie on my shoulders? And knowing that if *this* one's a clunker, then it's more than likely I'll keep getting offered lousier and lousier scripts, and if the next one bombs, too, and then the one after that one, that my career will be in the crapper? All because *this* day, of all days, started out wrong from the get-go, and now everything is quickly going to hell in a hand basket, and I feel like bloody shit anyway, which means I probably also *look* like shit—"

He was scared. And vulnerable. And oh, so human.

All that *despite* the fact that he was Louis Trollope: actor, heartthrob, and perfect male specimen.

"No, no, Louis, you don't! You look—well, just *look* at you! You're . . . you're Louis Trollope, for God's sake!"

That stopped him cold. Warily he glanced at himself in the full-length closet mirror.

Did he see what I saw? Louis Trollope, broad of shoulder, strong of chest, narrow of hip, with those slightly tousled gilded locks and those piercing blue eyes that held—as claimed in *O*—"a mouthwatering soulfulness?"

Of course he did. It was obvious by the loving look in his eyes as he scanned his own reflection in the mirror.

There was a knock on the door.

"Mr. Trollope? You're wanted in the makeup trailer."

"Thank you. I'll be right there." Louis cocked his head and grinned shamelessly at me.

"You're right. I *am* perfect. And no matter what, I should never let anything, be it bad luck, or trivial mishaps, or others' incompetence—yes, meaning *you*, my darling Hannah, beautiful fuck-up that you are—stand in my way."

With that, he clutched me close, gave me a heart-stopping kiss, and bounded out the door.

Exhausted, exhilarated, scared, I sat down. Hard.

That was no sisterly kiss. *And he had called me beautiful.*

Then again, he had also called me a fuck-up.

Fuck-up? Me? Why, what an overbearing, narcissistic blowhard—

And for the record, I had *never, ever* said he was perfect.

He stuck his head back in.

"Of course, I'll expect no more of these kinds of inconsistencies. Your trial period can't go on *forever*, you know. In light of that, I'll make you a deal: I won't dock your pay for today, but any further transgressions will have to be considered. That's only fair, right? Now, grab the script, go dig up another Jamaican Blue, then meet me in the makeup trailer in five. Hmmm. Make that two."

* * *

Louis was right: *Breakneck*, a modern-day cop-gone-bad noir-ish whodunit, had the potential to be thermonuclear at the box office.

Yes, it had Louis going for it as its star—no thanks to Randy, who'd talked him into it over a year ago in order to fill the newly transplanted Louis's dance card and, at the same time, bolster the crumbling career of another client, a third-rate director with a reel built on lascivious teen gross-out flicks.

In Hollywood, though, timing is everything. Once Louis had broken out with *Fast Eddie* and his career path was set, Columbia was hell-bent on holding him to his obligation with *Breakneck*. Unfortunately for Louis, by the time shooting began, any other A-list supporting actors who might have given its barebones script some heft were already signed up elsewhere.

That left Louis with a supporting cast of mostly B players. In other words, the other actors could say they were in a Louis Trollope film, while he could only grin and bear it—and pray that the studio would hold the film's release until February, when the news that he had indeed garnered those much-coveted Golden Globe and Oscar nominations for *Dead End* would either give this turkey some gravy or allow it to become a subtle reminder to Academy voters that Louis, too, had paid his Club Hollywood dues.

Did I say B players? Let me clarify that, since, in fact, Louis's cast members ran the gamut:

There was Simone Cavanaugh, who, in the 1950s, had been a winsome ingénue with a slew of Academy Award nominations of her own. Never having won, though, she did what all actresses of a certain age do: She took all roles offered—any role at all, no matter how bad the movie might be—then chewed up the scenery in hopes that the nostalgia bug would bite enough voting members to give her one more shot at Oscar gold. To do so with *Breakneck*, however, she'd have to convince her fellow SAG members that her role as a drunken down-on-her-luck Beverly Hills movie star wasn't just typecasting.

Donnie Beaudry, now fiftyish, was always the sidekick, never the lead, as he was here, playing Louis's partner on some prototypical L.A. police squad. Donnie was most definitely a B, having never ever gotten anywhere *near* an A movie. Still, to Donnie's credit, he had over a hundred films on his resumé. What, you don't remember *Western Horizon* or *Café California*? Perhaps that's because those films never made it onto a marquee. However, if you've got a couple of spare brain cells to kill, check out the straight-to-video titles in your friendly neighborhood Blockbuster and you'll find a trove of Donnie's duds. There was one way in which Donnie had put himself on the A-list, however. He'd married onto it: Bethany Revere, a starlet with an Amazon's body and a black belt in judo who had found her niche playing woman-in-terror-who-later-get-revenge-by-kicking-butt roles, was now being groomed by the producing powers-that-be to take it up a notch: say, save the world, as opposed to just her own skin and that of an interchangeable significant other. When asked by the curious tabloids (in the *nicest* ways possible, obviously) just what she possibly saw in Donnie (who'd had a walk-on in one of her very first made-for-TV movies), Bethany purred, "Let's just say he's got a *very* slow touch . . ." That immediately had the paparazzi asking the local L.A. madams if any of their girls, or, for that matter, their Bel Air matron clientele, could verify— off the record, of course—that his very slow touch was in fact accompanied by a *very* long schlong.

And, finally, Rex Cantor, a chiseled-cheeked Actor's Studio grad who'd had a couple of costarring roles in a few highly acclaimed indie films. And yet, somewhere in the past eight years or so, his path to stardom had somehow veered off course. Why? That was hard to say. Perhaps he had said "No thanks" to too many of the kinds of projects that might have catapulted him onto the A-list. Or, perhaps he had stuck it out with the wrong agent for too long. Or, perhaps he'd developed a rep for drug use that had film producers and their insurers running in the opposite direction. In any regard, playing the bad guy in a Louis Trollope film could only work for him if he had the chops to upstage Louis, which he did. (And maybe that was the *real* reason Louis was so rattled.)

While Louis played his scenes, I stood on the sidelines ever at the ready, gray cell in one hand, red cell in the other, finalizing the New York and London arrangements. By 10:30 the hotel reservations had been confirmed, Tatiana's tulips had been ordered, and all was good in the world—at least, good enough that I could sit down for a few minutes.

Donnie's pert PA, a chesty, corn-fed Midwestern blond cutie named Christy Tanner, offered up a hot cup of coffee and a croissant.

"Want to join us?" She pointed over to a table behind the set, where two other PAs were huddling, well out of audio range of their various bosses.

"Sure, I'd love to," I said, taking a long sip as we walked over to them. The only guy in the group, the slightly built baby-faced Freddy Pugh, who was cuddling a chubby pug dog with a rhinestone-studded collar, readily owned up to being "Simone's eunuch."

"And this is Bette," he cooed, introducing me to the dog. "She's Miss Simone's baby—and I *do* mean baby. Believe me: I ought to know, I've diapered *both* of them."

The thought of Simone Cavanaugh in Attends left a lot to be desired.

The other PA, Sandra Chapman, a plump, sturdy forty-something with a tentative smile, described herself as Rex's "executive assistant."

"Oh, drop the airs, Sandy!" Freddy sighed. "You're just like the rest of us: there to wipe brow and kiss ass. Or, is that kiss brow and wipe ass?"

Christy giggled knowingly. "Well, personally speaking, I've done neither—although, I have to admit, Donnie *did* once give me a kiss—"

"Do tell, sister!" exclaimed Freddy coquettishly. "Are we talking the noble brow here, or your very desirable ass?"

Christy blushed deeply. "It was nothing like that, really! What I meant was that I—well, Bethany yelled at me for making the temperature for her leg wax too hot, and Donnie saw that I was upset, and, well, he—well, he was sweet enough to give me a tiny kiss—on the cheek!" She paused, totally confused. "Believe me, it was all *very* innocent!"

"Of course, sweetie," cooed Freddy. "And if you had offered to blow him, I'm just *certain* he'd have turned you down."

"Freddy, that's just—well, that's *just disgusting*," sniffed Sandy. "Unlike you, Christy and I have a totally professional view of our jobs. We'd *never* cross that line with our employers, right, Christy? And they know that and appreciate it. Why, Rex has only the most honorable respect for me—as I'm sure Donnie has for Christy."

Christy had to think hard about that before nodding halfheartedly, obviously too chicken to admit a less noble rationale.

"Don't kid yourself, Sandy old girl! Rex ain't showing you 'respect.' He's just not into lollypop love that way. At least, not with the ladies!"

"And just what is *that* supposed to mean?" hissed Sandy.

"It means that Rex may treat you like a princess," Freddy intoned knowingly, "but that's only because he's one mixed-up queen himself."

Ah, so *that* was the reason for Rex's stilted career! Now a lot of things made sense. So, Louis had nothing to worry about after all.

"Those are just vicious rumors," growled Sandy. "And if people like you keep that up, it will ruin his career."

"Well, darling, take it from 'people like me': where there is smoke, there is fire. Your boy has hot pants, whether you want to acknowledge it or not. But don't worry, I ain't gonna be the one to out him. That old diva of *mine*, Miss Simone, keeps me too busy to make other people's lives miserable."

"More Dumpster diving?" Sandy asked haughtily.

"Nah, since she's landed this gig, she's cooled off on that—for now, anyway. Thank God the director's mother had a soft spot for her. All we had to do was have his mama over for tea and—voila! We were *in*. And hell, it sure is a lot easier pilfering from the studio commissary than the trashcans in some of those fancy Beverly Hills alleyways. Too many patrol cars, you know? Some of them Beverly Hills cops should work a *real* beat, like South Central."

He patted the big tote bag at his feet. I took a peek inside and saw several soda bottles, sandwiches, bags of chips and Saran-wrapped cookies—certainly a cheaper way to eat in Beverly Hills than trotting down to the Ralph's.

"Of course, this gig *has* put an end to our sleeping in, right, Bette?" He cuddled the pug lovingly. "Nowadays we're up-and-Adam by three, putting on Miss Simone's face."

Now, that was curious. "She doesn't get that done here, in makeup?"

"Are you *kidding?* Only her hairdresser—*moi*—knows for sure how many scraggly split ends are left on that eggshell she calls a head. Besides, you think these girls know how to fill those moon craters in her face? Miss Simone's got her own blend of SuperGlue. When I get done with her, even she can pass as one of those pseudo-'Simone' drag queens down at Micky's." Freddy licked his lips suggestively. "But enough about us, dear. Tell us a little about *you*—and that hunk you work for, of course."

All eyes locked onto me. Feeling a little uncomfortable—especially after what had transpired that morning in Louis's bungalow—I stammered, "Well, there's not much to tell, really. I just started the job last night."

Freddy gave a sly grin. "He didn't waste any time, did he?"

"What do you mean?" I asked, warily. Considering the suggestive innuendos that had been flying around the table, I knew I had to nip any rumors about us in the bud, and fast.

"Oh, don't get Freddy wrong, Hannah," murmured Christy. "He's just curious—well, since Sam disappeared—"

"Sam?" Now I was totally confused.

"Samantha. You know, Louis's last PA—that is, she was, up until ten days ago."

"Oh." So, Samantha was the mysterious "Sam" who was to be banned from contacting Louis. "No one told me about her."

We all sat there in silence. Christy and Sandy exchanged uneasy glances, while Freddy leaned in conspiratorially. "Well, we can certainly help you there."

"Now, Freddy—" Christy warned.

Freddy frowned at Christy. "She has a right to know!"

"Know what?" I asked, exasperated.

"You're right. She does," admitted Sandy. "And she certainly won't hear it from *him*."

That was it for me. I stood up. "I don't have time for this. Louis has an interview with *ET* during lunch—"

Christy's eyes were as big as saucers. "Hannah, as much as I idolize Mary Hart, this is even bigger than *her*." She yanked me back down into my chair.

I felt my heart go into my chest. "Okay, then, out with it," I hissed at them.

As I would have suspected, Freddy took the lead.

"Look, Hannah, we only knew Sam during these past four weeks of filming, right? But we got to know her pretty well, and we PAs have to stick together, understand? That's because everyone starts off the same way: you know, loving our jobs—well, maybe not *loving* them; but, okay, admittedly, it's nice to be sprinkled with a little bit of stardust, know what I mean? But the reality is this: we aren't treated any better—no, let me restate that—we are treated *worse* than this ugly mutt here."

He nodded down at Bette. "And no matter how much we do for them, they still treat us like second-class citizens, like they are doing us a favor to let us attend to them."

He paused. "Well, Sam was the best of the best, you know? They were both from 'across the pond' as they say, and they met when he got his first big BBC project there in London. She was a student, but she needed the money, and he was creating a buzz over there and needed someone fast, so she came onboard as his PA. She'd do anything for King Louie, including giving up her friends and family to come over here. And boy, was *he* demanding! Day in, day out."

Freddy took a deep breath. "Oh, that's not to say that he didn't throw her a bone every now and then." He laughed derisively. "In fact, he was quite free with the boners, if you catch my drift, at least where Sam was concerned. She lived for it, don't get me wrong. Like I said, she'd do anything for the guy. *Because she loved him.*"

"Where is all this going, Freddy?"

"I'm getting there, okay? You see, Sam thought she could fly close to the flame without getting burned. Know what I mean? Like, whenever he was between flavors of the month—and even when he *was* already hooked up—Sam made herself available to him, although she'd tell herself no strings attached."

"I see," I said softly. "Well, guys, thanks for the warning.

But don't worry. Louis is just a temp job to me, something to do for a few months, to pay the rent, that's all."

Christy sighed and nodded solemnly, as if those words were a distant memory.

"Yeah, that's what we *all* say," mourned Sandy. "And next week is *our* ninth anniversary."

"You're not married to Rex, Sandy, so it ain't exactly an anniversary," snapped Freddy.

"Well, *I* mean what I say." I rose again and turned to leave. "I'll be out of here in sixty days, tops. Louis means absolutely nothing to me. I've got an important project I've got to complete, and I'll walk away whenever I want."

"Whatever," said Freddy, kindly, knowingly. "Funny, that's what Sam said, too. She was supposed to complete her last semester of college. But she never did go back to school. Instead she got wrapped up in his life and fell in love with him. Until last week, that is, when he asked her for a favor: double up on him *and* a buddy. She did it, and she hated herself afterward. You see, all she *really* wanted was for Louis to love her as much as she loved him. But after that little episode, of course, he wouldn't. It was all the proof she needed."

A buddy.

Mick?

I muttered something about checking up on the *ET* camera crew, waved good-bye, and hurried out as fast as I could.

5

Equilibrium

*A situation when more than one force acts on a body,
but because the sum of the forces is zero,
no motion results.*

The band booked for Ethan Blount's premiere after-party at the Viper Room was obnoxiously loud, playing instruments that were horrendously off-key, and singing lyrics that were noticeably obscure.

That didn't seem to matter to the crowd, which was primarily made up of studio wonks; the few actual *live* actors who had starred in Ethan's latest special-effects-laden abomination; other actors, directors or writers who needed to be out and about hyping their own upcoming projects; all the usual suspects who show up at promotional freebees (a Paris Hilton or two, a couple of Tom Arnolds, a few *Survivor* contestants, and the last three "Bachelors"); Ethan's fan club members who were fluent enough in Klingon to have deciphered the anonymous email, circulated surreptitiously, that had contained the party's pertinent who-what-where info (hacked from the studio's promo department's computer files); and, of course, members of the Posse.

That is, everyone was there but Mick.

I wondered why and tried to think of a roundabout way to ask Louis if he knew if Mick might show, but then I thought better of that bright idea. After all, Louis hadn't seemed to notice his buddy's absence.

But then again, why would he? Louis was still high on that euphoric rush actors get when they've just walked the red carpet—the shrieks from hysterical fans still ringing in his ears, halos from the paparazzis' camera strobes still burning into his corneas, and the compliments still gushing from the entertainment reporters—on the movie he was currently filming, or the rumored Oscar nomination for *Dead End*, or what he was wearing (a taupe crewneck Zanone sweater, worn under a dark olive printed paisley suede trench coat by Sean John, along with Martin Margiela jeans, all chosen for him by the stylist he kept on retainer), and most certainly regarding his relationship with Tatiana. ("We've heard that there might be wedding bells in your future!")

All of which reaffirmed what he desperately needed to know: that he (and not his pal Ethan) was *really* the Man of the Evening.

And as such, he was being fawned over by everyone who was lucky enough to go shoulder-to-shoulder with him, including the many taut, tawny women cosmetically worthy enough to pass through the red velvet rope that held back the huddled masses now elbowing each other off the curb and into oncoming Sunset Boulevard traffic.

All in all, it was an appropriate celebration for *Tales of the Crystal Universe*, which, like most of Ethan's movies, flummoxed the critics with its confusing plot lines and stilted dialogue but dazzled his fans with never-before-seen special effects.

In an alternate universe—one in which he hadn't made so much money doing what he loves best, i.e., making techno-blockbusters—Ethan would have been ostracized for being a nerd. This being Los Angeles, however, he was hailed as a Hollywood Power Ranger, one of the chosen few whose innate knowledge of technological wizardry allowed him a paranormal connectivity with the basest (yet most coveted) of all movie audiences: *male teens.*

And because he was God in their eyes, he is deemed a deity to the Hollywood studio bosses as well.

Unfortunately for Ethan (although true to the Power Rangers creed), he was ill fatedly attracted to Sunset Slurpees.

What is a Sunset Slurpee, you ask? Believe me, you know the type: a woman whose physical beauty is too extreme for her to flourish anywhere else on the planet but here, in Hollyrude.

When the Sunset Slurpee is not trolling the boulevard that shares her name, she is misinterpreting the latest fashion statement, acting as a guinea pig for pioneering plastic surgeons, and—most importantly for her own survival—perfecting the art of felatio (hence the second part of her nickname). All of this is done in order to accomplish her one true mission in life: to evolve from a Rodeo Drive shopgirl to Arm Charm to Malibu Matron, prior to her thirtieth birthday.

Like the magnetic field that pulls planets into a sun's orbit, the Sunset Slurpee is always encircled by battalions of Power Rangers. Choosing carefully among them, she then picks as her consort the Ranger Most Likely to Succeed at the Box Office.

Teased and lured, the Ranger of choice takes great pains to

ignore all obvious differences—mental, emotional, and in most cases theological—that stand between them. The ultimate payoff: because his film has broken all box office sound barriers, he is allowed to sashay down the red carpet with his Sunset Slurpee at his side (in a sliced-and-diced Versace abomination no self-respecting dominatrix would be caught dead in).

And if the Sunset Slurpee is smart enough to hang in there, as opposed to joining Hugh Hefner's most current sorority, she and her Power Ranger will eventually seal their commitment in a nuptial extravaganza excessive enough to rate their very own four-page spread in *People* or, better yet, a special issue of *Us Weekly*.

Of course, there is a price the Hollywood Power Ranger pays for flying too close to the sun. Eventually his Sunset Slurpee will lay down the law: *On no uncertain terms will he be allowed to talk business when he is around her.*

She sees the town—what insiders call the movie industry—as "the mistress," and rightly so. However, the Sunset Slurpee will never admit this, most definitely not to herself. Instead, she not so subtly infers to him that his "shoptalk" is akin to an embarrassing illness, like jock itch is now, or homosexuality was in the 1950s—never discussed, let alone flaunted, in pleasant company. This allows her to strike an attitude of annoyed indulgence: it's all right for him to play with his buddies at the studio, to create fantasies that in turn bring him the prestige and money that they both enjoy (I mean, come on, would they rate that table at the Ivy if he were a top accountant with H&R Block? *I think not!*) But it is *not* okay to talk about it in her presence.

Which was why, I'd soon discover, Ethan practically lived at Louis's place. There, out of earshot of his own personal slurpee, Ophelia Randolph, he could talk movies to his heart's content.

As the band droned on, Ophelia stood there towering over him, a stunning vision in a vintage Pucci mini and three-and-a-half-inch Manolo Blahnik ankle tie ring sandals, even while sporting a visage of studied boredom. As Louis's PA, I was deemed too lowly for her to talk to, and that was fine with me. Unfortunately, Ethan eventually let out that I was Leo's daughter—which of course piqued Ophelia's interest.

"I saw him a couple of times at the Casa del Mar," she screeched, just slightly louder than the band. "In fact, I think he once picked me up there. Could that be right?"

"Oh, yeah, no doubt. Then again, you might have allowed him to pick you up anywhere, even the Farmer's Market, right?"

To prove she had been correct to ignore me in the first place, she wrapped herself around Ethan like a boa constrictor and pulled him over to the banquette where T was holding court, knowing that, there, both of them would be aptly appreciated.

She needn't have bothered. I was about to make my getaway to the observatory, where I could once again be among the only stars that really mattered to me.

I walked up to Louis, hoping to catch his eye, give him a quick good-bye, and warn him that I would be taking off tomorrow—Saturday—although I'd be available by phone should he need me, and certainly I'd be back at his place on Sunday in time for Malcolm to take us to Van Nuys that afternoon for the New York flight. I also wanted to remind him that, as promised, Malcolm was still waiting outside to deliver him home. Not that he'd have any trouble getting a lift if he wanted one, considering the throng of adoring, panting women around him.

Try as I might, though, I could not get him to see me through all that ordinance-busting cigarette smoke and teased tresses. Finally I just gave up. Seeing Randy standing over to one side enviously eyeing Louis's action, I weighed the odds that he'd actually do me the favor of giving Louis my message. Perhaps his agent code left him with some sort of fiduciary responsibility to deliver such missives to his clients. My guess is that it did, although I'd also wager that he'd broken it as many times as he'd seen fit. Still, he was my only alternative.

"What do *you* want?" was Randy's greeting to me. Undeterred by his sullen rudeness, I smiled pleasantly and began, "Well, I was thinking of cutting out, and I was hoping—"

His eyes narrowed, and his mouth twisted into a knowing smirk. "Sure, doll, I'll give you a lift." He put his hand around my waist and gave me a hard yank, which brought us nose-to-nose, then hissed, *"And it will be the ride of your life."*

It had been a long day, I was bone tired, and I truly didn't need this kind of grief. At times like this, I thanked God for Leo's insistence that he teach me the few jujitsu moves he knew, a little something he'd picked up while overseas making two or three low-budget samurai flicks in order to pay off Mr. Tax Man.

A simple wrist flex lock brought Randy to his knees, squealing like a piggy. I told him I'd let him on his feet, but only after he promised to pass along my message. Quite meekly he agreed to do that, so I let him loose—and soon regretted it. Still in shock and awe, he started blathering on and on about how he never realized I was into the whole S&M/D&S thing, and how that made me a goddess in his eyes, and would it be too much to hope that I, like he, was also a connoisseur of B&D? If so, as a platinum-card-carrying member of the Threshold Club, he would be delighted—no, he'd be *honored!*—to sponsor me for the club's upcoming "Mistress of Madness/Siren of Sadness" contest.

That idiotic offer was the cherry on the cake of my day.

I headed for the door.

I had almost reached it, too, when I felt a hand on my shoulder. Not in the mood for any more of Randy's games, I stopped short and was steeling myself for another altercation when I heard Mick's voice say, "Whoa, cowgirl! It's just little old me. And I promise I'll get on my knees willingly, if you promise not to hurt me."

Turning around, I couldn't help but cringe. *So, he had seen my little altercation with Randy!*

Well, that's just great. Now he probably thinks I'm some sort of psycho nut job who gets her jollies hurting guys, I thought miserably.

As if reading my mind, Mick said, "Let me guess. Randy was his usual gentlemanly self and said something totally endearing."

I nodded, relieved that he'd seen the situation for what it was. "Yeah, and I'm just too tired to put up with it. Unfortunately, I think my reaction gave him the wrong impression."

"I can just imagine. Unfortunately, I once walked in on Randy in his leather chaps and halter. Trust me, something like that is hard to forget."

I was relieved that I didn't have to offer any further explanation.

"So, you're not staying?" asked Mick. "Didn't you come with Louis?"

"Yep, but he's a big boy. Malcolm's on remote, so I'm sure he'll find his way home one way or another. Which reminds me: I should call a taxi."

"Don't bother. I've got my bike right outside. I'll give you a lift."

I didn't answer immediately. I had planned on going back to Louis's to get my car. Then I was going to go home to change into some jeans before doing my stargazing, which, I'm sure, would have sounded somewhat lame to a guy like Mick.

Now he'll know I'm a nut if I tell him about the great evening I've got planned, I thought.

I elected to stall. "Shouldn't you stay here, for Ethan?"

"Nah, I've already paid my condolences. Besides, when he's around Ophelia, he's no fun anyway."

I couldn't help but laugh. "Yeah, I get that feeling, too. Still, the place is hopping. I think you'd want to hang around—"

The band kicked off a yowling riff that had Mick cupping his ears. "What? I can't hear you!" Shaking his head, he gently steered me out the door with him.

The street was teeming with passersby, all dressed for a flirtatious Friday night on the Strip. In both directions, across all four lanes, cars were doing a bumper-to-bumper crawl, the better to ogle and hoot at the club-hopping crowds. It was noisy outside, too, but at least we could hear each other.

He was making it clear that I wasn't going to lose him easily—not that I minded in the least.

Okay, I thought, *I'll come clean. That should scare him away.*

"I appreciate the offer. But I'm sure I'll be putting you out of your way. You see, I have to go back up Laurel and grab my car from Louis's place, then I was going to go home and change, and then head out to—well, to Griffith Park. The observatory."

"But it's late. Isn't it closed?"

"There's a platform that UCLA has set up for its new planet research. That's my *real* job."

He gave me an incredulous look. "You're kidding, right?"

"No, I'm very serious. But since taking this job with Louis, I've been so busy that I haven't been able to keep up my research. So, it's now or never." I sighed. "Hey, I understand perfectly if you want to bow out on your offer to give me a lift. Don't feel obligated to stick around."

Out of the corner of my eye, I saw a cab pull over and disgorge a drunk, giggling couple. "See you when we get back from London, I hope."

"Look, I'll make you a deal," said Mick. "You quit trying to brush me off, and I'll give you a ride up the hill. In fact, if you let me, I'd like to tag along on your little stargazing expedition."

"Well—sure. But—but why would you want to do that?"

"Because I—well, I feel like a fool admitting this now, but, okay, I'll say it. Just don't laugh at me: although I've lived here for the past twelve years of my life, I've never been to the observatory."

I did laugh. Hard. And so did he. "I'm sorry," I gasped, "but I *can* believe you've never been there. Most of L.A. doesn't even know it exists, which is a shame."

"Then you won't mind being my guide tonight?"

I smiled. "I'd be honored. It's a fair swap for the lift—and the gas."

And (hopefully) your friendship.

While I was changing in the bedroom, Mick—keeping a gentlemanly distance in my small, cramped living room—peppered me with questions about planet searches and my interest in astronomy.

"What kind of telescope do you use?"

"A TeleVue NP-101. It's portable, but still bulky—about twenty-five pounds. It has a four-inch APO refractor. On it, I use a Carl Zeiss Monocentric lenspiece, which is around fifty years old but considered a classic among astronomers because of its two-lens design—as opposed to many modern telescopes, which have as many as nine lenses. This gives it a narrower field of vision, which means it sees more light transmission from objects farther away, which the newer multi-lens scopes can't see."

"Wow. I'm impressed. So which star will we be watching?"

"AU Microscopium," I answered, "but it's called 'Mic' for short and is a red dwarf'—or low mass—star, as are eighty-five percent of all stars. It's about seventeen thousand light-years away."

I also explained that scientists both at UC Berkeley and in Australia already suspected that a planet that is somewhat larger than Jupiter and three times farther from its star than the Earth is from the Sun is orbiting Mic somewhere within the expansive disk of dust emanating some 210 AUs—or, in astronomical units, 20 billion miles—out from the star itself. All bets were that this mysterious planet was somewhere within the first 20 or so AUs closest to Mic. The goal now was to verify their findings, and that called for around-the-clock observation by amateur astronomers like me.

"Mic, huh? Like me. Pretty neat," he exclaimed. Then, somewhat embarrassed at the pride in his voice, he continued, "How can you tell if a planet is following a star?"

While there were several methods, amateur astronomers such as myself used the Doppler Wobble method, which noted wiggles—or "wobbles"—made by the star as it pulls planets with a magnetic field. I don't know if he heard this explanation, though, because at the time, my head was buried in a too-tight Chetta B knit sweater that was caught on an earring.

"That means the star needs constant surveillance, and there just aren't enough scientists to do it—which is why they welcome us volunteers to pick up the slack. If we're able to confirm their theory, we all win."

"How long should the whole project take?"

"It's hard to say. It may take years," I said.

That brought a low whistle from him. "If you don't find it, will you feel as if you've wasted your time?"

I paused, both to collect my thoughts on that question and to zip up my favorite pair of old, faded jeans. Because I wanted to see his face when I gave my answer, I grabbed a jacket out of my closet, opened the bedroom door and walked out into the living room, where I found Mick peering into my telescope— which was pointed directly through the bedroom door's keyhole.

Caught red-handed, he looked up sheepishly. "Wow, this thing *is* powerful!"

I snatched it out of his hand and headed out the door. "To answer your question: sure, it's a crap shoot, with lousier odds. I guess that's exactly how you feel after writing a script, waiting for some producers to option it, watch them sit on it, have it go into turnaround, only to have it put back on the shelf. Then, if a movie actually gets made, first it's totally rewritten, or in fact could be rewritten two, three or more times, so that it's *really* not your script anymore. And that process may take a very long time, maybe even a decade or longer, soup to nuts, right?"

He nodded, chagrined. "You've got a good point there."

I pointed in the direction of the Beetle. "I'm driving tonight. Hop in."

Here is what I learned about Mick as we took turns watching the jolly red dwarf twirl and flicker:

1. He was originally from a small town in Missouri, which, he claimed, had absolutely no skyscrapers. Because of that fact, I pointed out, it was more

than likely his hometown had a great sky for stargazing.

2. He was allergic to cats. (Which made me glad I didn't have one.)

3. He preferred writing for film over TV, and although he had done both, he'd probably be richer by now if he had stuck it out in television.

4. His mother worried that he wasn't eating enough. (If she had been around for the boxing party, her mind would have been put at ease, because he'd been eating nonstop then!)

5. Like me, he couldn't stand Ophelia and was praying that Ethan would figure her out before she conveniently forgot to take her contraceptive pill and played on his natural instinct to "do good by her." ("No one really pulls that act, do they? "I thought that went out with *An Officer and a Gentleman*," I said, horrified. "Oh, you'd be surprised how popular that trick is . . . and, for that matter, the movie's DVD rental," explained Mick.)

Here is what Mick found out about me (and believe me, that's *only* because he asked):

1. How much I already missed Leo.

2. How angry I was at Leo for leaving me before we could clean up the crap between us.

3. How much I regretted not being able to tell Leo what I really needed from him when I'd had the chance.

4. How proud I had hoped to make Leo of me by doing something like this—*particularly* something like this, which had nothing to do with this town.

Neither of us mentioned Louis.

By five o'clock, enough light was piercing the sky to convince us that we had strained our eyes—and our voices—enough for one night. The ride back to my place was made in silence. Mick insisted on walking me to my door and lugging the telescope for me. I thanked him, then informed him that I now knew it was worth taking the time to put putty in my bedroom's keyhole.

When he leaned over to kiss me, I didn't try to stop him. Nor did I object when he moved us out of the doorway and, very gently, pulled me through the living room into my bedroom and onto my bed.

And I'll admit it: it was I who ripped the button off his shirt while pulling it out from under his belt. Granted, we took turns peeling off each other's jeans, but I'll give him full credit for how quickly he can unsnap a Victoria's Secret Second Skin Satin unlined demi bra, and definite kudos for his gentle touch while slipping off my lace low-rise Brazilian tanga, and for the tender way in which he explored every nook and cranny of my love-charged body . . .

. . . until the phone rang.

Reflexively I grabbed it, while Mick groaned.

Love hurts.

Unrequited love is an even bigger bitch.

Of course, none of that mattered to Louis, who was in full-fledged crisis mode.

"Love, where the *hell* have you been? I've been calling your goddam cell all evening!"

"I wasn't expecting you—I mean, I shut it off after I left the club. I've been—well, I—Louis, it's *Saturday*. Didn't Randy give you my message?"

"Randy? No, Randy said nothing. Look, something— something terrible has happened—" There was an ache in his voice, which broke before he could finish the sentence. "I need you."

"*Right now?* But it's—it's not even six o'clock yet!"

"Please, Hannah. Look, I'll—I'll explain when you get here."

The line went dead.

I stared at the ceiling, weighing what meant more to me: my obligation to Louis or my lust for Mick.

Mick made the decision for me. He got up, got dressed, and left me with nothing more than a kiss on the forehead.

And a broken heart.

It took me exactly 38 minutes to hightail it from my place to Louis's.

In the meantime, Louis had somehow found the strength to pull himself together. He was fully dressed, shaved and humming one of T's rap ditties as he munched a Zone-approved low-carb scone along with his glass of grapefruit juice. He didn't even look up from his *Variety* as I ran in.

"Change of plans," he said, smiling brightly. "We're leaving for New York immediately."

"Oh . . . kay." My mind went in a million directions. Suddenly I had a headache. "I'll have to call the jet service and let them know. And change the Ritz reservation. And the tulip order, I guess. Uh . . . may I ask what happened? You seemed pretty upset when you hung up forty minutes ago."

Could he tell by my tone that I was a bit peeved? I hoped so.

"I suddenly realized how badly I missed Tatiana. You know

how it is when you're in love, right? And you can't bear to be away one more second?"

"Yes. I know the feeling," I growled.

I punched in the reservation number for the studio's private jet on the gray cell and walked out of the room.

6

Penumbra

Means, literally, dim light. It most often refers to the outer shadow cast during eclipses.

It's true, for actors at least, that all the world's a stage. And since my primary assignment put me front row center in Louis's world (apparently, the job description wasn't fooling when it said 24/7), there was a part of him that pined for an ongoing standing ovation from me.

Well, as far as I was concerned, that morning he wasn't going to get it.

I was still fuming when Malcolm picked us up and shot us over to the private airfield at Van Nuys. Did this deter Louis from coveting my affections? Oddly, no, not in the least. At first he was a bit annoyed, however, and decided to show it in the best way he knew how: erotic flippancy. "What say we drop the icy indifference, eh love? Where I come from, we call that foreplay."

When that didn't work, he pretended to ignore my pouting altogether under the assumption that he could charm me into forgiving him. In the 40-minute trip from his house to Van Nuys, he chattered away: on industry gossip, the Posse's post-party antics; he even tossed me a bone about missing me in the Viper Room.

"I'd hoped you'd stick around and save me from all of those horny panting women. Not that I blame you for calling it a day as early as you did. Wish I could have done the same, but, hey, you don't make it in this town by clocking out after eight hours." He was hoping that would win him a grudging acknowledgement.

No go. No words were uttered through the polite, albeit frosty, smile on my lips.

Louis smiled, not one to give up so easily. "You left so early, I was sure you'd have had plenty of sleep by the time I called this morning."

"Oh, sure. I'm *always* up before the sun," I muttered. "If you must know, Louis, I'd been out all evening, too, catching up on some—some personal business."

"Of course. Understandable." He patted my hand sympathetically. "Hmmm. Mick must have been doing the same. I didn't see him, but Randy claims he was there, at least for a few minutes. Did you run into him?"

He asked it innocently enough, but the way his eyes bore into mine like two heat-seeking missiles, I suspected he already knew the answer to that.

If not, I'm sure the flush on my neck confirmed it. Still, I answered as noncommittally as I could. "Yeah, I saw him."

Nothing more. From either of us.

The rest of the ride was taken in silence.

The limo drove straight onto the tarmac, stopping next to the stairwell descending from the plane's forward door. We were greeted by the pilot and his navigator, both of whom

looked as if they had been hired by the studio's casting department, because they so perfectly fit their roles of stiff-backed
flinty-eyed flyboys. After making congenial small talk based
around their enjoyment of Louis's last film and the weather
patterns we might possibly encounter en route to New York,
they then assisted Malcolm with the luggage.

As we boarded the plane, Louis insisted that I go first.
Then, quite solicitously, he steadied my hand when I reached
the top step. Ignoring the fawning flirtatiousness of the flight
attendant, he introduced me to her as "the one woman in my
life I could never do without" (which had her practically curt-
sying to me).

From what I could see, the studio's jet, a Boeing 737-800
"executive" model, was tricked out with all the bells and whistles, including (as requested) a Zone smorgasbord, to be served
once we reached our cruising altitude on Vera Wang's "Em-
press Jewel" Wedgwood pattern; a fully stocked bar, with Brut
Réserve chilling in a William Yeoward crystal champagne
bucket; a custom-made Collezione-Divani built-in sofa and
four captain's chairs, all upholstered in leather so soft that
you'd have sworn it had been marinated in butter for a month
prior to being hand-sewn onto their frames; the prerequisite
in-cabin screening room with a 4700-lumens high-definition
digital projection system and a film library that included every
new release available, as well as every film the actor in transit
had ever made and every cinema masterpiece attributed to the
studio; a dining aft-lounge with a high-gloss Michael Graves-
designed mahogany table that could be electronically adjusted
for height but was currently set to accommodate that of the
typical leading man, who is—according to most studio publicity departments—five-feet ten (but is actually, if that same
source could be shamed into admitting it, more like five-feet

seven, and *that's* stretching it); and last, but not in any way the least, a "master suite" for the weary world traveler, which boasted a round Cal-King feather bed.

The flight attendant, aptly named Caresse, was a five-feet-eleven-inch raven-tressed Amazon tricked out in a way that would make any Hollywood player's flight less stressful, if not downright enjoyable. Her outfit included a form-hugging, jersey-Lycra Versace-designed catsuit with matching paperboy cap (both imprinted with the studio's logo). She had a tendency to hover at an arousing closeness, with a scent so enticingly musky that any airborne VIP wouldn't mind in the least when she did so and a soft, breathy voice emanating from lips plumped into a tantalizing liquid pout. She was trained as a sous chef, should Louis care to ditch his diet and indulge in a craving for, say, pan-seared tilapia with chile lime butter; and she was licensed in shiatsu massage, as well as the Heimlich maneuver *and* mouth-to-mouth resuscitation. And finally, her breasts were buoyed with so much of the requisite silicone that they could have qualified as flotation devices. In fact, I had no doubt that Louis would be clinging to them if, God forbid, our plane should end up in the drink. (I'm sure he was disappointed that this portion of our trip was over land.)

Frankly, I was thankful that the studio had been thoughtful enough to provide so many diversions, since I was in no mood to play handmaiden to Louis. Too little sleep, not to mention coitus interruptus, has a way of making me a bit peckish.

Prior to take-off, he insisted that *I* spread out on the sectional.

"That way, you can curl up and doze off if need be, love," he murmured. Taken with his sweetness, Caresse gave me an envious look that said, "You lucky, lucky girl!"

With a stony nod, I plopped myself down on the couch as if

I owned it and picked up that month's edition of *Esquire*, which Caresse had so considerately left on the coffee table. She was fully aware that its cover—which featured Louis in a white Armani suit sans shirt, four models dressed as mini-skirted nuns praying at his feet, and sporting the headline "Why Women Worship This Guy, and Not You"—would certainly be appreciated by the studio's precious cargo.

Clucking her tongue in shock at my apathy, Caresse commiserated with Louis, who was feigning crestfallen martyrdom, in the best way she knew how: After suggesting that we buckle ourselves up as comfortably as possible, she surreptitiously slipped him a business card containing her cell number, then made a geisha-worthy getaway to the galley.

As if his having it would have mattered to me!

Or that he would have given a damn if I did care.

Louis acknowledged my barely stifled guffaw at this contemporary comedia dell'arte with a knowing grin and a slight bow. I shrugged and went back to my magazine.

His A.D.D.—adoration deficit disorder—was now so great that he decided to take a more diplomatic tact to win my forgiveness. After flopping down beside me on the sofa (close enough to have scored well on that portion of the studio's flight attendant exam), he cleared his throat and began his new pitch with a serious tone.

"Hannah, my love, since this *is* a four-hour flight—"

"Five hours, twelve minutes, and forty-two seconds to be exact."

"Yes, right, excellent assessment. Be that as it may, I'm hoping that, at some point in those 312.7 minutes you will find it in your heart to put aside any reason you may feel justified in being disappointed in me—"

"I'm sorry. Did you say something? I must have dozed off. In my dream, it was a lazy hazy Saturday, and I was enjoying the fact that I had been granted a day off by my lord and master."

He sighed, then hung his head in shame. "You're right. I'm a self-centered bastard. I had absolutely no right to ruin your one day off. Who do I think I am, anyway? Tell the truth: I'm becoming one of those insecure, egotistical wankers who are so ubiquitous to Hollywood, aren't I?" He searched my face for any trace of forgiveness.

Well, yes, of course he was all of that, and more . . . which is why just the thought that Louis felt he needed clemency, from *me* of all people, put that much-coveted smile on my lips.

Pleased to have gotten the response he was looking for, Louis practically glowed. He was loved! Once again, all was right with the world.

Or so he thought. But I wasn't going to let him off so easily.

"Let's just say I was a bit surprised at your change of heart. Well, even if I don't appreciate it, I'm sure Tatiana will."

"Who? . . . Oh, of course, my beloved."

"If you say so." I plucked the card with Caresse's cell number on it from his shirt pocket. "And I'm sure you took little Miss Coffee-Tea-or-Me's card out of mercy, right?"

"If I hadn't, it would have broken her heart, now, wouldn't it?"

"Then how very considerate of you."

"Goes with the territory. What's a sex symbol without sex?"

Nonchalantly, he took the card out of my hand. He started to put it back in his pocket but then thought better of that idea. Instead, he pulled his wallet out of his back pocket and inserted it there.

"I couldn't tell you, Louis. No such animal has ever crossed *my* path. I live in Hollywood, remember?"

It was Louis's turn to laugh. "That's why I'm falling in love with you, Hannah. I don't have to sugarcoat anything for you because you already know the score, don't you?"

I laughed, too. *Yes, Louis,* I thought, *if anyone knows the score, it's me—which is why I refuse to play the game.*

The plane had started down the runway. Encouraged by my response, Louis tried another compliment—if you could call it that.

"You've got a great smile. Granted, you've got a bit of a space between your two front teeth, but personally speaking, I find that, in certain situations, it can be a real asset."

"Thanks. I guess." What, was I a horse or something? Over-spaced teeth, an asset? As it dawned on me that his remark might have been less equine than carnal in its inference, I blushed more than a bit. Having toppled me off my pedestal, he laughed heartily.

Primly, I retorted, "Now, if you'd like me to keep smiling, then you'll review these DVDs Monique sent of "The Actor's Studio" interviews. According to her, the last actor invited who'd starred in a film backed by this studio felt that dropping his drawers would gain him more empathy from James Lipton than some well-chosen anecdotes. She's assured them no similar antics will come from you, but—well, you *do* have a reputation for irreverence. Just think of it as another one of those 'sex symbol' obligations."

(Actually, Monique's exact words to me were, "While they're taping, make sure Louis keeps his cock in his pants. I mean that both literally *and* figuratively.")

He groaned. "But there's a Manchester soccer match scheduled today, and we can pick it up via satellite!" Then he paused, struck by some more alluring idea. Smiling mischievously, he countered, "Tell you what: I'll skip the match and go over the tapes, on one condition."

"And what would that be?"

"That we play our *own* little game between each interview. Say, Twenty Questions. You have to answer anything I ask."

Louis, curious about *me?* Hmmm. Sure, it was flattering. And scary. And *very* thrilling.

I hoped I was a good enough actress to hide the fact that I was pleased he was even interested. "Okay. You're on. But I have to warn you, it won't be half as exciting as Manchester, I'm sure. In fact, at any point if you get bored, as I imagine you will, we'll end it and you can switch over and get the Manchester score."

"Oh, I don't plan on getting bored," he teased.

"We'll see. By the way, I have a condition, too."

"Name it."

"That I get to ask a question for every one I answer."

He leaned back, thoughtfully. "Why not? I've got nothing to hide."

"Neither do I," I said, with a bit less bravado. "Who's up first, Depp or del Toro?"

The first three questions weren't so bad. In fact, I'd say we both found them much more entertaining than the tapes. His questions to me were: (1) What did I like best about my childhood (my answer: growing up on the waterfront); (2) What were my first impressions of Los Angeles (that it was hectic, hot—the weather; and cold—in regard to the people); and (3) What would I be doing if I weren't (in his words) babysitting him? (Planet hunting, full time!)

I thought his questions were quite thoughtful, so much so that I used them on him. At first, to avoid giving answers, he accused me of cheating, but I would have none of it. "A deal is a deal, remember?" I reminded him.

With that he shrugged and gave in: His best childhood memories were "sneaking into flicks with me mates"; (2) When he first landed in L.A., he said, "I thought it was heaven: the sun, the palm trees, all the great-looking birds—" (a.k.a. the pretty young things who couldn't resist him).

The third question—what would he have been doing if he hadn't been an actor?—wasn't so easy for him to answer. Staring off into the clouds through one of the cabin's windows, he muttered, "I'd probably be a lazy good-for-nothing tosser, like me old man."

Acknowledging the pity I'm sure he read in my face, he shrugged and turned back to the television monitor. "How many more of these do we have to go?"

"Too many. We'll never finish all of them. Maybe we can get in two more before the plane lands. That should put Monique at ease that both your posterity and posterior are safe and secure."

"I live to serve," he said dryly. "This time, what say we get the questions out of the way first?"

"Well, I dunno—" I hesitated. The happy, playful Louis was so much more comfortable to be around than the dark, bitter one I had just glimpsed. "If you want, we can skip the questions altogether."

"Indulge me."

"Okay, sure," I said warily. "So, what do you want to know?"

"What would you say to your father, you know, if he were still alive?"

Louis watched intently as I struggled with the words. "I—I guess . . . well, I guess I'd want him to know that I'm okay, and that I miss him terribly. And that . . . that I forgive him."

"Why?"

"Why? Why what?"

"Why do you forgive him? What for?"

I paused again, not just confused about how to explain this but more or less surprised that Louis would even give a damn. But apparently he did, at least enough to make me think that I could be honest with him if I truly wanted to—

—and yes, that was *exactly* what I wanted: to go ahead and say to him what I never had the chance to say to Leo.

"Okay, here goes: I forgive him for not putting me first."

"First?"

"Yeah, first: ahead of all of the loony wives and the bitchy lovers; ahead of this lousy studio deal, or that blowhard director. And most of all, ahead of his rep."

"Rep?"

"Yes, his—you know, reputation. As a lady's man. That's all I ever really wanted from him. To come first. *Just once.*"

There, I'd said it.

"So, you wanted him to put you in front of his career."

"Yes," I answered defiantly. "What's wrong with that? Doesn't every kid deserve that?"

"Well, whether we do or not, we all certainly *think* we deserve it, now, don't we?" he laughed wryly. "In my case, I was always coming in second to a pint of Guinness."

I laughed uneasily with him, then we both sat quietly for what seemed like forever.

Finally, very softly, he added, "That old man of yours must have been quite an education, eh?"

Our little game had so decompressed the levity in the cabin that I would not have been surprised if oxygen masks had fallen from the ceiling.

"My turn," I said, hoping that my question would be the breath of fresh air needed before we got to New York. "Are you looking forward to seeing Tatiana when we reach the hotel?"

"God, I hope not!" said Louis, in horror. "I *never* tell her where I'm staying. What a joke *that* would be!"

"Why? What do you mean?" I was confused. I'd done everything Louis had asked of me: ordered flowers for her, arranged their delivery to her apartment, along with his sweet little note: "My darling, I've been counting down the hours! From your Принц (the last word, which I text-messaged to the florist so that they would get it right, meant *prince* in Russian). I'd even given her agency our time of arrival at the hotel. And now he *didn't* want to see her? Was he afraid of a paparazzi stakeout? Was that why he preferred Tatiana to stay away from the hotel?

"I like to unwind first. She wouldn't understand that. Didn't they tell you?"

"Who? Tell me what?"

"Genevieve. About my usual routine. You know, how I need a massage when I arrive."

"Oh, yes!" I heaved a sigh of relief. "Of course, I know all about that. It's all taken care of, through Barry. Just the way you like it."

"That's my girl." He patted my arm but let his hand linger. "You *do* know the score."

"I . . . I guess so." I shrugged. I guessed his arrival massage was a good luck ritual or something. Leo's had been playing nine holes at the Bel-Air Country Club barefooted. Go figure.

Chances were that Tatiana's hectic booking schedule wouldn't allow her to be at the hotel in the middle of the afternoon anyway, so I decided to let the matter drop. And if she was there, maybe I could arrange a couple's massage for the two of them. I was sure Louis would like that.

"You've got one last question," I declared brightly. "Go for it."

"What is your ideal in a man?"

"My ideal? That's a—a funny question."

"Why is it funny?" Despite the nonchalance he showed as he flipped through *Esquire*, I got the feeling he'd be parsing every word that came out through the space between my teeth.

Pausing as I weighed my words, I finally answered, "I want a man who brings his heart and soul to our relationship. I appreciate men"—here I paused— "who aren't afraid to speak their minds, to be honest. Or, as you put it, I want both of us to *always* know the score." I gave him that gap-toothed smile he claimed to love so much. "How about you?"

"Well, frankly, I find honesty in relationships overrated."

"You don't say."

"No, I mean it! While every woman I meet claims to want exactly what you've just described, I've found that, in practice, they prefer the pretty lies. *Especially* in Hollywood." While I took time to digest this, he added, "I think we should go one more round."

"We can't. We're about to land." The consistent drop in the plane's altitude was coinciding with a rise in the intimacy of his questions, both of which I found a tad uncomfortable.

But Louis was not to be deterred. "I'll make it quick," he said briskly, then he looked me in the eye as he asked, "Are you falling for Mick?"

"What?" I could feel my ears getting uncomfortably hot. "What do you mean? I don't even *know* Mick."

"You're right. You don't. Then again, you'd like to think you know *me*."

I was unsure how to answer that. It was on the tip of my tongue to say, "I know you like a book!" But I didn't. Instead, I gave him the answer he wanted to hear: the sugarcoated answer. "I thought I did. But I guess I really don't."

"Exactly. And that's my point: He's a wanker, just like the bloody rest of us blokes, love." He gave me that dazzling smile of his. "I'm only telling you this because I'd never want anyone to hurt you—"

I was just about to ask him why he thought Mick would hurt me when, just then, Caresse came into the cabin. She was carrying two down pillows. Noting Louis's slight nod, she leaned beside him and slipped one under his head. As her breast grazed his forehead slightly, he grinned up at her, although I assumed he was still talking to me when he said,

"—I mean, what would I do without you?"

7

Comet

An icy object on an independent orbit about the Sun.

There are so many features that make the Ritz Carlton Suite perfect for an evening (or, for that matter, a 59-minute, $1,800 session) of naughty debauchery. And, while each amenity is unique in its ability to spark romance, collectively they create the absolutely *perfect* ambiance for fucking like rabid dogs.

Okay, well, perhaps like well-groomed highly pedigreed poodles.

Where to begin? For starters, there is its incomparable view of Central Park. As seen from the large twenty-second-floor picture window of this two-bedroom suite, and framed magnificently within the brocade drapes that complement the opulently furnished room's taupe, pale rose and celadon color scheme, it certainly sets the mood for romance!

Romantic enough to make you horny, you ask? Most definitely—particularly if someone else—say, the Hollywood studio you're shilling for—is picking up the tab.

And if that view doesn't ring your chime, try luxuriating in either of the two marble tubs while soaking in Frédéric Fekkai bath beads. Then dry off in the fluffy Egyptian cotton towels before swaddling yourself in thick terry robes and falling into one of the two king-sized beds swathed in 700 thread-count Pratesi jacard cotton sheets. To further set the mood, the hotel invites you to light as many of the fragrant Frette candles strewn about the room as you like. Or you can flip on the Bang & Olufsen stereo system and play a mood-setting riff chosen from the in-room compact disc selection, each CD chosen for its success in encouraging guests to just get it on (as determined by frequently conducted guest surveys).

And if none of this does the trick? Well, there is always the myriad of porn available via cable, as viewed through a Bang & Olufsen BeoVision Avant integrated home cinema system's 32-inch widescreen monitor.

While all of this was news to me, it wasn't to Prudence K., who, as Louis's regular "masseuse" during his New York journeys, readily partook in all of the amenities the hotel offered. Thanks to Louis (and other A-listers, VIPs, and expense unaccountable CEOs), the Ritz Carlton Suite was her home away from home. In fact, in preparation for her audience with Louis, Prudence K. even helped herself to the contents of the complimentary Floris shaving kit, which provided the necessary accoutrements—a tiny yet super-efficient razor and ultra-foamy scented shaving cream—to touch up her Brazilian bikini wax.

What a field day the hotelier's quality control team would have if they were allowed to survey her opinion as to whether the Stearns & Foster SilverDream Euro Pillowtop King mattresses were truly firm enough for marathon sexcapades, or how well the Teflon stain-resistant finish on the upholstery stood up to that potent combination of semen, sweat, vaginal fluid, and Glow by J.Lo Eau de Toilette Natural Spray, or the actual burn factor incurred when kneeling on the plush wool Oriental carpets!

All of these, and more, were her domain—or so I gleaned in the 18-second elevator ride we took together down to my room, a cubby which embodied the more marketable moniker of "guest suite" in describing its meager—and somewhat less opulent—425 square feet.

"Jeez, whattaya supposed to do in this cage, fuck standing up?" Prudence K. sniffed scornfully as she surveyed its much punier bed.

Since this was to be her temporary rendezvous site with Louis—thanks to my efficiency in relaying his whereabouts to his beloved Tatiana, who had been cooling her Rive-Gauche-satin-ankle-strapped heels in the intimate but still very public VIP lounge while Louis's onsite point man, the ever-vigilant Barry, frantically relayed the direness of the situation to a very irate Louis and me—I prayed that this was in fact the case, in light of the fact that, subsequently, I too would be sleeping on those sheets.

I certainly wouldn't be getting any sympathy from Louis on the matter; upon seeing Tatiana's petulant pout staring up at him from the lounge's reproduction Duncan Phyfe sofa, he hissed through his grim, teeth-gritting grin, "*Dammit, Hannah, I thought you knew the score!*" before sauntering over to "the face that has launched a thousand magazine covers" and sweeping her up in his arms.

Then, with a slight wave, he banished me to clean up the *merde* I had made.

After getting Prudence K. settled, I shot back up to Louis's suite and blathered out some lie about the *Vanity Fair* photo editor needing to meet with him to go over the wardrobe for the shoot later that afternoon.

"Should I come with you?" slurred the perennially annoyed Tatiana with a Slavic lilt. "That woman knows next to nothing about lighting! The photographer she chose made me look like a corpse!"

This from a woman-child whose alabaster skin was stretched so woefully thin on her bony five-feet eleven, 103-pound frame that her catwalk photos from Jean Paul Gaultier's Auschwitz-inspired fashion show brought tears to the eyes of Holocaust survivors.

"No!" both Louis and I answered in unison.

Shooting me a daggered smile, he continued, "I won't hear of it, my darling. She is *much* too temperamental, and I wouldn't dream of putting you through such torment. I'll deal with her alone. Hannah here"—with a steely grip, Louis pushed me forward into his lushly upholstered lair—"will be more than happy to keep you company while you wait. It should take fifteen minutes, tops."

With that, he left the two of us to get acquainted; that is, Tatiana studied her Opi-glossed nails with that world-famous look of boredom etched in Prescriptives Matte Foundation Velum No. 3, while I tried not to stare . . . too much.

As *if*.

It was certainly easy to see how Louis could fall in love with her, even if this infatuation, like all the others, lasted only a few months. Most certainly she was more beautiful in person than she was in her renowned partially nude Mario Testino photos, more so because, in 3-D and living color, those sharp green eyes acted like an ever-changing emotional kaleidoscope despite the placid countenance on her exquisite face.

Particularly when she was thinking about Louis, as she obviously was during the 52 minutes prior to her not-so-nonchalant inquisition of me on that very subject.

"You, Whatever-Your-Name-Is-That-I've-Already-Forgotten: how long have you worked for Louis?"

"Only for a couple of days."

"Oh, yes? How did you get the job?" The chill in her voice left nothing to the imagination as to her suspicions on how I must have accomplished this magnificent feat.

"I was referred to him by Jasper Carlton."

She grunted her grudging approval. But believe me, that guttural utterance took all the magic out of our budding relationship once and for all.

Not that I could blame her for having doubts. Heck, from what I could tell just from being with Louis for the past 44 hours, if I were his girlfriend I wouldn't trust him on the other side of the door unless he agreed to wear an electronic ankle bracelet.

Which is probably why, like me, she leaped to grab the phone when it rang. It was all the way across the room, and, thank God, I got there first. I attribute my win to the fact that she probably hadn't eaten in a week and therefore hadn't had the energy for anything longer than a short sprint.

"Yeah," I growled brusquely into the phone, praying it wasn't Louis saying he was "all tied up"—literally—and couldn't break away, and so was asking me to keep stalling.

"Hi, Louis! It's Caresse." To demonstrate that she was just as accommodating on the ground as in the air, our friendly flight attendant then purred, "Care for some company?"

"No thanks. Got it covered," I snapped back, then hung up.

"Who was that?" asked Tatiana, suspiciously.

"No one. Nothing important. Just the front desk, checking to see that everything is okay. With the room, I mean."

Tatiana said nothing, but she scrutinized every word that had come out of my mouth, like a human lie detector registering any deviating nuance.

Had I tipped her off to the truth? I wasn't to find this out until Louis came bounding through the door some 37 minutes later.

"*Finally!* What an unmitigated ordeal!" he moaned, taking Tatiana's granitelike visage between his hands and giving her a long, lingering kiss. "Hannah didn't bore you too badly, did she, love?"

"Not at all," murmured Tatiana. "I can see why you keep her around, Louis."

"Oh?" he laughed warily. "And why is that?"

"Because, dearest, she is too smart to fall in love with you."

Considering all that had transpired in the last two hours, I would have assumed that Louis would be relieved to hear that observation, but the way he raised his left eyebrow indicated that this was not the case.

Thankfully, she hadn't noticed. There was a mirror too close at hand, all the better to monitor the effect she made as she wrapped herself in his arms. Immediately, though, she pushed him away.

"Louis my love, how close did you let that woman get to you? You *reek* of Glow! Go shower, *then* we make love . . . Oh, and You-Whose-Name-I-Can-Never-Remember, you can go now, okay?"

Yeah okay, bitch, consider me out of here!

I made it back down into the bowels of the hotel and the (eeeuw-yuck!) comfort of my cubby—only to find Prudence K. still cooling her Manolo Blahnik–clad heels on my bed.

"Louis said you'd cover me," she said, slipping her hands into a pair of cashmere-lined black leather gloves.

"He—he *what?*"

"He said you'd have my cash."

I now saw how she lived up to her name. "How much?"

"Eighteen hundred."

"You've gotta be kidding!"

"Hardly. And believe me, *no one* ever complains." She licked her lips seductively.

"Yeah, I can imagine. Um, do you take credit cards?"

"Visa, MasterCard, Amex. No Discover. You can't get this kind of merchandise at Sears, ya know what I mean?" She laughed at her own cleverness. It wasn't the first time, I'm sure. From her Kate Spade striped tootsie, she pulled out a wireless credit card processing terminal, swiped my Visa, and handed it back to me with a printout to sign.

"I guess he expects me to add it to my expense report," I said, thinking out loud to myself.

Prudence K. clicked her tongue sympathetically. "Nah, I don't think so. He said something about this whole thing was your fuck-up, and that's why it was coming out of your pay."

And with a wave of her Gucci-gloved hand, she was out the door before I'd even finished saying, "Room service? I need a new change of bed linen—*now!*"

Vanity Fair's real photo editor was not wearing Glow.

Nor was she at all pleased with Louis's abuse of the magazine's renowned celebrity photographer, or his overt flirtatiousness with the stylist, makeup artist, hairdresser and the art director's barely legal but certainly awestruck intern ("For his own good, you need to lower your boss's dose of Viagra . . ."), or the way in which he second-guessed how the photographer lit the studio for the shoot ("Jeez, who does this prick think he is, Brad Pitt? That hasn't happened to me since that Russian-French cadaver they call a supermodel had the nerve to pull that same stunt, then went whining to my publisher when I told her where to stick her little light meter . . .").

As his handler, it was my duty to try to reel him in, but since it was me he was punishing with this outrageous behavior, I very seriously doubted I was up for the job.

Still, I had to give it a try. As the *VF* team set up the next shot, I followed Louis into his dressing room, where his next wardrobe change was already laid out: some duded-up urban cowpoke ensemble, courtesy of John Galliano. It was just perfect for the surreal fantasy in which a model, trussed up in strategically placed leather straps, was to be branded by Louis with a faux hot iron inscribed with his initials.

Upon hearing me enter, Louis sighed. "What is it you want, Hannah?"

"Louis, I think we need to clear the air about what went on back at the hotel."

"Oh, you do, do you?" he asked with a dark smile. "You have no need to worry. I'm not going to fire you over your slip-up."

"Oh." I don't know if I was more relieved or disappointed. "Why—why not?"

"I don't know. Let's just chalk it up to my magnanimous nature." He chuckled ironically. "Sure, I was pissed at first. Had every right to be, wouldn't you say? Then again," he broke into a broad smirk, "having Tatiana waiting her turn while Prudence K. and I were screwing in *your* bed was . . . well, let's just say that the love of one—or several, for that matter— good woman has a way of getting your juices flowing, know what I mean?"

No, I didn't. And I was hoping that he wouldn't go into any detailed explanation, either, considering that I'd actually have to *sleep* in that bed.

Alone.

I felt a tingle go up my spine as he walked over to me. He stood so close that I could feel the heat of his breath on my face.

Slowly he picked up the branding iron and examined it. "Frankly, love, I'm getting a bit bored with Tatiana. I mean, if I weren't, then why would I feel the need for 'a massage' every time I hit town? The truth is that she doesn't understand me."

He stroked my face with the branding iron gently, slowly. "Not like *you* do."

"Oh, I don't know, Louis," I nervously stammered. "I guess, after this afternoon, we are now both in perfect agreement that I really don't 'know the score.'"

"Oh, I think you do. In fact, I think you knew exactly what you were doing." His eyes were mesmerizing.

"And—what was that?"

"Encouraging Tatiana to see that the sooner she moves on, the sooner I can, too. Am I right?"

Even in my state of suspended animation, I was aware that I was witnessing a perfect example of the Hollywood spin on Newton's theory of universal gravitation: what was down—currently, his ego—could only be inflated again if those around him were willing to blow enough hot air into it.

Was I willing to pucker up?

I had no choice. A happy Louis made for a happier world.

I smiled uncertainly. "Okay, I guess you're right, Louis. It must have been a subliminal slip."

"I was afraid of that." He nodded knowingly. "Love, look, no one expects you to be perfect, not even me. But you can't be butting into my bedroom, no matter how tempting that may be."

Butting into his bedroom? What, is he crazy?

"Look, I know you just want to make me happy"—He

paused at that, as if considering the possibilities— "and I've no doubt that soon you'll become a pro at doing so. Still, the next time you have some grand scheme involving my love life, *just ask*. I don't bite—unless you absolutely insist on it." Playfully, he tapped me with the branding iron, his indication that I was now excused to go.

As I lurched toward the door, he called out, "Why don't we discuss some new ground rules, at dinner, after that taping? Make a reservation somewhere—but don't choose some place where we'll be seen—uh, interrupted. The paparazzi and stalkers are already staking out the lobby. Tatiana's visit tipped them off. Better yet, let's just order in room service. We both might just want to hit the sack early, right?"

Not me. At least, not on *those* sheets.

I stopped cold. *Was he insinuating . . .*

Flustered, I turned back around. "Um, Louis, I don't think—"

"You know, Hannah, that's just your problem: you *don't* think. But all that will change . . . once you know me intimately." Oh, which reminds me: call Barry. Tell him I won't need Prudence K. tonight."

Prudence K.—again?

But now . . . he wouldn't?

Why not?

Like all "Actors Studio" tributes, Louis's was comprised of various stills and film clips of his stage, BBC television, and film career, intermittently interrupted by flattering comments from the always officious Mr. Lipton.

The youthful audience, made up of up-and-coming actors, directors and future career waiters, was quite aware they were witnessing history in the making. They knew a soon-to-be

Academy Award winner when they saw one, by golly, and so they listened intently, and cooed and murmured at all the right moments.

Louis, ever the consummate performer, did not let them down. His unabashedly modest answers, spoken with unwavering intensity and periodically infused with wise cynicism (and in one instance, a faraway glance that bespoke a bittersweet longing), seemed astounding coming from someone his age—not that anyone in the audience could tell what that age really was: The filter used on the dimmed klieg lights shining on the stage gave him a rosy, boyish glow that shaved at least four, maybe even six, years off the age claimed on his official bio.

Standing in the back of the room and witnessing his triumph, I breathed a sigh of relief. The Day from Hell was finally over, I prayed.

The silent pulse of the red cell phone dashed my hopes. I flipped it open and found a text message waiting for me.

Mick B: Miss U. How R things?

Mick! A surge of longing swept over me as I remembered how comfortable I'd felt in his arms. I could never text message what I was feeling, so how was I to answer that? I chose to tell the truth—to a degree:

Hannah F: Interesting. Exhausting. Miss U 2. Wish U
     were here.
Mick B: I am.

I tried scanning the audience, but this was difficult to do, since, from where I was standing, I could only see their backs, and the only illumination was coming from the stage. As it turns out, Mick wasn't in the audience but standing right behind me, as I discovered when he wrapped his arms around my waist.

As happy as I was to see him, it also made me anxious to have him and Louis so close to me at the same time. But the way in which he nuzzled my ear told me that I—or, for that matter, Louis—would have to get over it.

He whispered, "So, Louis hasn't driven you to jump off the roof of the Ritz Carlton?"

"Almost, but not quite. Between him, Tatiana, and—"

"Oh, and let me guess: Prudence K.?"

"You *know* about Prudence K.?" I was more than a little disappointed that he did. What I was actually thinking was, *How well do you know her?*

"Louis likes to share his conquests," Mick explained, with a grimace.

Are we talking literally, or figuratively? I wanted to ask. But I couldn't.

Because then I'd have to accept whatever answer he gave at face value.

I turned back to the stage, where Louis had been answering the audience's questions. One wannabe actress, with the kind of assets that would certainly get her cast in a prime-time network soap with or without an ASDS diploma, breathily asked, "What do you look for in a leading lady?"

The audience giggled anxiously. Arching an eyebrow, Louis answered with a lascivious chuckle, "A woman who brings her heart and soul to the project. I appreciate women"—he paused, tantalizingly—"who aren't afraid to speak their minds. Bottom line: my perfect leading lady *always* knows the score."

With that, his eyes scanned the room, zeroing in on me—and Mick.

The interview was over.

* * *

On the ride back in the limo, Louis did everything to show his pal that he was glad to see him—and ignored me totally. "Man, I'm so glad you're in town. So, ready to see the sights?"

"Whatever, guy," said Mick noncommittally. "But, hey, I don't want to interrupt your plans. With Tatiana."

"She's winging her way to Paris as we speak," said Louis evenly.

"Oh. Too bad. Well, uh, yeah, so what say we take in some clubs?" He turned toward me apologetically, but I ignored him. Like me, he didn't have the guts to blow off Louis. From the look of things, *we* were the ones who would have to get over it.

Or get over each other.

"I've got an even better idea." Louis now had a reason to acknowledge me. "Tell Barry I've changed my mind . . . to get Prudence K. here pronto." He then turned to Mick. "You want some action, right?" When Mick hesitated, Louis added, "You remember her, right? Hey, don't sweat it, it's on the studio."

We'd finally reached the hotel. Yanking the limo door open with one hand, I speed-dialed Barry's number with the other.

"Hannah, wait—" said Mick, then he turned to Louis. "Look, man, I—I'll take a pass. I thought, you know, that you'd be tied up, and that I could keep Hannah company—"

"You did, eh? Well you were only right about one thing, I am tied up. *With Hannah*. Right, love?"

They both stared at me, waiting for my response. I looked from one to the other, weighing Mick's shock and hurt with Louis's annoyance and jealousy.

Just then, we all heard Barry's hazy voice coming through the phone, "Can I help you?"

I was confused, angry and upset. More than anything, I was bone tired.

So I threw the phone at them, headed for the front door and never looked back.

Housekeeping had forgotten to change my sheets. Since I was too angry to go to bed anyway, it finally didn't matter anymore.

8

Parallax

*The angular difference in apparent direction of an object
seen from two different viewpoints.*

By morning, I had decided that, if I was going to save both my
sanity and my salary, I'd need to have that talk with Louis
about our "ground rules."

Only *I* was going to be the one who set them. And *he* was
going to live by them.

Rule #1: No more guessing games. He was going to have to
start being honest with me as to what he wanted. Oh and hey,
if that was a hooker, he'd have to call her pimp himself. I was
out of the procurement business.

Rule #2: No more double entendres. If anything left his
mouth that even *hinted* at a sexual innuendo, I'd be out the
door so fast he wouldn't know what hit him.

Rule #3: This was a long shot, but I felt justified to have it as
a safety clause: If either of us fell in love with the other, I
would walk. Why? Because he was a guy with hot pants, and I
was a woman with a checkered history when it concerned men

with hot pants, starting with Daddy Dearest. Enough said. No hard feelings.

I never got the chance to lay out the new ground rules, because Louis fired me before I opened my mouth for anything other than a poached egg white on rye toast.

Granted, it was done in the gentlest way possible: After summoning me to his palatial chamber and insisting that I take a cup of chamomile tea and help myself to the Zone breakfast buffet already laid out by a retreating bellboy (smirking heaven knows why), Louis then proceeded to tell me how he hadn't slept all night (it was on the tip of my tongue to say that was Prudence K.'s fault, not mine, but I thought better of that), how he had been so upset at my "irrational behavior" that he'd called and blessed out Jasper for saddling him with "a Hollywood brat who assumes her job is to freeload at my expense—and the studio's of course"; and, oh by the way, what right had I to invite "my boyfriend" to do so as well?

"My *what?*"

"Don't play coy, Hannah. It is *so* unbecoming. I mean, what were you possibly thinking, inviting Mick here? We are supposed to be working, remember?"

I wasn't coy. I was livid.

"Wait—wait just a minute! In the first place, I didn't call Mick. He just showed up. He's part of *your* entourage, remember? Not mine. And in the second place, your idea of work— Ha! You've got to be kidding! It was you who—now, don't tell me you weren't planning to—I mean, asking me to 'order in room service,' and to—to call off Prudence K., and inferring that we were going to 'hit the sack early'—why, you wanted . . . didn't you? . . . Didn't you want—"

"Want what?"

Waves of emotion washed over his face: first anger, then confusion, followed by disbelief and finally (to my embarrassment) amusement.

"I don't believe you thought—you thought that *I*—I wanted *us*—" He paused. Then, with patronizing politeness, he added, "Hannah, I'm flattered that you'd even think about me that way, but the truth is, *you're just not my type.*"

Not his type.

"I'm . . . not?" That slipped out before I had a chance to think about what I was saying.

Wasn't any woman breathing his type?

As if I *cared!*

But I did.

I mean, if I wasn't *his* type, then whose type was I?

I was hurt. And embarrassed. And angry. Still, with all the dignity I could muster, I calmly rose. "Well . . . isn't *that* a relief! I'll—I'll just go pack my things. I've got to check flights back to . . . to Los Angeles."

"Look, Hannah, I didn't mean to hurt you—"

"I'm not hurt! In fact, I'm somewhat relieved."

"Relieved?" Nothing moved on Louis's face except that telltale eyebrow.

"Of course," I said blithely. "If I even thought you could be attracted to me, why, I'd just *have* to quit. I mean, there would be no way I *could* do this job . . . right?"

I laughed, hoping that it didn't sound as hysterical as I felt, but then again, exorbitant credit card debt and legal fees had a way of doing that to a person.

"Face it, Louis, you live to break hearts. But guess what? Mine has already been broken, so there's no way you could ever hurt *me.* So let me put your mind at ease that you'll never have to worry about hurting my feelings, okay? Not that I'd even give you a chance, because I'm out of here. And, I assume, with some decent severance."

I was already at the elevator when I felt his hand on my shoulder. He turned me around, cupping his hand under my chin so that I'd look right into those beautiful eyes of his.

"Look, I think we've both misunderstood what happened last night. What say we start with a clean slate? It's just a job, right, like you said." When he saw me shake my head doubtfully, he added, "And you're right about another thing: I am a heartbreaker—which is why I *want* you to stick around."

"I don't get it."

"We're a great team because you, as you so eloquently put it, *can't* get your heart broken. And since the last thing I need is an assistant who falls in love with me and complicates things, that one asset alone makes you invaluable to me."

In some cockeyed way, his logic made sense . . . *if* it had been true.

It was, as far as Louis was concerned. He made that abundantly clear by the way he assumed what my next move would be:

To do whatever he needed to have done.

"Now, go call the limo driver and tell him to be downstairs in ten minutes." Grinning, he gave me a gentle nudge into the waiting elevator.

Before the door closed completely, Louis called out, "Oh, uh, Hannah, one more thing: ask him to meet us at the side door, the one that comes out on Sixth Avenue."

"But why?"

"Let's just say that it's the best way for us to make a quiet getaway. You see, I, er, bumped into a couple of fans in the lobby last night . . . after your little drama queen scene. Seems that they'd been waiting hours for a glimpse of me, you know? Didn't want to disappoint them, right? Well, one thing led to another, and I asked them to join me for a nightcap . . . in my room." He grinned at the memory. "Wouldn't you know it, I had a *hell* of a time convincing them that the party was over . . . Mick, that bastard, was no help at all. He wouldn't take them off my hands! Well, the bellboy just tipped me off that they're *still* hanging out in the lobby. I think they're looking for an encore, know what I mean? Believe me, I can do without the tears. I wish every girl was as hard-hearted as you, love."

When I got back to my room, there were two dozen yellow roses waiting for me. The card read: "Didn't mean to interrupt your plans. Still missing U. So sorry."

Oh yeah? Well, so was I.

Which I guess blows my reputation for being a hard-hearted drama queen.

Our flight over was as uneventful as I could have wished for.

Did I use the word "uneventful"? Considering what the last 72 hours had been like, I guess that works. Sure, Louis exchanged telephone numbers with a couple of Virgin flight attendants. And of course he chatted up the girl lucky enough to have been seated across the aisle from him—some adorable young titled tootsie—and made a date to meet her later that night at some hot Europop nightclub.

But otherwise, he was the perfect gentleman. In fact, he was—well, *humane.*

For example, he insisted that I take the window seat.

Then when I dozed off, he covered me with a blanket.

And when I woke up, I caught him staring down at me, a look of immense sadness in his eyes.

"What's—what's wrong?" I sat up straight. Had they made some sort of announcement that the flight was doomed? Had he written off his chance of winning an Oscar?

Or had he changed his mind about my working for him and

was trying to come up with the words that would let me down easy?

He smiled wanly and pointed toward the window. "Look out there."

Below us, as we descended to 15,000 feet, I could make out a river coiling through a lush green terrain.

"That's the Thames," he said longingly. "Beautiful, isn't it?" Unconsciously, he laid his hand over mine.

It didn't move from that spot until fifteen minutes later, when it was announced over the intercom, in a very polite British manner, that we'd been cleared for landing, so it would be appreciated if we'd put our seats and our tray tables in an upright position.

There are many ways in which I could describe Louis's UK posse, which consisted of two of his childhood "mates" from Manchester—the stout, boisterous Andy and the redheaded Jim—as well as Nigel, a fellow actor from his BBC days, who was easily recognizable as a stalwart of the West End based on his ability to play characters of the "Yes Minister" variety and Louis's brother, Chaz, who, unfortunately for him, had none of his younger sibling's good looks. Friendly? Certainly. Flirtatious? Most definitely, if the terms they threw at Louis to describe his luck in having me with him ("Still being mollycoddled, I see" and "What a lucky bloke you are, finding *this* dolly bird to follow you around, eh?") were any indication.

They certainly weren't the types to cut him any slack because he was now famous.

Which, I came to realize, was just what Louis wanted.

Wanted? Make that *needed*. Instantaneously, the star attitude was gone. In its place, a happy, gracious, and *almost* modest human being emerged, one who insisted on carrying his bags himself (as opposed to having me run around and beg a skycap to do so), joshed around with his pals without feeling the need to lay them out and, with the utmost gosh-gee-golly politeness, signed autographs for the awed fans who came up and asked.

I was beginning to like *this* Louis.

But then his brother mentioned his father, and it all went to hell in a hand basket.

"Bugger it, what does that pain in the arse want?" Louis muttered when Chaz let it slip that "the old man" had been by to see their ma.

"The usual," Chaz grunted back.

"Tell her that I'll take care of him."

No more Mr. Nice Guy. Louis the Prodigal Son was home.

"Tell her yourself. She came in all the way from Manchester. She's waiting to see you, in that very nice hotel suite your gal here ordered. And Kathy and her brood are with her, too."

Was Ernestine J., as ordered by me in a more naive and innocent era, also there, ready, willing and able to give Louis his welcome-home "massage"?

That thought hit both Louis and me at the exact same moment. All the color that went out of his face must have flowed into mine, because I could feel my ears turn red.

Looking from one of us to the other, Chaz snickered, "It was sure sweet of Hannah to suggest that they meet you here. Why, it's a regular welcome-home party!" He and the others laughed riotously. "Don't worry, little brother, the boys here and I still remember fondly those 'little rituals' of yours. When Ma mentioned they were coming, we did you the favor of making sure the room was, shall we say, 'presentable'?"

Visibly breathing a sigh of relief, Louis gave me a look that said: *You're off the hook . . . for now.*

"That driver-pimp of yours, Alfonse, is keeping your little good luck charm safe and sound, in the limo," said Nigel briskly. "While you and Chaz visit with the folks, the boys here and I will take the li'l bird over to the pub around the corner. Oh, by the way, that reminds me: I take it she'll be satisfied with a couple of pints and a quid or two, am I right? No? *What—a thousand pounds?* Blimey, she's a posh one, eh? Well then, I'd better hold onto your charge card. You'll want us to keep her happy 'til you can join us, now, won't you? . . . Oh, uh, thanks, Hannah. I say, you *are* a sport!"

"So, you're taking care of me boy now?"

Edie Trollope, a fragile, porcelain doll of a woman whose faded cornflower blue eyes never once left the face of her youngest son as he hugged his sister, wrestled with his rambunctious nephews, and gamely jibed his brother, was able to convey anxious concern, bittersweet reminiscence, and maternal pride all in that one simple question, delivered in the distinctive cadence of her northern roots.

Louis would never have a more adoring fan.

I laughed uncomfortably. Considering all of my missteps to date, a more apt description was that her son and I were merely tolerating each other. And that was all.

Maybe.

But how do you say that to a doting mom? You don't. Which is why instead I answered, "He's a wonderful actor. It's an honor to work with him."

Reluctantly Edie forced herself to glance away from the most beloved of her progeny in order to look me right in the eye. "You're a lot like Sam."

I didn't know if, in Edie's mind, that was a good thing or not. Considering the sadness in her voice, though, I would guess that she saw it as unfortunate. For some reason, it mattered to me that she not assume Samantha and I were to suffer the same fate; and, more importantly to her, that her Louis was in better, more capable hands.

"I wouldn't know," I answered politely. "I've never met Louis's former assistant. Although I hear she was quite efficient. I hope Louis finds me the same."

I would have thought this would have appeased her and she would then return to the joy of reveling in all things Louis. But it didn't. Instead, she scrutinized me even more closely before coming to her verdict. "She was. And my guess is that he will." Edie sighed deeply. Pity."

"Oh? I'm—I'm sorry, I don't know what you mean."

"My son is a lot like his father—"

Just then Louis looked over, almost as if he knew he was the topic at hand. Smiling wickedly, he disengaged himself from the tangle of squirming little boys who'd engulfed him playfully. Despite the cavernous dimensions of the sumptuous suite, his suave swagger would put him beside us in no time at all. Realizing this, his mother concluded with a few well-chosen words—

"So, my dear, I'll give you the same advice I gave Sam: *don't fall pregnant, now.* Because Louis, God help him, isn't the type to stand beside you if you do. Sod it, if only someone had warned me to do the same when I was sweet on his father, I wouldn't be such a bitter old woman now."

Feeling Louis's arms envelop her waist, Edie indulged in her unwavering adoration once again.

"Fancy going for coffee?"

Louis's question took me by surprise. The suite was finally quiet, what with Edie, Kathy and the kids safely ensconced on the train back to Manchester (a trip that should prove to be three highly charged hours, thanks to all the naughty ideas

Louis put in the boys' heads about how they could "drive their mum narky"). The notoriously overbooked Ernestine J., payment in hand, had defected not long after being treated by the boys to a hearty breakfast of bangers, mash and ale, and, along with Chaz, Louis's mates were off attending to any obligations that might stand in their way of hanging with the King of Players later that evening.

Which meant that Louis and I were all alone.

He'd been granted a day's rest in order to facilitate any jet lag—which I was certainly feeling, despite the early afternoon hour. I'd assumed Louis was also tired, but obviously I was mistaken. He was up and raring to go.

Ah, my kingdom for an Ernestine J.!

"Hmmm . . . coffee . . ." Well, if anything was going to keep me from crashing, that would. "Ummm . . . does it have to be Jamaican Blue? Because, I'll be honest with you, I don't know where we'll find some in this town—"

"What do you take me for, some kind of sodding twit or something? Bollocks, no! Just . . . just a cuppa of something black. Anything at all." He reached for our coats. "In fact, I'll let you lead the way."

"No, this is your turf. I'll let you lead, but if I see a place I like, we'll stop."

"Agreed." He grinned playfully. "Blimey, it's been a while since I've showed someone around London. It should be interesting."

With him, it was. We didn't stop in trendy Kensington, or the beautifully-peopled Chelsea, the oh-so-posh Mayfair, or even hip Notting Hill. No, Louis's London was centered in down-and-dirty Soho, still—as in Louis's day—an edgy bohemia inhabited by those on the outer fringe of culture, art and, more importantly, infamy.

"It wasn't what I'd pictured at all," I murmured, squinting

up at the window of the grimy, three-story walk-up he'd once inhabited on Frith Street. Deceived by the morning's clouds, I had inconveniently forgotten my sunglasses. (Not Louis. His were always there, a not-so-successful deterrent to the inevitable tap on the shoulder that preceded that disingenuous question: "Aren't you—you know—*him?*")

Although I could not see his eyes, his voice, mellow with memories of a time long past, put his feelings into perspective. "To a bloke from Manchester who was going nowhere fast, it was a bloody get-out-of-jail-free card. My flat mate was Nigel." He laughed. "I still remember how pathetically long it took him to break me of my native Manchester brogue, to make me sound less—well, what we call 'Mancunian.'" He shook his head in wonder. "I must have cacked up at least forty auditions before I got the hang of proper British elocution. Bugger it! I was such a tosser back then, ready to quit and go home to Manchester each time they'd tell me to bog off—very politely, of course. Used to get so angry that they couldn't see past me accent."

"It was only a matter of time, right?"

"Yeah, right." He sighed deeply. "Bloody hell, those were glorious times! I worked me arse off and enjoyed every damn moment of it! Why, just look around you!" He pointed down the street, which was teeming with youthful exuberance clad in leather jackets, tattered jeans, colorful tights, and even more colorful hair. "It's just about perfect, isn't it?"

"Yes. It's perfect." It truly was. Because, right now, Louis was perfect.

He was so open. And honest. And *real.*

I was so enjoying the real Louis. And I was proud of him, proud now to be a part of his story.

We stood there for some time, just watching the carnival of Soho street life—the heavy conversations, the pickups, the put-downs, the street vendors, all still there, still very much a part of Louis—until a cloud once again overtook the sun.

"Time for that coffee now, wouldn't you say?"

We settled on one of his old haunts, Bar Italia, a twenty-four-hour hole-in-the-wall just a block down from his old flat. By the way he gulped down the thick brew of espresso the waiter put in front of him, it was obvious that he liked it even better than the Jamaican Blue after all.

Or perhaps it was being back in the old neighborhood that he liked so much.

Within an hour and a half, he was claiming it was due to the company: *me*.

But I'm sure that was only because I lent an interested ear as he talked about the very first London production he was cast in (Pinter's *Ashes to Ashes*), and the first time he'd gotten critical raves (Stoppard's *The Invention of Love*), and the production that got him noticed by American producers in the first place (a West End production of *Speed the Plow*).

"The damn American producers were looking for a Brit who could speak with an American accent. Well, hell, we were weaned on your cinema! I didn't know a dude who *couldn't* talk as if he'd grown up in the O.C., so I guess I was just lucky that I was the first guy they saw first," Louis explained, in a perfect O.C. drawl. "And to think I almost turned down the Mamet for another revival of *Julius Caesar*. Ha! Where would my life be if I had?"

"You would have made it 'across the pond' eventually. It was your fate. I know these things. I study the stars, remember?"

We'd moved from coffee mugs to beer tankards sometime during the unofficial happy hour of four o'clock. The fickle British sun, now fully encased in heavy, dense clouds, merited the switch. I was not used to thick dark British beers (let alone thin, pallid American ones), and I could feel my tongue get furrier with each sip.

"To paraphrase the Bard, 'the fault, dear Hannah, lies not in our stars, but in ourselves if we are underlings.'" He stared at me for just a second, then glanced away. His slap-happy grin couldn't disappear as fast, though. "You're an odd dolly bird, for Hollywood anyway, you know that?"

"In what way?" I demanded to know. Later I'd try to tell myself that it had been the beer that had made me belligerent, but of course I knew better. In truth, I was upset that he was so right, for so many reasons: I wasn't your usual Hollywood hottie, Malibu Barbie, or California surfer girl. Still, no woman wanted the obvious thrown in her face: *that she didn't fit in.*

Louis almost choked on his foam, he was laughing so hard at my reaction. "Don't get me wrong. You're certainly pretty . . . enough."

Enough? What, now there was a standard to be met?

But of course, in Hollywood there's *always* a standard. . . .

"I'm not being cheeky. I *mean* it—and not in a bad way at all. In fact, I think your . . . *ordinariness* is your most attractive feature."

"What? I don't get it." The fact that I *wasn't* pretty enough for Hollywood made me attractive? *To Louis?*

He took another sip of his beer before answering. "What I'm trying to say is that you're—well, you're not plastic. You know, not *fake*." He leaned in close—so close, in fact, that I could feel his breath on my face.

It felt warm. And nice. So much so that I felt it was worth staying awake for.

"You have *real* lips, not the blow-up-doll kind. Granted, your eyes could be just a bit larger—" He paused to scrutinize me more carefully. "And your hair . . . well, frankly, I *like* the fact that it's that—that sort of gingery brown color. Although maybe it could use a bit more red, too. . . ." He squinted to make sure, but there wasn't much light coming in through the café's windows. "You know what I mean—it's not just another shade of brass. And I must say, I find it refreshing to have finally met a woman in Los Angeles who doesn't spend every waking minute in some salon, or doesn't have an entourage of stylists trailing after her. The way you let it run wild all over the place—very Botticelli . . . well, okay, more like pinkie-finger-in-light-socket, but it seems to work. On *you*, anyway."

I snorted so hard that beer went up my nose. "Thanks. That's just what I needed: confirmation from the '*Cosmo's* Hottest Hunk' that I'm a total loser."

"I think you know better than that." All of a sudden, his voice got serious. "You're—*real*. Sure, your nose may be a bit too . . . 'pert' is the word, right?" He traced the pertness with a tapered finger. "And it's obvious that those are your *real* breasts—" His hand may have stopped, but his gaze hadn't. "Just the fact that they aren't anywhere near Hef's minimum is a dead giveaway that it's all you . . . I mean, I hope you started with *at least* that—"

Shaking my Botticellian mop, I warned him, "Watch it, pretty boy. You're treading on thin ice."

"Oh, don't I know it." He leaned back, but he didn't let up by any means. "And I like the way that you're always game to try something new, even though, as we've discovered, you have a propensity toward mucking things up. Most women in Los Angeles would rather play it safe. Then there's your very charming habit of speaking your mind, even at the most inappropriate times. Hmmm . . . and I find it endearing that you're not worried about breaking your face by laughing. What's truly more amazing is that you even laugh at yourself."

I groaned out loud, just thinking about the wrinkles he was

counting in the corners of my eyes. What was he truly dishing out: adoration, or insults? I was too tipsy to tell.

Whatever it was, though, it was too embarrassing to hear him continue.

"Enough already! Before this dissertation once again veers onto the subject of my gap-toothed grin, or how pigeon-toed I am, or the fact that my legs are too skinny, or that my elbows are too bony, or my ass sticks out too far—"

"As a connoisseur of the fairer sex's bum, I can assure you that yours is currently elevated quite nicely." He stopped and leaned outside the table. "But to make doubly sure, might I suggest we hasten back to the Portobello to measure its distance from the ground?"

"I've got a better idea." This I practically purred at him. "What say we complete our game of Twenty Questions?"

He blinked twice. "I thought we had."

"No, not really. You forgot to answer the very last question."

"Refresh my memory."

"On the plane, you had asked me what I considered were the traits of the ideal man. But you never answered that question yourself."

"Why, *I'm* the ideal man. For every woman, of course."

"I'm sure you think you are, but you know very well that's not what I'm asking! I want you to describe *the ideal woman*."

"I remember answering that very question in the 'Actor's Studio.'"

"No, you answered a question about your ideal *leading lady*. And, if *I* remember correctly, you stole my answer when you did. So, now it's time for the *real* answer."

He rose slowly and motioned the waiter for the check, but I made it obvious that I wasn't going to budge until he answered. After handing the waiter a £50 note to clear our tab,

Louis then sat back down, took both my hands in his, and looked me right in the eye.

"But I just gave it to you, Hannah dear, when I described *you*."

The conversations that took place every fifteen minutes or so between the hours of eight and eleven o'clock the next morning between me and the director of *Rebecca*, Dorian Lancaster (né Dragomir Levanat, an obviously fully Anglicized Croatian émigré), were a near-complete primer on the most colorful phrases in contemporary British slang.

Take, for example, *bang out of order*, which means totally unacceptable. (As in "It's bang out of order for that bastard prick boss of yours to blow off this final dubbing session!") Then there is *bugger it, mad for it, nadgers*, and *galloping knob-rot*. (The first term expresses frustration, the second is another way of saying *enthusiastic*, the third is slang for *testicles*, and the final expression describes an uncontrollable venereal disease— all of which Dorian used in this manner: "Bugger it! That bloke is so mad for it that one day he's going to wake up to find his nadgers covered in some galloping knob-rot!")

But the one phrase Dorian uttered that needed no translation was something to the effect that, if Louis didn't show up soon, the postproduction schedule for *Rebecca* would be "ballsed up" to the point that the studio might pull the plug on the project.

Would Louis be blamed? No.

I would. Again.

Bollocks!

I was too drunk to remember having stumbled into bed the prior evening. However, I did remember that our taxi had also picked up the rest of Louis's mates as it had wended its way back to the Portobello, and that, even in my much too sloppy state, I'd secured Louis's solemn oath—not to mention ones from Chaz, Nigel, Andy and Jim—that he'd be in his room, *alone*, no later than midnight that evening, to ensure that he'd be bright-eyed and bushy-tailed in time for his seven o'clock wake-up call the next morning.

Obviously, they'd lied to me.

Louis had lied to me.

Something told me I could take his last Twenty Questions answer with a grain of salt, too.

At 6:59 the next morning, after showering what was left of my hangover out of my Botticellian ringlets, I personally called Louis's room to wake him up as well. And while I wasn't panicking by the thirty-fourth ring, I was by the time my knuckles started bleeding from banging on his door—gently at first, then more frantically as each successive minute ticked by.

By 7:22 A.M., even Ernestine J., swathed in one of Louis's bedsheets, would have been a welcomed sight.

After securing an extra room key from the front desk and doing a sweep of Louis's suite to make sure he wasn't lying facedown in a pool of prostitutes, I hit the phones, calling hospitals, Chaz's cell phone, and every 24-hour disco the concierge suggested.

Finally, I got Nigel at his flat. "Louis? Dunno. The wanker got brassed off at me and stormed off," he mumbled. After too many pints of Guinness, Nigel's BBC elocution had been obliterated. What was left was pure Cockney.

"Why? What happened?"

"Dunno exactly. He disappeared for an hour, then came back into the pub already in his cups and whining about his father leaning on his mum again. Then when I mentioned the play I'm doing in the West End, he said something about wanting to come back to do some theater himself. I laughed and said, 'No you won't, not unless you cock up in America.'

That pissed him off! He said he was tired of apologizing to everyone for being a success. Then the bloody sod accused me of calling him a sellout, said I was a bloody poser, and stormed out."

"I'm sorry, Nigel. I'm sure it was the beer talking and he didn't mean it."

"The hell he didn't! Happens every time he comes home, the insecure bastard. But I guess that's why you're there."

"Why? What do you mean?"

"You know, to catch him when he falls and prop him up again. Blimey, I can certainly see how that would be a full-time job. Well, better you than me. Hope it's worth the salary he pays you. Bollocks! Sorry, must ring off. I forgot I had a rehearsal today."

With a click, he was gone.

When Louis eventually resurfaced—some three hours later— he was hung over, cranky from lack of sleep, and grousing about the absence of any decent coffee in London. I convinced him to take a hot, steaming shower, sent a bellboy over to the nearest Starbucks for a "cuppa" anything remotely resembling his favored Jamaican Blue Mountain (for once, thanking the corporate marketing gods for their strict adherence to conformity), put Alfonse on standby for our imminent departure, and called British *Cosmo* to beg off the interview and photo shoot until the early evening, so that Dorian wouldn't kill himself—or Louis—when it was time for us to leave for it.

"How unfortunate," sniffed the editor in a tone similar to the one used in Queen Elizabeth's infamous *annus horribilis* lament. "Monsieurs Mert and Marcus had planned on returning home to Ibiza sometime in early evening . . . but I'll see what I can do."

"Monsieur Trollope will be forever in your debt," I muttered.

Louis, toweling off as he gulped down his Starbucks Grande, was within hearing distance and cracked loudly, "The *hell* I will! They should be chuffed that I even agreed to talk to their feckin' rag—" before I could hang up.

Too late. She beat me to the punch, but not before letting out a telling *harrumph*.

"I hope you don't regret how she writes you up."

"When I get through charming the knickers off her, she won't remember why she was mad at me in the first place," he answered blithely.

But I knew better. For his own good, he needed to move beyond whatever ghosts he was seeing there in the back alleys of London, or else Louis's London bridges would be burning all around him.

Which meant I'd have to allow him to save face. At someone else's expense.

And I knew just who that sacrificial lamb would have to be this time around.

"I talked to Nigel—"

"*That* wanker? What did he have to say?"

"He . . . apologized."

"Really?" Louis narrowed his eyes into wary slits.

"Yes. He was worried that you might have taken something the wrong way. He didn't say what it was about; just that he hoped it would blow over."

Louis nodded grudgingly. "I'll have to think about it. To be honest, I'm tired of listening to him beg me for help with his career. There is no way he'd make it in America. They'd eat him alive."

Sighing from exhaustion, he made his way back toward the

bedroom to get dressed. As he passed his reflection in the foyer mirror, Louis stopped and scrutinized it. "I really do need to clean house; you know, clear out the bad karma and all that other California New Age bullshit. I *do* believe in that crap, you know."

Placing his thumb and middle finger over a frown line on his forehead, he spread it smooth. "Sadly, Mick's another one who's been leaning on me too heavily. I guess I should have dropped him a long time ago, too."

Catching my incredulous stare in the mirror, he added slyly, "But keep mum on that one, okay, love? It's what I pay you for, right?"

His eyes swept over me slowly, as if appraising my worth, too.

Then he shrugged and walked on.

So much for my role in Louis's life. Or anyone else's role either, for that matter.

"It's a wrap!" a relieved Dorian declared, in perfectly understandable English.

"Simply *adorable!*" the British *Cosmopolitan* editor gushed, after being charmed out of her Blahniks by Louis, and, thankfully, not her knickers.

"Stunning!" her photo editor murmured upon viewing Mert and Marcus' Polaroids of Louis, in profile, sans shirt, but with that devilish smile of his intact.

I, too, smiled, more wanly perhaps, but no less mischievously. For I had found the key to keeping Louis happy:

Just let him do whatever he wanted.

And medicate frequently.

Not him; *myself*.

Personally, I would start that night. Because all of his appointments had miraculously wrapped up ahead of schedule,

Louis insisted that we both take the night off, so that we could be rested before the late-morning flight back the next day.

"Sounds good to me," I answered, yawning widely. "I think I'll just turn in."

Not. If I dumped him now, I could make it over to the National Gallery. Luckily for me, this was the one night in which the gallery stayed open until nine at night, and now more than ever I wanted to see Botticelli's *Venus and Mars.* I needed a touchstone to my old life, and art and astronomy are eternally intertwined.

As, apparently, were Venus's unwieldy ringlets and my own. Afterwards I'd hit a bar.

"That was my thought, exactly." Louis smiled innocently. "See you in the morning."

For Louis, things worked out as planned: he did see me in the morning.

I, on the other hand, caught a glimpse of him a mere hour later, in, of all places, the National Gallery. There, where no cameras were allowed, in an alcove ignored by a public disinterested in Nicolaes Maes' *A Woman Scraping Turnips,* Louis, kissed, cuddled, scolded, then passionately kissed again a very sad, very haunted, sweet-looking woman about my age:

Samantha.

I knew this because, even *sotto voce,* his theatrically trained voice couldn't help but throw out her name while it denied her the love she begged for.

I was mesmerized by their pantomime for almost half an hour. Finally, as he cradled her, bowed and sobbing, in his arms and stroked her hair, I stumbled out from behind the statuette where I'd been hiding and headed for the front doors.

On my way out, a guard nodded sympathetically, apparently under the impression that I had been moved by all I'd seen.

He was *so* right: What had aroused me was the care and emotion I now knew Louis was capable of showing someone he had obviously loved at one time.

Or else he was one hell of an actor, which is why I dared not fall in love with him.

So, why *was* I still attracted to him?

9

Perihelion

The point in its orbit when an object is closest to the Sun.

Despite being born and raised in California, I have personally never bought into much of my homeland's conventional wisdom.

For example, I do believe that it is possible to grow old gracefully without the need to shoot collagen, silicone, saline, urine, animal placentas, bacteria or other alien organisms into my face, forehead, ass or chest.

And I don't buy into the theory that death is optional;

Or that a shrink is as much a necessary evil in your life as a cell phone.

And while I'm enough of a visionary to accept the logic behind the how and why of celestial bodies following predetermined orbits, I truly cannot believe that our futures are determined by anything other than the conscious decisions we make.

Then again, if I'd ever reconsidered hiring a shrink, maybe I would have realized that working for Louis was the most irrational, illogical, and deeply disturbed thing I could have done at that point in my life.

Instead I ignored any hints the universe threw at me that staying within Louis's orbit would be just as bumpy a ride as the one I had taken with Leo, and prayed that Jasper would recover my inheritance soon.

Very, very soon.

"Just hang in there, kiddo," Jasper counseled. "Something may break any day now."

In other words, if my lawsuit had been a script, you could say that it was stuck in Development Hell.

Until my golden parachute opened, I'd have to keep Louis's childish, erratic, egotistical demands from driving me crazy.

Right then and there, I realized that the only way to keep my sanity was to convince myself that Louis was nothing more than an employer with the desire to be happy, healthy and successful in his professional endeavors.

With that in mind, my mission was easy: help him achieve these goals.

In other words, *become the perfect personal assistant:* efficient, creative and indispensable . . .

. . . And totally immune to any of Louis's charms.

For three months, no task was too great or small, the latter of which included making sure Louis wouldn't want for any creature comforts, including the latest Humvee H2 SUT from the dealership—which he made me exchange twice, just because "the seat doesn't adjust just right, love. See what they can do about it. That's my girl"; the multitude of freebees (Las Vegas hotel and resort stays; or couturier and other luxury items) in return for Louis's nonchalantly made endorsements; and a kitchen stocked with his favorite foods (both on and off Zone).

However, some of my more trying tasks included juggling his appointments with:

- Candida Sage, the diva acting coach who charged Louis outrageous sums to verbally taunt him for having "the emotional memory of a Neanderthal," after which she would cradle him to her ample, sagging bosom when he broke down in fear that she was right, and he was in fact an acting fraud;

- Daniela Cross, his anorexic nutritionist, whom I caught upchucking in the guest bathroom after she'd stuffed a box of Zone cookies down her throat;

- Max Banks, the lascivious chiropractor who had Louis convinced that watching porn was a great muscle relaxant. I guess the fact that his shop backed up to a Triple-XXX video store should have been the obvious giveaway that he had a side business more lucrative than back cracking;

- Billie Buck, Louis's closeted personal trainer, who tenderly spotted Louis's bench presses but pouted jealously every time Louis went into the lurid details of his female conquests the night before;

- and "Dr. Manny" (Manolo) Lipschitz, celebrated quack therapist to the stars, who took full advantage of Louis's insecurities as an actor, as well as his anger at his father, by encouraging him to "pass along his hurt to others—lovingly, of course," then giving Louis "permission" to forgive himself for the subsequent bad boy behavior.

Worse yet, Dr. Manny actually had the audacity to ask me to grind up Valium and put it in Louis's coffee before he filmed his scenes.

"That should calm him down, relieve his performance anxiety," Dr. Manny lisped, spraying both me and the lapels of his Kenneth Cole suede shirt with a fine film of saliva.

"But won't he pass out?"

"Nah. Brando never did. Although it did make him a bit paranoid afterward. I'll leave you some restraints, too, just in case."

I passed on both recommendations.

And, finally, I was also in charge of supervising Lourdes, Louis's Mexican maid (whom Louis accused of stealing from his Zone pantry, when in fact it was his upchucking nutritionist who was swiping the food he'd just paid her for), and the Guatemalan gardening crew (who, unaware that I understood Spanish, had numerous interesting and somewhat convincing discussions as to whether Louis was in fact a pimp, based on the number of half-naked women who traipsed in and out of the house while they were there).

I also extricated Louis from the many ludicrous commitments he made to those who somehow broke through the front line of Team Louis—Monique, Genevieve and Randy.

And I quickly learned how to shoo away the Posse when they wanted Louis to come out and play while he was supposed to be studying a script or getting some rest in order to make it onto the set in one piece the next morning.

I also became adept at playing Russian Roulette—Louis's shorthand for lying to Tatiana—without stuttering from guilt. As Louis explained it, the truth only got her upset at him, which in turn got him upset with *me*. Still, no matter what time zone she called from, she instinctively timed her calls while he was cruising Sunset with his buddies—or with some fawning beauty he'd picked up. The upshot of our deceptions was that I got a great handle on both Russian and French curse words.

I could honestly say he appreciated my role in his life: the gatekeeper. But believe me, it wasn't always easy keeping the stallion in his paddock—even when he knew staying there was for his own good.

What about me, you ask? Had I figured out how to take some time off from the Louis Looney Bin? Well, to be honest, if I was lucky, that happened one night a week: When I knew Louis was out playing with the Posse, I'd go out and look at the stars—the *real* ones.

Usually I did this with Mick.

Then we'd go back to my place and indulge in the tenderest sex I'd ever had.

With my phones turned off.

Was Louis aware of our rendezvous? I had no doubt about this, although I know he never heard about it from either Mick or me. Still, it was evident in the little jibes he took at me ("You look a bit peaked, Hannah. Had a fitful night? Perhaps you'd prefer sleeping over here . . . in the cabana, of course . . .") and in the way he taunted Mick in my presence ("Ran into that piece of ass you once used and abused—what was her name? Sherry? Cheri? Cherry? That was it! The virgin, right? What, that *wasn't* her name? Well, for that matter, she wasn't a virgin either, was she?").

While Mick and I talked about everything—the scripts he was working on, my trials and tribulations with my star calculations, politics, food we were allergic to, the books we were reading—we stayed away from the topic of Louis.

Of course, Louis never believed that. And thinking otherwise made him paranoid when he saw us together—to the point that I almost wished I had taken Dr. Manny up on his offer for the restraints.

Mick chose another way to solve the problem. He avoided any Posse junket that might put us in Louis's presence at the same time. Instead, he'd claim he had some writing to do, or a late-night meeting with this director, or that producer.

Louis would laugh caustically—then take out on me his displeasure at being put off by his buddy. "Better watch it, Hannah. Mick isn't the innocent Boy Scout you think he is. Next to him, I'm a virtual wallflower. Trust me on this."

I couldn't believe him. At the same time, I never asked Mick, point blank, if Louis's teasing allegations were true. I guess Louis's warnings did the trick: I was too afraid of how Mick might answer.

Within those ninety days, I also took full control of coordinating Louis's professional life. For example, whenever Team Louis called up with a request for his participation in some media event, or a demand on his time, or his consideration of a possible role, I'd say brightly, "Sounds interesting!" Then I'd weigh its impact on The Big Picture of Louis's career, as defined by Louis's whims at any given moment, coupled with what Jasper knew were the realities of his financial situation, and leavened with what I remembered Leo saying were the three most important reasons to choose a role ("because the director has balls, the script has a soul, and the supporting cast are the best in the biz"). Then I acted accordingly.

Sometimes I'd pass adamantly. ("Louis is invariably tickled by *petite amusements*. He laughed aloud at this one! So sorry, but no go, dear.") On other occasions, I'd pass but feign a reluctance that left the door open for more appealing offers. ("Gee, sorry! Louis would have liked to have done it, but he's got a conflict that day/morning/evening/month/millenium.") Or I'd agree to a sit-down—albeit warily. ("Yep, it's on Louis's radar screen. But first he wants to be assured he's got final approval on all quotes/copy/photos/scripts/wardrobe/etc . . ." or

"Louis doesn't like the idea—at least, not as it's been pre-
sented. However, he's offered to allow me to sit down and discuss it with you; no, he won't be attending. *Yes, he's adamant
about that.* Would you prefer for Louis to tell you so, himself?
No? I didn't think so . . .")

While Monique learned to live with this, and Genevieve
groused about it but invariably accepted it, Randy went ballis-
tic over the thought that I had become an impregnable buffer
between him and his number one client.

"That cunt's going to ruin your career! She doesn't know
her tit from a hole in the ground when it comes to dealing with
Tom, or Amy or anyone for that matter. Hell, when Harvey
gets a hold of her, he'll carve her a whole new asshole," he
warned Louis as they worked out in Louis's home gym.

Randy was under the impression that I was nowhere within
hearing distance. I heard him, though, as his callous bark
wafted through the breezeway the gym shared with the cabana
guestroom, which I was using as Command Central while
bivouacked in Louis Land.

"My God, Randy, you're acting like a jealous little school-
girl! Besides, you're all wrong about Hannah. She's a natural
barracuda, just like you!" Louis's weights grated against each
other at timely intervals. "In fact, she just got Amy to agree to
my taking a pass on anything but a remote media tour for
Breakneck. And she had Tom practically going crazy over the
thought of greenlighting the *Moulin Rouge* sequel with me in
the male lead—for over twenty mil I might add, *and* a percentage equal to what they're paying Baz."

I then heard a clank, which indicated that either Louis was
changing the settings on the Universal gym, or that Randy had
just fainted.

I supposed it was the former, because then Louis added, "As
for Harvey, why just the other day he told me that if Hannah

weren't my girl, he'd make her his; says it was she who convinced her father to star in the first film of Harvey's to make its money back. Yep, he certainly has a soft spot for Hannah. Just like me." Louis chuckled. "Hey, guy, don't look so worried! With Hannah watching the shop, we'll both have more time to play. And just think what I could do with that extra fifteen percent I'll save because *she's* making my deals, instead of you."

Randy's fifteen percent.

The same fifteen percent that was his sole purpose for hanging with Louis in the first place.

As if they both didn't know *that*.

The clanking paused again, which was Louis's way of intimating that he was seriously contemplating that thought.

I supposed Randy was, too—unless that time he *had* fainted.

He hadn't. Instead he asked, "So, uh, what's really happening here, man? Oh, I get it: she finally let you into her pants, huh?"

The response: silence, except for the clacking of barbells.

That was it?

Louis wasn't going to deny it?

Of course not. Why should he? It was exactly what Louis wanted! He *got off* on the fact that Randy's Cro-Magnon pea brain—and, for that matter, those of all of his buds— instinctively assumed that it was out of sheer adoration and sexual longing that I killed myself making his life so easy.

"Well, it's about time. I thought you were losin' the ol' Trollope touch. Shit, I don't care if you've got her doing some of the piddly shit detail on your deals . . . saves me from handing it over to my assistant to cover, know what I mean? . . . Just don't tease about my percentage, okay, man? That hurt. Makes me think that all we've got here is some kind of—I dunno— coldhearted business arrangement. We both know better than that . . . right? We cover each other's backs, remember? So don't you worry, I'll be watching her like a hawk, making sure she doesn't leave any crumbs on the table."

"I know you will, Randy. You're my man," said Louis soothingly.

"Damn right, I am! . . . Hey, uh, can I get in on some of that Hannah action, too?"

My heart took a leap, just as much from Randy's sickening suggestion as from wondering how Louis was going to answer him.

"Why don't you ask her yourself? Hannah, love, what do you think of Randy's offer?"

So, he knew I'd heard every word!

My first instinct was to run away in shame. Instead, I chose to confront them, armed only with my fury at being a woman scorned so salaciously and the knowledge that Randy was more mortified than I was.

An AK-47 would have made the tableau complete.

Upon seeing the look in my eyes, Randy blathered something about being late for a meeting at Dreamworks and stumbled out the door.

This left me face-to-face with my tormentor and paycheck.

"Was that fun, or what?" he crowed, laughing. Peeling off his sweaty T-shirt, he wiped his neck and back with it, tossed it into a corner for Lourdes (or me) to pick up, and headed out toward the pool.

"Fun? *Fun?* What, are you *kidding* me?" Gasping for air, I followed him out. "You let him *denigrate* me! And then you let him think that we—that we—What *is* it, Louis? What more can I do to prove to you that—"

"Prove what, love? That you're the best personal assistant I'll ever have? That I need you in order to survive? That I wouldn't know what I'd do without you?" He stopped short. Slowly, he turned back and looked me right in the eye. "Why, you've already proven that, Hannah."

His words knocked the wind out of me. "I—I have?"

"Of course, love, of course!" Taking both my hands in his, he pulled me down with him onto one of the many double wrought iron chaises that were scattered poolside. "My darling, darling Hannah, did you actually think I didn't know you were in on my little joke on Randy?"

He laughed, as if any other assumption was absurd. "That sodding bag of wind! He's just a whoremonger, someone to pass time with while I'm stuck here in this glamorous Purgatory. Now that I have you, I just keep him around for laughs."

Of course, there was another benefit to yanking Randy's chain so hard: Now Randy squirmed, begged, and wheedled all the more pathetically when he *was* with Louis.

And Louis found those traits particularly appealing in sycophants.

"Why, you're worth *ten* of him! But you know how it is: I can't take a piss in this town without an agent, right? And since they're all alike, I'm better sticking to a known incompetent— even if I have to suck it up about the damned commission— and letting *you* watch my back for me. You're my angel. There is no one else I can trust."

Gently, he pulled me closer toward him until he was cradling my head on his chest. "I swear, Hannah, I don't know what I'd do without you. Admit it, darling, we need *each other*, don't we?"

I felt his lips graze my forehead.

Reflexively, I lifted my head. Our eyes met for an instant. Then his eyes roamed down to my lips, as if anticipating his next move.

He was wondering if I'd let him make it.

So was I.

All of a sudden, I wasn't at all sure how I felt anymore: Wasn't I still angry? Yes, of course I was. So, why was I so scared, too?

And aroused?

And then I thought of Mick.

"What the hell is happening here?" I whispered.

Louis narrowed his eyes, scrutinizing me for some indication that whatever spell he'd cast was still in effect.

Watching me glance away, he knew it wasn't.

His grasp on me loosened. Slowly he rose. As he stretched languidly, the few beads of sweat still clinging to his taut, bronzed abdomen glistened in the sun. Walking away with his patented pantherlike saunter, he tossed back over his shoulder, "So, am I forgiven for my naughty little joke at your expense?"

I nodded resignedly. What else could I say?

He was right. He *did* need me.

And he was also right that I needed him, too.

At least, I did for now.

The final scene of *Breakneck* was shot a week later, and not a day too soon. When the second the director called out, "It's a wrap," there was a collective sigh of relief. Considering all the histrionics that had taken place on the set over the course of the last two months—Louis's ever-increasing star turns, Donnie's obvious on-the-set cocaine consumption, the unexpected appearances of two of Rex's "associates"/lovers in his dressing room on the same day, the catfight that had ensued, and Simone's all-too-obvious kleptomania and the director's increasing exasperation over it—the wrap party was sure to be one hell of a hoedown.

Since Randy represented both the star and the director, he was invited, too.

Lucky, lucky me.

As soon as our bosses were ensconced in their own traditions of toasting cast and crew and handing out "remember me when Oscar Time rolls around" gifts, the Gang of Four—the nickname Christy, Sandy, Freddy and I called our little coven—grabbed a couple of bottles of Bouvet Brut off the craft table (not exactly a top-of-the-line bubbly, but, hey, this wasn't exactly a top-of-the-line production, either) and headed for a quiet corner we'd already staked out in the cavernous soundstage. The way Christy opened the first bottle—with a shake, twist and a pop—sent half its contents all over us, but by the time we'd downed the other half, we couldn't have cared less. We were all relieved that the production had ended without anyone being dropped, blacklisted or murdered. Yet at the same time, we were also melancholy at the thought that we'd no longer be seeing each other so often.

"I'll miss every one of you," blubbered Sandy, her staid demeanor in tatters after a mere two plastic cups of the Bouvet Brut.

"So, let's make a pact!" squealed a misty Christy, ever the Girl Scout. "Once a month, we get together! No ifs, ands or buts!"

"Aw, hell," hiccupped Freddy as he poured a bit of the bubbly into Bette the Pampered Pooch's saucer. "This always happens—everyone promises they'll make the time, but no one ever does."

There was just no *way* Freddy's dire prediction was going to bring me down. "Come on!" I scolded him. "We're not 'everyone.' We're the Gang of Four—remember?"

I was feeling no pain for good reason: I'd had three glasses of champagne, and as soon as Louis traipsed off with Randy, I'd be free to meet Mick at our favorite rendezvous point: the

Santa Monica pier. From there we'd watch the sunset and wait for Venus to appear, just to the right of the moon.

Then we'd head back to my place and make love.

It would be a perfect evening, followed by my first day off in over a week.

I showered the last of the champagne into their glasses. "Drink up, to tomorrow!"

"I'll drink up, but to something else," groaned Freddy. "Tomorrow, all hell may break loose: Simone is taping Penn & Teller's show."

"Why? Are they going to cut her in half, or something?" asked Christy, giggling from the champagne.

"What, you kidding? They're going to tear her up and spit her out. You know they tried to get Rex on that show. Of course, I vetoed it," sniffed Sandy.

"Yeah? Well, I'm trying to do the same, but the old bat is being stubborn about it. She doesn't get it that those two clowns are out for blood—"

"They're not clowns, Freddy," Christy corrected him gently, "they're *magicians*."

"Oh, they're clowns, all right. And if they put those little 'idiosyncrasies' of hers on the air, it will kill her in this town." He wiped away a mascarad tear.

"All of this celebrity spying and gossiping is getting way out of hand!" Sandy shook her head angrily. "If it were up to me, there would be a ban on those so-called 'infotainment' shows *and* those obscene celebrity gossip websites! I made Rex ask his attorney to send celebdish.com a cease-and-desist letter. Why, that *whole blog* is dedicated to putting out the rumor that he's gay! But his attorney wouldn't do it! Said it might open up a can of worms that Rex might regret—because he'd have to prove he was straight! *Can you imagine?*"

Freddy nearly choked on his champagne, and Christy took a very large gulp of hers. We all stared at Sandy.

"Sandy," I started, "aren't you even a *little* curious why Rex—why he always has these guys—that he likes to 'mentor'—well, you know—"

"What Hannah is trying to say, Sandy honey, is that Rex has been outed," finished Freddy. "Accept it, sweetheart."

"Not until I hear it from him myself," she growled as she stalked off.

"Bummer," moaned Christy. "Everyone has such bad news. But hey, not me!" She turned to us excitedly. "Guess what? Donnie wants to help me with my career. Isn't that great?"

"Just what does *that* mean?" I asked warily.

"That he thinks I have potential. He says the first thing I should do is get out there. You know, promote myself. And he's going to mentor me, like Rex does—with his associates."

"I'll just bet he will," guffawed Freddy.

"Don't laugh. I'm being serious. Look—" Christy unzipped her cardigan sweater. Beneath it she was wearing a thin, skintight, midriff-baring French-cut T-shirt that barely enveloped her chest and did absolutely nothing to hide the dark shadows of her braless nipples. Emblazoned on it was the logo for Ta-Ta's. While the restaurant's hamburgers were barely a mouthful, the same could not be said for its waitresses' breasts, which, disgustedly enough, were its main attraction.

I couldn't help but stare at it. "But you don't even *work* at Ta-Ta's!"

"That's okay. Donnie owns a chunk of it."

"And now he wants to own a chunk of you, too," muttered Freddy.

"Don't be silly," pouted Christy. "I'm not going to work there. I'm too important to Donnie for *that*. I'm just playing on their softball team. You see, they play all kinds of companies—movie studios, radio and TV stations, even Playboy bunnies—so I'll be getting all kinds of exposure." She giggled again at the thought. "He says that all I have to do is to be able to hit a ball and run the bases. They're excited, though, 'cause, in middle school, I was an all-star pitcher!"

She threw back her arm for a warm-up toss, then let an imaginary ball fly. Her shirt rose with the motion, exposing a plump, rounded breast, along with an already bared midriff.

"I can only imagine. But Christy, don't you feel a bit . . . uh, exposed?"

"Oh, I know: playing without a bra isn't the safest thing to do," she conceded.

"What I meant," I continued, "was that it may not be such a great career move."

"Oh, leave her alone, Hannah. She's certainly a *big* girl. I'll bet she can take care of herself just fine."

At the sound of Louis's voice, I looked up, only to find him mesmerized by Christy's breasts. Pleased as punch with his attention, Christy's cheeks turned pink. Unconsciously, she puffed out her chest even more.

Showtime. Zeroing in on her, Louis smiled, licked his lips, and headed her way.

The last thing I needed was Louis breaking Christy's heart. "Is the party ending so soon?" I asked brightly as I grabbed his arm and steered him back toward the table where the other actors were still holding court.

"Not soon enough," he murmured. "So, Donnie's doing some investing, is he? Smart boy." He twisted back around to get a second glance at Christy. "Say, speaking of Playboy bunnies, Randy and I are headed over to the Mansion now. Hef's having a poker party. You don't think your little friend there would like to—"

"Sorry, she's already got plans."

"Oh? Are you girls going out for a night on the town?" His eyes turned back to me. He watched me as I squirmed.

"We haven't really finalized anything," I answered warily.

"Got it. Well, if you change your mind, you'll know where to find us," he said evenly. "If you don't, then here, have a drink on me anyway." He peeled a hundred-dollar bill from his wallet and handed it to me.

"What? Gee—uh, thank you, Louis. That's very generous." As I stared at it, he closed his hand around mine.

"Just a little token of my affection. For all you've done." He smiled angelically. "Oh, and Hannah, I've told Genevieve to raise your salary—to $100,000."

Cha-*ching!*

Louis was doubling my salary?

For the first time since Leo died, I felt as if an anvil had been lifted off my back. The extra income would make a big dent in my debt load.

"Wow! Louis, I—I don't know how to thank you!"

"I've got a suggestion: how about a thank-you kiss?" He leaned in closer, his eyes half-closed in a lazy glaze.

"Well . . . I thought—"

"Thought what?"

"That we'd . . . that we had decided to keep things, you know, just friendly."

"What's friendlier than a peck on the cheek between friends?"

A little kiss wouldn't hurt. Would it?

No. Of course not. We were big people.

Just like Christy.

I nodded reluctantly. He lowered his head to mine and faintly touched my cheek with his lips.

Sweet.

Expertly he shifted his lips onto mine. I gasped, which he took as a signal to explore further the depth of my soul—and my mouth—with his tongue.

"*Shit!*" He jumped back, jerking me away before I had a chance to do the same to him.

"What?" I asked, not knowing what I had done, and why Louis was suddenly upset with me. Opening my eyes, I saw Bette scurrying away. Louis was slapping his pant cuff and scraping the sole of one of his $300 Bruno Magli loafers across the floor.

In more than one way, he was pissed.

Then again, so was Mick, who was standing right behind him.

Knowing the movie had wrapped, and assuming Louis would have been halfway to Hef's pleasure palace by now, Mick had thought he'd surprise me by meeting me at the studio.

He had. And I had surprised him, too.

I sighed, then headed off to find a towel for Louis.

"It was just a sweet innocent little thank-you kiss!" I was lying.

I was also arguing for my life, which so desperately needed Mick in it.

"No it wasn't. With Louis, *nothing* is innocent."

He had a point there. Still, I wasn't going to concede it; not to him, and certainly not to myself.

"He knows better when it comes to me. We have a pact. That's the only way it works."

Mick shook his head in disbelief. "Get real! Do you truly believe that this little pact of yours is working?"

"Yes, I do. Otherwise I'd be out of there!"

He looked as if he wanted to believe me, so I went for what I thought would be the most convincing point of all: "Besides, you're his best friend. He wouldn't dare try anything with me, just based on that."

He laughed hard and mean. "What, don't you get it? *It only makes him want you that much more.*"

"But I don't want *him.*" I put my arms around Mick's waist. "I want you. I need you. He's just my job . . ."

I pulled him closer to me in the hopes that he would kiss me. He did.

The kiss was hard, and deep, and erased anything that was left of Louis that still clung to me.

Then the phone rang.

Mick let go of me and gave me a look that dared me to pick it up.

I paused.

But I had to do it.

He shook his head and turned away.

"I'm surprised you haven't called me yet."

"Jasper?" Hearing me say that name, the tension went out of Mick's stance. "Is something wrong?"

"What, are you kidding? Everything is right!" He laughed. "Didn't Louis tell you?"

"Tell me what?"

"To call me. That schmuck! I ran into him late yesterday, at the Ivy. I'd just come back from the courthouse. It's over, Hannah. Sybilla agreed to the settlement."

Jasper had freed up my inheritance. Now I could quit.

"That's—that's wonderful news. Listen, Jasper, I've got Mick here. Can—can we talk tomorrow?"

"Certainly. Tell him I said hello. And call me before noon." He rang off.

I hung up the phone. *So, Louis had known since yesterday. That was why he gave me the raise. Because he needs me.*

Mick nuzzled my neck from behind. "What's up with Jasper?"

"The settlement went through."

"Isn't that great?"

"Yeah, sure." I forced my mouth into a smile before turning back around to face him. "How should we celebrate?"

"I know: let's write your resignation letter together." He moved over toward the desk. Spotting some paper, he pulled a pen from his pocket and started scribbling: "'Dear Louis, It's with great regret'—scratch that—'great *relief* that I can finally tell you what I really think of your whiny, egotistical bullshit—'"

"Hey, let's not talk about Louis." I picked up the paper, rolled it into a ball, and tossed it at the trash can.

"You're right. Let's talk about *us*. How we're going to take a long vacation, go somewhere there's a deserted beach—"

"I—Mick, *I can't*."

"What do you mean?"

"Well, I—I can't quit now."

"Why not?"

"Because we've got too much happening. We just got greenlighted on *Killer Instincts*, and we have a whole promotional tour for—"

"'We' haven't gotten greenlighted, and 'we' don't have a promotional tour. *Louis does*." He walked away from me.

"Well, I run Louis's life for him. And I can't just up and quit." I followed Mick into the living room. "It wouldn't be fair to him."

"Admit it, Hannah. You love being in the center of Louis's universe. You just love the fact that he can't take a piss without you."

"Okay, okay, I'll admit it." I was relieved. Maybe Mick understood after all. "I do like it. And I'm good at it. And Louis appreciates me for being good!"

"Louis never appreciated anyone in his whole life."

You mean Samantha, don't you?

I wanted to say it out loud, but I didn't. Instead I said, "Having my inheritance reinstated means I don't have to stay if I don't want to."

"But that's the point: *You want to.*"

"Yes. *For now.*"

"Okay. Fine." Grabbing his motorcycle helmet, he headed for the door.

"What do you mean? What's fine? Where are you going?"

"Out. For some fresh air." He clamored down the front steps, then right back up. "And, oh, by the way, you'll never quit."

"Oh yeah? What makes you so sure?"

"Because I know Louis a lot better than you. You won't quit, *because he'll fire you first.*"

Mick didn't have a chance to slam the door behind him, because I slammed it first.

And now that I could once again afford the comfort of Château Lynch-Bages 2000 Pauillac, there was none in the house.

The Bouvet Brut would have to do.

Part Two

Stardust

A cluster of stars too distant to be seen individually, resembling a dimly luminous cloud of dust. A dreamlike, romantic, or uncritical sense of well-being.

10

Perturb

*When a celestial body deviates from its predicted orbit,
usually under the gravitational influence of another
celestial object.*

Houston, we have a problem . . .
Jim Lovell, Astronaut, aboard Apollo 13

Jasper's usual table at the Ivy was nestled in the only perpetually shaded corner of the restaurant's garden, which, I'm sure,
was the primary reason the legendary entertainment attorney
was rumored to have never broken into a sweat no matter what
deal hung in the balance, despite his fondness for impeccable
lightweight wool suits. That was where I found him when I arrived (promptly, of course) for our meeting there, which was
to include not only Jasper and myself but Louis and Randy as
well.

That is, until Randy—who had picked up Louis earlier that
morning for a game of golf with Mick and Ethan at the Bel-
Air Country Club—called to say, "Hey, tell the old man we're

running late. They screwed us on our tee-time, the stupid bastards! Gave it away, to a bunch of old fart nobodies. Louis is pissed about it. I've been losing balls all morning just to keep him happy, so just hang in there and make nice-nice until we show up, okay? That should be easy for you: just whimper about the good ol' days, when Daddy Dearest was alive . . ."

It was on the tip of my tongue to say that I didn't know Randy had any balls to lose. Instead, I hung up on him and broke the news to Jasper that we should go ahead and place our orders.

"Yeah, well, that fourth hole is a bear," winked Jasper. "That's okay. This way, we can get some real work done without having to listen to Louis whine about the roles he's losing out to Jude, or hear Randy's inane bullshit, neither of which is good for our digestion, anyway."

Between listening to me recite Louis's agenda for the coming quarter, discussing the status of some of Louis's upcoming projects, and taking bites of the Ivy's renowned meat loaf, Jasper accepted the deferential homage proffered by Barry, Les, Bryan, and some of the other Industry movers and shakers who stopped by our table. A handshake from Jasper was a virtual Midas touch, assuring favorable future consideration from those who witnessed his acknowledgements and understood their worth in the Land of Awes.

If only Louis had had the brains to do so, he would not have been so brazen as to blow off this lunch with Jasper, I thought sadly.

As if reading my mind, Jasper said, "You know, Hannah, it never ceases to amaze me the amount of talent that this town will attract—then chew up and spit out. Few actors are capable of maintaining a career for longer than a few years, and that's only if they're lucky."

His hand swept out toward the other tables, where Holly-wood's elite were slicing up their ahi tuna steaks with the same thoughtful precision with which they cut their deals.

"You're wise as to how these guys operate. They're like lem-mings: one year, everyone's clamoring for Tom, or Brad, or Matt or Jude—and now Louis—to star in their next block-buster. Then the next year, it's a whole new set of names: guys who are described as the *next* Tom, Brad, Matt, or Jude. *Or Louis.*"

He reached for his wineglass, took a sip, then looked me right in the eye. "I took on Louis because I felt he had the po-tential to pull it off for the long haul. Now . . . well, I'm not so sure."

"Don't give up on him, Jasper." I don't know why I felt the need to plead Louis's case for him, but I did. "He's just new to it all. He hasn't figured out yet what he shouldn't be doing, or what things will blow it for him. He's one of the most talented guys out there, and the camera just eats him up. That's why so many directors want to work with him."

"They're *all* talented. The problem is that they're not all smart enough to know how to play the game—or to appreciate those who play it for them." He smiled knowingly. "I've always admired how you are able to keep all of this in perspective, to wade through the crap and come out the other end un-scathed."

"Well, I wouldn't say that I'm *unscathed.*"

He nodded. "I'm beginning to see that. So then, my dear, why have you chosen to stick it out? I thought you'd be out of there in a flash, focusing on your star project and other things that are more—well, permanent." He laughed. "I hope you don't feel you have to stick it out because of loyalty to me."

"I'm glad to hear that, Jasper. In all honesty, though, I'm not."

He held my gaze. "I can't imagine that you find it any more thrilling than you did when Leo was alive."

I laughed. "No, the one thing I'm *not* is starstruck, if that's what you mean."

"Ah. I see." His wan smile made me blush.

Why, he thinks I've fallen for Louis.

"It's not what you think. There's nothing—nothing intimate—going on between Louis and me. That's the only way in which a relationship like ours could work, and we both know it."

"That's good to hear. Still, I've always felt that a fulfilling relationship—professional or other—works on many levels."

Many levels.

"Well, whatever Louis and I have certainly fits that description, too. It's a lot like a carnival fun house: many doorways leading nowhere." I laughed, but there was no humor in it. "I don't know, Jasper; I guess that it's wishful thinking on my part to presume that at least one of those doors will lead to . . . to . . . well, I don't know what."

"Approval? Trust? Loyalty? Absolution, perhaps?"

"Yes. All of the above."

"Hannah, Louis can't give you what you didn't get from Leo."

It always came back to that.

Well, if Louis couldn't, then who could?

"Maybe not. Then again, maybe I'm sticking around because right now Louis's life is easier to deal with than focusing on my own."

"If you say so."

"You sound like Mick."

"Smart guy, that Mick. By the way, how's he doing these days anyway?"

While the question was asked innocently enough, I knew otherwise: the all-knowing, all-seeing Jasper was very much aware that there was trouble in Paradise. After all, he represented Mick, too.

"He's fine, really he is," I said brightly. "He doesn't fully understand why I need this right now in my life, but he accepts it."

In truth, my decision to stick it out with Louis had put my relationship with Mick in an odd place. It hadn't dampened our appetites for each other: on the contrary, our sex was just as fresh and exciting as ever. In fact, lately it had had a sense of urgency . . .

. . . as if both of us were waiting for the other shoe to drop.

At any moment, I expected to see some telltale sign that Louis's predictions about Mick were true, while Mick was anticipating my permanent defection to Camp Louis any day now. So we both held off on the one thing we both needed to give and get from each other:

Approval. Trust. Loyalty. Absolution, perhaps.

Not that I could say any of this to Jasper. So I said this instead: "We're taking it one day at a time."

"I think that's a great idea. In fact, that's a wonderful philosophy to have regarding everything in your life right now, including your job—particularly since you never really took the time to grieve for Leo. Hey, why not take some time off? Louis can survive for a few days without you, believe me. Besides, it might be the best thing that ever happened to you—and to Mick, if you allow him to tag along."

As I bowed my head, a tear dropped onto one of my crab cakes. Jasper handed me his pocket square, which I used to wipe another salty drop off my cheek.

"You're right, Jasper. I owe it to Leo. And I owe it to myself."

And I owed it to Mick.

I couldn't wait to see him, to tell him in person.

Par for the course, the boys never showed up. Back at Louis's, I spent the afternoon juggling the other appoints Louis had also blown off—his costume fitting for *Killer Instinct;* a meeting with one of last year's Oscar-nominated directors to discuss whether his and Louis's work styles were "simpatico" (which, Louis just proved, were obviously not); and a guy-to-guy telephone Q&A with *Maxim*.

Where was Louis?

The phone rang and I leaped at it, assuming it was Randy returning one of the several messages I'd left since leaving Jasper. Instead, it was Ethan calling: He wanted to know why Louis had never shown up at the country club.

"You mean he wasn't with you this morning? But Randy called and said that your tee-time got pushed back!"

Silence.

In Hollywood, either you're a creative genius, or you're a great liar who surrounds himself with creative geniuses and uses them to further your climb up the Tinseltown ladder. Leaving no doubt as to which talent he possessed, Ethan coughed nervously, then stuttered lamely, "Uh . . . well, I got called in to the studio. Gee, I guess they played without me . . . um, I'm needed on the set, now. Just have him call me—" and rang off.

By the time the phone chimed again, I was at my wit's end. Apparently so was Freddy, who, as predicted, was dealing with the fallout of Simone's 15 minutes of infamy on *Penn & Teller: Bullshit!*

"*Showtime* is promoting the show as the 'ultimate Hollywood horror story'! Those magician weirdos goaded her into putting on all her diva moves, and she came off as a pathetic nutcase!" Freddy moaned. "Well, that's the end of the road for milady Cavanaugh. Now, both she *and* the mutt will be eating Trader Joe's cat food!"

"Look, Freddy, I'm sure it's not all that bad. I mean, how many people watch the show? It's late night, and it's pay cable, right?"

"Yeah, you're right. And it ain't exactly *The Sopranos.*" He sighed. "Man, now *that* would have been sweet! Why couldn't she have gotten knocked off by Tony instead?"

"Look, I've got to keep the lines clear. We've got a little emergency here, too. Why don't we meet later tonight? We'll think of some way to spin it differently."

The "Central Casting" Denny's on Sunset near Highland, so nicknamed because it catered mostly to aging B-movie and movie-of-the-week actors, was the Gang of Four's usual hang-out. "Can you call the others?"

"Hell yeah, I'll make the calls," said Freddy. "I'll do anything to keep from having to inject the old lady's ass with sheep placenta, which is the next item on *my* agenda."

I blanched. "Doesn't that have to be done in a doctor's office?"

"Nah," he answered airly. "Miss Simone paid for me to get my cosmetology license. She figures that's cheaper than spending two hundred bucks a pop with the doc. And I figure, what the hey? It might become my fallback profession—if I can get used to staring at wrinkly old asses all day long."

Enough said.

I was contemplating my own fate when I heard Randy's car pull up. The Corvette C6—a test-drive loaner from one of the many dealers who catered to Randy's auto junkie habit—was low to the ground, which made it difficult for Louis, disheveled, distraught, and obviously stinking from too many scotch rocks, to uncoil himself and stand up without staggering. As Randy peeled off, Louis stumbled past me and out toward his bedroom, where he plopped down on his Cal King Dux. He ran a hand through his burnished curls just once, then stared forlornly at the infinity pool undulating outside his window.

I followed him in but said nothing. For ten minutes I waited for him to acknowledge me first, but by Minute Eleven it was all too obvious that he was going to keep pretending that I wasn't hovering overhead. I could live with that. But he couldn't ignore his obligations to his career, too.

"We missed you at the Ivy."

Annoyed, he growled, "Don't worry about me. I've already eaten lunch."

"I know. I can smell it on you."

He gave me a bleary-eyed stare. "What of it? What's it to you, Little Miss Goody Two-shoes?"

Why was he looking for an argument? Personally, I wasn't in the mood for his childish games. I opened my mouth to say something when he added venomously, "You know, Hannah, if only you'd been where you should have—"

"Where I—*what?* What are you talking about? With Jasper? Louis, I *was* there!"

He grabbed my hand and yanked me down beside him. "Not there, Hannah! Here! Beside *me!*"

There, with his face so close to mine that I could feel his warm, sour breath on me. I sat there quietly for a minute, then asked, "Louis, what's wrong? What happened today?"

He shook his head. "Nothing. No, that's not true, Hannah. Everything is—is so wrong."

"What? What is it?"

He turned to face me. "I'm an ass—a complete sod! You don't think I know that?"

"I don't think—listen, Louis, Jasper wasn't *that* upset—"

"Screw Jasper! This isn't about Jasper!" His eyes widened in disbelief that I couldn't read his mind. At the same time that his words poured out in a torrent of broken thoughts, he gasped for air: "My father did exactly the same thing! And me mum always said that I'd . . . ah, crap! My fans! When they— they'll hate my guts—Ha! What do I care if they think I'm a bastard, a fraud . . . *Bollocks!* I don't deserve—"

He's having a breakdown!

Should I get him a glass of water? Should I call an ambulance?

Damn it, why didn't I fill that prescription for Valium that Dr. Manny forced on me?

Why didn't I take those damn restraints?

Unconsciously, I put my arm around Louis and stroked his hair.

"Oh, Louis, Louis," I whispered. "Listen, whatever it is— whatever you're feeling, it will work itself out! *It will be okay.*"

As his gasps slowed down, I felt him collapse into my arms. Soon we were breathing as one. Without raising his head, which was now nestled on my shoulder, he murmured, "Thank God you're here. I've never really told you how much—how much you mean to me."

I felt his arms go around me. Gently, he pushed me down onto the bed's Anichini cashmere throw, all the while showering me with gentle kisses until, finally, his tongue parted my lips.

My heart leaped in my chest. He must have felt it, too, because he opened his eyes. No longer were they filled with doubt. *Au contraire*—he knew exactly what he wanted:

Me. On a platter.

But for right now, the Cal King would do.

How easy it would have been: I could have leaned back, closed my eyes and let his fingers do the walking—up and under my Anna Sui silk cami. Then, having discovered that my Damari's lace bra had a front snap, his long, thick fingers could have meandered ever so gently between my breasts and freed them from their lacy lair. Once my nipples were freed, his tongue could have titillated them into a frenzy. Then those ever-industrious hands of his could have begun the arduous process of untying my Frankie B. lace-up jeans (*Dammit! Dammit! I might as well have been wearing a chastity belt! Why, oh why did I have to wear those, today of all days?*), so that his lips could once again follow suit—

Then, in the morning, he could find a reason to let me down easy.

Despite all the wonderful claims he'd made just now.

And with absolutely no recognition of all I'd done for him these past few months.

And completely dismissing the torrid sex we'd had for sixteen or so hours prior to his grand announcement.

I shoved him away, hard.

"Louis, *NO*. We—we can't."

"Dammit, Hannah! *Why not?*" He was a petulant little boy whose brand-new toy had just been taken away.

"Because it won't work! You know that! We both know that! We have to stick to the pact and keep things between us totally professional."

I jumped off the bed. He looked as if he was going to pounce after me, so I took two steps back.

How he read that as an invitation for more of the same I'll never know, but somehow he did. He moved in until I was cornered up against the wall. "I can't. The truth is—Hannah, I'm falling in love with you."

"Oh, Louis, *puh-leez.*"

Placing his hands on either side of my face, he murmured, "I mean it, love! Truly, I do. I've never met anyone like you, who takes care of me like you do. But it can't go on—*just like that.*"

With a hand, he pressed one of my own against the wall and held it there while he leaned in to kiss me—

—So I slapped him with the other.

Hard.

Rubbing his jaw, he cried out in pain. "Dammit, Hannah! What the hell!"

"How could you do that to me?" I spat out. "Or—or to Mick?"

How could *I* do that to Mick?

Louis just stared at me. Then, he started to laugh uncontrollably.

"What's so funny?" I asked indignantly.

"Mick. That's what." His mouth twisted into a cruel smile.

"What about Mick?"

"Your Mr. High-and-Mighty, your Mr. Great Gentleman. I'll just bet you don't know where he is right now—and with whom!"

"Why—what would I—why is that so important?" Just talking about Mick made me want to hide my head in shame. I could only imagine what he would have thought if he'd seen me with Louis just moments ago—and could have deduced how much I had enjoyed it.

"It's important because I'm so tired of him standing between us, Hannah," he shouted angrily. "I meant what I said, about us! And whether you want to believe me or not, Mick *does not* deserve you."

"I know you find this hard to believe, but he's nothing like you. He's never given me any reason to—to doubt him. Face it, Louis, you're jealous. Of *us.*"

"Me? *Jealous?*" He snickered. "Look Hannah, I'll accept whatever you want to think of me. And if you want to keep things 'professional,' then okay, sure, that's fine by me! But I care enough for *you* to see that you don't get hurt. And Mick *will* hurt you."

"Cut it out, Louis," I said darkly. "I'm in no mood for your games."

"Oh, love, this is no game," he growled. "If you don't believe me, go see for yourself. Mick's at the Hotel Bel-Air. The Courtyard Suite. And believe me, he's *not* working on his golf game."

With as much dignity as I could muster, I headed for the door. Louis had already turned toward the mirror, where he was scrutinizing the very visible handprint outlined on his face.

"Oh, and love—the next time you want to play rough, let's pull out the paddles instead, okay? That is, if you don't mind being the bottom, because I always insist on being the dom. It's an ego thing, I guess."

Although he shrugged apologetically, his eyes never left the mirror. "Damn it, I wish you'd given me fair warning that you were going to slap me. I think you knocked a tooth loose! When you get back, if you're not *too* torn up, call Bill Dorfman's office and set an appointment for first thing in the morning, will you?"

I asked the valet at the Hotel Bel-Air to keep my car on the curb since I would not be staying long. I'd coordinated many of Louis's media interviews in the hotel's Courtyard Suite—it was his favorite—so I knew to follow the narrow garden path that rambled through the hotel's exquisite flora until it dead-ended at the boudoir's entranceway. I did not knock but instead went around to the double French doors that overlooked its very private terraced courtyard. As I suspected, they had been left open to take advantage of the mild fall breezes.

Mick's voice could be heard from inside. I couldn't make out what he was saying—only that it sounded, well, kind and gentle.

Similar to how it sounded when we made love.

Even that did not prepare me, though, for what I saw as I peeked through the door: Mick was on the bed, cradling Samantha, who lay naked in his arms.

Rocking her back and forth, he kissed her forehead tenderly.

Dazed and upset, I stumbled back out onto the garden path, but I only made it a few steps before I keeled over, gasping for air.

Why had I been stupid enough to believe that he had cared for me?

I don't know if it was the sense of betrayal I felt, or my anger at myself for having believed that Mick was any different from Louis—or Jean-Claude, or even Leo, for that matter—but suddenly, a wave of nausea swept over me. As I heaved all of my hurt and pain and crab cakes into one of the hotel's exquisitely pristine white rosebushes, the thought came to me that I owed Louis an apology.

I'd start by making that dentist appointment the minute I got back to the car.

"The biggest problem with Denny's," groused Christy, "is that it doesn't serve booze."

"You can say that again," I said, pushing away my untouched platter of eggs. "Frankly, I'd be more inclined to think that the Grand Slam lived up to its name if I were smashed before I ate it."

After what I'd told them of what I'd seen that afternoon, no one blamed me for having lost my appetite. However, my promise to ask Jasper to write a cease-and-desist letter to the Showtime Network on Simone Cavanaugh's behalf had restored Freddy's, who'd cleaned off his dish of French toast in just a few quick bites.

"Well, if living with that old diva has taught me one thing," he said, winking slyly, "it's that it's just as easy to carry a to-go cup *into* a restaurant as it is to take one out." Rustling through the bag in which he carried his constant companion, Bette, he came out with a thermos. "Who wants a cocktail?"

The Gang of Four downed its water glasses to make room for his expertly mixed cosmopolitans.

Ever appreciative of a host's generosity, Sandy raised her glass. "Well, here's to Miss Simone. May she survive yet another exposé of her poor pathetic life—and may other exposés follow, if only to grant her the satisfaction that her spotlight will never dim."

"Hear, Hear!"

"I guess what Donnie says is true: that there's no such thing as bad publicity," exclaimed Christy.

"Donnie's an idiot," Freddy said bluntly. "He'll finally realize it the first time he's caught with his pants down around his ankles and Bethany's attorneys are gleefully shredding his prenup."

She colored slightly. "Donnie's not like that. He's true blue to her!"

Was there a slight disappointment in her voice? I didn't want to go there, not today.

Not after what I had just seen of Mick.

Just then, all eyes turned to my Dooney & Bourke hobo bag, where, once again, the insistent buzzing of my cell phone had been beckoning all night long. Although its caller ID indicated that the number belonged to the very persistent Mick, everyone at the table winced reflexively. Personal assistants are the twenty-first-century equivalent of indentured servants, and as such, our instincts were to leap when summoned.

Well, too bad. At the moment, I was too angry to confront him over the obvious and to hear any lies he had to explain it away. Instead, I chose to drown my sorrows within a cloistered cocoon of true friendship.

Knocking back my cosmopolitan, I added my own two cents. "Freddy's right. You're a fool to trust him. Or any 'him' for that matter."

Christy sniffed, still unconvinced. "Look, Hannah, you've had a rough day—"

"That's an understatement!" I said, spilling the last of the thermos's contents into my glass. "They're all assholes. And the bigger they are in this town, the more they feel justified to use us." Stumbling over a hiccup, I added grandly, "I almost feel sorry for Samantha, that little sap! Well, she's welcome to have him."

Sandy and Christy traded guilty glances. Watching the interchange, I put down my glass. "What? What is it?"

Christy looked as if she was going to start bawling. "We knew, Hannah. Oh, please don't hate us!"

"About her—and Mick?"

I envisioned the silken strands of our friendship cocoon dissolving in my angry tears.

Watching my reaction, Sandy quickly added, "No, no! Not about that! Just that—that she'd come to town the day before yesterday. Said she was here to 'work things out.' We didn't say anything because—well, because we thought she'd have to go through you anyway, to get to Louis—"

But she didn't. She went through Mick.

Or, more accurately she went *to* Mick.

Christy interrupted her. "Omigod! You don't think that Mick . . . that he's . . ."

"That he's what?"

"You know: the *other* guy?"

In Louis's threesome.

No, I hadn't known for sure . . . until that moment.

Watching the color drain from my face, Freddy gave my hand a gentle squeeze. "Now that you know, you've got to walk away from them, Hannah. *Both* of them." He stroked Bette under her chin. "Look, doll, it may not be easy, but it will keep you from joining Simone at Betty Ford in a double room, 'cause heaven knows King Louie is too cheap to spring for a single at Sanctuary House."

"Don't worry about me, Freddy. Mick won't be able to deny what I saw with my own two eyes, so that takes care of him. And as for Louis—well, he and I have come to an understanding of what I'm willing to do—and *not* do, if he wants me to stick around."

"Just to set the record straight," Christy said solemnly, "Donnie and I have a similar agreement."

"Oh, I'll just bet you do," Freddy said under his breath.

"It's important to us, too, that we know where to draw the line, "Christy insisted, "particularly since we're now going to be working together as peers."

"What does that mean?" Sandy asked.

"Donnie's producing a movie, and he's got a role in it that he says is perfect for me," she gushed. "It's not a very big one, but it's certainly more than a walk-on. That's okay, because it's a small film, anyway. You know, an *indie*." She tossed her head with pride. "And we'll shoot my scenes at night, so it doesn't interfere with my day job, because that would make Bethany upset . . . Except, I don't know how we'll get back in time, since we're filming on location."

"Where?" Sandy asked suspiciously.

"Chatsworth."

"Christy, sweetheart, Chatsworth is only thirty minutes from L.A. It's in the Valley."

"Oh, it is? Well, whattaya know? Donnie made it sound as if it were at the other end of the world."

Freddy snickered. "That's an appropriate analogy, by our town's standards anyway."

"Why? What do you mean?" Perplexed, Christy took a dainty bite of a link sausage.

I frowned. "That's where the porn industry is based."

Gulping hard, she gave a little cough. "Oh . . . no."

"Something wrong?"

"No! Well, yeah. Well—it's just that—well, Donnie mentioned that I—that I might have to do a . . . a nude scene. . . . But he assured me that it would be shot *very* tastefully."

"How so?"

"The director—Harry Dickson—is really well known! He's won all kinds of awards."

"I'll say he has," murmured Freddy. "Have you heard of *Sponge Bobbie's Square Panties, Sex with the City*, or *Ladder 69?*"

Christy squinted in thought. "Uh . . . no. Not really. Should I have?"

"Those are some of the films he's directed. And you're right—they've won awards, but not any Oscars. We're talking *Adult Video News* awards."

"How do you know *that?*" While Christy frowned, I tried hard not to laugh out loud.

"Well, sweetums, it just so happens that I have a boyfriend in 'Holly Porn' as they call it. He was one of the—er—'stars' of *Ladder 69*. In fact, he won an award for that one, too. Ha! He may not recite Shakespeare or Ibsen, but with his kind of talent, he doesn't *need* to open his mouth. Others do that—*for him*."

Christy gulped loudly.

"I'll say! And you wouldn't believe the size of *his* 'statu-ette.'"

11

Moonstruck

*Dazed or distracted with romantic sentiment;
affected by insanity; crazed.*

The good news about *Killer Instincts*—the psychological thriller Louis was filming in a remote location deep within Oregon's mystical Klamath Forest along the banks of the Rogue River—was that it fit all the necessary criteria for being a hit movie, as defined by Leo: a first-rate director, a great screenplay, and a superb supporting cast.

The even better news was that my immediate departure with Louis allowed me to leave behind Mick and all the hurt he had caused me—at least, for now.

Not that he didn't try calling me at least four or five times a day after the incident at the Hotel Bel-Air. At first, his voice messages were filled with naive anticipation. ("Hey, babe, didn't we have a date? Tell that boss of yours you're calling it a night, and get on over here. I need a Hannah fix.") They quickly moved on to a mild concern that I wasn't responding. ("Honey, where are you? Call me, I'm worried . . .") Next was his annoyance at my lack of consideration in getting back to him, which was quickly replaced with sullen suspicion: ("Wow. Louis must be keeping you *really* busy. Okay, I get the message." *Click.*)

And finally, contrition. ("Hannah, please call me. I don't know what I did, but whatever it is, I think I have a right to know! It shouldn't be anything that we can't work out.")

Oh, yeah?

His final message, sent on the eleventh day after the Hotel Bel-Air incident, was a text message which simply asked, *What the Hell happened????*

Frankly, I was happy for a change of scenery—not that the set of *Killer Instincts* was any picnic. During the first week of shooting, Louis's own criteria for making the movie—the assumption that there would be a chance for some on-location hanky-panky with his leading lady, Marcella Kingston, coupled with the opportunity to work with his idol, the legendary Shakespearean British actor and recently knighted Sir Barnaby Chadwick—dissolved completely, like the early morning mists that shrouded the grove of Douglas firs in which the production had set up camp.

This all happened due to a series of misunderstandings on Louis's part, the first being that the radiantly beautiful and voluptuously proportioned Marcella, whose wonderfully salty sense of humor was all the more delicious for being delivered in her sweet, throaty lisp, would find him as irresistible as he found her.

She didn't.

But then again, being a lesbian, she wouldn't.

Louis was promptly informed of this fact by Marcella's very, very angry personal assistant (who, by the way, also happened to be her very, very butch lover) after he offered to run lines with the actress in her trailer and then suggested that she could reciprocate the favor by running her tongue over his body.

"Dammit, why didn't that git Randy warn me?" exclaimed a

truly disappointed Louis, after being escorted back to his own trailer (at his request) by two brawny grips who, luckily, happened to be passing Marcella's open trailer door just as her PA lunged at Louis with clenched fists. Marcella's scornful and incredulous laughter could still be heard echoing through the stately ponderosa pines.

"Why?" I asked. "Would you have changed your mind about doing the movie?"

I could tell that it was on the tip of his tongue to say yes. But knowing that I'd think less of him for doing so, he shrugged nonchalantly instead.

"Hell, no, of course not. . . . It's just that, well, I always find location shoots to be much more, shall we say, 'professionally stimulating' if my leading lady—particularly one as mad hot as that one—will at least *act* as if she wants me in her bloomers . . ."

"Oh, she's a pretty capable actress. I'm sure she'll be able to pull it off somehow."

"Sarcasm does not become you, Hannah," Louis growled. "Blimey, what a *waste!* Say, you don't think that I could . . . nah! Forget it. I've tried conversions before—I even did two simultaneously . . . but, alas, they never seem to stick."

He was straightening his collar, which had been mussed during the altercation with Marcella's PA, when another thought hit him.

"By the way, sometime in the next couple of days, see if you can get the name of Marcella's publicist from that cow she's got guarding her. Anyone who can keep the lid on *that* secret should be on my payroll, too, don't you think? Not that *I've* got anything to hide from the press, right?" He gave me a wink. "But don't feel you have to go 'beyond the call of duty' to get it, know what I mean? . . . Um, that is, unless *Marcella's* involved. Then call me. That way, at least I can watch."

I called him, all right, but from his expression, it was not a name he had ever been tagged with before.

At least, not to his face. Before this project was over, however, other voices would be joined with mine in a hallelujah chorus against Louis's lunacy.

Including that of his idol, Sir Barnaby Chadwick.

Sir Barnaby had earned his knighthood the old-fashioned way: one Old Vic play and classic BBC television production at a time. As a teen, Louis's first taste of legitimate theatre had been Barnaby's stately yet electrifying rendition of Shakespeare's *Hamlet*, and, according to Louis, it was why he'd chosen acting as a career—and why he had agreed to do *Killer Instincts* in the first place: because Ben had been able to get Barnaby to sign on as well, for the role of the father of Louis's character.

It was also why Louis was letting his insecurities get the better of him. The last thing he wanted to do was blow this opportunity to impress his idol. That said, after introducing himself to Barnaby, Louis made pointed jokes at everyone else's expense—Marcella, the movie's screenwriter, Begley Holt, even one of the film's many hovering associate producers. He then proceeded to chastise the director, Ben Grisham, in front of the whole production crew for allowing the extras, many of them locals, to strike up conversations with the cast's leads.

His audacity had the opposite effect on Barnaby: the commanding but soft-spoken man, who always went out of his way to treat the whole cast and crew with an appreciative deference, blanched visibly and retreated to his trailer at every break.

Needless to say, this affected Louis immensely. In fact, it made him work all the harder to prove that he was a star, with a capital *S*.

The cast and crew, all one hundred or so of them, willingly granted him that capital *S*. In fact, they did so every time they called him "Shithead" behind his back.

They treated me no better, particularly since it was I who did Louis's bidding. At the start of each day, I was sent forth to negotiate a fresh set of irrational demands, each more outrageous than those made the day before, with Ben, a director who was legendary for the insightful way in which he dealt with his actors, and who enjoyed the undisputed loyalty of those lucky enough to be a part of his crew.

To my immense regret, in time Ben grew to dread the sight of me. It wasn't the request for certain delicacies from Louis's favorite Los Angeles restaurants that had him scowling even before I'd opened my mouth; or Louis's demand for a larger, more ostentatious trailer than the other actors, tricked out with, in Louis's words, "the necessary accoutrements to turn this hellhole into a livable ambiance," including a Cal-King Dux bed with the requisite 700-count sheets and four cashmere throws on top of that, and of course, a Universal gym. No, it was Louis's whim for the daily delivery of water from the frigid prehistoric Crater Lake some 121 miles away—which was to be specifically used for his daily bath, since its unique "oxygenation" was supposedly blessed with incredible healing and age-reducing properties—that sent Ben over the top.

"He wants to sit in fucking *ice water?* What, is that supposed to be some New Age way to shrink that supposedly mammoth cock of his, or something?" yelled Ben, running a hand through what was left of his graying hair. "Jeez, that boss of yours is some whack job! Look, I don't believe in shooting the messenger, so I'm going to level with you: feel free to grab a bucket and pull as much 'special water' as you need out of the river there."

He jerked his head toward the raging Rogue thirty feet beyond. "In fact, you can even tell him that I told you to do it, if you want. At this point, *I really don't give a shit!* Hell, Clive was my first choice for his role anyway. And guess what? Clive's current project was just put on hold. So, if Louis walks, it's a win-win for me."

Of course, *I* cared. And so did all of Team Louis, who would blame me if I allowed Louis to be miffed enough to quit over some damn lake water.

So I nodded resignedly to this alternative, bit my tongue about Louis's next request, and headed down the road in search of it or, rather, them myself: members of the Yahooskin American Indian tribe, who were known for the uplifting mysticism (not to mention the innate eroticism) of their incantations.

Louis had dreamed up his latest harebrained scheme after talking to the most buxom and definitely most starstruck member of the local catering service. "She claims their mantras are pure aphrodisiacs! Oh, and most importantly, they should help realign my chakras." He sighed, as if exhausted from just the thought of going another night in karmic turmoil.

"Louis, you've got to be kidding! Where am I supposed to find these—these—what did you call them?"

"Ya-hoo-skins," he mouthed patiently. "Try the local phone book."

"Under what, 'Indian tribes'? 'Native Americans'? 'Native tribes'?"

"Bollocks, Hannah, how am I supposed to know? If all else fails, Google them!"

Impatiently, he shooed me out the door. "I'd like at least two of those people here, no later than ten every night, as soon as possible. They are to stay at least an hour. That should exorcise the negative karma of this godforsaken place . . . particularly if the chanters are women . . . yes, I think that would be best . . . and virgins, preferably."

Oh, sure. It's not like I have anything better to do than to turn your trailer into a playpen for an underage harem!

Instead, I'd conjure up a couple of old tribal chieftains in the hopes that Louis would change his mind within a night or two. End of story.

Borrowing a four-wheel-drive vehicle from the production fleet, I drove the fourteen miles of rough hairpin turns to the closest place with a land line and a local phone book, a tiny country store known as the Gas-n-Gulp.

That treacherous dirt lane might have been the road less traveled by others, but I was coming to know it intimately. Maybe it was the river, or its roaring waterfalls, or the adjacent cliffs, or the tall pines that enveloped the location—or perhaps even Louis's bad karma—but obviously *something* was repelling my cell phone service, and rarely could I make out the frantic phone calls I received almost hourly from Randy, Genevieve and Monique. I found it easier to check in on a daily basis via the Gas-n-Gulp's land line, for which I was charged a dollar a minute by the store's enterprising owner, who was smart enough to recognize a desperate sap when he saw one.

He laughed his head off when I asked him whether or not he knew any Yahooskins willing to come to the set after hours and chant.

"Lady, what, are you drunk or something? That casino of theirs rakes in tons of dough. Hell, if they wanted to, they could *finance* several movies!"

Shaking his head in disbelief, he wrote down the telephone number of the tribal council, then headed over to cut a piece of rhubarb pie for the only other customer in the joint, a balding, bearded guy who had walked in not long after I had.

The tribal council's telephone receptionist seemed to take

my request for chanters seriously—that is, until I meekly added that, despite the late hour in which the chanters were to appear, it was preferable that they be underage females. After calling me a sicko and threatening me with a lawsuit, she hung up.

I could now tell Louis I'd done my best to honor his request.

Next I had to appease a very agitated Randy, who warned me that "Marcella's people have been on the horn, threatening to toss out some embarrassing rumors about Louis if he's the source of any dirt *at all* about her fuckability . . . or lack thereof—"

"Look," I shot back, "I don't know what the hell they're talking about. Okay, it's true she shot him down. But you know Louis—do you think he'd want anyone to know that happened? Besides, he's barely talking to anyone on the set, not even Ben! Besides, Marcella had her reasons—"

"Yeah, I'll say." Randy snickered. "Hey, has she come onto *you* yet? Be honest now."

"Don't get nasty, Randy, or I'll hang up," I said darkly.

"Okay, just wondering, no harm in asking, right? But listen, Hannah—the ball's in your court. *Louis needs this one.* But if Marcella gets pissed enough and walks, Louis may get canned over it. Jasper's already gotten an earful from Ben, so make sure Louis keeps it together."

Hanging up, I groaned and plopped down into the portion of the store considered its "diner": a couple of rickety tables surrounded by a few plastic chairs, where the store's owner made casseroles created from whatever canned goods were due to expire that month.

At the next table sat the chubby bearded bald guy. He wore tan Dockers and a worn plaid shirt stretched so thinly over his large belly that the buttons were straining not to pop. I'd seen him before. In fact, many times. Gulping down that day's blue plate special along with whatever pie had been defrosted, he'd pretend to read the same magazine he carried with him at all times: some fly-fishing rag, which was always turned to the same page. It made me wonder if he was in fact listening in on my embarrassingly exasperated remarks to Team Louis.

Then again, maybe I was wrong. I mean, hadn't I also seen him hanging around the craft table on the set, too?

Aware that I was staring at him, he looked up and grinned broadly, obviously recognizing me, too.

"From the shoot, right?" he said, as if reading my mind.

"Yeah," I nodded. It was great to see another Industry warrior. "I'm Hannah."

"Nice to meet you." He stuck out his hand, wiping it on his khakis first. "Jerry."

"You too, Jerry." I took it warily.

Why was he here, and not on the set, like everyone else?

"It's getting hairy over there, isn't it?" he said conspiratorially.

"Oh, I don't know," I answered. "Par for the course, I guess." From the snickers that followed in Louis's wake—and therefore, in mine—I had learned to be cautious of everyone else on the set, including the other PAs. I wasn't about to break that rule now, even while I was away from that insanity, if only for a few minutes. "Why? What do you mean?"

"Nothing. Nothing at all." He smiled benignly. "I guess your boss keeps you on your toes, eh? Underage Indian chanters? And that fight he had with Marcella—what was that all about, huh?"

I didn't answer. Something wasn't right, although I couldn't put my finger on it.

As if sensing my concern, he grinned broadly and added almost too quickly, "I have to say, though, I've got a lot of respect for him."

"Oh, yeah? How's that?"

Even after all you've heard and seen? I really wanted to ask.

"Why, the guy's a—an acting genius! A real pro! He's going to be the next—I dunno, the next Russell, I guess. Don't you think so?"

"Probably."

"Well, there's one way in which he's even got Russell beat." He winked at me.

"What do you mean?" I answered coolly.

"Hey, honey, you got to admit, your man Louis has got quite a rep—in the sack, I mean. Why, that's one place he even puts *Russell* to shame . . . right?"

"Look, I've got to get back." I started for the door.

"Hey, uh, do you think you could give me a lift back?"

I hesitated. For some reason, I didn't feel comfortable having him anywhere near me, although I didn't know why. I looked out at the gas pump. Beyond it was the old truck belonging to the Gulp-n-Gas's owner, and what was obviously a rental car.

Jerry's car.

So, why did he need a lift?

A cold chill went down my spine.

For a minute, I stood there, as if contemplating his request. Then, slowly I turned back to him. "Sure . . . aw, *shoot!* Um, look, I'm out of cash, so would you mind awfully if I borrowed your cell phone? My service is lousy up here. Can't get a signal."

I licked my lips coyly, then smiled at him, all wide-eyed innocence. "It'll only take a second. I promise! But if I don't make this call, Louis will be mad as all get-out,'cause it's *sooo* important!"

He hesitated for only a second, then grinned. "Sure," he said, as he tossed his phone to me.

I saw immediately that it was a camera phone. I held up a finger apologetically, pretended to dial a number, and sauntered slowly out the front door. Glancing back at him, I saw a look of disappointment flash over his face because I'd be out of his hearing range. He waved, though, to indicate that he was fine with granting me these few seconds of privacy.

By the time I'd made it to my car, I had reviewed the last five or six photos he had taken—of Louis, Marcella, and Barnaby, but he also had a couple of Louis with me.

As I'd suspected: Jerry was paparazzi.

And he'd heard everything I'd said. About Marcella. And the chanters.

Not to mention all the other calls he'd eavesdropped on during the past couple of days. And it would not have surprised me in the least to learn he'd been paying the store owner for any tidbits he may have missed.

I groaned. No wonder Marcella's people were on the warpath!

Angrily, I yanked out the phone's memory card, slipped it into my sock, and started my engine.

Hearing it rev up, Jerry rambled onto the front porch of the Gas-n-Gulp. As I pulled away, he stumbled down the steps and made a beeline for my Jeep.

I tossed his phone back at him. "Thanks!" I said brightly, as I waved and made a U-turn.

I almost ran over him as he slid momentarily onto the hood of my Jeep and banged on the windshield. "Bitch!" he shouted. "What did you do with the memory card?"

"Too late. Gone with the wind," I answered blithely, turning the wheel sharply to shake him off.

"Wait! WAIT!" He was breathing hard and was certainly not used to the workout he was getting. I pulled up short, making him roll off the hood. If I rolled forward, I'd flatten him. Before I could put the Jeep in reverse, though, he got to his knees. Catching his breath, he knocked on my window.

"Truce! Truce! I mean it!"

I didn't roll down my window but yelled through it, "Why should I believe you?"

"Because—because I know what it's worth to you, sweetheart!" He stuck his hand in his pocket, pulling out what looked like a wad of bills.

It was hard for Jerry to look as cool as he hoped he sounded, what with the rhubarb pie crumbs clinging to his grizzled beard. I wanted to blanch, but I don't think that even that visceral reaction would have convinced him that I couldn't be bought somehow.

He put a sweaty paw on my door handle. I couldn't help but shiver in revulsion.

"What say we have a little talk?" he smiled encouragingly.

I glanced away, sighed, then rolled down my window, but just partially. "Okay, okay. But listen, Jerry, whatever I say—it can't come back to haunt me! Understand?"

"No prob! Sure thing."

I shrugged, as if still not convinced. "Can we shake on it?"

"Whatever makes you feel good, honey." He stuck his hand through the window.

I rolled it up and drove off.

His screams shook the birds out of the treetops. Somewhere before I reached the second hairpin curve, he'd finally fallen to the wayside.

I made it back to the set just as the cast was breaking for lunch. Upon hearing that I could not procure his chanters, Louis took to his trailer—for the rest of the afternoon. "Make my excuses for me, love," he pouted. "Maybe I'll feel better tomorrow, but who knows? Tell that blasted director we'll play it by ear."

I was loath to break this news to Ben. All I could think of were the hundred plus cast and crew member sitting around twiddling their thumbs.

And pointing their middle fingers at Louis's trailer.

"Please, Louis," I whispered frantically. "You can't do this! Ben's at his wit's end with your shenanigans. And Randy said—"

"At *his* wit's end, you say? Why, that prat has *me* at his mercy, out here in the middle of nowhere. No wonder they call it Hellsgate! And he dares to complain about my needs as an artist?"

"You're no artist. *Why, you're nothing but a damned fool!*"

Both Louis and I turned toward the trailer door. There stood Barnaby Chadwick. His cobalt blue eyes were flashing in anger, and his regal stance all but dared Louis to contradict him.

Louis, quite aware that the older man's fury was more legitimate than his own, turned white but kept his mouth shut.

Satisfied he had Louis's attention, Barnaby continued. "Don't be such a prima donna, lad! Hell, life is too short! And for that matter, so is your so-called career."

He was now nose to nose with Louis. "So far all you've got to show for it is a few BBC historicals, a well-chosen indie or two, and, admit it, two or three bombs. Am I right?"

Watching Louis turn beet red, Barnaby continued, "Don't you get it? Sure, you have *Dead End*, and your performance was great—but it's *just one movie*. Understand? Why, even if your studio *is* able to buy every SAG vote that's up for sale this year, you'll still be just a flash in the pan if you blow it now—and over what, eh? Some New Age baloney?" He laughed caustically. "You're only a legend at thirty-two if you're dead. And you certainly don't have to be fifty to be a has-been."

Louis closed his eyes and clenched his fist. Knowing him the way I did, I could see that it was taking a lot for him to control the many emotions streaming through him.

So did Barnaby. The anger left his eyes as he softened his approach.

"I'll be honest with you, Louis: I was looking forward to working with you. You gave an incomparable performance in *Dead End*. Why, I haven't seen acting like that since—well, since her father starred in *Tomfoolery*." He turned to me and gave a slight nod. "Hannah, I was honored to be in that cast, I'm glad I have this opportunity to say so."

I had forgotten about that! No wonder Barnaby had sought me out when we'd first arrived. At the time, his wide, crooked smile had struck me as familiar, but until now I couldn't remember why: I'd met him years ago, when I was eight and had visited my father on the set of the one movie they'd made together.

"Leo was a prodigy, granted. But he was also stupid enough to piss it all away. And why? *Because he didn't trust his talent, and he didn't trust posterity to appreciate it, either.* So instead he's going to be remembered for having a solid-gold wanker and little else."

Louis looked over at me, as if he needed my assurance that I felt the same way. Without thinking, I bowed my head in acknowledgement.

Poor Leo.

Poor Louis.

Watching this interchange, Barnaby gave a weak smile. Suddenly the air seemed to go out of his body, as if he were a blow-up doll that had been punctured and had begun to deflate. Slowly he turned to leave, but by the time he reached the trailer door, he was shaking so hard that I was sure he was going to fall down.

Both Louis and I leaped to help him. Louis reached him first. Putting his hand on the older man's shoulder to steady him, Louis muttered something that I couldn't hear. Whatever it was, Barnaby looked Louis in the eye, nodded, then patted his shoulder.

As he limped down the trailer steps, I noticed that a crowd had gathered a few feet away. It was obvious by their whispers and the curious looks on their faces that Barnaby's stentorian rant had been heard through the trailer's thin walls.

Louis was still standing behind me. Unconsciously, he put a hand on my shoulder. As I looked up at him I saw that his eyes never left Barnaby until the older man was out of view.

On the other hand, Marcella's PA, who was standing in the midst of the curious onlookers, couldn't take her eyes off Louis and me.

In fact, she looked right at me—and smiled, if you could call it that.

More likely, bared her teeth.

Oh great, I thought, *just what we need: a little tit for tat.*

Barnaby's cold corpse was discovered by the production assistant who had been assigned to him, but only after the girl—a shy, sweet coed who was there in order to fulfill her college internship requirement as a film study major—had knocked a minimum of 103 times, called through his window at least twenty more, then mustered the courage to enter the trailer of the great revered actor.

Shaken up from the event, she immediately resolved to change her major to something less stressful: say, accounting—and promptly left both the backwoods of Oregon and any hopes of a film industry career behind her.

Calling the rest of the shell-shocked crew and cast together, Ben explained that, according to the set's doctor, Barnaby had expired sometime during the night. The local coroner was on his way, and in the meantime, no one was to enter Barnaby's trailer. Ben assured every one that, as much as he'd have liked to shut down the set for mourning, he knew that Barnaby would have preferred that they continue to rally on despite this tragedy so that the production could stay within some semblance of its budget. Oh, and not to worry, because he and the producers already had calls in to those they considered acceptable replacements—not that anyone could in fact replace the revered actor. In the meantime, the scenes in which his character did not appear would take precedent—

In other words, the show must go on.

But not for Louis, it seemed.

Not even waiting to hear Ben's windup, Louis, ashen-faced and hollow-eyed, slowly walked up to one of the crew's many drivers, who nodded, took the tip Louis handed him, then tossed Louis a key.

As Louis peeled out in a Jeep, I ran up to the man. "Tell me," I asked, catching my breath, "did Louis say where he was going?"

"I'll say," the guy smirked. "To find a nice deep bottle."

Seeing my grimace, he added, "Don't worry. Hell, no way I'd let him get anywhere near Grant's Pass or some other place where he could get into trouble." The man smiled. "Been with Ben for too many years, and I've got too much respect for him to let that happen. I sent your boy a little over an hour west of here, to the Marial Lodge. Trust me, no one will recognize him there."

I thanked him, grabbed another Jeep key, and went to look for Ben so that I could plead for Louis's professional life.

Grudgingly, Ben gave me 24 hours in which to work a miracle. But by Hour 25, he warned me, he'd be calling Clive's agent.

In other words, no one—not even Louis—was irreplaceable.

* * *

I reached the lodge in the midafternoon. As late in the fall as it was, Louis had wasted no time in securing one of the two rooms the lodge had, and I had no problem getting the other.

After tossing my bag on my bed, I steeled myself to face him. I knew it wouldn't be pretty. Whether it would be as bad as his mood after the London run-in over his father, or similar to the day of Mick and Sam's deception, I didn't know. In any case, I'd have to get him to realize that Barnaby's death was not his fault.

And that his career depended on him getting over any insecurity he had about that and anything else that was holding him back.

As Barnaby said, only Louis could keep himself from being a has-been.

I placed my ear on the shared wall between our rooms. Not a sound.

Maybe he had decided to take a nap. If that was the case, shouldn't I let him sleep?

Or perhaps he'd passed out in a drunken stupor. That made the sleep/wake issue a definite toss-up.

Then again, was he capable of doing something stupid, like slashing his wrists?

My heart leaped into my throat at the thought that he might die. But then the calm voice of reason came over me:

Nah, not Louis. If he survived, he'd be pissed to come to and find he had scars on his otherwise perfect body.

Still, I couldn't take that chance.

I crept out into the hall. Hesitating to knock, I decided to try the knob instead.

The door opened. *But there was no sound beyond it.*

My heart was thumping so loud that I would have been surprised if I'd heard anything anyway. I took a few steps inside and tried to see something, anything at all, in the vast gloom that enveloped the darkened room, but I couldn't make out much.

Certainly not the bed, which I was clumsy enough to bump into.

"Stop or I'll shoot." The tone of his voice, although muffled, was tense enough to raise the hairs on the back of my neck.

"Louis, it's just me. Hannah." I paused, suddenly scared.

He had a gun? So he had *planned on killing himself!*

I tried to keep my voice steady. "So, uh, where did you get the gun?"

He flicked on the light. "Blimey, Hannah. You believed *that?* My God, it's the oldest line in the book!" he smirked caustically. Then he closed his red-rimmed eyes, as if he was too tired for polite conversation. "Well, I'm glad to see that I still have the old Trollope touch."

A half-empty Dewar's bottle was on the nightstand. Obviously he had been sleeping.

And drinking. And crying.

Other than the sheet that was coiled around his legs, he was naked. I blushed.

Still, I was relieved to see he was okay. "Of course you do." Gently, I sat down at the edge of the bed. "Louis, look, I know what you're thinking—"

"I know you do, Hannah. That's why I love you: because with you around, I don't *have* to think. You do it for me."

His sarcasm made me wince. "No! That's not what I meant."

"I don't care *what* you mean." The words flowed out of him in a torrent. "What you mean doesn't matter to me. Nothing matters. Not now."

"Why not?"

"Because I—" He choked on the words. "I killed Barnaby."

"No, no, Louis!" I ran to him. "You didn't!"

"Bollocks! You were there! You saw what happened!"

"Yes, I was there—and I saw him get angry and put you in your place, and make you realize that you have a lot to lose when you act like an ass! But you did *not* kill him!"

"Granted, I might not have physically injured him, but all of my—my asinine stunts probably . . . probably put a strain on his heart—"

I pulled Louis close to me. He buried his face, now wet with tears again, in my angora sweater and slowly stroked it with his hand for what seemed like an eternity.

After a few minutes, I countered, "Look, Louis, I'm not going to lie to you: things have been extremely stressful on the set these past couple of weeks. And . . . and you're part of the reason it's been that way. But still"—as I paused, I looked him right in the eye—"can't we both safely agree that Barnaby's fondness for Gauloises and rare steaks might have had *something* to do with his heart attack?"

Realizing the truth in what I said, he looked up, gave a hollow chuckle, and nodded.

He kept stroking my sweater.

And his eyes never left my face.

Suddenly, I noticed that Louis's eyes were the same shade of blue as Leo's.

That startling turquoise blue.

How ironic.

Softly, I added, "It would be wonderful if we could save the ones we love the most from themselves. But we can't."

That in turn released a flood of other memories of my father, and I started to cry.

It was Louis's turn to cradle me; and to cry with me.

And to kiss me all over, as I dreamed he would, so many times before.

And then to undress me, slowly, lovingly, desperately.

And to trace every curve and crook and ingress of my body with his hands, then with his lips, then his tongue.

And for me to do the same to him, before exploding with him—*inside of me.*

Again.

And again.

So many times, over so little time:

Alas, a mere 22 hours.

Because, by the twenty-fifth, a very sober Louis was back on the set: clear-eyed, refreshed, relaxed, and ready to go to work. . . .

. . . with me—the one person, as he'd professed so ardently in those 22 hours, that he just couldn't live without—at his side.

12

Worm Hole

Hypothetical shortcut through the space/time continuum.

Sheer bliss.

Each day of the next four weeks of our lives took on a dreamlike quality.

At daybreak, cocooned together in Louis's trailer, our senses were awakened: by the mournful conversations between the owls that hovered in the branches overhead; and the soft shimmering shafts of the sun's rays that warmed our faces and our bed, somehow making it through the sentry of tall trees that surrounded the trailer; and most certainly by the musky aura of our lovemaking from the night before.

Once aroused, the inevitable happened: Our bodies hungered—insatiably, obsessively and uncontrollably—to be joined together again.

Our lips, thirsting for passion, could only be quenched from the liquid lust that flowed out of each other. My fingers, tantalizing the tip of his penis with gentle strokes, were instantly rewarded for their endeavors when, inch by glorious inch, a hardened Louis fervently unleashed himself inside of me with an obsessive zeal that awakened my broken soul and brought me to joyous tears.

Ah, sweet, crazy, rapturous delight!

In other words, all the rumors were true:

Louis Trollope was one hell of a lover.

And now, he was *my* lover.

Mine alone.

Elated, we were also anxious to get on with the rest of our day: We'd quickly pull ourselves together and show up on the set early, where Louis was courteous, alert, prepared, professional, insightful and inspiring—to the awe of all who watched.

Then, when Ben was satisfied with the last scene of the day, we'd watch the digital dailies.

It was during one of these sessions that Louis realized that this could be the best performance of his professional career. Out of the corner of my eye, I caught him watching me. When I turned to face him, he squeezed my hand and whispered, "I could not have done this if it weren't for you."

After viewing the dailies, we'd sequester ourselves in Louis's trailer for another night of blissful lovemaking . . .

. . . followed by a late-night stroll through the jet-black woods, me leading with a flashlight while he carried my telescope, over to the water's edge, where the roar of the river was the symphony that accompanied our stargazing.

Away from any city lights, the thick blanket of stars was multiplied tenfold beyond what we were used to seeing in L.A. They were layered in such a way that they seemed to float away, and us along with them. After adjusting the telescope, I'd invite Louis to look through it as I divulged the science and myth that was our rationale for their existence.

As he learned about the stars, I learned about him: his impoverished, wretched childhood in a home dominated by a father who'd drowned his love and sorrows in bottle after bottle of scotch; his mother's frustration with her own predicament, and eventual resignation to it; and Louis's own fears and insecurities in light of his innate talent, exceptional looks, and the guilt over his own good luck.

"Oh sure, I'm lucky. I've been blessed," he noted ruefully. "But sometimes our blessings are also our curses." He turned from the telescope to look at me. "I never know if my friends love me for me, or my fame. The women I meet only see Louis the star, not Louis the person. Hell, even when I'm a monster to them, they love me all the more! It seems that they can't get enough of that Louis."

"I think you're wrong. I think they are sad around that Louis but keep hoping for a glimpse of the real you; the Louis who is here with me, right now."

He thought about that for a while, then shook his head in wonder. "Hannah, how do you know that this *is* the real me? Even I don't know that! In fact, I doubt very much that it is." He turned back to the telescope. "You bring out the best in me. Unfortunately, the rest of my life brings out the worst."

Whether I wanted to admit it or not, Louis was right.

Which brought up the question: would this Louis, my wonderful Louis, disappear, like the stars overhead, in L.A.'s hot bright spotlight?

Not if I could help it.

Already we were open with others about our intimacy with each other. Not that our feelings would have surprised the *Killer Instincts* cast and crew: on-location trysts are part and parcel of the filmmaking process. Even before Barnaby's death, any of the innocuous trips I'd made into Louis's trailer—to bring him dinner or to help him prepare for the next day's scenes—had been met with no more than a raised eyebrow, or at worst, a leering wink and a nod. Besides, with Louis's legendary reputation as an insatiable cocksman, the real shocker to the others would not have been that we were having an affair but that we hadn't consummated it until then.

Still, we weren't prepared for the media hailstorm that met us the day after *Killer Instincts* wrapped.

Shouldn't the twelve desperate voice messages that Monique left on the red cell the day of the wrap party have been some indication?

Perhaps.

Or, how about the thirty or so frantic messages from Tatiana, each more shrill than the next, that came in over the course of those final 24 hours?

Didn't I even suspect what they were calling about?

Okay, I'll admit it: We were both a little bit in denial. I'd convinced myself that keeping Team Louis on a need-to-know basis about our situation would allow Louis the time he needed to concentrate on the role of a lifetime—

—and for me to do the same, in *my* role of a lifetime:

As the one and only woman for Louis.

Which was why I didn't return Tatiana's phone calls, either.

Or suggest that Louis do so.

That policy ended the moment Malcolm's limo pulled up to the tarmac. At Monique's behest, he handed Louis a manila envelope filled with clippings from the tabloid magazines for the past week.

All of them had fuzzy cover shots of him—*with me*.

Flinging them onto the seat, Louis laughed raucously.

One had him holding me in his arms, obviously taken during one of the breaks on the set. The caption read: "Louis' On-Location Lover Is Leo Fairchild's Love Child!"

Another, which must have been taken with a night filter, showed us kissing down by the river. The robe I'd been wearing had fallen off my shoulder, allowing the photographer to capture Louis cupping my naked breast, although the photo editor had superimposed a black band over my nipple. The headlined screamed: "British Rogue on the Rogue: Hot Pix of His Wet and Wild Sex Romps!"

Why Louis found that funny was beyond me.

As I flipped through the articles, I noticed that none of them mentioned Louis's run-in with Marcella, although she did appear in some sidebars, in which her red carpet gowns were praised to the hilt.

Interesting: So Jerry had gotten his scoop after all. Having been banned from the set at my insistence, I could only guess who had helped him:

Marcella's PA.

Her reward: Marcella stayed in her closet, along with all of her designer duds.

A third tabloid cover showed what looked like Louis pushing an irate Barnaby out of his trailer, with me looking on. The headline heralded: "Barnaby's Mysterious Death: Over Louis' New Love?"

Upon seeing that one, Louis frowned as he slumped back onto the limo's leather seat and slapped the paper with his hand. "What, are those bastards crazy? They're insinuating that I knocked off Barnaby? And over *you?*"

I knew what he meant. And of course, I was just as outraged at the insinuation as he was. But still, it hurt when he put it that way: *As if I would not have been worth the fight.*

Pulling up to Louis's house, we were met at the gate by a flock of paparazzi gone wild, shouting questions while clicking their cameras at the same time.

"Hey, Louis, does your new arm charm know any tribal chants?"

"So, Louis, when Barnaby said 'Knock it off,' did you think he meant it literally?"

And then there was this one:

"Over here, Hannah! We want to give Tatiana a good look at who's been treading on Louis's runway while she's been in Paris!"

Neither she—nor I, for that matter—had ever dreamed I'd fit that role.

Unruffled as always, Louis was ready for his close-up: His devilishly handsome, angular face was set in a piercing stare that made love to the cameras even as he muttered out of one side of his mouth, *"Get us out of here, Malcolm. Now."*

I, on the other hand, looked like Bambi caught in the head-lights of an oncoming truck: a big, unwieldy eighteen-wheeler that was swerving out of control and crushing beneath its wheels any remnant of privacy I had in my life.

Turning to me, Louis said, "Had Monique given you any inkling about this?"

Guiltily, I shook my head. "I—I guess the crew was gossip-ing about us in Oregon. It's my fault, Louis. I should have warned Monique first. But I never dreamed that it would be such a big deal, so I ignored . . . well, I guess I thought it best if we just focused on your performance."

I tapped Malcolm on the shoulder. "I think you'd best take us to Randy's office." Then I turned back to Louis. "I'll call the private security detail and ask them to clear these clowns out of here for us. I'll also call Genevieve and Monique and ask them to meet us at Randy's, too."

"Call Jasper first. I want to see what legal recourse I can take to stop this rubbish."

I put my hand over his. I'd hoped he would respond with a comforting pat. Instead, he moved it slightly away from mine and looked out the window again. Although he didn't show it, he was annoyed. "No doubt Tatiana knows about us now, too."

My stomach clenched at that thought. I had witnessed the way in which Tatiana perused the tabloids, parsing every photo of her and Louis—or, for that matter, anyone else, particularly anyone who might be conceived as her competition for his love.

Our honeymoon was over.

Did this mean that our relationship was as well?

Jasper's advice was the following: Don't supply. Don't deny. In that way, today's tabloid headlines quickly become yesterday's garbage. "Unless, Hannah, you can say under oath it wasn't your breast, or that wasn't you kissing Louis."

My silence spoke volumes.

"That's what I mean." Now he was silent, but I knew what he was thinking: that I had done the one thing I had sworn not to do—fallen under Louis's spell. "I'll threaten something, don't worry. Just don't expect miracles in light of the truth."

What *was* the truth about us?

I didn't seem to know anymore, and I couldn't imagine that Louis had a clue. By the way in which Louis wrapped his arm around my waist as we entered Randy's office, or patted my ass so territorially in front of him, or tossed commands at me like so much confetti, it was less than implicit that he saw me as his . . .

His what? Lover? PA? Chattel?

All of the above?

Not that this even mattered to the rest of Team Louis. As we huddled in Randy's office that afternoon, neither Monique, Genevieve, nor Randy seemed to give a hoot whether Louis and I were in fact in love or not.

All they cared about was that Louis was happy.

And more importantly, that we make the most of the situation that had put him in even greater demand than he had been before.

Which was why Randy heartily agreed with Jasper's recommendation—sort of.

"Fuck what the tabloids are saying. The bottom line is that our man is on every one of their goddam covers! Shit, we couldn't *buy* this kind of publicity!"

He tossed down the latest *People*, *In Touch*, and *Us Weekly*. "And Fox is ecstatic! Ticket sales for *Dead End* are moving again. It's back up to third place at the box office! Not bad for a movie that's been out twelve weeks already." He slapped Louis on the back, then gave me a once-over that made me cringe. "My only regret is that the photographer didn't catch you two doing it doggy style over the stump of a sequoia tree! Just think how *that* headline would have read!"

Genevieve, Monica and I blanched at Randy's crudeness. Realizing it would be best to change the subject, Genevieve touched on one just as sensitive.

"I'm getting calls every fifteen minutes from Tatiana." She looked at Louis. "She says that no one is returning her messages to your private line." Then she looked pointedly at me. "How do you want me to handle it?"

Louis smiled and followed her gaze to me. "Don't worry, Genevieve. Now that we're back in civilization, Hannah will take care of it. Right, love?"

As he stroked my arm, I saw Genevieve and Monique exchange glances. Randy, on the other hand, guffawed loudly. "Jeez, I'd like to be a fly on the wall for *that* one!"

Me—tell Tatiana? No way! No way in Hell.

As the meeting broke up, I tried to wangle Louis away from the others so that we could discuss this further in private, but Randy got to him first. I couldn't hear what Randy said, it was murmured so low. Louis's reaction was to laugh uproariously and shake his head no.

Later, when we were back in the limo, I asked him what Randy had said.

"Believe it or not, love, he paid you a compliment."

"You're right. I find that hard to believe." I faced him straight on. "So, what was it?"

"He said that those pictures are proof positive that you're not a frigid bitch after all. Bollocks, Hannah, I just *knew* you'd take that the wrong way! And no, we are *not* turning the car around so you can beat him black and blue. . . . Besides, he'd like that too much. Darling, *let's go home!* You can run my bath for me, then join me in the tub. That will make you happy, right?"

The tub would have to wait, because Tatiana would not. We could hear the house phone ringing even as Malcolm went through the motions of pulling up to the front entrance, opening the back car door, and carrying our luggage into the house.

Once more I tried to convince Louis that the very least he could do was call her himself to let her know that things were over between them.

He gave a very good reason for disagreeing with me: "Love, trust me. I know Tatiana better than you do. If I get on the phone, she'll beg me to see her. Even if I say no, she'll be on our doorstep in no time, or worse yet, she'll ask me to meet her at the Bel-Air. I . . . I couldn't do that. It would bring back too many memories."

Of what? I wanted to ask. Of them, together, making love?

Or of him with Samantha?

I had never asked him how he'd known about Samantha and Mick, but now was certainly not the time. I had to make a decision about Tatiana instead: If I kept insisting that Louis call her, I'd be risking the chance that his guilt would drive him back into her arms. However, if I called her myself, I'd have to face her very justified wrath. After all, I knew how much she loved Louis. And I also knew how much he had taken that love for granted.

I had played an integral role in allowing him to do so.

So that would be my penance, I reasoned: *I'd have to listen to her tell me what a conniving bitch I was.*

Besides, I wouldn't be able to stand it if Louis fell back under her spell—

—or slipped out from under mine. I'd die if I lost him. I knew this.

So I dialed her number.

Louis watched silently as I asked her assistant to put her on the phone. He said nothing as she screamed Russian epithets at me, then cursed at me in French. He glanced in another direction as I held the phone away from my ear while, in the human language of pain, she howled and sobbed.

He bowed his head as I whispered, over and over, how sorry I was that all of this had happened, and that I hoped that one day she could forgive us.

Hanging up the phone, I collapsed in his arms. He carried me to his bed, undressed me, and made love to me.

Afterward, while I was curled in the fetal position, he ran the bath water. Then, scooping me up again, he gently placed me in the tub so that he could sponge the hot, soapy suds over me.

Finally, he wrapped me in a towel and carried me back to his bed.

I still felt dirty.

When I woke up an hour later, he'd already gone to the Fox lot to begin the postproduction sound dubbing on *Killer Instincts,* but there was a note on the bedside table that read, "You prove your love to me in every way. I thank God I have you at my side."

It also asked that I move my things into the house—and *not* into the cabana.

Most of my clothes fit into a big old steamer trunk I'd salvaged from Leo's estate. It was too unfashionable for Sybilla to have coveted. Luckily for me she hadn't thrown it away prior to the settlement. Leo had used it on all of his many safaris, and it had also made it around the world with him on his many on-location projects.

It had brought him home safe and sound. I was hoping it would work the same magic for me as I made my way to my new home.

I was dragging it from the bedroom and into the living room when I bumped into something that should not have been in my way:

Mick.

I hadn't heard him come in. But I could see from his stance that he wasn't leaving—or, for that matter, going to let me leave until he got some answers.

To get the ball rolling, he tossed the *People* magazine at my feet.

"Is it true?" The pain in his voice rivaled what I had just heard from Tatiana. But I wasn't going to lie to him.

"Yes." Still, I held my head up high. "I'm sorry. About us."

"Yeah, uh, about that: *Could you at least tell me what the hell happened?*"

"What happened? You want to know what *happened?*" The nerve of him!

Before now, I hadn't been able to confront him about Samantha. Well, now I could, in a way that would hurt him as he'd hurt me.

"Louis and I fell in love."

"Louis, in love? What, are you kidding me?" He looked at

me as if I'd gone crazy. "And I don't believe you love him, either, just like that!" Angrily he leaned into me. "Or were you stringing me along all this time, to make him jealous?"

"Stringing *you* along! Who—who are you to accuse *me* of stringing you along?" I started dragging the trunk again. "Get out of my way. I've got to get this over to Louis's."

"What's the rush? Are you on babysitting duty 24/7 now?" He jerked my hand away from the trunk. "Or are you afraid he may find someone else to keep him company if you stay away too long?"

"How dare you! Louis has changed, Mick. We both have. You wouldn't understand."

"Yeah, I'll just bet. He's just a regular guy, right? Well, have you noticed that great guy of yours isn't even here to give you a hand?"

"He had to get back to the studio. Or he would be here."

As soon as I said that, I regretted it. Louis, help me move? More than likely he would have just insisted that I call a moving service.

Or that I just buy whatever I needed instead, and have the bills sent to Genevieve.

Mick laughed long and hard. "Right, that's a joke! Why, I'll bet he's never even asked to see your place."

"What difference does that make? Why should he want to come here?"

"Because if he had, it would mean that he wants to know all about you, instead of what you can *do* for him." Mick grabbed my hand to force me to face him. "It would mean that he loves you for the *right* reasons, Hannah, not his usual selfish ones."

I wrenched my hand away. "Who are you to say what the right reasons are for him to fall in love? Or for me, for that matter?"

He flinched. "I thought I knew what reasons were right . . . once."

"I did, too." I sat down hard on the trunk. "Look, Mick, I know for a fact that I wasn't what you really wanted."

"What makes you say that? Because he told you so, and you want to believe him?"

"Yes. No! I mean—I mean if there ever was a time you felt you loved me, then maybe it was for the *wrong* reason."

"And what reason would that be?"

"Maybe you were attracted to me only because of what I meant to *him.*"

He looked at me as if he could not believe his own ears. Then he laughed incredulously, mirthlessly. "Hannah, you are so wrong. In the first place, you don't mean anything to him!"

"No, Mick, you're the one who's wrong. About Louis. You always were! He does know me. And I know *him* now, too. In fact, I know everything about him, the good and the bad . . . which is more than I can say about you."

"What's that supposed to mean?"

"It means that—that you've never really told me the truth!"

He seemed confused. "The truth? About what?"

"About—about Samantha." There. I'd said it.

"Samantha?" He was confused. "You *know* about Samantha?"

"Of course I do! What do you take me for, an idiot?"

"I don't know, that depends. Just what do you think you know?"

"Well, I know you had a tryst with her, at the Hotel Bel-Air."

"Me? A—what?"

"*You made love to her!* There, in the Courtyard Suite. I saw the two of you—"

"You saw *us—making love?*"

Now *I* was confused. "No—well, not exactly! I mean, you were—you were holding her. And I—I know she was naked at the time. That's true, right?"

He looked angry. But still, he didn't answer. Instead he asked, "Tell me, Hannah, how did you know that I was there with Samantha in the first place?"

I hesitated, but of course he knew.

Louis.

"You go ahead and believe what you want to believe— which, I assume, is anything he wants to tell you." He started out the door but turned back around. "Oh, by the way, did he even mention that he was there, too? I'm guessing no. Well, he was, Hannah! He was there because . . . because . . ."

He stopped to find the right words. Seeing the pained expression on my face, though, he quit trying. Then, very quietly, he said instead, "Just take my word for it, he was there, too. With her. But then he left her, without even having the courtesy to tell her he was going. That was *my* job."

He pulled me into his arms. Searching my eyes with his, he added, "That's how he dumped her, Hannah! Do you see a pattern here?"

I did.

But I didn't want to admit it, because I didn't want to be wrong about Louis.

Not now. Not any more. Not after what Louis and I had been through these past four weeks.

Which was why Mick *couldn't* be right.

By my silence, he knew what I chose to believe. *It's our loss,* the look in his eyes seemed to say. Then he was gone. I heard his motorcycle growl down the street.

I stood there for a moment, thinking about Louis and Samantha.

So, Louis had lied to me about her.

And he doesn't like to break up in person.

Did I see a pattern there?

Yes, I did. And yet I didn't want to believe it. There had to be a better explanation.

I'd have to ask Louis what that was.

I loaded up a few more items then headed back over to Louis's place, something the Beetle could now do on autopilot.

By the time I got there, both the red and the gray cell phones were ringing. On the red line was Genevieve, screaming something about Louis's broken nose, and that I'd better get over to Cedars-Sinai as fast as I could.

"What? What are you saying?"

"Just do it! Now!" she screeched, then hung up.

On the other cell was *In Touch* magazine: Did I care to comment on the information they had that Mick Bradshaw had punched out Louis Trollope on the set of his movie, now filming at Fox Studios?

Was it true that I had been the subject of their altercation?

Was there any word as to how long Mick would be suspended from the Fox lot?

Would the break in Louis's nose mean that plastic surgery would be involved?

I gave no comment, got back in the Beetle, and began the trek back down the hill.

13

Zenith

The point on the celestial sphere directly above an observer, or the highest point in the sky reached by a celestial body.

From what the doctors could tell, Louis was lucky: His nose had not been broken. Still, they could do an X-ray to confirm this only after the swelling went down in a couple of days. In the meantime he'd need ice packs to reduce the puffiness and plenty of Vicodin for the pain.

And a whole hell of a lot of reassurance for his bruised ego.

Being in no mood to counter the stares he would get if he decided to go out in public with a swollen nose, Louis spent the next four days at home, poolside. Because he wasn't supposed to drink while taking Vicodin, he chose to forgo any painkillers and to live with the soreness. He did, however, use plenty of ice.

In his perpetually filled glass of Dewars.

Naturally, his pain put him in a lousy disposition, which he took out on anyone who dared to tread onto his path within the now heavily guarded estate: Lourdes, who burst into tears when he yelled profanities at her for moving his empty drink glass; the Guatemalan gardeners, who cursed the *puta* who had put him in such a foul mood, then flipped coins to determine who would dare trim the bougainvillea bush adjacent to the pool, only to incur his wrath for having gotten too close to him; Randy, who stopped by daily with the latest box office stats on *Dead End* and had to put up with Louis's threats to move to another agent "who can appreciate me"; and, of course, me, who had been delegated the job of keeping his spirits up at all costs—including my sanity.

"Bloody git! He coldcocked me when I wasn't looking!" With the ice pack and bandage on his nose, Louis's voice now had a nasal cadence to it. "Listen to me! I sound like a bloody pouf or something! So much for the dubbing. . . . Bollocks! Well, Ben can't blame me for this! Fox's security people never should have let that bastard through. In fact, if my face is ruined, I'm bloody suing the whole lot of them, starting with your boyfriend!"

"He's not my boyfriend, Louis," I said calmly, although I could feel the blood rushing to my cheeks. "You are, remember?"

That brought him back to earth for a moment. He turned away from me. "Sorry, love. I'm not blaming you—"

Oh, aren't you?

"—it's just that I can't stand the thought of that wanker ever having touched you."

"We can't change the past, Louis. Neither of us can, right?" I said pointedly. I had yet to ask him about Samantha. But that would have to wait now.

Instead I reached for the phone. "Don't worry. Ben is already working around you until your nose heals. And I asked Monique to cancel all the interviews you had scheduled, until next week. Otherwise, any opportunities you have to plug *Dead End* will be squandered in questions about the—the altercation."

"Oh yeah, great! As if I'm giving Mick any more publicity." He punched the wrought-iron chaise with his fist. "Once again he's hanging onto my gravy train."

"Well, Mick did write the screenplay for *Dead End*. I mean, he deserves credit for that at least, right?"

"No one gives a shit who wrote the bloody screenplay! All they care about is the star's performance: *mine*." His eyes narrowed with suspicion. "Hey, whose side are you on, anyway?"

"Why are you so paranoid all of a sudden? Haven't I done everything you've asked of me?"

"I haven't quit asking," he shot back. "For example, it would be nice to know why he was there in your house in the first place." He raised an eyebrow.

"Why is that strange? Before . . . well, before we were . . . us, Mick used to come over all the time."

And you've never been there at all. And now you never will.

"But how did he know *you* were going to be there? I just don't like the timing of that whole scenario." Louis stared coldly at me. "And by the way you're acting, Hannah, I'm beginning to wonder if you actually planned to meet him there."

"Louis, please! Don't be ridiculous!"

"No? Okay, I believe you . . . I guess." He picked up a pebble and tossed it into the pool, turning its glassy surface into a bull's-eye of ripples. Without looking my way, he asked, "Mick didn't say anything that would make you change your mind about us, did he?"

There it was: the opening I was looking for.

It was my chance to ask him to level with me about Samantha.

But I didn't take it.

Instead I answered him with a trembling voice. "No, Louis. He just said that—that you're a pro at using others. And that eventually you'd use me, too."

The tremor in my voice was a dead giveaway that Louis's suspicions were confirmed: *I knew about Samantha.*

But, for the sake of our relationship, I was going to pretend that I didn't.

He turned back to me. The mere shadow of a smile acknowledged my obvious lie, as well as his appreciation that I was willing to do that for him.

For us.

He too was willing to make sacrifices for us. He said so in this way:

"I'll be the first to admit it: I've done some things—to the other women I've known—that I haven't been proud of. *But I'm different with you, Hannah!* That's because I love you more than I've loved any other woman I've known. You do believe that, don't you?"

He'd asked me in such a way that I knew his heart would break if I didn't.

Yes, I want to believe that. I really, really want to. . . .

"Yes, Louis. I know you do."

"That's good, love. Very good." Gently he traced my face with his finger. "But I have to ask this, and I want you to be honest with me, or else what we have here won't work: Do you feel the same way about me, love? There is no one standing between us, is there?"

Of course, he meant Mick.

Mick, who created the cinematic heroes Louis had been born to play.

Mick, Louis's best bud, his loyal pal.

Mick, who, for all I knew, had shared Louis's other women with him but was forbidden by Louis to share me.

Which was why neither of us could now share Mick's love, loyalty and friendship.

I hesitated about a fraction of a second. "No. I love you more than anyone I've ever loved, too."

I'll be the first to admit it: I'm a lousy actor. My unconscious blink as I spoke was a dead giveaway, I was sure of that.

But Louis, like the rest of us, only saw what he wanted to see and heard what his ego needed as confirmation: *That I was his.*

All he had to do was ask.

"Is that so, love? Then prove it." He pulled me down onto his lap and moved in for a kiss. His lips brushed mine for a second . . .

. . . then he pulled back. "Shit! That hurts! I can't—I can't even kiss you now!"

He put his hand to his nose and tapped it gingerly. I rose to get off, but he held me firmly. "That's okay. Kissing is just the appetizer, right? We can move on to the main course without it—"

"Louis, I don't think we should do that—out here."

"Who cares that we're out by the pool? The gardeners are working in the front now. . . . No, don't worry about the security guard, he's watching the gardeners! . . . . Look, love, we both know that I shouldn't have to beg for it! I mean, if you're being *truly* honest with me. Right?"

He wanted proof that no one stood between us. Was that too much to ask for?

Not Mick. Not Tatiana.

Not Samantha.

No one.

"Good, now that's better! . . . *Right* . . . *Right* . . . um, now, *that's* therapy . . . Damn, I wish you could get a hold of a naughty nurse's uniform somewhere . . ."

*   *   *

Despite my trying to appease Louis in every way possible, his incarceration made him grumpy.

I have to admit that I had a bad case of cabin fever, too. In fact, I couldn't run the simplest errand without having a swarm of paparazzi on my tail as I bobbed and weaved down Laurel Canyon Boulevard until I ducked down one of the many side streets that dropped me onto Sunset, where, if I was lucky and the lights worked in my favor, I was granted anonymity in the form of three lanes of traffic.

I was somewhat miffed, however, to discover that my new problems garnered no empathy whatsoever from the other members of the Gang of Four.

Showing up late for our infrequent confab at the Central Casting Denny's, I undid my scarf and took off my glasses only after the waitress—plump, timeworn and smacking her gum loudly as proof that she had better things to do than to worry about who I was—sauntered off with my order of poached eggs on rye.

"Hey, what's with the Mata Hari couture?" asked Freddy as he sliced up a sausage for the ever ubiquitous Bette.

"The press," I answered miserably. Then I threw down some Fred Segal gift bags. "Go ahead, open them."

Christy and Sandra pounced, while Freddy gave a raised eyebrow before opening his bag and squealing out loud. Each bag had a trove of goodies unique to that elite boutique. For the girls, designer perfumes, scarves, earrings, and metallic hobo totes. And for Freddy, aftershave, a cashmere scarf and some angora socks.

"I was in Fred Segal picking up some shirts for Louis, and for some reason the salesclerk insisted that I take some items from their VIP closet for myself. I thought you guys might not be so mad at me for being late if I came bearing gifts."

"Oh, sweetie! You didn't have to do that," murmured Sandy.

"Bullshit. I, for one, would have never spoken to her if she hadn't," teased Freddy. "Now we'll be expecting these goodies every time we meet. So, tell us the truth, girlfriend: why the Trojan horses?"

"It's just my humble way of saying thank you. I'm beginning to realize that you three are the only ones whose friendships I can count on. Particularly in light of all that's happened this past month."

"Works for me," said Freddy. "So, how *is* life in the fast lane?"

"Frightening." I sighed. "I can't go anywhere without a paparazzi escort. I just know I pissed off the security people at Fred Segal."

"Well," sniffed Christy, "they must not be too upset at you to give you all this VIP stuff." Even as she dabbed the store's signature cologne behind her ear, it was obvious to everyone at the table that Christy was having a hard time with my sudden fame.

But not as hard a time as I was.

"What, do you think I enjoy living in a fishbowl? That this is how I want to spend the rest of my life?" I asked her incredulously.

"Don't be such a little drama queen," laughed Freddy. "You're proof positive that Warhol was right. So sweetheart, now that the clock has started running on *your* fifteen minutes of fame, why settle for the kiddie table when they're inviting you to sit with the adults?" He patted the banquette. "Don't worry. Your spot will be waiting right here, after you've have that inevitable fall from grace."

Well, I had to admit, it had been a while since I'd had others treat me so deferentially.

And offer me nice pretty things.

And fawn over me, as if my every word were golden.

Although my work as Louis's PA had meant running into

stores all over L.A. to pick up and drop off items that had caught his fancy (or ones the stores hoped would), those tasks had been for business, not pleasure. However, since my meta-morphosis from Hannah-the-PA to Hannah-Louis's-Girlfriend, I was once again encouraged—no, make that required—to shop.

And shop well. Yep, my favorite Rodeo shop girls had missed me (or at least my Amex card), that was true; and once again, I was on a first-name basis with the girls at the Grove.

But now, not only was I back, *I was back with a vengeance.*

Better yet, I was back with the kind of cachet that came only through celebrity.

Just like Leo.

Just like Louis.

"You don't have to feel guilty about it, Hannah," Christy echoed, then added, "but just don't make us feel bad if we fol-low in your footsteps."

"Just what is that supposed to mean?"

"It means that—well, it means that I'm going to reconsider my stance on Donnie."

Freddy turned from feeding Bette in order to give Christy the once-over.

"Oh? Do tell, darling! Why the sudden change of heart?"

"It's not exactly sudden." She flushed brightly. "I've been reconsidering it for quite some time. Besides, if Hannah can do it—"

"Do what?" I asked exasperatedly. The last thing I wanted was to be blamed for Christy doing something stupid—and getting canned for it. "Fall in love?"

"Yes, exactly—*with a star*—well, then, so can I. That is, if he'd ever leave Bethany." She hit the table in frustration, caus-ing Bette to hide her head behind Freddy. "He's so unhappy with that bitch!"

"Is Donnie trifling with your affections?" asked Sandra worriedly.

"That's just it: *he's not!* I mean, sure, he—well, he's sweet, and kind, and gentle with me. And yes, I'll admit it: he will try to kiss me—"

"*Try?*" Freddy guffawed. "How can he mess *that* up when you play the role of Little Miss Ready Willing and Able to the hilt?"

"Well, Freddy, believe it or not, he's got a conscience!"

"Madame, methinks it is more likely that he's got a smart attorney who's warned him not to fuck up his very, very generous gravy train." Freddy shook his head knowingly. "And I'm sorry, but Bethany's not just a meal ticket: she's the whole Sunday brunch buffet at Polo Lounge. While you, my sweet, are the stale soda crackers from Cantor's Deli. That boy has never been on a diet in his life, and he's not starting now."

"Once I get in front of the camera, he won't have to," she sniffed. "I'll put us both on the map, and then *that* won't be an issue."

I glanced over at Sandra, whose eyes were suddenly rimmed with tears. I patted her wrist. "Sandy, are you feeling okay?"

"It's nothing." She shrugged off my hand. "It's just that when Christy used that term—*putting us both on the map*—it made me think of this creep who's been hanging around Rex lately—"

"Gee," pouted Christy. "Thanks for that! So, now I'm some sort of *creep?*"

"No! Not you . . . this guy, Franklin. He's done a few commercials and he thinks he can act. Rex has been 'mentoring' him. Ha! If you want to call it that. All hours of the night and day. It's just . . . it's just . . . well, it's . . . so weird . . ."

Christy and I decided that now was the best time to scrutinize our silverware. As Sandra sobbed, Freddy put his arm around her.

". . . And *so loud*." She groaned, then buried her head in Freddy's shoulder.

The waitress's arrival with my food gave Sandra time to pull it together while the rest of us collected our thoughts. After a decent interval, Freddy spoke up.

"Honey, it's time you face facts: that closet door of Rex's is not just cracked open, *it's revolving.*"

"Freddy, believe it or not, I hear you loud and clear." She turned to face him. "But I can't just let his career go down in flames! Or *flaming*. He's up for a big important movie part, and he's worried sick about it. I'll just have to do my best to— to keep that boy from distracting him!"

"What does that mean?" I asked. "How can you stop him from being—himself?"

Sandra drilled into me with her large, jade green eyes. "I can do whatever it takes. That's my job, right? You know what I mean by that. You did what you had to do, too, for Louis. Right?"

No, I thought, I didn't do it to save *him*.

I did it to save me.

The party T was throwing for his wife Takiyah's twenty-eighth birthday at their stately 32-room English Tudor mansion in Beverly Hills came just in the nick of time—on the fifth day after what we now formally (albeit euphemistically) called "the Altercation." With Louis's having been granted a cautionary, but certainly clear, bill of health by the doctors, the party gave us the excuse we needed to put on a happy (albeit in Louis's case, slightly bruised) face.

We easily outraced the reporters in Louis's Ferarri F430. However, our euphoria was short-lived as we pulled up to T's place and found another swarm of photographers buzzing around his front gate as well. So that we could slip through without too much interference, Louis honked loudly to get the attention of T's gatekeepers: two former football-players-cum-bodyguards, both of whom were sporting T's plum-hued signature suits with the requisite blue bandana as a pocket square. (Some say that this touch was an homage to his former gang, the Crips, although you wouldn't hear that from T, who, under the guidance of legal counsel, had disassociated himself from these former and most formidable pals.)

The guards scowled at Louis's obvious attempt to jump the line, but seeing who he was—and recognizing him as a frequent visitor to T's palace—they motioned us to drive on through and up to the cul-de-sac that encompassed a large fountain in which ten chubby cherubs danced in a misty spray.

Another hulking sentry then signaled us to get out so that he could park the car.

"Bullshit," said Louis. "Only one ass gets into the driver's seat of this two-hundred-thousand-dollar car, and that's mine."

Despite the giant's stare, Louis didn't flinch. In the meantime, three other cars pulled up behind us. T was watching from the terrace balcony with Ethan, Bennett, Ophelia and Randy. No Mick, of course. Needless to say, after the Altercation, he had been stripped of his Posse membership.

Used to things on his estate running like a finely tuned Swiss watch, T was not at all happy at the reception Louis was receiving from one of his homeboys. He hollered at the guy to leave Louis alone. The big guy shrugged, pointed to a spot on the far side of the fountain, and began yelling obscenities at some poor schmuck who had already parked his car himself without either permission or T's absolution.

T greeted Louis at the door with the kind of bear hug that only a man who had already proven himself in the streets of East South Central could get away with. Randy, Bennett and

Ethan knew better than to hug; they settled for the kind of hand-eye shorthand that signaled to Louis that the party wasn't anywhere near the foyer but in the dark recesses of the house, which was wall-to-wall deep in players, gangstas, slurpees, and the wannabes that fill out any self-respecting celeb's entourage. The five of them then took off for parts unknown, leaving me with Ophelia, whose tiny, delicate foot was encased in a plaster cast, to find common ground.

What would that be? Not her orthopedic surgery, in which the middle toe of her left foot had been shortened with an oscillating saw in order to accommodate her vast shoe collection, which, she informed me, was her most visible trademark.

"The toe might be a little floppy at first, but my doc *swore* I'd be back in stilettos in fourteen days," she said breezily. "Hey, we all have to make sacrifices in life, right?"

I might have nodded in sympathy, but little remarks like that had had me avoiding Ophelia like the plague since our first encounter at the Viper Room, which now seemed like a whole lifetime ago. A lot had changed since then, the biggest thing being that I was no longer Louis's assistant but now his girlfriend.

In other words, I was Ophelia's equal.

Of course, I didn't flaunt that, but boy, did she know it anyway. In fact, the way she practically genuflected to me, you would have thought that I was the queen of some surreal Hollywood homecoming court.

"Eight hundred and sixty-one inches! Isn't that exciting?" Ophelia squeaked loudly above the hip-hop din as we walked—well, she hobbled—through the cavernous rooms of the mansion. She grabbed my arm conspiratorially, then tossed her head in a way that was sure to draw attention to us from the several dozen or so guests milling around us.

"Huh?" I was drawing a blank. What did that number represent? The name of the band that was bombarding us? A new brand of jeans? Some wishful thinking on Ethan's part about the size of his endowment?

"The press you've had this week, silly!" Despite her foot cast, she undulated to the music's beat, and, in the process, ensured a rising quota of admiring glances. "In 'Celebs Ink'! You know, in the ' 'Tab Fab' column on E Online?"

I shook my head, still confused. "I don't read 'Tab Fab.' "

She looked at me as if I were lying or crazy or both. "Well, babe, you better start, if you want to keep your standing. I guess Monique is clipping for you, right?" She put her arm around me, a sure indication to any prying eyes that we were tight buds for sure.

Not.

Clipping gossip articles? About me? I almost laughed out loud. "Monique? Uh, no. At least, I don't think so." Diplomatically, I tried to disentangle myself from her leechlike grasp.

"Then Randy should have a talk with her."

"What? Randy? Why should he talk to Monique about me?"

"He's now rep'ing you, too, right?"

Obviously she and Ethan had been smoking something on the way over. Whatever it was, it was certainly stronger than Wild Lettuce.

"No," I said emphatically. "*Hell*, no."

"Oh, that's funny. I thought he and Louis had worked something out. Hasn't Louis said anything?"

Numbly, I shook my head.

"Well, don't worry. Now that we're BFs, I'll be right there beside you to show you the ropes. In fact, what are you doing tomorrow? Wanna go to the Grove? I'm craving a real spree. . . . Oh, shit! I have a coloring appointment at Canale. Hey, do you want me to see if Michael can fit you in, too? No offense, but some highlights might, you know, warm up your complexion some, you know?"

This parasitic Sunset Slurpee, my "best friend"? Oh yeah, right sure, that was all I needed: to have Ophelia show me the ropes, so that I might become her clone.

Or Sybilla's.

If that was to be the case, the only rope I'd need would be a thick one tied in a hangman's knot.

Which was why my stomach lurched at the thought. As bile crawled quickly up my throat, I choked out an apology and headed toward a door I hoped was a powder room.

Considering the white powder on the tip of the noses of the couple coming out of it, I had guessed right.

"Hey, I know you . . ."

The man now staring at me was waiting patiently for the woman who was upchucking in the enclosed toilet stall to be done with her purging so that they could get back to the party. Having beaten me to the stall, I was left to flush my lunch down the bidet instead, with her boyfriend as my unwilling witness.

Lucky dude. Retching in stereo, no less.

I moved over to the sink so that I could rinse out my mouth. I know I sounded like a fool as I stammered back, "Yeah, uh, hi. Sorry, but I just couldn't wait. When nature calls and all that, ha ha."

He said nothing else but just kept staring at me. Then his eyes moved from my face down to my breast.

That now famous breast, which, for this party (as with all other events I attend, excluding well-publicized trysts in the woods) I'd had the decency to cover up.

And trust me, not every woman at the party could make that

same claim. Least of all the Stare Master's date, whose top was so low-cut that she popped out of it with each new spasm she gave.

If you don't already know this, then believe me when I tell you that fame is a surreal experience. Even having grown up around it, I never truly realized how awful it was to have others stare at you, scrutinizing every inch of your being as if you were an object in a store window. Or a museum.

Or worse yet, the zoo.

I snapped my fingers to get his eyes to move back up to my face. "Hey, shouldn't you be checking in on her to make sure she's okay?"

He shrugged. "She's fine. Happens all the time, right?" He winked at me, as if I should have known better, what with how I had just unloaded my own lunch. Then he pulled a business card from a gold-plated case.

"I'm in development over at the WB. You know, you're *really* hot right now. All celebutantes are. We could build a whole reality series around you, like Paris and Nicole? Whattaya say?"

Celebutante? Me? What, was this dude high or something?

"And since we're cable, no prob at all with, um, nudity, you know?"

His girlfriend gave one last heave, then she flushed.

"Just think about it," he grinned broadly as she reemerged, paler and a pound or two lighter.

He couldn't help but watch vicariously as I took her place in the closet. Had I meant to leave the door open? Yes. Why? To take care of business, in a way: I tore up his card, flushed it, and walked out of the powder room suite with my head held high.

At least it was high until I got out into the hallway—and realized I'd have to confront Louis about what he and Randy were cooking up.

I wandered through the labyrinth of rooms and suites that made up T's castle. He had personally redesigned it, unfortunately without the help of an architect. My hunt moved me through a gauntlet of stares and whispers from the partygoers—actors, agents, songwriters, musicians, record industry producers, all prominent in their own right. Their seemingly nonchalant head turns were a dead giveaway that they recognized me as Louis's new (newest?) arm charm.

Not fun.

Just when I thought I might have to find another bathroom before I could find Louis, I caught a glimpse of him sitting out by the pool with Bennett, Randy, Ophelia and Ethan. Their Insiders Only intimacy created an imaginary 40-foot bubble around them, which allowed others the opportunity to observe them jealously as they laughed and conspired but deterred anyone not already in on the joke from joining in.

Glancing up just at that moment, Louis smiled, winked and waved me over into the bubble. I smiled back, but I wasn't happy. I wanted to leave so that we could have the conversation in private, but I knew I'd never get Louis to agree to go home yet. So instead I steeled myself to grin and bear it for now. When we were home, just the two of us, away from Randy and all of this glam and glitter garbage, we'd talk about it.

Then we'd cuddle. Or better yet, we'd make love.

"We were just talking about you," Louis said as he wrapped his arms around me. "Randy is trying to convince me that you may someday be a bigger force in Hollywood than me." He chuckled at the thought. "Well, certainly bigger than him. Right Randy?"

Randy winced. "Sure, whatever. Another Paris maybe. But your boyfriend here wants to keep you in your place. He doesn't believe me when I tell him that you're a brand, now, too."

"Don't tease the poor girl, Randy," Louis retorted. Ever so gently, he tightened his grip on me. Suddenly I found it hard to breathe. I took a few quick gulps of the L.A. night smog and glanced skyward. Only a few stars were twinkling through it. "Hannah doesn't have an ego of any sort. Why, she could care less about all of this celebrity crap! You live to be at my beck and call, right, love?" He stroked my arm with his finger.

Ego, me? Of course not. You're right: I couldn't care less.
Sort of.

And as for being at your beck and call—yeah, right. That's how I envision spending the rest of my life: forgetting my own dreams.

Somewhere to the left of Saturn, a star flickered.

My star?

I sighed. Later, when we were alone together, I would convince Louis that it was important that I continue my work.

For us. *For me.*

"Hey look, guy, I'm just as shocked as you are about it. But Monique tells me that the phone is ringing off the hook about you. *And* her." Randy nodded toward me. "They want to know everything: about her life as Leo's little girl, what she wears, where she eats, how she was able to wangle you away from Tatiana . . . Hey, what have we got to lose? If it keeps you in the limelight, I say the more the merrier." He leered at me. "You wouldn't mind that, would you, hon?"

I looked down into T's pool. He had it filled with gigantic golden koi fish. They were all swimming in different directions, chasing each others' tails.

Ophelia piped up with a pout. "Well, I, for one, don't see how it would hurt, Louis. It didn't hurt Tom and Nicole. Oops! Okay, well, they're not a good example. What about Brad and Jen—oh . . . duh, sorry. My bad! You've got to admit, it has *helped* Madonna and Guy. And Ethan and I love being a power couple, don't we, honey?"

She glanced at him for encouragement. He nodded uncertainly.

Looking into the pool, I noticed that some of the fishes' tails had been eaten off.

By other fishes. *Scary.*

"I don't know. I mean, I really don't think our relationship is anyone's business! And besides, supervising Louis's career takes up all my time. And that's the real priority here."

"So get some help, silly!" laughed Ophelia. "You can hire a PA and then delegate some of the grunt stuff, right? Heck, even *I* have a PA. I had to get one because Ethan was getting too much hate mail about me. Can you believe it? His fans like to blame *me* when they don't like his movies. So now my PA burns all the stuff that gets us both so upset." She tossed her head so that her tresses danced in the breeze, surely a crowd pleaser for those watching from outside the bubble.

"Hey, there you go!" seconded Randy. "If you want, I'll even help you screen the prospective candidates." He grinned slyly at the thought.

"Thanks, but no thanks," I said coolly.

"I don't know, Hannah. That might not be such a bad idea," Louis put in. I turned to him, incredulous that he'd go along with the concept. He smiled sweetly. "Love, look, I'll admit it. Sometimes I ask too much of you. And I know that I've been wearing you out lately."

I felt the palm of his hand move down the small of my back. It stopped just above a belt loop of my low-cut jeans. He massaged my hip suggestively. "Besides, if you're out running errands, then who is going to stay at my side and look after me?"

Translation: Between all the running down into town, and the phone negotiations, and the studio meetings—not to mention being on the set whenever Louis was—I had been falling asleep too often when he wanted sex.

And now, with the requests flowing in to be the newest power couple on the party circuit, I'd have to make some hard choices:

Was I his PA or his girlfriend?

I got the message loud and clear.

"Okay, Louis. If that's what you really want. I'll start interviewing on Monday."

"Good. Then after the postproduction on *Killer Instincts* maybe you and I can get away. You know, take a long vacation, go somewhere there's a deserted beach . . ."

Funny how familiar that all sounded.

"Yeah, well, you'll have plenty of time to do that, now that *Mind Bender* is off your calendar," said Ethan offhandedly.

Louis's touch went cold. "What? What do you mean?"

Ethan froze as the realization that he was breaking bad news suddenly dawned on him. Randy blinked twice, indicating his own knowledge of this. Ophelia, although totally in the dark, caught the subtle change in temperature around the pool and shivered.

"Um, well . . . well, I just happened to be over at Paramount the other day, and the guy I deal with in development let it slip that Mick made the deal—"

I barely contained my gasp. Whenever Louis and Mick had gotten together, they had talked nonstop about that project. Mick had written it with Louis in mind. And, despite having been asked by several other A-listers to see the script when it was finished, Mick had been too loyal to show it to any of them. After the fight, however, Louis had naively (or egotistically) assumed that Mick would just shelve the script. Besides, Louis had reasoned, Mick would never have been able to find a producer to finance it, what with the 140-plus-million-dollar budget it needed to do it justice.

Louis was silent. Then he added, *"Without my permission?"*

"Well, Randy never formally optioned a first look deal for you, right? And you and Mick haven't actually been talking since . . . since—"

"Paramount, eh? Well, they won't put any real money behind it, not without any star power already attached. It'll die of natural causes. So what else did he say?"

Ethan, looking uncomfortable, mumbled, "Just that Mick came with Cruise, who's coproducing. The studio's slating it for Memorial Day weekend, the year after next."

Cruise's name was all that was needed to put a deal over the top.

Randy, Bennett, Ethan and Ophelia exchanged glances, waiting to see how Louis would respond. He didn't say another word. He just walked to the edge of the terrace and stood there, staring up into the inky sky overhead.

"Getting late," grunted Bennett. Ethan nodded. Ophelia scooped up her Prada Venice print bag and Hermes scarf from the teakwood settee and hobbled after the guys, who were already scurrying back into the house without saying goodnight.

Why should they? Louis wouldn't hear them, let alone respond.

I didn't know what to say, or do, either, but I walked over to him.

Louis felt my presence behind him, but he didn't turn around.

Instead, he simply said, "This is *your* fault, you know."

Part Three

Resolution

*The amount of small detail visible in an image
(usually telescopic);
low resolution shows only large features,
while high resolution shows many small details.*

14

Absolute Magnitude

If all stars were placed at the same distance, then their apparent magnitudes would only be dependent on their luminosities. Thus, absolute magnitudes are true indicators of the amount of light each star emits.

In the world of celebritydom, I had arrived.

The proof was in black and white, and read all over the world.

Vogue put me on its cover. To indicate that I played muse to the men in my life, I was photographed by Steven Meisel in a sheer, frothy, ethereal concoction by Christian Dior, with hair extensions cascading down my back in ringlets, making me the über-Boticelli goddess. When Freddy heard about that, he laughed and said, "You're more like a conscience, or better yet, a pain in the neck!"

On the other hand, Louis's reaction was a pout. By the way he carried on about *Vogue*'s policy to use only women on the cover, I could tell he was more upset that he couldn't be there than the fact that I was. *I think.*

According to the *National Enquirer*, I demanded that Louis dress up in Leo's old clothes so that I could sit on his lap and call him "Daddy." (For the record: *Not*. I mean, come on already! I never even called Leo "Daddy.") Oh, and by the way, the *Enquirer* also clamed that Louis put up with this because he thought doing so would help him beat Leo's Oscar wins. (For the record, two.)

InStyle gushed over our "love lair," which, it declared, "is decked out like a Moroccan sultan's harem, accommodating both her obsession for richly-hued sensual fabrics—velvets, damasks and silks—and his fondness for pleasuring playthings . . ." (Correction: the stylist Monique hired to decorate the bedroom prior to the photo shoot had much better taste than I could ever claim; and unfortunately, we didn't have time to hide Louis's treasure box of sex toys before the editor and photographer got to the house.)

The Globe insisted that Louis and I were into hot sex with little woodland creatures. (A retraction was requested. What we got instead was a reprint of that photo of Louis touching my naked breast—but this time the shot was widened to show that a couple of owls had been watching from a tree branch. The retraction's headline: "Louis and Hannah's Kinky Wild Kingdom!")

Life & Style Weekly made us number two on their list of "Most Beautiful Couples." For that photo, the photographer suggested that we re-enact the bare-breast-in-woods shot. Louis was up for that, but it was only after I threatened to walk off the set that the photographer agreed to drop the idea. The compromise: Yes, we were photographed in the woods. No, I was not naked. And to put your mind at ease, no woodland creatures were harmed in the making of the photo, let alone were there animals anywhere *near* any vulnerable body parts.)

And *Page Six* intimated that I was pregnant with Louis's child.

That was wrong, too.

Sort of.

You see, what happened was this: My period was six miserably wretched days late. And so, for six long, sleepless nights, while Louis snored beside me as contentedly as a newborn babe, I'd wake up awash in sweat and ask myself why I was so terrified at the thought of being pregnant with Louis's child.

Didn't I think we'd make beautiful babies? Yes, yes, of course I did!

Didn't I know I'd make a wonderful mother? Totally! Why, I'd be June Cleaver, Carol Brady and Lorilei Gilmore all wrapped into one. My impishly adorable child would always know love, inspiration and security . . . and happiness.

Didn't I think Louis would make a great dad? Yes . . . eventually . . . because he certainly did not want to make the same mistakes his father had made with him.

Didn't I think Louis would be happy to hear I was pregnant?

That was the question that made the sweat bead up on my forehead and a cold chill crawl up my spine.

And then I'd throw up.

Bad sign.

By that sixth night I couldn't stand it any more. Sure, I could wait for the morning, then go see my gynecologist—and read about my visit the next week in the *Star*. Instead, at two o'clock in the morning, I got out of bed quietly, so as not to wake Louis, shoved a baseball cap on my head, and ran into the Savon Pharmacy on Wilshire to pick up a home pregnancy test.

I was naive enough to assume that no one else would be in the store. Or, if someone was there, that he or she wouldn't recognize me anyway.

Well, someone was, and that someone did. *Page Six* got its scoop the next day.

To my immense relief, however, the pregnancy test showed me that I was due a retraction.

Within a few days, my bleeding finally started.

"Bollocks, you're on the rag? *Again?* Weren't you just on it last week?" asked the ever oblivious Louis. "I think you're just creating an excuse to avoid making love."

"Louis, we make love every night! Come hell or high water. No matter what my mood, or even if I'm, you know, bleeding." Or cramping. Or bloated.

Or feeling used.

I could not turn my head quick enough. He saw my grimace and matched it with his own.

"Complaining, love?" His eyes narrowed. "Well, if you're so bloody worn out, then maybe you'll finally find a PA that meets your high standards. Because if you haven't figured it out already, Priority Number One is making me happy."

He flopped down on the bed and flicked on the flat-screen TV with the remote. "Or better yet, maybe you need to lower your standards, because heaven knows my libido isn't going anywhere. And we both know you wouldn't accept the alternative."

"The alternative?" I felt my heart jump into my throat. "What does that mean, exactly? Are you asking my permission to go to bed with other women?"

He was silent. Then he said, "Of course not. Don't be so melodramatic."

We both knew that the only reason he wasn't asking had nothing to do with whether or not he felt he needed my permission in the first place.

Needless to say, neither of us enjoyed our lovemaking that night.

In truth, we hadn't had great sex since the Altercation. In fact,

Louis had been distant—both emotionally and physically—since the night he'd found out about *Mind Bender*.

Even the Hollywood Foreign Press Association's formal announcement that he was a first-time Golden Globe nominee for best actor in a dramatic movie for his performance in *Dead End* did not change his mood—most certainly because, a few moments later, it was also announced that Mick had been nominated as well for the movie's screenplay.

I cannot honestly say that we made love the night of the nominations.

Not unless you can call a marathon of raw copulation devoid of any tenderness whatsoever making love.

I know, on that night, *I* couldn't.

To make the most of Louis's nomination, we hit every must-see party and red carpet event on Hollywood's celebrity circuit.

Yes, we were at the Tisch School of the Arts West Coast Gala and Madonna's "Heavenly Bodies" album release party.

And there was no way we'd miss either Puffy's annual Bad-Ass Bowling Party or MTV's *Holiday Hip-Hop in the Hollywood Bowl* Christmas special.

And, on the same night, we breezed into both the *Vanity Fair* Celebrity Pajama Party and the premiere of Bennett Fielding's between-seasons project, *Dude, Where's My Karma?* in which he picked up that very dated, very tired franchise in the hopes of following Ashton's flat-footed missteps onto the silver screen.

Would this, Bennett's third movie outing, be the charm? From the number of people who snuck out before the credit roll, that was doubtful. The word on the street was that ABC was going to cancel Bennett's show in January, and I'm sure that's what compelled Bennett to get downright sloppy drunk at the after-party at Forbidden City.

Louis, pissed that his friendship with Bennett obligated him to be there, and doubly pissed that neither Ethan nor T felt likewise duty-bound, was not in the greatest of moods when a photographer had the audacity to ask me to turn toward him in order to get a shot of me in my Elie Saab frock, one of the many freebees that had been proffered to me during this see-and-be-seen marathon we were running.

Gritting his teeth, Louis murmured to me, "Don't bother. He's just being polite." And headed on.

Oh, is that so?

Louis's rudeness—or was it jealousy?—left me angry.

And ready to prove him wrong.

I'll be the first to admit that I am no supermodel. However, I've been around enough star power to know how to turn on the heat.

To ensure that the photographer got more than he asked for, I was provocative. I was captivating. I was hotter than New Orleans in July.

And so was Louis, when he reached the front door of the restaurant and realized that I was not in my usual place: at his side.

He turned back around, stormed up to the photographer, seized his camera and tossed it up against the wall. Then he grabbed my arm and yanked me along.

The photographer yelled after us, "Hey, Hannah, admit it! Louis is a letdown after growing up around someone with real talent like Leo, right?"

Louis turned back around, ready to beat the man to a bloody pulp. I grasped him by the wrist and pulled him inside the restaurant. Thank God the retro techno/rave music was pulsating so loud that Louis's rant could only be heard by me.

"Fucking let me go, Hannah! I *mean* it!"

"Don't—don't lower yourself, Louis! He doesn't know what he's talking about!"

Louis took a couple of quick breaths to calm down. He nodded to indicate that he wouldn't go back out, but his eyes were blazing.

"He's full of shit, you know."

"I know, Louis. I know."

"That's good." Looking into the mirrored tiles on the wall, he straightened his shirt and jacket. "Because I'd feel like bloody hell if my own girlfriend didn't believe in my talent. But of course you do." Catching my eye through his reflection, he added, "You *do* believe I'm more talented than Leo was, right? You even admitted that, to Barnaby, remember?"

He waited for my response. I hesitated.

Too long.

During that time, his eyes never left mine. At the same time, as the seconds ticked past, his own expression registered each emotion in the order he felt it: assurance; surprise; disappointment; hurt; and finally distrust.

"No, Louis, Barnaby never said that Leo didn't have talent. He said that Leo *wasted* the talent he had, and I agreed. . . ."

Either Louis did not hear my answer above the restaurant's raucous din, or he didn't care to hear what I had to say. In either case, he made his way to the VIP room without me.

That night, for the first time since the day we opened up to each other at the Marial Lodge, I caught Louis flirting.

When I confronted him, he laughed and called me paranoid.

I called him a liar and told him that I would never put up with it.

He called my bluff.

"You're imagining things, love! Oh, alright, I *may* have given that waitress a little love tap on the bum, but I did *not* exchange phone numbers with the girl. If you don't believe me, go ask her yourself. . . . If you do, though, you'll be embarrassing me, so don't bother to come back here. Things will be *over* between us. . . . That's a good girl, stay put before you make a fool of yourself."

Had I been making a fool of myself? Had I been kidding myself that Louis could love me, and just me alone?

According to Leo—who made a cameo in my dreams later that night—I was being hoodwinked.

"Jeez, Hannah, didn't I teach you anything? This is the kind of guy who will always be tempted by other women."

In my dream, Leo and I were sitting poolside at Lion's Den. He was wrapped in one of the many pale blue plush bathrobes that were usually found hanging in the cabana. For some strange reason, he was practicing his putting with my telescope. I found that even more irritating than his accusation.

"But I was there for him when he needed me most! We have that bond! Doesn't that count for anything?" I shielded my eyes from the glow emanating from Leo.

"Maybe it did . . . once. A woman like you always brings out the best in guys like us, for a month or two, anyway. And, if we're lucky, then maybe even a couple of years. But that's a mighty big maybe. . . . Look, sweetheart, I hate to break it to you this way, but unfortunately for men like Louis and me, the rest of whatever is happening in our lives brings out the worst in us."

What he was saying sounded so familiar. *Where had I heard that before?*

"Well, I think you're wrong, Leo."

Looking beyond the pool, he sighted a spot somewhere out

in the dreamy infinity, then took careful aim with the telescope.

"Hannah, honey, I know it would be easier to just go on believing whatever you'd like. I mean, most women do, God
knows why. They hang in there under the assumption that the
guy will change, or that they can reform him. Then they get
upset when he doesn't. And that gets them inconsolable, which
makes them appear pathetic to us. Why, I remember once,
when your mom caught me in bed with a waitress from
Chasen's, she was so upset that she had me exorcised by an In-
can shaman. Talk about desperation!"

"But he told me he loved me! Now you're telling me that it's
already over between us? So, what am I supposed to do, just
walk away?"

"Before I answer that, let me ask you this: why are you in
this relationship in the first place? Is it because you truly love
him and want to save him from himself? Or are you trying to
make up for not having been able to save *me?*"

I teared up. "Sure, I'll admit it: I will always regret the fact
that I couldn't have done more for you. As for loving Louis,
well of course I love him. And yes, I feel I can save him. I'd be
a fool not to try."

"Darling, if that's the case, then let me be the first to tell you
that you are a fool if that's what you think, because you can't.
No way, no how. Only Louis can save himself."

That said, Leo busied himself with setting up his next shot.

This was it? This was his sage advice? Here I was, desperate
for his help, for his insider's tips on how to get Louis to love
me forever—and all he could do was tell me that I was wasting
my time?

So then why had he shown up in my dream, anyway?

And, for that matter, why was he ruining my telescope?

"You know, Leo, I wish you wouldn't do that! It's not exactly a toy. It cost over four thousand dollars!"

He stopped mid-swing. "What do you care? You've quit using it, anyway."

He had a point there.

I'm sure that's why I woke up crying.

15

Out of Orbit

*Orbit: The path of one body around another
due to the influence of gravity.*

"That is *sooo* mack, dontcha think?"

If anyone knew what was mack, it was certainly the
seventeen-year-old behind the counter of that little hole-in-
the-wall boutique on Melrose, what with her butterfly tattoos,
sterling silver piercings, and wafer-thin body swathed in sheer
chiffon over barely there denim.

The object of her admiration was the dress I was trying on:
a simple floor-length aquamarine sheath held aloft by a chain
of tiny smooth turquoise stones running from one shoulder
and crisscrossing the gown's open back.

It was definitely beautiful. And I should have known, since
I'd spent the past two weeks going to fashion designers' trunk
shows and to personal appointments at their ateliers, to find
just the right gown for the Golden Globes.

Was this the one? Because I would have to look perfect, for
Louis. *For us.*

I never wanted him to regret leaving the perfect Tatiana. *For me.*

"Who's the designer?" I asked as I reached around the back and tried to read the tag upside down. "It says . . . Axis of Evil? That's an odd name. Could that be right?"

"Dunno. *Could* be. Like, see, most of our designers are anarchists who work outside the typical capitalist system. They'd rather create just one beautiful perfect something, not make a bundle off the backs of third world slave labor. That's why stuff flies out of here so fast. You snooze, you lose."

Having made a truly heartfelt political statement and perfect sales pitch, my little socialist shopgirl went back to reading the latest by Sedaris.

I hesitated just a second before looking back into the mirror. She was right. The gown was gorgeous.

In fact, in it, I *was* mack.

Besides, I could always hedge my bets with another gown. Or two. Or three.

I was finally beginning to enjoy the fringe benefits of dating a Hollywood heavyweight.

"I'll take it," I said, as my cell phone chirped. Carefully, so as not to tear the web-thin gossamer strand holding the bodice aloft, I rummaged in my purse until I found the culprit that was keeping the salesgirl from enjoying the darkness of Dave.

It was Freddy, calling to remind me that the Gang was getting together that evening at the Sunset Room to celebrate Christy's first day (or in this case, night) as an actress on a bona fide movie set—if you could call any endeavor involving Donnie Beaudry bona fide. True, the Sunset Room was a bit pricey. But because the restaurant had numerous celebrity investors, it was Christy's contention that partaking in a White Russian and a Caesar salad at the trendy locale might bring her good luck.

Unfortunately, the date had somehow slipped my mind. I groaned so loud that the kid actually looked up from her book.

"Damn—damn it, Freddy! I . . . well, I just can't be there tonight! I'm—gee, you see, I have something that I just can't cancel."

"Do tell." Freddy sounded unperturbed, but I knew better.

He was upset that I was blowing them off.

Again.

"I know it may not sound so important, but I've got one last private trunk show to go to, for Dolce and Gabbana. I mean, I still haven't made a final decision about what I'm going to wear to the Globes! I'm so sorry, but it will look really bad if I don't show up there, after Monique cleared it and all. Please tell Christy I'm sorry, and that I'll make it up to her somehow. I promise."

Shop Girl snickered and shook her head. Whatever panache I had gained by recognizing true cutting edge genius in this hovel on Melrose, I had lost through the mere mention of the couture team revered by arm charms everywhere.

"Oh, I'm *sure* you will make it up to her," Freddy leered. "Your friendship is turning out to be priceless."

Of course, Freddy's jibe hurt. In his defense, though, since Louis and I had become an item, I had pulled a few no-shows on the Gang. And the few times I had made an appearance, I'd either come in too late to join in on the fun, or I'd had to leave early for some other event.

Granted, I had tried to make it up to Sandy, Freddy and Christy by bringing along some sort of a "forgive me" trinket or two. The last time I'd done this, Sandy had seemed somewhat upset with me.

"You don't have to feel as if you have to buy our forgiveness with a consolation prize, Hannah," she sniffed. "We're your friends out of respect and love, not obligation."

Now Freddy was questioning whether I felt the same way.

I wanted desperately for him to know that I did. "You know, Freddy, that hurt. I can't feel any guiltier than I already do about this thing tonight! Okay? I mean, really! Do you think I enjoy all of this bullshit?"

"Since you're asking my opinion, then, yes, Hannah, I do. So, why don't you just admit it to yourself?"

I didn't answer quickly, because he had a point. I *was* enjoying the attention, beyond how it tied me irrevocably to Louis. And I was enjoying it because finally, for the first time in my life, people were paying attention to *me*.

"Tell me the truth," I asked quietly. "Am I a bad person for—well, for liking it?"

Silence.

Then he answered, "No, sweetums, you're not. Any one of us would be gaga over all of that adoration. But if you let it consume you, if you become stupid over it, then you'll become *one of them*."

"What do you mean? A celebrity?"

He laughed as only Freddy could: caustically, sympathetically, and soulfully all at once. "You wish! No, my dear sweet Hannah, celebrities have talent for something, even if it's only for staying in the spotlight. You'd be something worse."

"You mean—a *Sunset Slurpee?*"

"There you go. By the way, how's your supply of Altoids holding up?"

Without saying another word, I hung up the phone.

I was hurt when I read, in Ted Casablanca's column in E!Online, that I was considered "that sublimely tarty Mr. Trollope's delectable dragon lady. Studio wonks cringe when their assistants inform them that she's on the line. Her demands, made ostensibly on Louis-poo's behalf, are too outlandish even for the LaLa Land moguls who have seen and heard it all before. The most recent request, reflecting said b-f's Golden Globe nomination glow, was for the use of Vatican Studios's very own private plane for a weekend jaunt over the pond—just in time to make Stella McCartney's fashion show, in order to pick up that perfect Globe-worthy gown. . . ."

Wrong! That was so wrong! And I thought I had a good rapport with Ted! If he had called me directly, I would have told him that I already had my gown and that Louis had already been promised the jet in order to attend the London premiere of the *Rebecca* remake.

Louis was almost cavalier about my being raked over the coals.

"Love, you can't go through life afraid to ruffle some feathers just because it might get you a few lines of negative ink."

"That's easy for you to say! I'm the one coming off like the bitch from hell, not you."

"I thought you enjoyed running interference for me. Well, you can't have it both ways: running my life *and* being liked for doing so by those who live to take advantage of me. And as my very public girlfriend, they can take potshots at you out in the open."

As a concession, he brushed his cold lips on my forehead. "Look, darling, I can just imagine you've had a horrendous day. I hate those bullies a Vatican, too. You know that! Which, my dearest, is why I truly do appreciate you holding firm on my request for the jet. And hell, with all the box office I've made for him, you'd think that he would at least have the decency to send me a couple of tickets to a bloody Manchester game while I'm there, wouldn't you?"

As he was walking out the door, he added breezily, "And, oh, by the way, don't feel obligated to tag along. Bad timing, this premiere, coming just a few days before the Globes. You might as well stay and finalize your dress and all, right? In fact, why don't you tag along with Ophelia? She knows the ins and outs for that kind of thing. Don't worry, the studio will send someone from publicity to babysit me. Genevieve will fill them in on my routine."

Not going with Louis meant that we would be apart for the first time since Oregon.

Not going with Louis meant that he didn't want me along.

As for Louis's routine: Did that mean he was back to having "massages" in his hotel room?

In the week prior to his departure to London, I lay sleepless beside Louis.

Sleeping meant visits from Leo, visits in which I was told what I didn't want to hear:

That I was losing Louis.

Then again, staying awake meant fretting over how, why and when that would actually happen.

What had I done wrong? Why was Louis growing tired of me? Couldn't I stop it from happening?

Or was it inevitable?

Mulling over these questions was why I couldn't sleep. And why dark circles were forming under my eyes. And why I was losing weight.

Great for trying on gowns, bad for my self-esteem.

Up until the day Louis left, we were in a holding pattern: by day, I'd fight his battles with all the various forces within the town that pulled at him. At night, after we'd attend yet one more star-studded event, I'd battle my suspicions that he was leaving me, as well as my desire to fall asleep.

On the morning before Louis's departure, he woke up to find me staring down at him.

"That's some bloody look, love. You're giving me the willies! Had a nightmare or something?"

"Or something," I answered hollowly. "I dream about Leo now. All the time."

"Damn!" He laughed. "So, now I'm sharing my bed with him, too?"

"What's that supposed to mean?"

"Nothing. Nothing at all." Louis was no longer smiling. He ran his hand through his hair, yawned and stretched. The sheet fell to one side, revealing his omnipresent hard-on. He smiled as I glanced up. "Well now, since we're both up—"

"You have to be at Lion's Gate in an hour. The Brownstein project, remember?"

"Damn! How did you let me get roped into that one?"

"You insisted, remember?" Since there had been—as Ethan had so eloquently put it—a hole in Louis's schedule with *Mind Bender* going to the wayside, Louis had chosen to fill it with something different. Independent. Edgy. And with a low enough budget—except for his salary, of course—to get it quickly greenlighted.

Besides, it sure beat hanging out on a deserted island with me.

"Saved by the bell, eh?" He rose up from the bed. "You're beginning to look like a raccoon. Very unbecoming. I think you should see Dr. Manny."

"Ha ha. I don't think so."

"Why? Are you enjoying Leo's visits too much?"

"I didn't say that."

"For once, Hannah, I think you should let me take care of you. You never allow me to act on that primal male urge."

Louis wanted to take care of *me*? It had been weeks since I'd ever thought I'd feel that was possible.

"Go to Dr. Manny. Do it for me. For us."

For us.

"Okay, Louis. I'll go, if it will make you feel better."

"Trust me on this one. He'll have you feeling like a new woman. And right now, I wouldn't mind a new woman."

I'll just bet you wouldn't.

During the three days that Louis was in London, I made a visit to Dr. Manolo Lipschitz, as promised.

While I gave him the rundown on myself in extreme detail as per his instructions, he listened intently, his hands clasped over his eyes and his chair angled away from me, toward the window behind him.

At least, I thought he was listening. Until I heard him snoring.

I almost snuck out, when he woke abruptly. "The session is not over yet," he said unsteadily. "Did I doze off?"

"I'll say."

"No reason to be sarcastic. I had—a late-night session, with Hef and some of the girls, at the Playboy Mansion." He tried hard not to smile at the memory. "A couple of the ladies are having jealousy issues."

"Gee, I don't know why."

He gave me a sharp glance.

"You know, Hannah, from what you've said, you may share some of their symptoms."

"As long as that's all we're sharing."

"So, what you're saying is that you'd find it hard to share Louis?"

"I do share Louis. With the world. He's a star, remember?"

"I mean intimately, with another woman."

What, was he kidding?

"Dr. Manny, I think you'd agree with me that most women would have a problem with that."

"But you're not most women, are you? You're your father's daughter, so you understand better than most women. And Louis certainly isn't most men."

"Granted, you're right on both those counts. But still, I don't see why that should mean carte blanche to—"

"Hannah, admit it: You and Louis need to take sex to a new level. It is no longer fresh, spontaneous. Am I right?"

"Well, yes and no. I mean, it's certainly frequent."

"I'm not talking quantity. I'm talking *quality*."

Ah, yes. When all else fails, there is always that cliché.

"So, what exactly are you proposing, Dr. Manny?"

"Nothing so drastic as you might think. I could suggest a sex surrogate—"

I'll just bet you could. Which Bunny wouldn't be willing to work that *trade?*

"—but I don't feel that a surrogate would be necessary—for now, anyway. Of course, there is only one way to know for sure."

He leaned forward in anticipation. A bit of spittle formed at the side of his very thick lips. "For now, I'd suggest that you videotape your lovemaking. Nothing so cinema verité as a handheld camera. Just a simple tripod setup."

Do tell.

"Enlighten me, Doctor. What do you anticipate doing with these tapes?"

His glasses fogged up at the thought. "Well, of course, I'd examine them. In that manner, I can better assess the issues that are blocking your mutual happiness."

Oh, yeah? And who else would be "examining" them? The boys in the grotto, during movie night at the Playboy Mansion?

I don't think so. "Neither Louis nor I would agree to something like that."

At that declaration, Dr. Manny beamed knowingly. "In fact, Louis is very open with the concept. *Very* open indeed."

"I beg your pardon? You've already asked him about this, even before this session?"

"Well—yes. Why, we discussed it prior to his leaving. You know, Louis and I have a long history as patient and doctor. We discuss *everything*." A bit of drool gave away the underlying meaning of his remark. "But you already knew that, didn't you?"

Not until now.

I told Dr. Manny I would think about it.

Instead, I thought about all the other poor, foolish saps who'd fallen for his line.

And all the celebrity porn he must be distributing, for a mint.

I prayed that none starring Louis would surface.

As for me, well, I'd already had *my* money shot, and once was enough.

Louis came home from London the day before the Golden Globes. He was a happy boy. I assumed that seeing his friends and family had been a soothing tonic.

I hoped that was *all* that was making him smile.

He did not ask me how it had gone with Dr. Manny. My guess was that he had already been given a full report, straight from the quack's mouth.

My visit to Dr. Manny taught me something, however—to pretend to be asleep, even if I couldn't doze off.

That mission was stymied the very night of Leo's return, with a single phone call, at two in the morning, from Christy.

"I just ran off the set! I—I've been . . ." Christy, sobbing uncontrollably, couldn't finish her sentence.

"Calm down, and tell me what happened exactly!"

I was whispering so as not to wake Louis. The last thing I

needed was for him to be grumpy and upset before the preparations for the next day's event.

"Everything was fine—at first. You know, we were getting only a few pages of script at a time, because apparently they were always changing the plot, or something, I guess. At least, that's what they told me."

"Christy, get to the point."

"I am! You see, last night they didn't give me any portion of the script to read. They said it wasn't written yet." She gulped down her sobs. "Okay, I thought, no prob. I'll just improv when I get on the set. So, when I get here, Donnie comes up to me with these two actors who are starring with me. He tells me how beautiful I am, and how blown away they both are with—with my skills, and he says that he still needed to cover some of the financing—"

"You mean to tell me he hasn't gotten all the financing yet? What is he, an idiot?"

"No. I mean, well, *maybe*. I don't know! But that's not the point! What I'm getting at is that—that they wanted me to be *nude*."

"And you said no?"

"Not exactly. I said okay—that I was okay with nudity. But that was *it*."

I let that sink in. "Then what?"

"Then Donnie said, 'Well, you're supposed to have sex, too. With the guys.'"

"Both of them?"

"I know! *I know!* I kind of freaked out, too, when he said that! I'm thinking, 'What will my folks think?' You know?"

"Yeah, hon, I know. So, what did you say?"

"I said no. At first."

At first.

"But then he started to tear up. Said it would ruin him if I didn't go through with it. Said he'd lose everything. He begged me, Hannah! Said he always felt he could count on me! What else could I do?"

I said nothing. It all sounded so familiar.

"So I said okay. But just—just one guy."

"Oh."

"Well, it wasn't 'just one guy.' Donnie—he was standing on the set, sort of coaching me, you know?—well, there I was with the first guy. We're, like, standing up, doing it. And then I feel something—someone—*behind* me. And it's the second guy! So I'm like, 'What the hell is this?' And boy, is he rough! I've never done it that way, with two guys . . . and you know . . . *anal.*"

She whispered the word. "So I start screaming, and I can see Donnie and he's giving me the thumbs-up! As if it's all an act or something! Only it was real! The guy—that creep—*violated* me! And—and Donnie didn't do a fucking thing!"

She broke down again. This time it took her a full five minutes to come back onto the line. "I'm bleeding! And I hurt all over. I've never been this sore! Please, Hannah, please! Can you come get me? I grabbed my clothes and ran to an all-night diner. On the corner of Roscoe and Canoga. Please say yes!"

Picking her up meant driving almost an hour and a half, round trip to Chatsworth and back, tonight of all nights.

I didn't want to say yes to Christy, but I had no choice. I was her friend.

"Okay. I'll be right there." I rose, stepped into my jeans, and carried my sneakers with me as I crept to the door. I had almost made it when Louis flicked on the light.

"Where are you going at this hour?"

He sounded suspicious. Great, just what I needed, on the eve of the Golden Globes. He was already as wired as a cat about whether he would win.

"That was Christy. It's an emergency. She's stranded, and she needs me to pick her up in Chatsworth."

"Donnie's PA, right? The one with the big tits?"

"Yep, that's Christy." I sat down on the bed to put on my sneakers.

"Why can't one of those other people go get her?"

"Louis, it's too late now. She called me. I *have* to go."

Louis chuckled. "Chatsworth? So, old Donnie's backing porno films, eh? Who would have thought that?" He paused, then added, "And this friend of yours is starring in it? The rest of her must not be so bad either, eh?"

Obviously on that last day on the set of *Breakneck*, Louis had been so enamored by her breasts that he'd forgotten to check out the rest of her.

"I really hadn't noticed," I retorted. "She's not my type."

"That's too bad. Then again, three-ways aren't all that they're cracked up to be, particularly if the two girls get so carried away that they forget about *me*."

I couldn't help staring at him. Here was my chance to ask the one question I'd always wanted him to answer:

"What about when it's two guys and a girl? Is that more fun? You know, having a buddy there, to share?"

He quit smiling and turned to the other side of the bed.

"Poor kid. I guess she'll be leaving Donnie and Bethany after this fiasco . . . Hey, you still haven't hired anyone for your PA, right? Why not your little friend?"

If he had been facing me, he could have watched the blood drain from my face. As it was, he could only hear my anger, although I didn't shout. In fact I whispered. "Oh, I don't think Christy is going to want another PA position anytime soon. Samantha didn't get back into it so quickly, did she?"

I left him with that.

So Leo was right after all.

16

Retrograde

Rotation of a planet, or orbit, opposite to that normally seen.

Next to the sun, the brightest star in our sky is Venus.

In fact, if you happen to glance up at the sky at dawn, you'll notice that, despite the sun's growing glow, only Venus is still visible to the eye. Like two lovers, they cuddle closely, so closely that it is easy to envision them as lifelong partners, floating through the cosmos together for eternity.

Having effectively walked away from my planet-tracking project, I took consolation in the premise that Louis and I were the human equivalents of the sun and Venus; that our pairing would last a lifetime.

For this union, I had given up my late-night planet search around Mic.

And I had also given up Mick.

Regrettably, one I could never get back. The other, however, was still within my reach.

It was dawn when Christy and I finally left the emergency room, where she had a full rape kit and HIV tests performed. I brought her back to my cottage on the Venice Canal, where I made her some tea, tucked her into my bed, and suggested that she stay as long as it would take for her to find a job to replace her old one with Donnie and Bethany and to get a place of her own.

She was so relieved that she burst into tears. "I've been such an idiot! I guess I thought that being close to the two of them would give me my big break. Now I know that all I did was waste the last year of my life."

"We all do stupid things. Your goal now is to move on and never make the same mistakes again."

Ha ha. Like falling for some guy who is just like Dear Old Dad.

No, I reasoned desperately. Louis was *not* Leo. We were good together. We loved each other and trusted each other and . . .

. . . and I was the one person he could never live without.

At least, that's what Louis had said.

It seemed like an eternity ago.

I made up my mind that, as soon as possible, I'd find Louis the PA he needed so that I could be where I was supposed to be—by his side.

That is, as long as we both felt I belonged there.

And most definitely, I would do everything I possibly could to ensure that this was the case.

Just as significantly, though, I would also make time in my life for all the things that were important to me. Otherwise, I'd be living my life through Louis, and Freddy's prediction would come true:

I'd be nothing more than a Sunset Slurpee.

'Nuff said.

I'd get back to tracking Mic.

When I walked back to the house, I noticed that, despite the early hour, Louis was already up and about, still on Greenwich mean time. On the coffee table in front of him was this week's issues of *Variety* and *Entertainment Weekly*—and a scotch rocks.

Not a good sign.

"You're certainly up early," I said brightly. "What's up?"

"Golf," he grunted.

Now I remembered. Louis and the Posse were inaugurating what was to be their new tradition: golfing on the day of any awards ceremony in which Louis was in the running. To the outside world, that implied *It means nothing to me* when it really did but he didn't have a snowball's chance in hell of winning. It could also be interpreted as *It's in the bag* when the truth was that the race was too close to call.

Considering how tense Louis was, I was sure that now, only eleven or so hours before the awards ceremony, his real feelings leaned more toward the latter.

"I think it's smart that you're getting out, getting your mind off the ceremony this evening. Leo liked to do that, too."

"Don't worry," he answered caustically. "I won't be playing barefoot, like Daddy Dearest. The press would have a field day with *that.*"

"I never assumed you would. You know, Louis, I'm not the enemy. I certainly don't confuse you with Leo in any way, shape or form—"

"Oh, really?"

He picked up the *Entertainment Weekly* and tossed it at me. Bannered on its cover, over a photo of the two of us, was the headline "Oedipus Sex?" There was an inset shot of Leo right next to it. The teaser claimed that the article would compare Louis's movie roles to date with that of Leo's, as well as their track record with women, and the odds of Louis racking up as many Globes and Oscars.

Great. Just what Louis wanted to hear: that Leo, he and I were some incestuous celebrity ménage à trois.

Still, from the murderous look on his face, now was not the time to remind him why he should not believe his—our—own press clippings.

"That's nothing. *Variety* says that the Vegas oddsmakers have pegged me to come in a 'distant third.' Behind Sean—again, damn it!—and that lucky Prat Jude. *Again.* Hell, it's over. We might as well stay home tonight."

"Louis, you're kidding, right?"

"No, I'm not kidding. Why go? What's the advantage of being humiliated in public that way?" He grabbed his glass and sucked down the rest of his scotch. "It's the same old shit, year after year, like it's rigged or something! Why don't they let some new blood through? Haven't I paid my dues, too?"

Uh . . . no. If I wanted to be honest with Louis, I'd have to point out that he *was* the new guy in town.

In a town with a lot of new guys.

And at the same time, competing with a lot of very seasoned, very well-known, well-revered icons, too.

But now was not the time for honesty with the man I loved above all others.

Instead I would say what I knew he wanted to hear first and foremost, now more than ever. So I sat down beside him on the couch and, stroking his cheek in my palm, put on the performance of a lifetime.

"Why, that's great! Don't you see? This makes you the dark horse! Heck, we should put a couple of thou on that bet. We'll clean up!"

The shadow of a smile nudged the corner of his mouth. "Yeah," he said grudgingly, "that would be a pisser, now, wouldn't it?"

"Heck, *yeah!*" I grabbed the phone. "I'm not joking. Let's do it. We'll laugh all the way to the bank."

"Or not." Uncertainty clouded his eyes. "Bollocks, Hannah, who am I kidding? Who do I think I am, anyway? All anyone in this town cares about is what kind of box office I deliver. And all my so-called 'fans' want to know is who I'm shagging, how much I'm drinking, or who I'm punching out, not what I can do on the screen. I'm not an actor, I'm a bloody circus act!"

"Louis," I said seriously, "tell me you don't believe that *Dead End* isn't your best performance to date."

He was silent. Well, of course he *did.*

"Or that you believe that any of the other nominees even came *close* to giving the audience what you gave." I took his hands in mine. "That's all that matters. When all is said and done, no one will remember the gossip columns or the head-lines. But what they will remember is how you moved them. *On that screen.*"

In his eye was the merest glimmer of pride.

That was it. Louis was back.

I hit the 0 on the phone and was immediately connected to an operator.

"Hello, operator? Yeah, for Las Vegas, please . . . Bally's betting line . . . thank you . . ." I turned back to Louis. "What-taya think, five grand? Ten?"

He threw up ten fingers. I nodded.

After the bet was placed, he scooped me up in his arms and kissed me.

A long, lingering kiss.

A sweet, tender kiss.

A probing lover's kiss.

Among other things.

And afterward, he said the sweetest thing: "Hannah, darling, please don't ever leave me. I don't think I could stand living in this town without you."

Which was why I could forgive him when he added, "Of course, you should feel free to leave town if I dump *you*. In fact, I'm sure that would be best for both of us."

Within the hour, Randy was honking the horn, shouting that they'd lose their Bel-Air tee-off time to some old fart nobodies if Louis didn't hurry it up. As Louis waved good-bye, I suddenly felt very happy.

And very tired.

And thankful I'd have the rest of the morning to nap before getting ready for the evening's festivities. Then, about noon or so, I'd have the sheer girlish pleasure of getting ready for the equivalent of Hollywood's homecoming dance. (But of course, the Oscars have already secured the more esteemed comparison with the senior prom.)

The turquoise gown had won out over all the others as the fairest in the land. Between its exquisite color, wonderful cut and unique detailing, I could proudly hold my head up and answer, "Why, Axis of Evil!" when, as I glided down the red carpet on Louis's arm, *Entertainment Tonight*'s gushing gadfly, Steven Cojocaru, begged to know which couture house had created this heavenly vision for me.

I could see it now: A second after I'd utter that unlikely moniker, an avalanche of orders would swamp the tired secondhand fax machine of Axis of Evil's anarchic creative genius, who toiled for prêt-à-porter perfection, albeit one gown at a time. And my thanks for pulling him out of his socialist burrow and into the fascist fashionista limelight would be any cutting-edge frock from future collections that suited my fancy.

All right!

Truly, what was the value of celebrity if you couldn't share it with others, particularly those who were so much more deserving of it?

But alas, my role as Lady Bountiful was not to be.

Just minutes after Louis pulled out of the driveway, Ophelia pulled into it—along with a battalion of beauty pros who were to ready us for our big night on the arms of two of Hollywood's most eligible bachelors. Her SWAT team, commandeered with Louis's approval but without my knowledge, included the stylist we shared (who came towing a portable wardrobe filled with gowns), as well as two manicurists, a facialist, a makeup artist, and a trio of hair pros from Canale, who were sporting more tattoos than any biker mob this side of Bakersfield and enough hair spray to ensure that our 'dos would hold up under a blast of red carpet hot air.

"Isn't this *fun?*" she squealed, ignoring my look of shock. "Louis agreed with me that you needed to look great for tonight. I mean, in light of his past with Tatiana and all . . ."

"Is that what Louis said?" I felt my stomach turn flip-flops.

Ophelia's smile got even broader (if that had even been possible, considering the fact that her cheeks had recently been injected with whatever fat they could find in her previously lipo'ed ass) and her eyes glossed over, both telltale signs that I could take whatever syrupy words came out of her mouth with a grain of salt.

"No! Of *course* not! *My* bad! Hey, if anyone can compete with a—a supermodel ex-girlfriend, it's you!"

Darn tootin'.

Omigod! Who am I kidding?

I shook as I sat down in one of the portable salon chairs brought in by the Canale carnival. Immediately, a manicurist attacked my bunions with the rosemary-and-ground-cactus-needle scrub that was the first torturous step in my pedicure.

Just breathe. Everything will be okay. Don't think about yourself. Try to remember that this is Louis's night, and be there for him.

Louis, who had already crashed and burned once this morning, angsting over whether others thought his craft was worthy of their notice and their praise.

Louis, who had confided in me all of his fears of failure and loss.

Louis, who had chosen me over Tatiana, who was already crowned a princess in that elite aristocracy known as celebrity.

Okay, sure, for Louis's sake I could quell the overwhelming urge to throw Ophelia out on her cute little ass, along with her stylist and facialist and manicurists and the hair care coven from hell, as well as any other partridges-in-a-pear-tree that were in the trailer out front.

Because I'd do anything for Louis.

"Thanks for the vote of confidence, Ophelia. You're quite a pal, and don't I know it. And you know what? You're absolutely right: for the next twenty-four hours, my role is only that of Louis's consort: I'll be gorgeous, serene, and unobtrusive, and as invisible as a mouse."

"You're joking, right?"

"Not in the least. I really don't want to do anything that might steal his thunder." I frowned at the thought of his reaction if that happened.

Shocked, Ophelia batted away the manicurist buffing her cuticles in order to point a tapered Opi-glossed nail at me. "Now, Hannah, don't do anything stupid on that red carpet, like some sort of PA perp walk, do you hear me? You've got to stay *in camera range* with Louis the whole time!"

"Why? What difference will it make if I don't? I thought we just agreed that this is his night, right?" It was hard to make my case while wearing a facial in which the main ingredient was processed nightingale droppings, but I was bound and determined to do so.

"Be real! Aren't you afraid that might give the wrong impression?" Ophelia asked.

"To whom? Louis?"

"No, silly. *Other women!* If they don't see anyone on Louis's arm tonight, the rumors will start. Everyone will assume that he's up for grabs. Other women will envision that *they* should be there, if you're not." She shivered involuntarily. "Jeez, I'd be scared to let him walk alone!"

"Well, I'm not," I answered defiantly. "Tell you what. I'll leave it up to Louis whether or not he'd like to walk ahead a bit. I imagine he'll say no, but it will be his call."

At least, I *hoped* he'd say no. I mean, wouldn't he *want* me by his side, to share his moment in the sun?

Of course he would.

Right?

"Besides, even a wedding ring means nothing if the guy is looking around anyway."

"Tell me about it! But, hey, personally, I'd never be stupid enough to give up on collecting that ring, no way, no how! That ring means power. And it means financial security." She sighed despondently. "Hell, I've been with Ethan for over a year now, and I still can't get him to pop the question. In fact, just yesterday I gave him an ultimatum: I told him I need some *real* show of commitment, or I'm walking. Well, at least now he's agreed to take part in a Rabi snip."

"A snip? What's that? You don't mean a rabbi, you mean a mohel, right? Like some sort of bris?"

"No, it's not Jewish or anything. It's that ceremony from the te I-Matang people, in the Rabi Islands." With an arched brow, she dismissed a hot pink frothy gown held up by the stylist for her approval and pointed to a copper satin concoction instead. "You see, a holy man snips off a bit of Ethan's foreskin. Then he takes some of my breast skin, and we toss both into a fire, where it burns up together. The ashes and smoke intertwine as proof of our eternal love."

"Jeez, I'll say! Won't that, uh, *hurt like hell?*"

"We're anesthetized, so not initially. I think it's *ever* so much more spiritually binding than exchanging vials of blood, like Angelina and Billy Bob did, you know, right before their divorce. That was *so* creepy!"

She tossed her head with that declaration, causing the hair designer working on her golden locks to cut a tendril a quarter-inch too short. I watched the poor man bite his lip in fear of her wrath. Luckily, she hadn't noticed his faux pas.

"But, yeah, for a few days we'll be smarting. More so Ethan than me, I guess. You see, I'm going to get the holy man to clip a skin tag that my dermatologist missed. I mean, this crap wouldn't be worth doing if I were going to be, like, deformed afterward, right? Besides, I'm getting my boobs redone anyway. I'm going up a cup size. My operation is scheduled for later that week."

"Can't you both just clip a toenail or something, or maybe some hair?"

"You know, Hannah, you just don't get it! True love is a give-and-take. And sometimes what you have to give must be *really* painful."

Oh yeah? That was easily said, coming from someone who had nothing more to lose than a skin tag. As for Ethan, well, I wondered why he felt it was worth the price of some foreskin. Perhaps he'd been informed by his attorneys that, when it came to appeasing Ophelia, the Rabi snip was the less painful way to get shafted than a pre-nup.

Yanking the copper dress out of the fashion stylist's hand, Ophelia roused me from the salon chair and held it up to me. "Whattaya think of this one? Stunning, right?"

"Well, um, gee . . . I don't know. I sort of had something else in mind already."

As carefully as I could with two undercoats of polish on my nails, I opened the dress bag hanging in the foyer closet and brought over my gown for her to see.

Her eyes immediately went to the label. *After all, it don't mean a thing if it ain't got that couture zing.*

"Axis of Evil?" she sniffed. "What, is that some kind of joke?" Gingerly, so as not to get infected with any off-the-rack cooties, she tossed it into a corner, where it slid under the makeup artist's mobile cosmetic cart.

In the movie that was my life, my role as Lady Bountiful now lay on the cutting room floor.

Ophelia draped the copper gown over my shoulders. "With the right highlights, you *just* might be able to pull it off." She turned to her hair patrol: "Coco, pray tell, whattaya think? Too too red?"

"Honey chile," purred the SWAT leader, so designated because he was the one with the most tattoos. "Can there ever *be* too much red in a girl's life?"

"You're a *savant*, you know that, right?" She blew him an air kiss, then perused the tag and held it out to me triumphantly.

"I must be one, too! See? D&G!"

Well, she was partially right.

That night Wilshire Boulevard was a virtual milky way, lit up by those who glowed the brightest in Hollywood's celestial firmament as they made their way to the Beverly Hilton in their earthbound stretch chariots to eat, drink and be merry at the gala that predicted (or, some insisted, jinxed) Oscar's ultimate nod.

To ensure that theirs was a party to be reckoned with, the international press corps provided an elegant setting, a decent enough meal, and enough liquor to relaunch another *Titanic* sequel *and* lure their honored guests (industry bigwigs, revered film legends, television's latest veterans, talented up-and-comers from every medium, and flash-in-the-pan fly-by-night celebrities of every ilk) to let down their perfectly coiffed hair and be happy, silly, tense or tearful—preferably during the ceremony's live satellite feed as opposed to one of its many commercial breaks.

As Malcolm opened the back door of the limo to let us out, Louis smiled and waved to his adoring fans. Then, leaning so close to me that all watching assumed he was nuzzling me, he murmured in my ear, "Oh, darling, I hope you don't mind too terribly, but I would really appreciate it if tonight you walked in *after* me . . . you know, on the red carpet? We don't want to remind them that I'm competing with Leo too, now, do we?"

Competing with Leo?

I was crushed. I was hurt.

I was sad that Louis was too damned insecure to share this very important moment with me.

Still, I was willing to accept that.

I'd have to, if we were going to stay a couple.

Out he went, debonair in his white Armani tux jacket, sauntering down the red carpet with the kind of assurance that implied that he was truly worthy of the adoration of his screaming fans. And yes, true to my word, I hung back somewhat, waving at the crowd, stopping to talk to anyone who did not look like someone the paparazzi would care to photograph with me, while Louis schmoozed with the bevy of gushing infotainment reporters who, one by one in their private audience with him, parroted the mantra sure to garner his biggest smile: *"Why, Louis, you're a shoo-in for the Best Dramatic Actor award!"*

Out of the corner of my eye I felt someone watching me. It was Mick, handsome in a black-on-black tux. He, too, had seen Louis stroll into the limelight without a second thought to my being left behind. The involuntary shake of his head let on how incredulous he was at what he'd just witnessed. Seeing me glance over, Mick gave a hesitant wave. I nodded in return, then followed after Louis, hoping that the smile I forced onto my lips wouldn't give away my own feelings of regret, not about the fact that I wasn't on Louis's arm but that I wasn't on Mick's.

To my relief, no one else was on it, either.

It was inevitable that someone would pull a Lathi (be otherwise predisposed with relieving bodily functions when his or her name was announced as the winner in their category), or perhaps a Jack (take enough painkillers to give the press something to write about, or perhaps let some part of his anatomy sum up how he felt about the evening). As the night wore on and the speeches wore thin, I was afraid that person would be Louis, who seemed to belt down a scotch every time he heard the phrase ". . . and I'd like to thank the Hollywood Foreign Press Association . . ."

Mick's category came up before Louis's. When he won, he bounded onto the stage, thanked the movie's crew, took special note of the producers and the director, expressed his gratitude to various cast members for bringing his characters to life, but pointedly skipped any mention of Louis. The cameras were ready for that, cutting to a close-up of Louis and me.

And Louis was ready for them. By reminding the world that he'd stolen Mick's girl, he'd effectively steal Mick's thunder, too—which is why he pulled me close, gave me a soulful look, and moved in for a long, lingering kiss.

Just as his lips came up to mine, I turned my head. Louis's lips brushed my cheek instead.

The effect was sweet—and not at all what Louis had wanted the world to see.

Too bad. I was disgusted with his behavior, and I wasn't going to play along.

For the rest of the ceremony, Louis ignored me. And since our table was filled with a fair amount of Hollywood's up-and-coming women-to-watch, that was certainly easy for him to do.

When Louis's category was finally announced, he won as well. Leaping onto the stage, he took his award from Renee, then he, too, thanked the movie's crew, the director, the producers, and his cast members.

It was no shock to anyone that he did not mention Mick.

What did stun everyone, when the incident was discussed afterward and incessantly by the media, was that he hadn't mentioned me, either.

The wounded look on my face was later described by the media as "reflectively melancholy."

With Renee on one side and the official onstage eye-candy-cum-statuette holder (i.e., one of Hollywood's many second-generation princesses) on the other, he was led off the stage and into that den of wolves known as the press room—where, with backslaps, air kisses and handshakes, along with the clicking of flashbulbs and the gushing softballs pitched by reporters, Louis was once again assured of his position as the brightest, most recognized star in that social constellation known as Hollywood.

As for me, I had to sit at our table and smile serenely as Ben or Hilary or Julia or Steven nodded and shrugged sympathetically at my exclusion in Louis's speech. It was inevitable that Louis would forget someone's name, right? They'd all done it. No big deal, right?

Of course it was.

When Louis finally made his way back to the table, his unabashed apology said it all. "My God, love, I'm truly and awfully sorry! Must have just slipped my mind somehow. But I'll make it up to you, later tonight, right?"

With that he winked patronizingly, then punished me further by giving his undivided attention to two female *Fear Factor* contestants who were proclaiming to be his biggest fans, and explaining how they could prove it.

Together.

Mick got up and left.

I wished I had followed him out, but I just couldn't.

17

Eclipse

*A chance alignment between the Sun and
two other celestial objects, in which one body blocks
the light of the Sun from the other;*

or

*to obscure or diminish in importance, fame,
or reputation.*

The PA I found for Louis was perfect in every way: efficient, discreet, highly experienced (having been employed previously by two other film actors of Louis's caliber), and most importantly, vetted with a clean record by a private investigator hired by Jasper.

The PA also happened to be a man.

As I explained this to Louis, who was floating in the pool, he raised his Ray Bans in disapproval and frowned.

"He's got to be a pouf, right? Oh, come on, Hannah! Now, why would I want some fag hanging around here? It gives the wrong impression."

"As a matter of fact, he's as straight as you are," I countered.

"Look, Louis, if you're really worried that people question which team you bat for, then why do you hang around with Randy? I mean, come on already! Despite all of his macho bullshit, the jerk practically lives in tranny bars, right? And haven't you seen his paddle collection? I mean, the guy proudly admits he lives to be a bottom. Haven't you asked yourself what *that's* all about? The way Randy fawns all over you, I'd be willing to bet that you'd feel more comfortable sharing a bar of soap in the shower at The Sports Club with your new PA, Jeremy, than with your esteemed agent."

Louis's nod was barely perceptible, but it was an acknowledgement just the same. Ah, so some of these same suspicions had crossed his mind before, eh? With any luck, Louis might now actually reconsider his "relationship" with Randy and shop around for another agent: a real he-man, like Ari, say, or Guido or Jeremy.

If only.

"Besides, Jeremy was the most qualified candidate I interviewed. Also, he's a total stickler for details, has a photographic memory, and was the hungriest candidate for the job. Oh, and by the way, he's got his choice right now of working for you or Ewan. He's choosing you. Go figure."

"Oh . . . well, of course, he *would.*"

Surprise, surprise: I'd taken every single objection Louis could think of, added a reason he could feel superior about, and turned it around on him. I tried hard not to smile at my triumph.

Louis lowered his shades and got back to his sunbathing. "I trust your judgment, love. Do what you think is right."

"Good, then that's settled. Jeremy's waiting in the foyer. I'll go get him so that you two boys can get acquainted."

I'd almost made it to the door when Louis stopped me cold with this one: "In hindsight, Hannah, having a guy as a PA might be the smartest thing I've ever done. Another bloke would understand things about me that women just can't grasp. No offense to you, darling! Of course, you're more to me than just 'another woman.' And you're certainly more than just my lowly PA. . . . Can't wait to meet him. I'll break him in right, go over a few things with him, like my usual routine—"

Louis's usual routine.

His words ripped through me, like a knife.

Now I knew how Louis had spent his time in London.

"And all this time, I thought that *I* was your 'usual routine.' Well, thanks for clearing that up, Louis." I tried to keep my voice calm, but I couldn't. "I'm doing this only because we both felt it would save—strengthen our relationship, remember? If bringing on Jeremy, or anyone else for that matter, male or female, means that we have no relationship at all, then maybe I shouldn't hire anyone, or maybe we should just break—"

"Damn it, Hannah! Why are you always jumping to conclusions? I mean, *really!* Are you that insecure?"

He waded through the water until he reached the steps, then climbed out and wrapped a towel around his waist. Water droplets, clinging to his well-oiled shoulders, glistened in the sun.

"In case you've forgotten, my management company has devised a multi-page dossier on my likes, dislikes, needs and preferences. The fact that I've offered to go over them with Jerry—"

"Jeremy."

"*Whoever*—is just my way of shouldering some of the burden that always seems to land on your fragile, delicate shoulders."

He took hold of those fragile, delicate shoulders and nuzzled them seductively. "You know, love, you'll never lose me as long as we're both happy."

"So, tell me you're happy, Louis."

He stopped, thought a moment, then said, "Couldn't be happier, love . . . just wish I—we—weren't so bored . . ."

Bored? Did I say I was bored?

Or was he saying that I was boring?

That afternoon, while Louis reviewed his dossier with Jeremy, I familiarized myself with the contents of Louis's toy chest of sexual paraphernalia. I was determined that my name and the word *bored* would never come out of Louis's mouth in the same sentence ever again.

True to his resumé, Jeremy took to the job like a fish to water. Nothing his master requested of him went unfulfilled.

In fact, the very first thing he did was to change the passwords on both the gray and the red phones, as well as the one on Louis's PDA.

In other words, I no longer had access to Louis's voice mail or his calendar.

Jeremy did, however, present me with my own phone and PDA—on Louis's orders.

"He wants me to copy you on all important meetings," Jeremy explained in that calm, rational, happy singsong voice that I was already learning to despise.

"Frankly, I'd like to be copied on *all* of his meetings. As a double-check system, okay?"

"Already got that covered. With *Genevieve.*"

"But that's not necessary if I have—"

"Louis would prefer it that way."

I was beginning to hate it when he said that. Maybe because he said it much too frequently, in response to every question I had about Louis's "routines."

"Louis feels that you're too weighted down by stupid details. It's his desire that you focus on his big picture—"

His big picture.

"—because that frees you up to be with him more of the time."

"More time with him, huh? Not according to this." I jabbed a finger at my PDA, which only had me scheduled for press interviews, broken up intermittently by some "play time" (at least, that's how Jeremy had written it up) with Ophelia—a mani/pedi, spa day, trunk show at Barney's. . . .

Oh yeah, I was beginning to see the "big picture," all right.

"Thanks for your consideration, Jeremy," I answered coolly. "I'll just take it up with Louis tonight."

"Sure, whatever you want to do, Hannah," he chimed in. "Oh, and by the way, just so you know, we'll be getting back late tonight, after midnight. Randy scheduled a—a dinner. With Mr. Brownstein."

"That's nice. Where is it taking place?"

"I'm really not at liberty to say."

I stared at him. *Hollywood Reporter* had already noted Brownstein's penchant for dives where the steaks were served lukewarm but the pole dancers were red hot. I could only guess that their destination was one such hole, perhaps Fantasy Island.

Imagine the tattoos they'd see, and where.

By the eighth minute of our staring contest, a bead of sweat popped up on Jeremy's forehead.

Still, he didn't break.

Boy, he's good. I really know how to pick 'em, don't I?

If I was going to suffer separation anxiety from Louis, then at least something good could come of it. I'd devote my night to stargazing. After telling Jeremy to inform Louis that I'd be at the observatory that evening, I called Christy to see if she'd have an early dinner with me.

Unfortunately, Christy couldn't join me: she was working a double shift at Dublin's. Although it enjoyed a coveted location on Sunset, the bar catered to a less-than-desirable crowd, mainly frat boys and blue-collar Neanderthals who preferred shooters to premium brands and waitresses with bountiful breasts to Sunset Slurpees with credit-rating services programmed into their speed dials.

"Sorry, Hannah. I've started taking acting lessons again, and so my bosses here are letting me fill in for anyone who calls in sick." She sounded breathless but happy.

"I understand, sweetie. By the way, were you able to get any of your things out of Donnie and Bethany's place?"

"They had Manuel, the gardener, drop off my clothes." I could hear her tear up. "He also left a note from their attorney. Bethany is threatening to sue me if I say anything to anyone about Donnie and the rape."

"As if she could shut you up! I think you should go to the police, *right now*—"

"I can't, Hannah!"

"Why not?" I asked indignantly. "Those pigs need to understand that they just can't do something like that! If you go to the police, they'll make sure that Donnie and those—those 'actors' don't get away with it!"

"Hannah, no! I'm not going to the police, and that's final." Although Christy whispered it, she was resolute. "In the first place, I don't want people to think of me as 'that girl that did the porn flick for Bethany's husband Donnie Beaudry.' What will that accomplish, other than keep producers who are afraid of getting Bethany mad at them from working with me, or get me more offers to do porn?"

Her sigh echoed through my cell phone.

She had a point there. "Okay, Christy. I understand. I can't stand the thought that they're getting away with it."

"They are. But, you know what? I just can't afford avenging my pride right now."

* * *

Mic, my little red dwarf star, was happy to see me again.

I knew this because, four hours into my observation—12:43 P.M., to be exact—he let me in on his little secret: No dust was visible at around 17 AUs inside the debris ring that encircled Mic.

That was the telltale sign I needed that a planet was orbiting it.

I made the necessary notations, then packed up my telescope.

Like most realities, we don't really believe in them until they prove themselves to us over time. I'd need to come back each night in the coming weeks to verify these findings.

For the first time in weeks, I slept through the night, without a visit from Leo.

I also slept in. When I woke up, Louis—and, subsequently, Jeremy—had already left for Lion's Gate, where a read-through of the new Brownstein project, currently untitled ("in homage to Woody Allen," Jeremy informed me seriously), was taking place.

When my new aquamarine cell phone rang, I leaped at it. I fully expected it to be Louis calling, to tell me how much he'd missed me last night. He'd already gone to bed by the time I'd come home from the observatory.

"Damn, girl! Have you gone underground? And who's the nerd you've got asking twenty questions of your minions?"

It was Freddy, apparently upset. For the past two days, he'd been calling the number of the gray cell phone in order to reach me. Only in the past few minutes had Jeremy deemed his call important enough to return and deemed Freddy friend, not foe or press, and therefore worthy of my new private number.

"That's Jeremy. Louis's new PA."

"Lucky Louis. Or should I say lucky Jeremy?"

"Down, boy. Besides, you already have a gig."

"Not as of forty-one hours ago, babycakes. Simone passed away." He was trying to be flip, but I could tell he was heart-broken.

"You're kidding! Was it—expected?"

"Hell, no! But then again, when you've told the world that you're only sixty-three when you're really eighty-one—"

"You're kidding! *Eighty-one?* Who can get away with something like that?"

"A helluva great actress, that's who!" He started sobbing. I could hear Bette whining pitifully in the background. "Hush, baby girl! Papa's just—just in a tizzy, is all."

"Gee, I'm so sorry, Freddy. Really, I am. Look, is there anything I can do? Are—you homeless?"

"No, believe it or not. At least not yet. Her estate attorney told me to sit tight. I'm supposed to stay here, with Bette, until the will is read."

"He doesn't want you to do anything? What about an inventory, or packing up her things?"

"Nah, that was done *years* ago . . . ha! That diva had me doing that in my spare time." He gave a soggy giggle. "Hey, well, finally I'll get to lay out by that old cracked pool of hers and pretend the place is mine, for a few days, anyway. Speaking of which, gotta run, sweetums, and look for the garden hose. She lied about her age, so maybe she was kidding when she said the pool leaked, too."

"I wouldn't put it beneath her." I faked a laugh, for Freddy's sake. "Hey, speaking of Bette, what's going to happen to her?"

"I asked the attorney if I could keep her. As the song says, I guess I've grown accustomed to her very ugly mug. Simone had no relatives, and Bette wouldn't last a day in the pound. My baby has too delicate of a disposition." He made some purring sounds, obviously directed at her and not me. "I'll call you back as soon as I figure out what's going to happen to Bette, okay? Glad the Gestapo deemed me worthy enough to get your new private number. Hey, now that you've found him a PA, I suppose this means that you and Louis can have a normal relationship, right?"

A normal relationship? Is there such a thing in Hollywood?

I spent the next ten nights confirming what I'd suspected: That Mic's shadow was in fact a three-dimensional companion, a planet it could call its own.

It was time to celebrate. Although Louis and his shadow, Jeremy, had been working late each night, they still managed to beat me home. Well, for one night at least, I was bound and determined to make it home before Louis. I wanted to be waiting for him, with open arms and an open bottle of Château Lynch-Bages 2000 Pauillac.

No problem, I made it home before him.

Then again, no matter what time I'd come in before 7:30 the next morning, I would have won *that* booby prize.

Or maybe *I* was the boob for not walking out on him before he finally walked in.

I let him have it: about all I'd done for him and about his lack of respect for me.

About how abused I felt, and how I wasn't going to take any more crap from him.

"I don't know what you're so upset about," growled a very drunk, very disheveled Louis. "If anything, I'm the one who should be ranting and raving. Instead, I chose to celebrate—without you."

"Celebrate? Celebrate what, pray tell?"

"Ah, yes, I forget. You're not *really* in tune with my life anymore, are you? Too busy playing the diva, or divining the cosmos, or some other bullshit." His eyes flashed as he spoke. "Well, my sweet, here on Planet Earth, we put on a little event they call the Oscars—"

The Oscars.

They had announced the nominees yesterday morning.

I'd slept in because I'd been at the observatory all night.

Louis had gotten the word that morning. He had been nominated.

Naturally, he had assumed I would have heard about it, too, at least sometime during the day, and that I'd have stopped by the set to be with him, to share his joy and excitement.

I'd blown it.

"—so, when you didn't show up, I did some celebrating of my own."

"I would have been there had I known. Besides, you could have called me."

"I did call. Check your voice mail. Bollocks, Hannah, for once you've got no one to blame but yourself."

I took the turquoise cell phone out of my purse. No outstanding call was indicated.

"Where is your other phone?" he asked. "Don't you carry the red phone anymore?"

"No. Jeremy carries that one now." So that was why I'd missed him. Of course, actually knowing my phone number was too minor a detail for Louis. Still, I wasn't going to let him off that easy.

"So, where did you go, and with whom?"

"Out. With friends." He waited to see if I'd push further.

Did I really want to know?

Before I could admit to myself that I didn't, he added, "I doubt that your evening was a total loss without me."

"No, it wasn't. In fact, it was quite an evening for me, too—"

I wanted him to share my excitement about Mic, but he interrupted me.

"I'll just bet. I'm sure Mick just couldn't wait to see you." He watched my reaction like a hawk.

Mic? He already knew about Mic?

Then it dawned on me: "What are you talking about? Mick Bradshaw? See me?"

Louis smirked. "To tell you in person. About his nomination."

Louis pointed to the bottle of wine opened on the table. "You don't have to play coy, Hannah. Do you think that I believe you've been out for the past ten nights doing that 'stargazing' bullshit?"

He started stripping down as he headed for the shower. "You act so prim and proper, making a fuss about me 'sharing' women with my buddies. But you don't mind my sharing you with Mick—*just not at the same time.* Well, okay, if Mick wants my leftovers, he's welcome to them."

What nerve!

"I am *not* your leftovers. I left Mick for *you*, remember? Because, according to you, he was being disloyal to *me*." I was so close to him that we were standing nose to nose.

Good. I wanted him to look me in the eye for once.

"And now that we're on the subject, tell me the truth: How did you know he and Samantha were at the Bel-Air? Just who was Samantha there to see, you or Mick?"

Did he blink?

No.

Did he feel any compulsion whatsoever to assure me that I had nothing to suspect?

Hardly.

So much for his primal urge to protect me, even from myself.

Instead he smiled, looked me straight in the eye, and gave me what I asked for:

The truth.

"You saw her and Mick with your own eyes, so that's one piece of the puzzle. Did she see me too? Yes, Hannah, I admit it, *she and I made love that day*. But you already knew that, didn't you, love? And you've chosen to stay with me, anyway."

As Louis took his shower, I poured the Château Lynch-Bages 2000 Pauillac down the kitchen sink. I have no doubt that I could have easily downed the whole bottle by myself, but I no longer felt as if I had anything to celebrate.

18

Meteor

*Also known as a "shooting star" or "falling star,"
it is a bright streak of light in the sky caused by a bit
of space debris as it burns up in the Earth's atmosphere.*

That's one small step for man, one giant leap for
mankind . . .

> Neal Armstrong, during the first lunar landing,
> July 21, 1969

The news of my research traveled quickly.

Not only was I the toast of the astronomy department at
UCLA but, because my statistics confirmed that of the planet's
discoverer, Paul Kalas of the University of California at
Berkeley, and his colleagues at the James Clerk Maxwell Telescope on Mauna Kea in Hawaii, they could now announce
their findings to the world.

I was invited to the banquet honoring the naming of the
planet, to be called "Azkaban," which would take place in
Berkeley very soon.

Too soon.

In fact, the ceremony was scheduled to take place a mere 72 hours before another little shindig: that one thrown by the National Academy of Motion Pictures Arts and Sciences and fondly nicknamed "The Oscars" by its world of fans.

It was then that I realized that timing was everything. At least, it was to Louis, whose reaction was less enthusiastic than I'd hoped when I asked if he'd attend with me.

"What, are you *crazy?* Don't you know how busy we'll be? Hannah, don't be a dolt! Besides, some egghead awards dinner is not my cuppa tea. Count me out."

He took a breath, but only to grab a second wind in which to bolster his case.

"And frankly, love, I don't know why you feel you can just prance off to this nonsensical event, either. In fact, I insist that you stay."

"You're kidding me, right? You 'insist' that I stay? Just what is *that* all about?"

"*That* is all about *our* priorities. And Priority Number One is me. Remember?"

Always. Without fail.

"Louis, when will something I do ever matter to you?" I whispered.

The question seemed to puzzle him.

But only for a moment.

"Why, darling, *everything* you do for me matters immensely. That's why I keep you on."

"You 'keep me on'? Oh. I get it. And when I stop doing the things that matter to you—"

"That's right, love. You *do* get it, after all." There was no warmth to his grin, just a fake, frosty sheen. "Which reminds me, I'd like you to put in a call to Jon, over at Lion's Gate. That Brownstein kid is too wet behind the ears for this project.

They'd be better off with Mann, or better yet, Tarantino, at the helm. Make that clear to him."

"I don't think—Louis, there is *no way* they're going to can Brownstein now! That would blow the budget to smithereens, since preproduction is already underway. Besides, they'd have to pay through the nose to get one of those guys, and they'd have to pay Brownstein, too, since he owns the rights to the story in the first place—"

"Of course they will make the change. If *I* insist."

"It would help if I knew whether or not Randy put a director approval clause in your contract. Knowing Randy, though, if the deal was made anywhere within sniffing distance of a pole dancer in a G-string, I wouldn't be too surprised if that tiny detail got overlooked—"

"Why *don't* you know? It's your job to make sure he doesn't fuck up the details, isn't it?"

"Is it? I thought my first priority is to be your girlfriend, remember?"

His eyes narrowed as the smile vanished.

"How can I forget? If *you* don't remind me, some godforsaken magazine cover does."

In the weeks leading up to the Azkaban banquet, neither of us would give in on our respective stances about attending. Still, we were civil to each other. In fact, for our performance as lovebirds while on the pre-Oscar party circuit, the Academy Awards should have awarded us a special statuette.

Alas, these very public displays of affection were inevitably offset by Louis's less-than-discreet flirting.

Many times, sometimes even at the same event.

Like the time we were at a rooftop pool party at the Standard downtown, celebrating T's latest release. Using the thickening crowd as cover, Louis disappeared into one of those lipstick red, cocoonlike waterbed cabanas with the most recent acquisition of T's label. She was sultry-voiced, under-age, and agile enough for her MTV video to be banned after one showing.

I took the elevator back to the lobby and called a cab.

Louis never came home that night.

On that memorable evening, I couldn't fall asleep; I just cried uncontrollably until dawn. When he finally walked through the door claiming that he'd fallen asleep in his studio bungalow but smelling of a fragrance more pungent than my own signature scent, I called him a liar, threw something expensive and irreplaceable, and locked him out of the bedroom.

That was all the excuse he needed to stay away a second night. Before a third rolled around, our negotiator, Jeremy, secured from me a solemn promise that I would, as he so delicately put it, "act somewhat humane in Louis's presence."

Act somewhat humane?

How could I do that if Louis never let me feel human in his presence in the first place?

With my sullen permission, Louis moved back into the bedroom, but we were still as emotionally distant to each other as two wooden horses on the same merry-go-round: We might be moving in the same direction, but we always kept our distance, and we certainly never touched.

Unless it was for sex.

A raw, dispassionate if-not-for-this-than-why-is-this-relationship-worth-the-hassle kind of sex.

Ironically, we weren't the only ones who were questioning whether it was: Later that week, "Page Six" in the *New York Post* predicted "Trouble in the Tropic of Trollope."

When the call came in from Freddy asking me to join him and the rest of the Gang over at Simone's Beverly Hills mansion for cocktails, believe me, I was out the door as fast as my legs could carry me. By now I welcomed any excuse to get away from the sense of dread that hung over Louis's estate. The way we politely ignored each other when occupying the same room, we might as well have been two ghosts whose only connection was that we were sharing the same haunt.

Not that Simone's place wasn't any less otherworldly, thanks to its décor: retro Eames, intermixed with some original French Provincial sideboards and settees, the total effect of which created an ambiance worthy of *Peyton Place*. And Freddy, decked out in a smoking jacket and ascot and shaking up martinis, looked right at home.

"Here, have an hors d'oeuvre," said Sandy, motioning to a butler who held a platter laden with such delicacies as steamed pot stickers, Dungeness crab cakes, Polynesian chicken skewered with pineapple, and shitake mushroom puffs.

"Butlers? Hors d'oeuvres? *Ascots?* Wow! What's the occasion?"

"Got me beat. For once in his life, Freddy is actually being discreet." She gulped down her martini and grabbed another off the butler's tray before popping a crab cake into her mouth. When a crumb escaped her, it was immediately sucked up by the ever-watchful Bette, who hovered at our feet for just such an occasion.

Just then Christy walked through the door, breathless and excited. "So sorry I'm late, but hey, gang, it was worth it!" Her eyes glowed brightly. "My acting teacher kept me after class. He says that I've got real potential! In fact, he's offered to coach me in private sessions!"

Freddy sighed heavily. "Girl, we need to keep you on a *very* short leash. Haven't you learned anything by now?"

It had been a long time since we'd heard Christy's sweet giggle, but there it was, fully restored in the echo of her most recent conquest. "That's just the point, Freddy. I *am* learning. And just think what I'll know when I get through with *him*. For free!"

No, Christy, I thought, *there is* always *a price to pay for the most important lessons we learn in life.*

By the looks on both Sandy's and Freddy's faces, they were thinking similar thoughts, but they said nothing—which was unusual for Freddy. Had he suddenly realized that discretion was indeed the better part of valor? Hardly. He was just antsy to get the ball rolling, which he did by waving the butler away and closing the door behind him.

"Well, my graceful girlfriends, I'm sure we'll hear more of that saga as it plays itself out. In the meantime, I have good news, too. And I'm glad you all were able to take a few minutes out of your very busy days in order to celebrate it with me."

"Enough already, Freddy!" sighed Sandy, her mouth filled with a mushroom puff. "If you don't get to the bottom of all of this, I'm going to burst!"

"Now, now, we can't have you regurgitating those fine vittles all over this antique Persian carpet"—he closed his eyes, took a deep breath, then continued—"because, as the executive director of the Bette Cavanaugh Humane Foundation, I'd have to get the butler in here to clean it up before Bette decided to make it her dessert."

"A foundation? For—for the dog?" Like the rest of us, Sandy was flabbergasted.

"You got it. According to what I heard this morning at the reading of Miss Simone's will, li'l Ms. Mutt there is as rich as Croesus."

"Rich? But I don't get it." I had to sit down. Gingerly, I found my way onto one of the many gilded Louis XVI chairs scattered about the room. "I never heard of anyone who was tighter with a dollar than Simone."

"You can say that again!" Christy echoed.

Freddy nodded. "No argument there. Apparently that old diva saved practically every dollar she ever made after the Second World War . . . and put it in little things like telecommunications, banking and Microsoft stocks. Who knew, right?"

Christy blinked twice. "Let me get this straight. All of that money now goes to *the dog?*"

"You betcha. And as the executive director of Bette's foundation, I'll be in charge of making sure that Bette is kept in the style to which she has never had the luxury of being accustomed. It's about time, too, eh, baby?"

He scooped up Bette in one hand and scratched her under her chin with the other.

"Besides making sure she lives high on the hog for the rest of her life, I'll be administering to the foundation's other mission, which is making sure that five percent of its interest, compounded annually, is distributed to animal shelters and sanctuaries in need—*and* collecting a six-figure salary for all my time and trouble. Pretty nifty, huh?"

I smiled. "Yeah, I'll say. But, Freddy, that dog isn't going to live forever. What happens after she, uh, joins Simone in the grand hereafter?"

"Miss Simone thought of everything. My gig is for life, or as long as I want it. And who wouldn't?" He winked. "After fifteen years with her, I guess I proved I could be just as resourceful as she was. And I certainly do love this little dog. This was her way of taking care of the both of us."

Christy was still confused. "But, if that's the case, why put it in the mutt's name in the first place? Why not just leave it to you outright?"

"Who cares, honey? Heck, my diva might not have shown it while she walked among the living, but in her own way, she loved me. And she certainly recognized love and devotion when she saw it, too. Maybe she was worried that whatever was left of her adoring public wouldn't understand what she shared with a prissy black man with a little stardust in his eyes. But I'm certainly not one to look a gift corpse in the mouth."

Christy and I both laughed, but Sandy didn't. As Christy proposed that we raise our glasses one last time in honor of Simone, two large tears rolled down Sandy's cheeks, not out of fondness for Freddy's dearly beloved boss but for something she was now too obviously holding inside.

I caught Freddy's eye and motioned with my head for him to find some reason to keep Christy busy. The ever astute Freddy knew what would fit the bill. "Hey, how about a tour of all forty-eight rooms in this hovel?" That was catnip to Christy. Off they went.

Once they were out of earshot, I took Sandy's hands in mine and moved her to the silk settee in front of the salon's blazing fireplace. We sat there silently for what seemed like forever, just listening to the fire crackle and pop, until she was ready to speak. Finally, gulping back her anguish along with another mushroom puff, she began.

"Rex got passed over for that Grazer project." As she dusted her hands of crumbs, Bette pranced at her feet. "But that's okay. He's been asked to star in the newest *Law & Order* series." She emptied her glass again.

We both knew that TV was a step down for Rex's career. "Is he going to take it?"

"He'll have to," she said sadly, "now that he's got a family to support."

"*What?*" To Bette's immense pleasure, the pot sticker I was holding fell to the floor.

"Yep, you heard it here first—although I anticipate it will be all over town in twenty-four hours. Rex married his agent's assistant last night." Her knees buckled, perhaps the consequence of her overwrought emotions, but I had a feeling that her tipsiness was vodka-induced. I gently grabbed her arm to steady her.

"Is that . . . a *woman?*"

"Not just 'a' woman. A very, very pregnant woman."

"Jeez." Now I'd heard it all. "He's—*the father?*"

"Get real."

Sandy's blinders had finally come off, but by the way she grabbed another skewer off the butler's tray, I was worried that the pounds would go on in their place. Not that I could blame her for binging through her pain.

"It's a marriage of convenience. The baby's father is Rex's *very* married agent, who will *never* leave his wife, and the assistant—the mother of his child—says that she'll never have an abortion. Religious reasons." She stuffed a pineapple cube in her mouth and licked her finger. "But her religion doesn't forbid her from marrying a gay movie actor who desperately needs a beard." A tear trickled down her cheek. "The agent paid for their wedding and honeymoon. In fact, his unsuspecting wife planned the whole thing herself! Go figure. And because he's forever indebted to Rex for getting him out of a jam, he's making sure that Rex comes up for anything and everything. Can't allow the bastard to starve, now can he? By that I mean the baby . . . which is how Rex landed the TV gig. I guess it's a win-win for everyone—except for me. *I'm* out of a job."

"What? Why? You're everything to Rex!"

"Not quite everything." She tossed her skewer into an antique urn. *Bull's-eye.*

"Seems that Rex's boyfriend—you remember, the wannabe actor?—well, he's got some talents that I obviously can't measure up to. And since the agent wrote in an assistant's salary in Rex's TV contract, Rex has asked me to 'retire' so that he can put Pretty Boy on the payroll without raising too many eyebrows."

"And you're going to just walk away from a job you've done for the past nine years? That just seems so unfair, so cruel!"

Sandy nodded. "Particularly since I"—she paused to clear the catch in her throat—"*I still love him.*"

Even after all that.

On the way home, I thought about how Louis and I had lost our perspective, and how it was affecting our love for each other. I thought about how wonderful we had been together in Oregon, where we had shared trust, and passion and the kind of secrets you only tell the person you love with all your heart.

I'd seen Louis at his worst, and I loved him anyway.

Even when he lied to me.

I'd always believed that he could be a good person—a *wonderful* person—if only he'd realize that he didn't have to lie in order to be loved.

He didn't understand that now, and certainly not here in Hollywood, where lies were the currency for success—at least, for those without talent.

But Louis *had* talent, which was why *he didn't need the lies.*

I could convince him of that.

Of course, it would be easier if we were alone, just the two of us. Perhaps under a cloudless night sky, just like we'd had in Oregon.

Most definitely, we had to work things out as soon as possible.

We had to do it *now.*

And I knew just the place.

"We're in the bloody desert, Hannah!"

"Yes, darling, I know we are. It's Palm Springs, remember?" The two ends of the Emilio Pucci scarf I had tied around my head whipped across my lips as I turned to face him.

"But Palm Springs is back there. We just passed the turnoff. This looks like the middle of nowhere." Louis's words were lost to the wind as the Ferrari zipped off Highway 10, and, at my behest, up the more desolate Highway 62. He was staring straight ahead, trying to get a handle on how the chalky earth, scattered prickly cacti and errant tumbleweeds translated into velvety verdant golf courses, stately Royal palm trees, and undulating kidney-shaped pools with mirrored surfaces that perfectly mimicked the endless clear azure sky above.

"Seems that way, doesn't it? But don't worry. Where we're going is a little out of the way, but it's still close enough to go into town . . . *if* that's what you want to do. I'm guessing you'll be happy to just stay put." I gave him a big smile, which left him even more perplexed.

In truth, our final destination was further than the town of Twentynine Palms—renowned as the home of the largest Marine Corps base in the country—and even beyond Desert Hot Springs, a resort built around a natural underground river, where the hot mineral water flows out of the earth at a scalding 207 degrees.

In fact, we were going even further out than Pioneertown, a remote movie set built in the 1940s to accommodate the number of Westerns Hollywood was shooting at the time, including anything starring Gene Autry, Hopalong Cassidy, the Cisco Kid and Roy Rogers. As we drove by this tribute to the Old West, I thought it was appropriate that we'd be only a few miles from the site of many a Hollywood shoot-out, since Louis and I would also be facing down the demons that were killing our relationship.

I pointed to a dirt road that ran adjacent to the entrance to the mystical 800,000-acre Joshua Tree State Park. We turned into it, and within two miles we came to a gate that I opened via remote control.

We had arrived at our destination: "Le Shack," Leo's "high desert adobe castle." At least, that was how it was being described in the eight-page, four-color brochure put out by the realtor who now had the listing.

Although the 28-acre property had been put up on the market when Leo's estate had finally been settled, its $8.2 million price tag, coupled with the fact that it was forty minutes beyond the tonier gated enclaves within Palm Springs's city limits, was making it a hard sell.

It was for that very reason that Sybilla had never used it. So, thank goodness, it was free of any of her negative karma.

The house itself was one of those 6,000-square-foot midcentury modern monstrosities: white-on-white and angular, with a flat roof, a huge wraparound verandah that separated a massive salon and master bedroom from two additional guest suites, and an oasis of a playground that included a fire pit, tennis courts, its very own nine-hole golf course, and a 70-foot infinity pool that butted out over the mesa on which the estate sat.

Some of my most treasured childhood memories had been formed when I'd visited Leo there: he had taught me how to swim in that pool, and, roaming through the scrub brush that surrounded the outskirts of the property, I'd caught a whole menagerie of lizards, on which I'd then bestowed ridiculous nicknames like Esther, Horatio, and Geraldine.

And it was there that, under the cool, cloudless canopy of night, I'd taught myself the names and origins of various stars.

Here I was, once again, focusing on one star in particular: *Louis.*

Getting him to join me for a mini-holiday at Le Shack really hadn't been all that difficult. For Louis, the Oscar nomination had created an emotional pendulum, weighted on one side by euphoria and on the other by unfounded insecurities. Out in the desert, a hundred miles away from Los Angeles, we'd be trading in a very frenzied Team Louis, the stalkarazzi, and the media's pre-Oscar infogasm for leisurely games of golf, interspersed with sunbathing and exhilarating swims, followed by poolside massages that (I assured him) would inevitably culminate in some passionately unbridled lovemaking.

I had left strict orders with Jeremy not to call us, for any reason whatsoever.

Then I left my cell phone behind, to ensure that he couldn't break this one and only rule.

I'd sworn to myself that sometime within the 36 precious hours we'd spend here at Le Shack, Louis and I would recapture the attraction we'd felt for each other that afternoon in Soho. And while these few precious hours certainly couldn't rival Oregon, where we'd first professed our love to each other and lived without secrets and lies, I had all the confidence in the world that it just *might* allow us to rediscover why we'd loved each other in the first place.

As we followed the sentry of palm trees to the portiere that fronted the frosted glass double-door entrance of the house, I saw Louis give an imperceptible nod of approval. The realtor, having fully comprehended the added advantage of saying "Louis Trollope slept here," had followed my directions to a tee in readying the house. A bottle of Château Lynch-Bages 2000 Pauillac had been brought up from the wine cellar and uncorked. A tin of caviar rested on a bed of ice, beside a platter with a sliced loaf of fresh-baked Tassajara bread and organic fruit. Vases holding fragrant flowers were strewn about the sunken living room, which was adorned with classic Eames chairs, Le Corbusier sofas, and curtainless floor-to-ceiling windows that boasted breathtaking panoramic valley views.

Entranced, Louis walked out onto the patio to the pool's

edge, breathed deeply, then moved on through the doors leading into the master suite, where the slow-moving overhead fan nudged the early afternoon breeze over the large kingsize bed. Its white chenille duvet was already turned down, and its smooth, lavender-scented sheets called out to be rumpled in the heat of passion.

"You've thought of everything," he said finally.

"I hope so." I jumped on the bed, pulling him down onto it with me.

He needed no other invitation.

We undressed each other, slowly at first, then furtively, as if we would burst if we couldn't feel each other's skin beside our own.

As if we'd die if we couldn't consume each other: body, mind and soul.

The first orgasm, a magnificent, spontaneous combustion, was followed by a mutual and exacting exploration of each other's longings and desires. Tentative and oh, so tender at first, our love play grew hungrier as the afternoon shadows grew longer, finally voraciously raging into a wet, throbbing passion that left us both weak as we collapsed side by side.

Afterward, neither of us could speak. When he finally caught his breath, Louis murmured, "I've missed you."

A tear rolled down my face. I sobbed, then answered, "I missed you, too."

We fell asleep in each other's arms.

When we awoke, the sun had already fallen beneath the horizon, and the evening desert chill had settled in. We tossed on some robes, grabbed the wine and caviar platter and headed out to the pool.

"I'm a cruel sod, aren't I?" Louis stared off into the shadowed hills, but by the huskiness of his voice, I knew his thoughts were with me, not out there, or even back in L.A.

"Thoughtless perhaps . . . yeah, okay, and cruel. No doubt about it, you are both." I put my arms around him.

"You can't say I didn't warn you, eh?" A crooked smile pierced his lips.

"Yes, I was duly warned." I turned to face him. "I guess I know the score."

"I'm glad to hear that. Because having to break in a new girlfriend every few months is a pain in the arse."

"Boo hoo hoo. I feel so sorry for you." I took off my robe and dove into the pool. By the time I resurfaced, he had joined me. We kissed underwater. Then, gasping for air, we came up once more.

He jumped out first. "Bollocks!" Scalded by the hot Mexican pavers that encircled the pool, he reached for his robe before offering me his hand. Pulling me up beside him, he held the robe open so that I could share its warmth. *His* warmth.

We sat together in a cabana chaise as Venus appeared to join the moon in their nightly duet. But in no time they were surrounded by other friendly lights.

This starry promenade danced above our heads as we talked the whole night through.

I listened as he opened up: about his concerns over how poorly the Brownstein project was going; his fears that if it bombed it would irreparably damage his career; his realization that his reputation was fragile and that any destructive move might bring it down like a house of cards; and his inevitable qualms over whether that Oscar statuette was truly going to be his next Sunday night.

At dawn, I made him his favorite breakfast of bangers and mash. I no longer did Zone. That was Jeremy's job now, and Jeremy wasn't here. *Thank God.*

And of course we made love again, as if nothing else mattered.

Not his past cruelties, insecurities or infidelities.

Not my fears of abandonment or my anger at his betrayals.

It was almost as if all was forgotten.

Perhaps even forgiven.

Afterward we just lay there in bed, his body spooning mine. Drifting off, I realized he was whispering something in my ear, but I didn't catch it.

"What?" I asked. "I didn't hear you."

"I said, don't go. Blow it off."

I sighed and turned around to face him. "We've already gone through this. It's important to me. Why is that so hard for you to understand?"

His face was caught in the one shaft of early morning sunlight now seeping through the drapes. He stared at me blankly. Then it registered so clearly on that face of his that was like a moving canvas: Finally, for the first time since Louis had professed his love for me, he understood how there could be something just as important to me as him.

He would have to share me with the galaxy.

But he couldn't.

In Louis's mind, there should only be one star in my life.

Him.

Then and there, realizing that this would never be the case, Louis sighed, shook his head sadly and turned his back toward me.

It was my turn to sigh.

All of Hollywood had Oscar fever, including me.

This time, I was organizing my own transformation from ugly duckling to swan. It would go something like this:

Oscar Blandi would come in to do my hair. He does not sport any tattoos, thank goodness. Any *visible* ones, anyway.

Diana Ayala would be there for my makeup. No nightingale droppings, thank you very much.

Ophelia would be nowhere near Louis's place. In fact, if she showed up, I would order the now omnipresent guards to shoot on sight and ask questions later.

Despite being deluged by calls from every couture house on the planet begging me to take anything from their showrooms for my walk down the red carpet, I had already made up my mind about what I'd wear. Once again, the ethereally elegant turquoise Axis of Evil gown would have its shot at stardom.

And despite any traumas Louis might incur prior to the event, I'd be wearing a smile on my face, too.

And yes, I *would* be by his side as he walked into the Kodak Theatre and into cinematic history.

Hey, not that I was adverse to *all* loaners: The House of Harry Winston had the perfect pair of aqua-hued sapphire-and-diamond earrings and a matching bracelet for my gown. In fact, now that my trust fund had been fully reinstated, I might even consider the bling worthy of a splurge after the big night.

On the day of the Azkaban dinner, Malcolm picked me up at two o'clock in the afternoon to take me to the airport.

Louis was home, but he stayed out by the pool all morning while I pulled together the few things I needed for my overnight stay. I knew he was still upset at my decision to leave, because he didn't even get up to see me off when Malcolm rang the doorbell. I stood there for three or four minutes, hoping that he wouldn't make this so hard on me, but he didn't move. I couldn't even tell if he saw me blow a kiss good-bye, because those stark turquoise eyes of his were shielded by his pitch black Ray-Bans.

I'm guessing he did.

*   *   *

The whole trip took less than twenty-four hours.

My name was called, and the tiny role I'd played in making Azkaban's whereabouts known was lauded with hoops, hollers, and claps from a roomful of eggheads delirious over their new-found notoriety, an additional outpouring of grant funding, and too many bottles of Cristal. As I walked to the speaker's podium to collect my plaque, all I could think about was the fact that no one I loved was here to celebrate this with me.

I wished Leo were still alive.

I wished Louis wasn't so selfish.

I wished Mick was still in my life.

In the Hollywood you know, here's how the love story ends:

As she steps off the plane, there he is, waiting for her, contritely, with a bouquet of roses in his arms and a lopsided grin on his face.

She smiles beatifically, runs into his arms, and kisses him longingly.

The camera pulls back, the shot fades to black, and the credits roll, validating what the audience has been conditioned to believe:

All endings are happy.

In the Hollywood I know, here's how my love story ended:

My plane was met by Jeremy, not Louis.

And he was not carrying a bouquet of roses. He did, however, have a copy of Liz Smith's column in his hand, which carried the item "Rebound! Louis and Tatiana Give It a Go, Again!" Next to it was a file photo of the two of them, wrapped in each other's arms.

"Louis feels it's best that the two of you go your separate ways. He no longer feels that you are loyal to him, or that you even care about him and his career."

His tone, albeit tinged with the right degree of sincerity,

was stern enough to indicate that he would brook no form of emotional outbursts.

I was too stunned to emote, anyway.

Realizing this, Jeremy immediately launched into his canned spiel—something I was sure he'd have plenty of opportunity to practice in the future.

"Obviously by your current actions you no longer put Louis first in your life. While that hurts him deeply, he will weather this disappointment and move on with his life as best he can."

He was hurt deeply? *He* was disappointed?

He was moving on with his life . . . without *me?*

"I took the liberty of packing your things and sending them to your Venice abode."

As I stood there staring at the magazine cover, Jeremy scurried away as fast as he could.

This is where you learn that not all Hollywood endings are happy.

Which is why I had to grab my gear and get the hell out of Hollywood that very minute.

Despite being home to the sprawling Joshua tree, which derives its name through biblical reference, the 22,000-acre Mojave Desert certainly is no promised land. Not only is there no Ritz Carlton in which to flop and order room service but there isn't even an Econolodge in which to hang your hat—that is, unless your destination is Edwards Air Force Base Shuttle landing or the tourist-friendly Red Rock Canyon.

And anyone looking for me certainly wouldn't have found me *there*.

Another little-known fact: In January, while temperatures can get as high as 75 degrees, they can also go as low as a frigid 12 degrees, so it is advisable to bring your thermal underwear and a well-made sleeping bag when sleeping out under the stars.

Which was what I planned to do, for at least a month or

two—or however long it would take me to lick my wounds over losing Louis and lousing up the rest of my life.

And last but certainly not least, should you decide to sleep outside, know that you will be sharing these wide open spaces with hungry coyotes, venomous rattlesnakes, and tarantulas— although hardly lethal, certainly not shy.

Of course, Mick knew none of this as he drove into my campsite, cold, hungry, almost out of gas, and deathly afraid he was lost and wouldn't be found until all that remained of him was something even the coyotes wouldn't want to touch.

When I saw him, I'll admit it, I could have murdered him myself. And no one would have known the better.

Of course, my only regret would have been that he hadn't brought Christy with him so I could have wrung her neck, too, the traitor! I knew it was she who had given him my where-abouts, because only she had the exact GPS coordinates of my location.

"Jeez! I thought the desert was always hot," he began. Al-though it was just now turning dark, he was already shivering. That would teach him to trot out into the Mojave with noth-ing more than Tommy Bahama Hawaiian shirt and shorts.

"And I thought I was alone. What do you want?"

"To take you home, silly." Hearing the howl of a coyote, he ducked. "And the sooner, the better."

"Feel free to turn around. Me, I've already got plans for the evening."

"I can see that." He walked over to my telescope, already set up on its tripod, and took a look through the eyepiece. "Wow! Look at what you can see already, and it's not even totally dark!"

I pushed it out of his hand. "Look, Mick, I'm here because I want to be here—and not there." I looked him straight in the eye. "I'm through living the Hollywood lie. I've had my fill of actors, and industry types, and writers, too, I might add! You're all too wrapped up in your egos!"

To toss off the hand he put on my shoulder, I took a step back. "L.A. is a measly fleabite on the ass of the world, and there's a whole, big universe out there, or haven't any of you noticed?"

And I was just warming up. "Besides, wouldn't you prefer to take Samantha?"

"Samantha wasn't there for *me*. She was there for Louis. The two of them hooked up again in London."

"I know. I saw them together there. But I thought it was to break up with her."

"Well, they made love that night." He paused, embarrassed. "And she got pregnant. She flew here and arranged to meet him at the Bel-Air because she thought he should know."

"I never knew about—about the pregnancy!"

Mick nodded. "I figured as much. I didn't think Louis had the guts to tell you. I certainly didn't feel that it was my place. And besides, since you had already made up your mind . . . about him . . . I didn't really know if that would have made a difference to you, anyway."

It was my turn to hold out my hand to him. "I don't know if it would have, either," I murmured.

Mick winced at that. "Well, you know Louis: he turned on that infamous Trollope charm and convinced her that a baby would ruin his career—*and* ruin them ever reconciling. He got her to agree to have an abortion. He even called Genevieve in front of her and arranged everything, including sending Malcolm to pick her up and take her to the doctor's office that afternoon. Nice guy, huh? Then, after they made love, he left the cabana on the pretense that he had to make a call to the studio. Instead, he just—walked out on her!"

I had to sit down. He sat down beside me, his eyes never leaving mine. "I was the call Louis made. He asked me to come over and stay with her until Malcolm got there. He called it a 'mercy shag,' to appease her for the time being, and to keep her from approaching you. Of course, by the time I got there, she was hysterical. She threatened to commit suicide. I got Louis on the phone. He was with Randy. He refused to get on the phone with her. Instead, he told me to tell her that if she didn't follow through, he would never allow her to see him again."

Mick paused. "I guess that's when you saw me holding her."

I was silent for a moment. Then I whispered what I needed to know: "Mick, did you ever make love to her, with Louis?"

His pain made me wince. "Heck, no! My God, Hannah! That—that was Randy!" He paused, shaking his head in disbelief. "Is that what you thought?"

"I didn't know what to think! Particularly after I saw you holding her—"

He came over to me and pulled me into his arms. "I don't remember it being anything like this . . ."

Holding me as if he'd never let me go, he kissed me.

No. I now knew it had been *nothing* like that . . .

When he finally pulled away, he turned to face me.

"Look, Hannah, you and I both know that only in the movies would someone like Louis come to his senses and get the girl. Heck, I know it because I've written enough of those scenes. Well, this is no movie. *It's real life.* It's *your* life."

He stood up, pulling me along with him. "That kind of guy doesn't deserve you. *I* deserve you. And whether you believe it or not, Hannah, you deserve me, too."

Well, of course I deserved Mick. *Every girl* deserves a Mick.

And a night in the desert, making love and looking up at the stars.

When I woke in the morning, he was already awake, just watching me, with a smile on his face.

It was nothing like the predatory, calculating way in which Louis had watched me that first time we met.

Very matter-of-fact, Mick asked, "Will you marry me?"

I answered, "Perhaps."

"I'll just take that as a yes. . . . Oh, and by the way, you *do* have a dress for the Oscars tonight, right?"

We made love again.

I can tell you firsthand that it's great to be with someone when they win their Academy Award.

It's also great when the guy you love holds up that award and thanks you—his fiancée—for walking into his life . . . even if you were not wearing any shoes at the time.

And believe it or not, Mick thanked Louis, too, for being, as he put it, "the only actor living who could have embodied our hero." Considering the fact that Louis had played a real bastard, I had to agree with him.

Louis, who (gladly, I'm sure) walked the red carpet by himself, since Tatiana was on some runway in Rome, didn't flinch a muscle at Mick's acknowledgement, but I guess he was flattered.

Then again, he wouldn't have gotten the joke.

It's also wonderful when the man in your life shares something that you never knew about him—and consequently, never knew about yourself. For example, in my case, I never knew that Mick had originally written the screenplay with Leo in mind, when he'd first gotten to Hollywood some twelve years ago. But Leo had turned down the role!

Upon hearing that, I suddenly realized that, despite all my love and adoration for him, Leo had never been perfect.

He hadn't been a perfect father, and apparently he'd made some really dumb business decisions, too.

And you know what? *That was just the way it was.*

Nothing I could have done would have changed Leo: his flaws had been his own, and despite them, I should have no shame in loving him—just the way Mick loved me, flaws and all.

From Mick, I finally got what I always wanted: Approval. Trust. Loyalty. And absolution.

By now I'm sure you're wondering: Did Louis win his Oscar?

No. It went to Adrian again.

Ladies, pucker up.

Poor Louis. He was stunned, but he was a real pro and kept a smile on his face.

Believe it or not, I felt sorry for him. I wanted to tell him not to worry, that he had the chops to pull it off again someday.

If he chose to focus on his craft instead of his libido.

If not, well, if Leo taught me anything, it's that you have to live—and die—with the choices you make in life.

Wow! Just think: If Leo had agreed to do the role Mick had written for him, I might have met Mick earlier in my life!

Now, what would *that* have been like?

Not that it matters. One way or the other, we were meant to be together.

I suppose you could say it was written in the stars.

Want More?

Turn the page to enter
Avon's Little Black Book—

the dish, the scoop and the
cherry on top from
JOSIE BROWN

Transcript of
John Gray's Mars & Venus *TV Show*

JOHN: *All right!* Welcome to my show, everyone! Great day we're having, yeah? Right? *Okay!* Well, today, I've got some *very* special guests for you. Believe it or not, talking to one of Hollywood's most celebrated couples, *and* the writer who has chronicled their lives—and their very, very public breakup. How about that? Truly heart-wrenching, I've got to say. Please give a warm welcome to Hannah Fairchild . . .

(The audience applauds)

Josie Brown . . .

(Somewhat more subdued applause)

. . . and Louis Trollope!

(Delirious screams, wildly ecstatic applause, and whistles from the audience)

Now, ladies . . . ladies . . . Hey, I know it's hard to control yourselves.

I'll let you at him in a minute . . .

(More chuckles, unabashed giggles and more screams)

Still, you have to try. . . .

Hannah, I'd like to start with you . . . Josie's book, *True Hollywood Lies,* is really your memoir about your relationship with Louis. How difficult is it being a significant other of a very, very public, very sought after public figure?

HANNAH: You know, John, having grown up around celebrity, I can tell you honestly that charisma is 24/7, and no one—not even your loved ones—are immune to it.

LOUIS: (Giving the audience a knowing grin)

That's good to hear, love. So, you still have feelings for me, eh?

HANNAH: (Blushes deeply but shakes her head adamantly)

Funny, Louis, very funny. No, what I am trying to say is that, while you and other celebrities inspire awe in all of us, you can also be just as untouchable to those who love you most.

LOUIS: Oh, THAT old chestnut.

JOSIE: I certainly understand what Hannah is saying. I saw that play itself out in so many ways as I was chronicling Hannah and Louis—

LOUIS: What you mean is, when you were making our lives miserable. Quite frankly, Josie, I thought what you wrote was *very* one-sided.

HANNAH: By that you mean that it wasn't YOUR side, right, Louis?

LOUIS: You got THAT right. You women all stick together—

(Groans and hisses from the audience)

—No, now, I mean it! Nowhere in the book does Josie touch on MY heartache and anguish—

JOSIE: Um, yes I do: page 43 . . . then again on page 76 . . . and from 142 to 144 . . .

LOUIS: That's just my point! A couple of lousy paragraphs, in over 300 pages? I wouldn't exactly call that "even-handed." Why, the whole bloody book is told from Hannah's perspective, right? Gab, gab, gab, whine, whine whine, "me, me, me . . ."

HANNAH: (To John)

You see? This is what I had to put up with!

JOHN: Certainly he's got that Martian introspection . . . But some women *do* find that endearing—

HANNAH: Yeah, well, *not me.* To paraphrase Tom Hanks in *Forrest Gump*, one of the world's greatest actors in one of his finest roles, "Adorable is as adorable does."

LOUIS: You see, John, the inference there is that *I* will never be the caliber of actor that Mr. Hanks is . . .

(He gives the camera a bereft look)

I guess we all know emotional abuse when we hear it, right?

HANNAH: (Snorting)

My goodness, Louis, can't I even *mention* another actor without you feeling slighted? Too bad you're not on a movie set now, because that was *truly* an Oscar-worthy performance!

JOHN: Now, now, Louis, Hannah . . . The wonderful thing about my show is that you get to hear, from each other *and* from the heart, the things that you *know* went wrong, and what may be possible to put things right again.

LOUIS: I'm right there with you, John. Believe me, I haven't written off Hannah completely, and I don't think you should, either. Sure, she's stubborn—

(WIDER CAMERA ANGLE to include Hannah, whose eyes have opened up wide in disbelief)

—and certainly she is overly jealous, but . . . well, I still have a soft spot in my heart for her.

HANNAH: From what you've just said, I think it's more likely that you've got a soft spot on your *skull*.

JOHN: Now, now, Hannah. It's obvious that Louis still has feelings for you. That's got to count for something, right? Josie, tell me: what's *your* take on these two? Do you see them getting back together again anytime soon?

JOSIE: As much as Louis would like to believe that Hannah is still enthralled with him, from what I observed, she's a smart enough cookie to understand that old adage "Fool me once, shame on you; fool me twice, shame on me."

HANNAH: You've got *that* right!

JOSIE: Besides, Mick, her fiancé, isn't exactly dog chow. He's sweet, sensitive, loving, fun to be with—

LOUIS: Oh, puh-*leeze*! Heck, he's just like every other man . . . he's exactly like *me!* I'm telling you, Mick's got an eye for the ladies.

JOSIE: I beg to differ, Louis. From what I've seen, Mick is *nothing* like you. In fact, not too many men are as self-centered as you are.

HANNAH: I'll vouch for that!

(The audience also murmurs and claps in agreement)

LOUIS: Come on, now, is this fair? Two on one?

HANNAH: Gee, Louis, I'm surprised you're complaining, I mean, in the past, you certainly loved *that* combination.

(Audience roars and whoops with laughter at this double entendre)

JOHN: (Laughing)

Ooooh . . . she's got you there, Louis. . . .

LOUIS: (He acquiesces with a smile directed at Hannah, but his fangs are showing)

In any regard, I'm used to being on top, right, love?

(Hannah is boiling over to answer him, but she just shakes her head in annoyance.)

JOHN: (To the audience)

Well, it looks like there's a new top dog, and, unfortunately for Louis, it isn't him. Would you like to meet him now?

(Audience claps enthusiastically)

Great, let's bring him out. Here's MICK BRADSHAW!

(Mick bounds on the stage, waves at the audience, then sweeps Hannah up into his arms and gives her a knock-her-off-her-feet kiss. Louis ignores this, studies his nails instead. Josie claps along with the audience.)

JOHN: Hannah, you are one lucky girl. Why, this guy just dotes on you . . . right, audience?

(Audience coos in agreement.)

But, hey, Mick, you've got to admit, the competition was pretty stiff, right?

(Camera does a close-up on Louis before cutting back to Mick.)

MICK: Yep, totally. Although I can only say that, in my opinion, the best man won.

(The audience chortles in anticipation of Louis's reaction, which is that patented raised eyebrow.)

JOHN: Still, Hannah, it must have been difficult dating your boss's best bud, right?

HANNAH: It was . . . stressful, to say the least. I know that it was difficult on Mick and Louis, too . . .

LOUIS: (Caustically)

What makes you think *that?*

HANNAH: Well, the biggest clue was that you teased us both unmercifully about it . . . and the way in which you tried to make me doubt Mick's fidelity. I'd say that you may have been—well, just a *little* insecure about the whole thing.

LOUIS: Ha! I've no doubt that you were the one doing the teasing, both to Mick and myself, playing one against the other—

HANNAH: Me? Teasing *you?* That's—that's just TOO funny, Louis! Besides, there were also all those mixed signals you gave me—

LOUIS: As I told you in New York, you were fantasizing any attraction you may have felt—

HANNAH: When was it no longer a fantasy, Louis? Perhaps when you were pushing me up against the wall and sticking your tongue down my throat? Now I *know* I didn't imagine *that!*

JOHN: Aw, now Louis, there's that "top dog" issue again. Right, audience?

(audience twitters and giggles)

You know, Louis, Martians don't need force to make their point. All they need is to be open with the women in their lives. That's the most important way to show your love—

LOUIS: Frankly, John, I think I've been quite open with the *"love"* I show the women in my life.

(He winks at Hannah suggestively. Audience goes wild!)

JOHN: Um, Louis . . . I don't quite think that we're talking about the same thing here. But I'm talking about opening *your heart* now . . .

LOUIS: (drawing a blank)

Heart? Ummm. . . . You've lost me, love. . . .

JOHN: (sighing sadly)

Louis, Louis, Louis . . . Look, dude, the *whole purpose* of this show is to show you, who is most certainly one of the most celebrated studs on earth, that it takes more than macho bravado to win a woman's heart. Louis, *true love can be yours, too* . . . Love similar to what Hannah and Mick share . . . but *only if you don't run away from it.* Only if you *truly want to let it* into your life. . . .

(SFX: Upsweep in music . . . Studio lights fade to black, Video on blue screen . . .)

VOICE-OVER OF JOHN: For Louis Trollope, the youngest of three children born to Jack and Edith Trollope, a couple eking out a hardscrabble existence in the mostly blue-collar city of Manchester, England, love was always a struggle . . .

(PHOTO MONTAGE, including pictures of Louis's parents in a younger era, the toddler Louis with his father, and young Louis with his brother and sister.)

His mother, Edie, worked as a maid, and his father, Jack, when he worked at all, was one of many day laborers in the factories that ring this industrial city. But Jack's alcoholism and philandering kept him from being an ongoing presence in the life of his family.

(Close-up on Louis, whose face now reflects the pathos of John's words. Audience moans its sympathy.)

Like most boys, Louis's dream was to leave for a better life. And although he set his sights on a soccer career . . .

(Camera swipes to a photo of a tenderly handsome teenage Louis, in a soccer uniform)

. . . His natural good looks—and love of the ladies—led him to the stage . . .

(Quick montage of his stage roles)

. . . Where his natural charisma won him starring roles in sold-out West End productions of plays by Harold Pinter, Tom Stoppard, and David Mamet. Then that illustrious British television training ground, the BBC, made him a favorite on the small screen . . .

(A shot of Louis in an "of the manor born" costume, leaning over a costar's heaving bosom . . .)

. . . But he quickly made the leap to film. His first American movie was as that rascally lead in *Fast Eddie,* where he met Mick, who had worked on the script that won Louis instant acclaim . . .

(Camera cuts to Mick, who nods reminiscently . . .)

. . . For his second project, Louis chose another film penned by Mick, *Dead End*—

(Wild hysterical audience applause.)

. . . Which, believe it or not, had originally been written for Hannah's father, film legend Leo Fairchild.

Today, Louis Trollope is one of the most sought-after leading men, both on and off the screen . . .

(Another quick montage of Louis's many "leading ladies")

Including supermodel Tatiana Mandeville . . .

(Video clip of Tatiana begins)

TATIANA ONSCREEN: I can honestly say that Louis was the most ardent lover I ever had

(Camera now goes close-up on Louis, who is nodding and most certainly full of himself)

But he was also the biggest [BLEEP] I ever dated. No one should have his assistant break up for him. That is inhumane!

(Audience murmurs its obvious disapproval. Camera cuts to Louis, who shrugs. The video clip fades into another of Samantha Wellesley, Louis's former personal assistant)

V/O JOHN: The string of broken hearts Louis has left behind includes a young woman who worked for Louis . . . *and paid too dear a price.*

SAMANTHA ONSCREEN: (Timidly, in her clipped British accent)

Can one person love another too much? I did. I loved Louis. And I thought he loved me, too. Until he asked me for the cruelest favor one lover can ask of another—

(The audience holds its collective breath)

That I go to bed with both him—and his best mate!

(A disapproving murmur rises from the studio audience. All eyes now go to Mick. Close-up on Mick, who shakes his head as if to say, "Nope, it wasn't me!" Hannah pats his hand in acknowledgement. The video clip of Samantha fades to black.)

JOHN: We'll now take questions from the audience.

(He points to an angry woman in the third row)

WOMAN IN AUDIENCE: Wow! I'm in shock! I had so much respect for Louis—until now! I mean, he's just as sleazy as my third husband!

JOHN: Louis, would you like to comment?

LOUIS: Well, since I've never met her third husband, I can't vouch for how sleazy he is.

JOHN: I don't think that's the point here. I think she's commenting on *your* actions, not his.

LOUIS: Oh. Well, in that case, I assure you, madam, you would have never made it into bed with *me,* so essentially your accusation is unfounded.

JOHN: Uh . . . Oh-*kay*. . . . Way to win friends and influence enemies, Louis. . . . How about a question from the guy over there?

GENTLEMAN IN AUDIENCE: I agree with this dude. Three-ways are no big thing. Only I woulda thought a stud like you would bring another woman into the bed, not another guy. What's with that, man?

LOUIS: Just generous, I guess. Besides, my staying power always impresses the other blokes. So, why not share and share alike, right, mate?

GENTLEMAN: (Appreciatively)

Yeah, I see your point. Hey, I think *I'll* try it. Thanks.

JOHN: (Incredulous at what he's hearing)

Whoa, whoa, Louis! You can't give pointers to other men on how to pump up their libidos *and* their egos, at least, not on *this* show. We're about communication, strengthening relationships, honoring each others opinions and needs—

LOUIS: Bollocks, John! It was a perfectly legitimate question. Right, audience?

(He looks out into the crowd)

How many of you are truly interested in why a man might prefer *not* to be tied to the same ball and chain, day after day, month after month, year after year—

(Several hands go up in the audience, including some bashful women. He looks jubilantly at John)

I thought so.

JOHN: (Somewhat puzzled)

Earth to Louis! Look, dude, I'm not trying to scare men back into their caves; I'm trying to help them get in touch with their hearts. And as far as you're concerned . . . well, I've got to be honest with you: I'm questioning if you even have a *pulse.*

LOUIS: (Bored, yawning)

Yeah, well, that would surprise me. Look, John, to be perfectly honest with you, the only reason I'm even *on* your bloody show is because my idiot agent, Randy, thought it might be good for my image, which recently has taken a blow, thanks to that bloody book of Josie's. Right now, I'd say that Randy's a sodding idiot. Hannah, remind me to fire him when we get back to L.A.

HANNAH: All I can say, Louis, is that it's about time you dumped that clown. But for once, you're going to have to remember that yourself. Since you dumped me in Chapter Eighteen, I don't clean up your messes anymore. Remember?

LOUIS: (Looks incredulously at Josie)

Bollocks, Josie! Why did you have to go and do *that* for? *I'm* supposed to get the girl!

JOSIE: No, Louis, in the end, the girl gets Mr. Right, *not* Mr. Wrong.

(Audience whoops hysterically and claps their approval.)

JOHN: I couldn't have said it better. Now Josie, you're coming back on the show after the publication of your next book, *Impossibly Tongue Tied,* am I right?

(Josie nods happily, with obvious gratitude to her host.)

JOHN: Audience, I tell you, it's going be *another sizzler*! It's about that brand-new up-and-coming hunk, Nathan Harte, and his adorable wife, Nina—and of course, Hollywood's *Number One* diva, that femme fatale, Katerina McPherson—

LOUIS: *Hmmm.* Now, *she* sounds likes my type. I say, Josie, can you write me into that one?

(Camera pulls back. Mars & Venus *theme song cues up. Closing credits start to roll . . .)*

JOSIE: Uh . . . No, Louis, I don't think so . . .

LOUIS: Not even a cameo? You know I'll make it worth your while . . .

(Close-up on John)

JOHN: Yep, it certainly is shaping up to be another *hot* show! So, stay tuned . . .

(Shot dissolves into the Mars & Venus *logo, then out.)*

JOSIE BROWN is a feature writer whose relationship articles and celebrity interviews have appeared in numerous publications. She is also the editor of the internationally syndicated "John Gray's Mars Venus Advice" newspaper column, and the co-editor of the *Relationship News Wire*.

Her most recent book, *Last Night I Dreamt of Cosmopolitans* (St. Martin's Press) will be released May 2005. She is also the co-author, along with her husband, Martin, of *Marriage Confidential: 102 Honest Answers to the Questions Every Husband Wants to Ask, and Every Wife Needs to Know* (Signal Press).

Josie lives in Marin County, California, with Martin and their two children.